A Tiding of
MAGPIES

STEVE BURROWS

**POINT
BLANK**

A Point Blank Book

First published in Great Britain, the United States and Australia
by Point Blank, an imprint of Oneworld Publications, 2018

First published in English by Dundurn Press Limited, Canada.
This edition published by Oneworld Publications in arrangement
with Dundurn Press Limited

ISBN 978-1-78607-438-6
ISBN 978-1-78607-439-3 (ebook)

Printed and bound in Great Britain by Clays Ltd, Elcograf S.p.A.

Oneworld Publications
10 Bloomsbury Street
London WC1B 3SR
England

Stay up to date with the latest books,
special offers, and exclusive content from
Oneworld with our newsletter

Sign up on our website
oneworld-publications.com

MIX
Paper from
responsible sources
FSC® C018072

For Tom, and for Diana,
who both chose to join their stories with ours

And for Steve, Randy, Stacey, and Shannon,
who really had no choice in the matter

ACKNOWLEDGEMENTS

My thanks to Kirk Howard and the rest of the team at Dundurn, with special mentions to my publicist Michelle Melski, and my editors, Allison Hirst and Jenny McWha. I am extremely grateful for the continuing advice and guidance of Bruce Westwood, Michael Levine, and Meg Wheeler at Westwood Creative Artists. In the U.K., the overwhelming support of Oneworld's Juliet Mabey, Jenny Parrott, and Margot Weale reassures me that the Birder Murders couldn't be in better hands, while in the U.S., Becky Kraemer's energy and enthusiasm have already made her a valuable addition to the team.

On the home front, my sincere thanks go to fellow author and soccer teammate, Steve Lloyd, who passed on the details about a great setting. I'll never complain about his passing again! I am particularly grateful to Mike Burrows, who, at very short notice, gave the text his usual expert scrutiny and suggested a number of improvements. The birder who stopped me at Point Pelee to share some entertaining collective nouns will note that one of them made it into this book, even if I couldn't find room for the funnier one.

And finally, as always, my love and thanks go to my wife, Resa, for her inspiration and unfailing encouragement. Resa has offered her predictions for the Birder Murder series for so long now, we have come to consider it as her right. Some readers might think I should claim this role for myself. However, I just don't think I could bring myself to claim Resa's right.

PROLOGUE

The hunter was closing in. It had pursued them relentlessly, silently stalking them as they ran, splashing water all around them in their panic. Now it was here; a menacing grey curtain, hovering over the surface of the water, ready to take her. To add her to the victory it had already claimed.

She didn't know how long she had been standing out here, hunched against the dampness and the cold. She had stopped moving when Monte left, just as he told her she should. *I'll check ahead. Better you wait here.* Now, she was frozen in this place. She couldn't go back, she knew that. But her mind wouldn't allow her to take even one step forward. The hunter was waiting. The hunter that had taken Monte.

The inexorable approach of the fog had gradually shut down her senses. First, the horizon had dimmed to nothingness, then the waters around her had faded from her sight. Now, even the air itself seemed to have gone. Only this deep, impenetrable greyness remained, surrounding her, filling her world. The sounds had disappeared, too, sucked up into this void until there was nothing. No foghorns, no bird calls, not even the soft lapping of the waves around her feet. It was as if all the voices of the world had ceased. Only the echo of silence surrounded her now. And the terror that came with it.

She felt the life slowly ebbing from her body. She could sense the wet patches on her skin where the thin dress was sticking to it; feel the dampness in her hair and on her bare arms and legs. There were water droplets beneath her eyes, too, and on her cheeks. But those were different. Those had been for Monte, when she could still weep. Now she couldn't even raise a single sob for him. She had no tears left.

The waves washed over her shoes. The water was deeper than before, cold and cruel. *Tide's coming in fast. We got to keep moving.* But she couldn't. She could only stand here, with the fog and the sea all around her.

It was time. She would sit down and let the rising sea gather her in. It would be a relief, from the terror, the sorrow, the uncertainty. She wondered where she would be found when the fog lifted and the light returned to this place. Perhaps someone would discover her on the distant shore, lying peacefully on her side, looking like she was only sleeping. Perhaps she would drift with the tide and be found miles away, days from now. Perhaps her body would never be found at all. Her poor parents; they would never know what had happened to the daughter they loved so much and who had never really loved them enough in return. The thought pierced her heart with sadness. And it made her stay standing. Not to fight — there was no longer any point — but just to stave off the inevitable, to hold back the insidious creeping advance of death for a few moments more.

The water was at her ankles now. Her feet were aching and the dampness seemed to be seeping inside her. The air was getting colder, but she had stopped shivering. Her body had nothing more to give. Now it was just a matter of time. *I'm sorry, Monte. I can't do this anymore.* For it to end like this, after all she had gone through, all they had both gone through, in the past few days. Once, she had believed it would all end well. Monte's notes had said so. *Hold on. Be brave. We'll make it.*

But they hadn't. *You didn't make it, Monte. And you left me out here alone, far from the shore, with the sea all around me, coming in to claim me, while the fog hides its sins.*

Perhaps it would have been better to end it the way Monte had, pushing on into the unknown, the unknowable. But she knew she didn't possess that kind of courage. So she would wait. It would be over soon. Like him, she would simply disappear into the fog. Or the water. She had heard splashing once, before the swirling grey blanket had stolen the sounds from her. But there had been no calls. Monte had gone without crying out. It was his way. *Be brave.*

She didn't know why she looked up. For so long her eyes had been cast down, towards the water she could only feel, towards her feet that had gone numb inside her shoes. But when she stared ahead, a shape coalesced in the fog, slightly darker than the surrounding greyness, almost human in form. And then she saw the arm, extended in her direction as the shape advanced towards her, through the fog, across the water. Sounds were coming from the form, but she couldn't make them out. She was frightened, confused. It seemed so life-like, this apparition, she wanted to believe it. The cruelty of her hope stung her. The arm had almost reached her now. It looked real; flesh and blood she could grasp onto. The sounds, too, started to distill into meaning, penetrating the awful silence of the fog.

"Are you alone?"

She nodded, still unsure if this spectre was real.

"There's no one we should wait for?"

She shook her head dumbly. It was a real voice. She knew that now. But it sounded strange, the words odd and distorted.

"We have to start moving. We don't have much time."

And then she realized what it was about the voice, and tears started to roll down her cheeks. "It's you. Monte said you would come for us. He knew you would."

"Take my hand," said the voice. "It's over now."

She reached to take the outstretched hand.

1

Perhaps it was the frame that focused the scene so clearly. Through the single diamond of the chain-link fence, the objects seemed thrust towards the viewer in sharp relief. blocks of shattered concrete, shards of broken piping and twisted metal, mounds of bricks and plaster. Everywhere, debris and rubble littered the hard-packed earth in a silent, still-life tableau of destruction.

The spring sun was already high, casting shadows that turned the site into a checkerboard of light and dark. Ridges of hardened earth lay across the ground like healed scars, wounds of an earlier life, when metal blades and heavy industrial tyres had moved over the terrain like an army of mechanized invaders, gouging the history of their passing into the landscape as they went.

On the far side of the site, a row of scrubby poplar trees traced the boundary. Each cast a narrow finger of shadow, and sunlight fell in bright patches onto the ground between them. Beneath the trees lay the tangled remains of a collapsed fence. A few sparse weeds, dust-covered and water-starved, dotted the hard, stony ground. Pale-yellow flowers trembling uncertainly on thin stalks of washed-out green provided the only splashes of colour.

In the midst of this bleak landscape, caught between the shade of the trees and the bright sunlight, two men stood side by side, heads bowed like mourners at a graveside. At their feet was a shallow pit.

A black-and-white bird leapt onto the top of a mound of earth near the far end of the pit, flicking its long tail and tilting its head to one side as if in curiosity.

"That's four. Perhaps that means it's a boy," said Sergeant Danny Maik flatly.

Detective Chief Inspector Domenic Jejeune looked across at him, puzzled.

"Magpies," said Maik. "That one is the fourth I've seen since we arrived."

"And that makes it male?"

Maik moved his head slightly. Jejeune knew so much about the big picture of English life now, but there were still these small pockets that had escaped the Canadian DCI. Local lore, references to a shared English past of which he had no part; childhood memories, nursery rhymes, like this one.

"Magpies: *One for sorrow, two for joy, three for a girl, four for a boy* ..." There was more to the rhyme, but now that Jejeune was nodding his understanding, Maik saw no need to continue.

Jejeune watched the Magpie as it hopped boldly over the ground. He had seen a pair sitting motionless in the lower branches of one of the poplars as they arrived. The birds had been flitting around a lot since then. Perhaps the sergeant had seen four individuals, but it was more likely he'd seen only those two in various locations. A momentary image of another Magpie flickered across Jejeune's memory. Another Magpie; another death. His mind recoiled from the thought and he turned his attention to the bottom of the pit.

A man in blue coveralls knelt beside a fire-blackened corpse. He looked up and pointed to the nearby rifle and the photographer above nodded to indicate he had already captured the image of where it lay in relation to the body. The medical examiner slid the rifle to one side and swivelled the charred head slightly to examine it.

Maik seemed unwilling to watch the proceedings. He looked around and his attention was drawn to a plant that appeared to be growing directly out of a crack in a concrete block near the edge of the pit. Slender clumps of colourless flowers dangled at the end of the arching stems. "It's surprising anything could grow in a place like this," he said.

"Buddleia," said Jejeune. "It's an invasive. From China, I think. A lot of alien plant species are more resilient and adaptable than native ones. They tend to thrive in these areas, where the resources are poor."

Jejeune's mind didn't seem to be on his words as he spoke, even though he was staring directly at the sprig of vegetation. Life sought out every advantage in its fight for survival. It clung on tenaciously, desperately drawing the faintest threads of sustenance from its surroundings. Had the life in the bottom of this pit fought so hard to hold on to its existence? The thought only seemed to magnify the callous brutality of the crime that had taken place here.

"It looks like the M.E. is about to wrap up his preliminary examination. He seems very thorough."

"You've not had the experience of working with Dr. Jones before, have you, sir?"

Jejeune noticed Maik had not described it as a pleasure.

Dr. Mansfield Jones scrabbled up out of the pit and made a note on his hand-held tablet. "Male," he told the detectives, without looking up.

Four for a boy. Jejeune stared down into the excavated pit. He was fairly sure the charred body they were looking at was an adult. But Maik was right, of course, it was a boy.

Someone's boy. Everybody was someone's child.

"There's still some residual heat," said Jones. "The burning occurred no more than twenty-four hours ago."

"So the body has been here no more than a day?" Jejeune caught something in Maik's expression that could have been a guarded warning. But against what?

Mansfield Jones looked at the DCI directly. "All I would be prepared to say is the body was set alight within that timeframe."

Jejeune nodded. Logic suggested either the person had been killed here and the body set alight, or a corpse had been transported here and put into the pit to be burned. But the M.E. had a point. There was no way of ruling out the possibility that the body had been left in the pit earlier, possibly much earlier, than when it was set alight. Jejeune couldn't immediately come up with a scenario where such actions made any sense, but it wasn't outside the bounds of possibility.

"Was an accelerant used?"

"Petrol." Jones inclined his head towards Jejeune again. "Gasoline, I believe you'd call it. A great deal of it, as a matter of fact."

"More than would be needed to burn the body?"

"Far more." Jones looked back at the hole. "The entire pit was doused with it."

Maik's expression showed his surprise at Jones's willingness to provide so much information. Reluctantly, perhaps, but he was still volunteering it. Except that *volunteering* wasn't quite the right word. Jejeune's style of questioning was leaving the M.E. little alternative but to answer.

Jones began to peel off his latex gloves, bending his thin, overly tall frame awkwardly as he did so, in order to tuck his tablet under one arm.

"Is there anything else you can tell us?" asked Jejeune. "I saw you turning the head."

Jones allowed himself a slight nod of acknowledgement. "There are single entry and exit points near the base of the skull."

"A bullet?" Maik's eagerness to pursue the information overcame his earlier caution. "From the rifle?"

Jones drew up to his full height again and settled his gaze on the sergeant. "The wounds are consistent with bullet trauma. Fired from what, I couldn't say at this stage." He turned to encompass them both in his next statement. "I'd prefer to deliver my findings after I've had time to examine this person in my lab. I'm sure you can appreciate they'll be of more value to your investigation than hasty conclusions offered in the middle of a construction site."

Maik appeared to accept the M.E.'s point, though judging from his expression, *appreciate* might not have been Jejeune's way of putting it.

The two men watched as Jones packed up his mobile examination kit and headed out across the rubble-strewn site to his car.

In the lower branches of the nearby poplar tree, one of the Magpies was preening its blue-black feathers carefully. It raised its head to survey the landscape, looking first one way and then the other; a disinterested sentry at this place of death. Jejeune watched the bird for a moment and then looked beyond it, at the crowd gathered near the chain-link fence.

Maik followed his DCI's gaze, and his thoughts. Beyond the members of the Saltmarsh Serious Crimes squad gathered here, the person with the most interest in this examination would be the one who had left the body in this pit. Perhaps that person was in this crowd. It was unlikely; most killers would have done all they could to put a healthy distance between themselves and this place long before the body was discovered. But killers were as individual as their crimes, and there were those amongst them who revelled in observing the responses to their acts. Watching as the body was recovered and the police pondered over the situation would be a draw that might prove hard to resist. Perhaps he should have uniforms round up all the onlookers, thought Danny, a surprise sweep on the pretext of asking if anyone had seen anything prior to the police's arrival. Get them in an interview room and look for signs — wariness, agitation, evasiveness — signs that shouldn't be there in an innocent person. But if Danny's mind was now racing ahead, drawing lines between dots that didn't even exist, his DCI seemed to have gone the other way. Domenic Jejeune had withdrawn into a silence that suggested he was already on his way back into the past, where they would need to start if they were going to solve this case.

"How long has this site lain undeveloped?" he asked.

Maik thought for a moment. "Eight, nine years. It's been a brownfield site. Used to be heavy industry here; they had to wait until they were sure all the contaminants had cleared from the soil before they were allowed to begin redeveloping it."

"And construction was due to begin today? Was this common knowledge, would you say?"

"The local papers have been all over it, what with the promise of jobs, both during construction and after. You'd have to work hard not to know what was going on here."

Jejeune thought about the sergeant's comment. He had heard about people deliberately avoiding newspapers and television as a way of combatting the incessant stream of negative news stories. Even if he could understand this approach, he had his doubts about whether it would be successful. It seemed to him that bad news had a way of tracking you down, whether you hid from it or not.

"An out-of-towner might not know, or a recent incomer, I suppose." But Maik's tone suggested he was already a long way toward rejecting the idea, as he knew his DCI would be.

Randomly choosing a site that sat neglected for years, only to have work begin there the very next day, smacked of the kind of coincidence they had both long ago learned to distrust.

"I might as well go on back to the station and get started on the missing persons database," said Maik. "You'll want to stay on here for a while, I imagine?" He knew his boss would want to take in the scene, trying to draw something from it, as it settled again to stillness once the disturbance of the body's examination and removal was over.

Maik began picking his way carefully across the uneven terrain, leaving his DCI looking out over the site, deep in thought. On his way, the sergeant did his best to avoid stepping on the plant life, these non-natives that were, like his boss, now rooted in the Norfolk landscape, if not perhaps in its folklore.

The undulating land rolled across the space between the watcher and the younger detective. A safe distance. It had been hard not to draw back when the man had looked over this way. Certainly, this watcher would be nothing more than another indistinguishable shape on the far side of the wire, one of a growing number of people gathering along the fence to observe the proceedings inside the taped-off police perimeter. But he had a reputation, this detective, for seeing the things the others missed, for drawing connections that eluded everybody else.

Through the fence, the watcher's eyes had tracked the older officer's departure from the site. He had walked with his head down, staring at the ground, like someone lost in thought. Perhaps his mind was travelling beyond this place, reliving memories of other bodies, evoked by this scarred, rubble-strewn landscape.

That the younger detective had remained troubled the watcher. What was he seeing, as he stared around him? Perhaps the medical examiner had told him things that had given him a new perspective. It seemed unlikely the M.E. could have told him anything significant at this stage, but his comments seemed to have made an impact on the young detective. He was acting now like someone looking for a context into which he might place his thoughts.

Look well, detective, thought the watcher. *Drink it all in, every detail, every feature of this place, because you will never be this close to the truth again. From this point on, everything you learn will lead you further away from an understanding of what really happened here. In the end, the evidence, the clues, all of it, will convince you that you know the truth. But you will be wrong. You will have only facts. And you and I both know that the truth is something very different.*

2

Domenic Jejeune sat in the quiet gardens of Titchwell House, leaning back in the wicker chair and turning his face towards the sun. He closed his eyes, listening to the early spring birdsong that filled the air around him. A high box hedge screened the garden on three sides, the square completed by the glass wall of the hotel's dining room. This had once been a place of refuge for Jejeune, when his brother's problems were threatening to unravel his career, and his life. He remembered the deep reluctance with which he used to leave here to go out again and confront the turbulence Damian had brought to Saltmarsh. But even now, when Domenic did not need this garden setting as a bolt hole, it remained a favourite spot of his; a place for quiet reflection, a place to bask in the sun and watch the birds. The garden's well-stocked feeders and varied vegetation attracted a wide variety of species, both local and migratory. On one remarkable occasion, he had seen a Hoopoe, an exotic visitor from the tropics, wheedling its way across the manicured lawns, looking for insects. He retained a birder's illogical hope that the bird would one day return to this same spot, but, of course, it never had. There were other prizes, though, that he could rely on; the dainty Long-tailed Tits that came to the feeder, the Wren that fidgeted through the base of the hedgerow, the House Sparrows that flitted constantly back and forth through the curtain of ivy draping the rough stone wall above the dining room.

Jejeune opened his eyes and saw a couple at a table in the restaurant. Though the windows looked out onto the lawn, these people had eyes only for each other, leaning in intimately and parting only reluctantly as the waitress arrived to take their order. He thought about his last trip here with his girlfriend, Lindy, smiling at the memory of her indignant expression when he had remarked on the prices on the menu. "As the cost of bringing Lindy all the way up to Titchwell so she can sit in the Reserve's car park while you go birding," she had told him archly, "I'd say you're getting off cheap."

How close they had come to losing all this: these wide, blue skies, this air filled with the early spring fragrances of bluebells and violets, this abundant birdlife. Lindy had shared his despair when he'd been transferred following his return from Colombia. But since his reinstatement here, it was as if they had discovered Saltmarsh anew, revelling once again in all the wonders of the area. The reprieve had reinvigorated Lindy in other ways, too. She was back to her full-blooded best at work. Today, she was due to confront her editor, Eric, about another of his arcane journalistic policies. She would return home flushed with success — there really was no other possible outcome when Lindy had her dander up — but it would not be until later this evening, after the post-match analysis with her friends, over a glass of Chablis at the Boatman's Arms. Going home now, to an empty house, was one more argument against leaving this garden oasis, where not even the sound of a passing car on the coast road beyond the hedge disturbed the tranquility.

Where had these times gone from his life? he wondered. How had he allowed them to slip away for so long? It seemed he had spent so much of the previous few months stumbling from one crisis to another; family, personal, professional. And now, all of a sudden, this; gaps in his day, chunks of time upon which no one was making any claim. He saw the waitress making her sweep of the gardens, and on a whim he decided he would order tea and scones. Jam and cream, too. But which cream was it that he liked? Clotted? Double? Were they the same thing? He realized that without Lindy to guide him through the intricacies of an English cream tea, he was lost. In the end, he settled for ordering just another cup of tea.

As he waited, he thought about the case that faced him. It had some troubling aspects to it already, but he was unlikely to receive any pressure from DCS Shepherd to arrive at a quick solution. In previous cases, Shepherd's timetables had so often been set by someone else's agenda — superiors, diplomats, politicians. But this time, no one would be pressing them for a result, at least until they located the victim's family. So far, all they had was a body. And the dead have all the time in the world.

From the top of the hedge, Jejeune heard the distinctive, multi-part call of a Yellowhammer. He located the bird, the full sun catching its bright yellow head as it moved around. For once, he had no need to regret leaving his bins in the car. The bird was so close that even with the naked eye he could see the tiny throat muscles moving as it churred out its song. Birding, even snatched moments like this, had always had a way of driving the cares from his mind. Even during Damian's situation, it had managed to provide some respite from the swirling madness he had faced. *Damian's situation.* The decision of whether or not to acquit his brother of manslaughter now rested solely with the Colombian authorities, but Jejeune knew he had done all he could to assist in his brother's case. There was a kind of reassurance in the thought, and if that was not quite the same thing as closure, for now, it would do.

The server delivered his tea and disappeared inside to take the lovers their lunch; cellophane-thin slices of cucumber on squares of flimsy white bread with the crusts removed. It seemed to Jejeune that if you were that intent on avoiding nutrition, you might just as well eat the paper napkin that came with the food. But he enjoyed these snippets of English eccentricity. Perhaps it was the guilty pleasure of forbidden access, an intimate look at a country's unguarded self, a peek into this delicate, genteel world to which he was still, in so many ways, an outsider.

He looked around at the carefully landscaped gardens. It was still mostly evergreens this early in the season: Italian cypress, Japanese umbrella pine, Hungarian gold cedar. He had not realized how many were non-native. *Exotics* they were termed in settings like these. It was a garden landscaped for the humans that visited, rather than the birds. But the birds, too, had adapted, taking the seeds they found, gleaning insects from the alien branches and leaves.

Overhead, a single cloud plotted a leisurely course across the sky, a lone white blemish on the pale-blue canvas. Only one cloud remained on his own horizon; a review of an earlier case that he knew would be coming, had to be coming, all because of the unsafe conviction of a man named Ray Hayes. Jejeune had no wish to revisit the events surrounding his rescue of the Home Secretary's daughter, but he had no need to fear them. He could have done things differently. He should have. But he knew no one would ever hold him accountable for his actions. Only he would blame Domenic Jejeune for what he had done, and what he had failed to do. And regardless of the outcome of the review, he knew he always would.

The cloud had drifted in front of the sun, turning the garden into a world of cool shadows. It was time to head home. Jejeune slid away his half-finished cup of tea. He hadn't developed the unquenchable capacity for it the English seemed to have. He wondered if he ever would. He realized the Yellowhammer had stopped singing and looked over. There was a small flicker of movement deep in the hedgerow. The bird would reappear again soon enough. Perhaps he would wait, after all, just a few minutes more. For once, like the dead, Domenic Jejeune had all the time in the world.

3

Silence was one of Danny Maik's particular talents — that, and standing still. Few people could fill a space so completely with the force of their presence alone. But the brooding dormant volcano Detective Chief Superintendent Colleen Shepherd and the other officers were familiar with wasn't the Danny Maik standing at the front of the Incident Room today. He seemed strangely distracted, disengaged almost, barely registering the usual commotion as the rest of the team settled into their seats. As Maik surveyed the room, Detective Constable Tony Holland saw the sergeant's gaze flick to the empty desk of Lauren Salter.

"Don't worry, Sarge. She hasn't forgotten."

Maik's puzzled expression was its own query.

"Your birthday. While Lauren's away, I'm under strict instructions to have a whip-round and get you something. Just between you and me, though, I think it makes more sense if we do away with all that paper and ribbons and crap, and you just pick something up for yourself. Let me know how much it is, and I'll make sure these tight-fisted gits all chip in to make sure you're not out-of-pocket."

"Thank you, Constable. After all, it's the thought that counts."

"My feelings exactly," said Holland, for whom irony sometimes seemed to be a foreign country. "There's a second-hand shop on the high street that has some vintage Motown albums. Vinyl ones, with artsy covers and sleeve liner notes. You know, the way you lot used to like them. I thought you could grab yourself one of those. That is, unless you've already got them all."

"I'll give it some thought." Despite his evident detachment, Maik still clearly recognized it as his duty to call the meeting to order, and once he had done so, he took up the black marker, ready to begin sketching out their lines of approach on the whiteboard behind him.

"The body we discovered yesterday belongs to an adult male, but the burning was so intense it has prevented the recovery of any usable DNA."

The cold detachment with which they were discussing the calculated incineration of another human being seemed to occur to them all at the same time. A moment's reflective silence fell across the room.

"So I suppose dental records are our best hope for an ID?" said Shepherd finally.

"There's little to go on, apparently," said Maik. "The teeth are in very good condition. There's some evidence of light cosmetic work, but trawling through the databases to try to match our victim against everybody who's had a bit of capping and straightening done would be a monumental task. I can't see it being worth taking that route until we've finished looking at the serial number on the rifle. Although an attempt was made to file it off, it's probably still our best lead."

"An attempt?" said Shepherd.

"I could make out a couple of markings with the naked eye, so I'm fairly confident we can recover something once Dr. Jones puts it under a luminescent light. Even if it's only some

STEVE BURROWS

of the digits, it'll help narrow down the search. The rifle is a Brno. They're not all that common."

Shepherd nodded with what might have been slight satisfaction. "And what about the significance of the location? Any thoughts on that?"

The response came from the back of the room, where Domenic Jejeune had perched himself on a desk, as usual, feet on the chair in front of him. "I'll take this if you like, Sergeant."

Heads spun to look at Jejeune as he dismounted from the desk and began to make his way to the front of the room. Well, this was certainly new. Was it a manifestation of the DCI's relief at being re-instated, after so nearly losing his position? Did it portend a new era of engagement, a more conventional leadership style in their murder investigations? Whatever it was, it was definitely going to be preferable to having to drag contributions out of him one syllable at a time, the way they had in previous briefings. DCS Shepherd, for one, looked particularly pleased with the new turn of events.

Jejeune took up a position centre stage. Maik was hovering just beyond the DCI's shoulder, as if he feared he might have to step in, should Jejeune's newfound resolve suddenly fail him.

"Before we start, I need a little background on the site itself," said Jejeune.

"Certainly, Domenic," said Shepherd. "Ask away."

"Obviously, I wasn't around at the time the site came on the market." The small self-conscious smile was new, too. Whatever had brought on this new approach, Jejeune was clearly determined to give it his best effort. "But a prime piece of land like this, at such a strategically important location, I'm sure there would have been no shortage of interest in it."

"Blimey, you can see how he got his detective's badge, can't you?" said Holland, making sure his own smile was broad enough to keep things nice and friendly. "Residential, industrial, commercial; they all went after it like the last pint at a darts tournament. Not to mention the enviro nutters. No offence, sir," added Holland hurriedly, "just how they were categorized at the time … by the other groups…. Remember?" He looked around the room for support, but none came.

Jejeune nodded. "The land could have formed an important wildlife corridor between the two protected areas. I can imagine environmental groups wouldn't have been too pleased to see such an important opportunity lost."

Lost, thought Shepherd. It was an interesting term for a project that was going to provide a much-needed boost to the local economy. "They certainly caused enough fuss at the zoning hearings," she said. "We had to issue a couple of public order notices, if memory serves. Eventually, there was some sort of settlement reached whereby the environmental groups would agree to drop their protests if the developers promised to set aside some land as a conservation area."

"That the local council would then have to pay to maintain," added Holland, with a sour expression. "Which was great, because, you know, we were all hoping they'd find another way to flush our taxes down the drain."

Shepherd's expression suggested they might be able to move things along a bit more quickly if the constable could dispense with the editorials. Clearly, for all his new enthusiasm, the DCI was going to need some practice keeping a daily briefing on track.

"I have to say, Domenic, if you're thinking this murder might be related to the decision to zone this area for development, I'm not sure the timing makes sense. Those decisions were made years ago. Even the plans to turn the site into a shopping centre have been public knowledge for months."

Jejeune nodded as if to acknowledge he'd already taken the DCS's point into consideration. "Yes, they have." The room waited for something more, but it wasn't forthcoming.

Holland stepped into the silence with another idea. "I suppose leaving a body at a construction site is an effective way of stopping the work," he said, "if you are thinking this is about opposition to the construction project."

The remark was directed at Jejeune, but it was Maik who shook his head slowly. "I can't see anybody going to all that trouble to bring about such a short-term delay. It's only going to hold things up for a matter of days, at most."

"Speaking of which," said Shepherd, "there is some urgency to conclude our evidence gathering and release the site. The local Chamber of Commerce is not best pleased, to put it mildly, to have found a body in the middle of the most important piece of commercial land to have come available in decades. An ongoing police presence only serves to remind people what happened there. There's a concern that it might deter shoppers from coming, once the new centre is opened."

"You're joking, right?" From long practice, Holland's tone fell just the right side of contempt. "Even now, it's all uniforms can do to keep people far enough back so that we can do our jobs. A shopping centre built on the site of a violent murder? Once the place opens for business you could charge admission and the lineup would still go from here to Sheringham."

Shepherd tilted her head slightly to acknowledge the sad truth of Holland's remarks. "Nevertheless, the sooner we can turn the site back over to the developer, the fewer phone calls I'll be receiving from on high. Any idea when that might be?"

Maik had spent the previous afternoon extracting from Jones what little bit of information they now had. He reached for his formal tone, to hide any lingering personal feelings he might have about Dr. Mansfield bloody Jones. "The M.E. would prefer to share his conclusions only after he has explored all possible interpretations of the evidence."

"Well, I'm sure that'll be worth us all coming out of retirement for," said Holland. Like the others, he knew Maik found the man's refusal to enter into any kind of speculation particularly exasperating. He had watched with amusement as the sergeant sat at his desk when he returned from his meeting, headphones on, staring blankly at his laptop screen as he sought to let his music bring his blood pressure back under control.

Shepherd nodded, but not with indulgence. "I'm sure we all appreciate Dr. Jones's thoroughness," she said diplomatically. "Nevertheless, the entire population of Saltmarsh shouldn't have to sit in abeyance waiting for him to make his pronouncements. Try and hurry things along, would you, Sergeant?"

"It strikes me," said Holland, "it might be helpful if the sergeant spent his days shadowing Dr. Jones. You know, working side by side with him. That way, he'd be on hand to report any findings as soon as the doc made them."

Maik's expression suggested the idea might not be the only thing to strike Holland, who was doing his best now to portray a look of wide-eyed innocence.

Shepherd looked at the pair of them carefully. So much of her time at these meetings seemed to involve ensuring they didn't disappear down these rabbit holes of irrelevance, and instead stayed focused on the task at hand.

"So, Inspector," she said briskly, "any other thoughts at this point?" It would have been unusual for the old DCI Jejeune to be very forthcoming at such an early stage, but perhaps this new, engaged edition was more inclined to share his ideas.

"Large amounts of petrol were used to burn the body. It was likely done to ensure the burn temperature was high enough to make DNA recovery impossible."

"So you believe the intent of the fire was to conceal the victim's identity?" said Shepherd cautiously. She nodded. "Yes, I think I'd be ready to go along with you on that."

Jejeune wasn't sure if Shepherd was already along with him on the rest of it. But Danny Maik was. "It seems to me the best way of concealing a murder victim's identity is to make sure the body is never discovered in the first place."

"Exactly, Sergeant. So why go to such trouble to disguise the victim's identity and then leave the body where you can virtually guarantee it will be found within twenty-four hours, when construction work begins on the site?"

Shepherd nodded in understanding. "So you're saying whoever committed this murder wanted people to know about the act, but not about the victim." And just like that, the case had morphed from a straightforward murder investigation into one that was undoubtedly going to require the inspector's special talents. She would have been grateful for her DCI's involvement at any time, but she had a feeling that watching this new, fully-engaged Domenic Jejeune at work was going to be something to behold.

4

A matter of life and death.

It was the kind of hyperbolic drivel that reminded Lindy Hey why they rarely listened to local radio talk shows anymore. In fact, they rarely listened to the radio at all when they were driving. Usually, it was a CD by one of Dom's obscure Canadian bands, or something from this century if Lindy was at the controls. But today's discussion topic was relevant to the investigation, so they had tuned in to listen. People wanted to know just how long the discovery of the body was going to hold up construction of the new shopping centre. And in Saltmarsh, "people" generally meant those with enough juice to put DCS Colleen Shepherd, and consequently DCI Jejeune, under significant pressure.

The callers were clashing over whether the delay would cause further traffic backups on the area's narrow roads during the tourist season. Things had become heated and the host had felt compelled to intervene. *Clearly, passions are running high on both sides, but I'd urge you all to keep some perspective here. I mean, it's hardly a matter of life and death.*

Few things are, thought Lindy. Even for this poor man whose body had been discovered on the site. It was simply a matter of death for him, now. His life was no longer of relevance. His existence, his achievements, his place in the world, they had all been consigned to the past. And that is where most people would be content to let them remain. *But not you*, she thought, looking over at Domenic. *For you, this person's life will still matter. Because you'll be relying on the secrets it held to lead you to the reason for his death.*

The Range Rover drifted towards the centre of the lane as Jejeune guided it along the narrow country lane. Lindy waited for him to correct it, but it continued to drift further still as he craned forward to look up through the windshield.

"No birding while we drive, Dom. Remember," said Lindy calmly, "wheels stopped and handbrake on if you're going to watch birds from the car. What are they anyway?" Her own eyes followed the small group as it crossed overhead and disappeared from sight behind the tall hawthorn hedge.

"Little Terns, back from West Africa." He eased The Beast back into the proper lane. "The first ones of spring are always nice to see, but I'm surprised they're here so soon."

They turned onto an even narrower track and drove along in silence. In the waning light of the spring evening, Lindy could see the faint outline of the full moon hanging low over the newly tilled fields. It seemed so alien to the landscape that she stared at it for a long while. She was surprised when Dom drew the vehicle to a bumpy stop at the side of the road, and looked around her.

"Where are we?"

"Far side of the construction site. There are a couple of things I want to check out." He jumped out and rounded to Lindy's side to open the door for her. Dom occasionally sur-prised her with genteel courtesies like this, and they never failed to bring her a tiny frisson of delight. They scrambled up the low bank and began to pick their way carefully over the uneven ground. The traces of human activity that were so much in evidence on the far side of the site were absent here. The natural colonization that had begun after the destruction of the old buildings had continued unhindered, and the rubble now lay under a thick, tangled mass of ground elder and nettles. Dom and Lindy crested a small rise and emerged onto the dustbowl of the main construction area.

"It was here?" asked Lindy quietly.

Jejeune pointed to an area on the far side of the site where a perimeter of yellow police tape fluttered in the light breeze. Lindy drew her shoulders together slightly. It seemed worse, somehow, than a domestic murder. You could almost accept that as being a random act within the confines of somebody's private space; a one-time event that happened when all the controls broke down. But a body left out in the open like this, abandoned on public ground — this crime seemed to belong to everybody, drawing them into the horror, the tragedy.

"You're wondering if the killer brought the body up through the way we've just come. I don't know, Dom." Lindy shook her head uncertainly. "That's a long way to drag a full-grown person."

"I don't see any evidence that happened," agreed Jejeune.

She looked at him now, surveying the area enclosed by the yellow tape, the place where a man's body had been so callously discarded. There must be somebody who was missing this person, she thought. Didn't everybody hold a place in somebody's life, no matter how small? Perhaps. But if he did leave any connections behind in the world of the living, it was now up to Domenic to find them. He needed them if he was to discover why this person had been murdered and then had all traces of his human identity scorched out of him.

She left him to his thoughtful silence and wandered off between a low canyon of rubble that led to the far side of the site.

* * *

On the still evening air, her voice came to him like a siren's call. "Come and have a look at this."

Lindy was standing at a gap in a section of chain-link fencing that had collapsed. Just beyond was a large pond surrounded by steep-sided mounds of construction rubble. In the last of the low, slanting sunlight from the west, small waves rippled over the surface of the water like light along a serrated blade.

"Did you know this was here?" asked Lindy as she heard Jejeune approaching.

He shook his head. "It's a construction pond, a man-made scrape that rain and runoff have filled up over time. If they're allowed to survive for long enough, some of these ponds become a viable environment."

"Viable for what? Look at all the concrete in there, not to mention the bricks and the rebar and the rest. God knows what that pretty little duck is finding to eat. It's disappeared now. Dived. It'll be back up in minute. It had a blue beak."

Jejeune snapped a look in her direction. "You saw the blue clearly? It couldn't have been a trick of the light?"

Lindy cast an exasperated look at him. "It was bright blue, Dom." She began to protest as he opened his phone app. "Come on. You know I'm not going to have noted its scalloped primaries or partially indented septum." But she nodded as soon as the image came up. "That's it: Ruddy Duck. The tail sort of stuck up a bit, just like that." She leaned forward to read the text. "*North American vagrant*. Interesting description. Friend of yours?"

Jejeune didn't see her cheeky grin. He was already scouring the water surface again. There were so many weed-strewn islands in the water, so many piles of demolition debris around the edge. A small duck could be concealed behind any of them.

"That one was there, too," said Lindy, scrolling down to another image. "Oh, it's the female. That explains it. He's probably brought her out here to this picturesque spot for a date. He seems to have the same flair for romance as another North American male I know."

"There was a pair? Are you sure?"

Again her humour seemed to have missed the mark. She was used to Dom's passion when it came to potential sightings, but the urgency charging his voice surprised her. "That eye-stripe's hard to miss, even in this light, and she had that same pointy tail thing going. Are they rare? Has Lindy earned a slap-up dinner for finding her man a listable bird? Providing, of course, that he's a good enough birder to re-find it … them."

If Jejeune wasn't rising to the bait, he was certainly taking up the challenge. She couldn't remember when he had scanned an area for a particular bird with such unwavering intensity.

"Relax, Dom. I'm sure they're still around. I would have seen them if they'd flown off."

"I should have grabbed my bins. I never thought …"

"You won't need them. They're really close." She flung out her left arm. "There, ten o'clock, in front of that island on the left. The male. Both now."

By the time the female had bobbed up from her dive to join her partner, Jejeune had spun and focused on the spot. Together, he and Lindy watched as the ducks puttered around in tight circles before diving again suddenly and disappearing from view. The light was almost completely gone now, but he had seen enough for a positive ID.

"So, is that a lifer for you?"

He shook his head. "No, I've seen them before, plenty of them."

"But not over here, I take it?"

He nodded. "Even here."

He didn't seem to want to say any more, to explain why it had been so important to him to see a bird he'd seen so many times before, why there had been such a desperation about his search this time. Lindy let it go. He continued watching the water, observing the ducks until the last vestiges of the day disappeared and the full moon bloomed on the horizon, spilling its milky light over the landscape. Lindy had already tired of the vigil and wandered along the fenceline. He found her now, resting her forearms on the top of a fencepost, her chin set on them, staring unblinkingly at the perfect yellow disc. She didn't turn at his approach. "The moon has some of the most fantastically-named features I've ever heard," she said. "The Sea of Tranquility, the Bay of Rainbows." Jejeune looked at the moon carefully. Even with the naked eye it was possible to make out some of the topography, the suction-cup craters and the hard, bony ridges of mountain ranges.

Lindy sighed heavily. "How can another world have such beauty when there is so much horror down here on this one? To leave that man out here, to burn away everything that made him a human being, everything that might tell people who he was. Who could do that?" She gave a slight shiver. "We'd better get back to the car," she said. "This bumpy ground is going to be no fun in the dark."

They picked their way over the moon-gilded landscape in silence. Though she couldn't risk taking her eyes from her path to check, she had the sense that beside her, Dom was deep in thought. As they approached the Range Rover, he paused and turned to look at her. "We can't say anything about seeing these ducks, Lindy. Okay? Not even to Eric."

Not sharing a sighting was so out of character for Domenic that she was taken aback. She'd already decided that the only reason he hadn't already texted one of the bird lines was because it would have been so dark by the time anybody got here it would have been impossible to see the ducks anyway. Apparently, though, there was another reason.

"I'm going to need an explanation as to why I'd be jeopardizing my career by failing to inform my boss about such an apparently important bird. If he finds out I've seen these ducks and he ends up missing them, I'm going to be reporting on construction site developments like this one for the rest of my days."

"I just need to check out a couple of things first. A day or so at most, I promise."

Lindy nodded uncertainly. A day or so could be a lifetime in birdwatching, when even a few seconds could mean the difference between seeing a bird and missing it. But Domenic didn't make frivolous requests, and certainly not with the urgency he was making this one. Whatever his reasons, she knew it was important. And that was enough for her. For now.

The night had filled the narrow lane with shadows. The sudden flurry of two shapes in flight flashed across in front of them as they drove and Jejeune spun his head to track the birds. He heard Lindy scream and felt the jolt as The Beast swerved wildly off the road, the two offside tyres mounting the grassy verge beside the hedgerow. The front tyre slipped down into the ditch beyond the verge, sending the vehicle lurching towards the hedgerow, branches scraping along the windshield and bodywork, squealing as the vehicle hurtled alongside them. He fought the steering wheel as the ditch threatened to snatch it from his grasp, the muscles in his forearms bulging with the effort as he held on and yanked the wheel hard to the right. The Range Rover began to tilt further in, and he accelerated, the big engine roaring with the effort of dragging the front wheel up from the ditch. With a final surge, The Beast remounted the verge and bounced down onto the road surface, the chassis rocking violently as it landed. As soon as he had righted it, Jejeune pulled the Range Rover to a halt and put it in neutral.

Lindy let her hands fall from the brace position against the door and dashboard. She drew a deep breath and patted her chest. "You idiot," she said, giving him a hard slap on the shoulder. "I swear, you're going to kill us one day with your car birding."

"I'm sorry," he said sincerely. "I thought it was the ducks flying over. I wanted to track their direction. Are you all right?"

Though she was still shaken, there was a part of Lindy that would never allow fear its complete victory. She needed to show her recovery even before she felt it, and irreverence was often the way. "*Here lies Lindy*," she announced solemnly, "*Birded to death*. Not much of an epitaph, is it?" She fell quiet and looked out through the windshield for a second. The headlights lit up the hedgerow ahead of them, but the rest of the lane was in darkness. "Sorry," she said. "That was wrong, considering that poor man who was left out there."

Jejeune reached down to put the car into gear again, but before he did so, he paused and turned to her. "Listen, Lindy," he said earnestly. "I can't emphasize how important it is that we say nothing about having seen those ducks."

It wasn't like Dom to restate something. They were tuned in enough to each other to pick up the nonverbal clues that a thing was important; a sudden stillness that accompanied the words, or the slight leaning in to close the space between them. That he should mention this again now surprised her, especially when he should still have been offering her his apologies.

"Jeez, Dom, I get it," she said testily. "Not a word. A matter of life and death."

Jejeune paused for a moment. Finally, he slid the vehicle into gear and pulled away. "As a matter of fact," he said, "it is."

5

In other police stations, getting hold of a medical examiner's report was easier than this, Maik thought ruefully as he made his way down the steps to the basement. You called down and had it sent up. If the findings it contained were sensitive enough, perhaps the M.E. might even deign to bring it up himself, blinking in the light, no doubt, as he emerged from his lair. But to get anything of value from Dr. Mansfield Jones, it was apparently going to be necessary to go down to where he held sway. Maik gave a small sigh of irritation. He only remembered having to do this once with Jones's predecessor. A popular television show at the time had featured a medical examiner in the lead role. For his own part, Maik didn't understand the appeal of a show where the main focus seemed to revolve around dissecting bodies. Then again, there were a lot of things about television that Danny Maik didn't understand, which no doubt went a long way to explaining why he spent most of his nights listening to vintage Motown tunes on his turntable instead. But the Saltmarsh M.E. at the time seemed to consider himself elevated to something of a celebrity along with his TV counterpart, and found himself far too much in demand to deliver mundane forensic reports to the detectives on the upper floors. Maik had been advised that if he wanted reports, from now on he'd need to come down to get them. Neither the arrangement nor the medical examiner had lasted very long.

At least this trip wasn't the result of an outsized ego. Jones, to his credit, had no illusions about his own importance. He simply refused to sign off on anything until he had subjected every finding to a seemingly inexhaustible series of tests and verifications, to eliminate any possibility that he could be wrong. To get him to part with information any earlier was going to require somebody to come down and pry it from his grasp. For *somebody*, read Danny.

The stairwell was well-lit, but Maik was still unprepared for the glare of ultra-bright fluorescence that flooded the lab as he entered. It seemed to bounce off the pristine steel surfaces like a pulse of energy. A shiny pink skull showed through Mansfield Jones's wispy hair as he bent over a body on the examination table. Maik couldn't be sure, but he thought he heard a quiet murmuring as the M.E. went about his work. If so, it ceased as soon as he became aware of the sergeant's presence.

Jones straightened as Danny approached, drawing himself to his full height, a good couple of inches taller than the sergeant. The height only exacerbated the cadaverously thin frame and added to the man's overall sense of frailty. He offered Maik the sort of guarded welcome the sergeant had come to expect. "You're feeling well yourself, Sergeant?"

Not least among the things Maik dreaded about these visits was the M.E.'s solicitous inquiries into his well-being. Perhaps there was a need for Jones to connect to the living, but Maik still felt there was something vaguely unsettling about a forensic pathologist asking after your health. It didn't help that Jones himself hardly looked to be in tip-top condition. His skin seemed to have a particularly sickly pallor.

Perhaps it was just the relentless glare of the overhead lights, but it wasn't the best sign when you were working in a morgue and you weren't the healthiest-looking person in the room.

"As well as can be expected, I think is the phrase, Doctor." Maik regretted the words as soon as he said them. His comment opened the way for other, more pointed questions.

"I'd heard you were prescribed a fairly strict diet after your health scare. I trust you're still managing to stay on it."

Maik greeted the reference to his earlier heart condition with all the tolerance he could muster. "Doing what I can. The job doesn't always make it easy. You know how it is, irregular hours and such."

Jones looked into Maik's face, as if to read something in it. "Your health should be of paramount importance these days. A cavalier approach may well have been understandable as a younger man, but we experience great changes as we get older."

"Like becoming less tolerant of medical advice, for example?" asked Maik, as pleasantly as he could manage. Jones himself was a devoted vegetarian. The sergeant could understand how an M.E. might veer in that direction, after the things he must see during the course of any given day, but Maik had once been on a survival course that consisted of eating roots and leaves for a week. He didn't know if Jones's diet was actually going to extend his life much, but he was fairly sure it would make it seem like an eternity between meals.

"At this stage, there's really not very much I can tell you with any certainty, I'm afraid."

"Any information you could offer would be most welcome," said Maik. "Even if we get height, build. It could all help to narrow the field for a potential match from missing persons." With anyone else, such an explanation would have been unnecessary, but with Jones, Maik always felt strangely compelled to justify the reasoning behind even the most straightforward statements.

"I've taken some of the bone measurements, but I'd prefer to complete them all before I make any calculations. One set of results so often informs the other, you see."

"I understand," said Maik, more indulgently than he felt. "How about location? Do you have any indication of where the victim might have been shot?"

"Indeed I do. At the base of the skull."

A sigh seemed the safest outlet for Maik's frustration. For both of them. "The physical location, Doctor. SOCO have not recovered a casing from the pit, or any evidence that one was previously dug out of the soil. We don't think the man was shot in the pit."

"Ah, my apologies. Your question, you see. Perhaps if you tried for a little more precision …" Maik's expression seemed to hurry Jones on. "There was no evidence to suggest the victim was moved from another location. Are SOCO absolutely sure? Just because they didn't find the casing doesn't mean it's not there. I'd remind you that absence of evidence is not evidence of absence."

"Let's call it a premise we're working on." Maik tried for another smile, but they seemed to be getting harder to come by.

"I can confirm the two wounds are consistent with a rifle bullet," offered Jones. The gentleness with which he turned the charred head to indicate the two sites seemed to Maik to go some way beyond simple concern for preserving the evidence. The M.E. noticed his expression. "I doubt it would be possible to do this job effectively if one wasn't prepared to consider them as people, Sergeant."

Maik wondered what the man could have been murmuring to this person from which virtually all evidence of human existence had been stripped. Solace? Apology? Perhaps even a prayer? He realized there was a great deal about Mansfield Jones that he didn't know. But now was not the time to begin that particular journey of discovery.

"Calibre, by any chance?"

"The wound matches a .22 subsonic hollow point, possibly around forty grains in weight."

Maik nodded thoughtfully. It was very light for a human target, though it would prove effective enough at close range. It meant it was still possible the weapon had been chosen specifically for the job. It might be an important point.

"Two wounds," confirmed Maik.

"Through and through, I believe they call it where the DCI hails from. Though quite why it's necessary to repeat the word, I'm not sure. Saying a bullet passed through a body is clear enough, surely. I don't have much tolerance for redundancy," said Jones redundantly.

Maik regarded the M.E. carefully. He was struck by the loneliness of the man's situation down here, where he squirrelled away gossip about other people's modified diets and dwelt on redundancies. *What a terrible wilderness he must exist in,* thought Maik, *surrounded by his uncertainties.* What did you hold on to as your anchor? What could you trust?

"And you're sure," Maik hesitated, "confident, shall we say, that cause of death was a single bullet to the back of the head?"

"Not necessarily."

"You said there was an entry wound and an exit wound," said a calm voice that seemed to come from somewhere outside Maik's body. "You're saying you believe someone could survive a bullet passing through the skull like that?"

"No. But I can't say for certain that the wound was pre-mortem."

Maik stretched his neck from the confines of his collar, like a man developing a heat rash. "And why might anyone want to shoot a dead man in the back of the head, Doctor?"

"Why indeed, Sergeant? It's extremely unlikely, I'll admit.

But I couldn't say categorically that it didn't happen."

There was a long moment of silence as Maik digested this idea. "But you would be prepared to concede the victim was shot once in the back of the head, at some point."

"It's the most plausible explanation for the wounds."

"The Brno CZ is a .22-calibre rifle. I don't suppose ..."

"Without the shell casing, it is impossible to say definitively if the bullet came from that rifle."

Given that it looked like he might not be getting much more ballistics information from Jones, Maik considered what else he could remember about the Brno CZ. It was a rimfire rifle. Single load. Beyond that, nothing.

"For a hollow point to make it all the way through like that, it would indicate the shooter was close, wouldn't it?"

"It could," conceded Jones, dragging the last word out to emphasize the conditional nature of his response.

"Okay, thank you, Doctor. I think that's all for now," said Maik, extending a hand as he prepared to leave. "If you've been able to recover all you can of the serial number digits from the rifle, I'd be prepared to have a guess at the rest of them."

"No need. I treated the surface with an etching reagent. It's known as 'raising' the number. All the digits became legible. I've already run the serial number against the gun registry database." He handed Maik a sheet of paper. "The registered owner is one Jakub Kowalski. The address is local, as you can see."

"There's a person of that name on the missing persons database," offered Jones, since Maik suddenly appeared incapable of speech. Jones had come up with the name of the gun owner, and he'd still begun their conversation by informing Maik there really wasn't very much he could tell him? Just what must constitute definitive information for this man hardly bore thinking about.

"Jakub Kowalski," Maik said finally. He looked down at the

charred form on the table. "Is this him, do you think?"

"Unfortunately, there's no longer any way of telling whether this man ever even handled a firearm, let alone owned one. However, now that we have a name, it would be helpful to compare the victim's dental work with Mr. Kowalski's charts, if his dentist can provide them."

Helpful? For anybody else, it would decide the matter beyond question. And yet, for Dr. Mansfield Jones, perhaps it really would be only one more marker on his path towards some unattainable certainty.

"I'll see what I can find out," said Maik. He felt he should offer something more, perhaps try to draw some connection between the work Jones did down here in his abstract, isolated world and the rest of the policing community. But he suspected his efforts would be misunderstood, at best, and possibly even be taken as patronizing. In the end, he decided there was little to be gained by trying to convince a man of the value of his work if he couldn't see it for himself.

"Well, if there's nothing else, I'll get back upstairs. I'll make sure any information from the dentist is passed on to you as soon as we receive it." And with that, and one final forced smile, Maik took his leave of Jones and went off to rejoin the world of the pseudo-living.

6

Perhaps it was the sunshine that gave DCS Colleen Shepherd's office such a welcoming air as Jejeune entered. The golden light was flooding in through an east-facing window that looked out over a flat tract of farmland. The hedgerows along the boundaries of the fields were beginning to acquire a greyish haze that would soon explode into a full cloak of green. Only the faintest of breezes seemed to be moving them. The earth looked rich and fertile, ready to receive the first of the year's plantings. Reminders of their rural setting were never far away for the officers of the Saltmarsh Division, and like many of them, Shepherd seemed to embrace the fact, eschewing window blinds so she could enjoy the full vista of the north Norfolk countryside whenever she chose.

Shepherd's demeanour held plenty of sunshine, too, and she offered her DCI a pleasant smile as he approached her desk, indicating with an open palm that he should take a seat. It was to be an amicable meeting, then. In the past, when relations between them had been less cordial, they had stood either side of this desk, facing each other like gladiators.

"Eric tells me migration season is just about upon us. The time of year the birds come to you, for once." Her partner's growing obsession with birding was one of the few conversation topics they had been able to retreat to during their recent troubled times. Now, Shepherd seemed to be signalling that it would be a building block in the renewal of their relationship. "I take this to mean you'll not be gallivanting off on any more foreign birding trips any time soon?"

"Spring migration along the north Norfolk coast is about as good as it gets. I can't imagine why a birder would want to be anywhere else."

She nodded. "If Eric's staying local, too, perhaps this means I'll actually get to see him now and again. So, this awful case at the construction site," she said, initiating the abrupt shift of topic for which she was renowned. "We have a name, I understand — the registered gun owner." She consulted her notes. "One Jakub Kowalski."

"It's a Polish name."

"Well, that will save me checking with the Scottish police, then," said Shepherd with heavy sarcasm. She had long ago come to realize that Jejeune's occasional condescension was unintentional, but it was nonetheless irritating for all that. "The victim, we think?"

"There is a missing person's report on file, but we're still waiting for confirmation. Or otherwise."

"Dr. Jones is being his usual contrary self, then?"

Jejeune wanted to correct her. The word implied deliberate obstructiveness, whereas according to Maik, Jones was merely cautious — overly so, perhaps, but not with any malicious intent.

"Your first stop will be to talk to the local Polish community, I suppose? They've quite a large presence in the area, what with all the agricultural labour out here for itinerant workers. I'd imagine they keep fairly close tabs on each other."

Jejeune hesitated slightly. "There's a mother on record. She lives at the same address as the missing man."

Shepherd nodded thoughtfully. It was always the most difficult visit, the one advising a parent that a body was possibly their child. The despair mingled with the uncertainty, the grief with the hope, so that the information sat like an open wound, waiting for the kind of closure only certain knowledge could bring. Sometimes, it never came.

"Sergeant Maik will be going with you?" Jejeune's nod was all the assurance she needed that the visit would be handled as well as it possibly could. "Is there anything I should know about? He seemed out of sorts at the briefing. It's not like him," she said. "His nose is not out of joint because Lauren Salter has finally decided to take her sergeant's exam, is it? To be honest, it's about time, though for the life of me I can't see why she'd feel the need to take a leave of absence to study for it. It's not an unduly arduous test, is it Domenic? They don't ask you to come up with ten positive points about your DCS, anything like that?"

Jejeune forced a smile that suggested on his own list of the DCS's talents, her wit might not come at the top. He shrugged. "I'm not sure he finds working with Dr. Jones all that easy."

"I can see his point. I sometimes wonder if there isn't something else behind Jones's reticence. Caution is all very well, but with the arsenal of forensic equipment at his disposal, I'd expect a little more than a series of singularly non-committal remarks."

"I think he's just wary of issuing information before it's been confirmed. He wants to establish what is known, and what is not known, as clearly as possible." Jejeune both understood and appreciated an approach like this. Like Jones, he knew it is in those empty spaces, those silences between the facts, that the truth is to be found.

He looked past Shepherd at the fields. On occasion he'd seen Curlews from this window. On one glorious late-autumn morning, he had seen a Pallid Harrier. He couldn't remember what they had been discussing, but he had been sitting, so he presumed it must have been a friendly meeting. What he did remember was the bird's long V-shaped wings and its curious flight pattern, bouncing skyward as if tugged by an invisible string. That, and the glorious deep-orange of its underparts, caught by the early morning sun as it banked to avoid the pursuit of a building of Rooks. He had resisted the urge to race from the room, but he had followed the bird's flight across the fields with such intensity that Shepherd had simply abandoned her sentence and waited for him to return to her.

The DCS shifted slightly in her chair, and the movement brought him back to the present. She picked up a sheet of paper that had been lying on her desk and pushed it across to him. "The Met would like to interview you about a past case." She paused and looked at him. He would not need to be told which one. "It was inevitable it would come up, Domenic. Ray Hayes was released on an unsafe conviction, over questionable handling of evidence. You must have known they'd want to have a look at all the other cases that passed through the division around that time. There's no suggestion they'll be looking into your own conduct. They're simply hoping you'll be able to verify everything that went on at the time, as documented. They want to reassure themselves, and everybody else, that all the *i*'s were dotted and *t*'s crossed in this case. *Especially* in this case." She saw his look. "I understand there are aspects of it you'd prefer not to revisit, but perhaps it may even help."

To look again, she meant, at the death of a young man, for which Jejeune had never forgiven himself. To look again at a verdict he had never quite trusted, at evidence he now had reason to doubt. And to know that controlling this review would be the man who had overseen Jejeune's meteoric rise through the ranks, and could just as effectively ensure his fall.

If Domenic Jejeune shared Shepherd's view that revisiting the case might somehow be beneficial, his expression failed to show it.

"They wanted you to go down to London for a couple of days, but I've told them I can't spare you at the moment, so they've decided to send somebody up here. Clearly, they want this thing wrapped up as quickly as possible. Better for all of us, I suppose. A few days, I'm promised, at most. And I'll make it clear that your current investigations are to take priority." Her eyes searched his face for a moment. "Nothing for us to worry about, is there, from a procedural standpoint?"

"The file contains an accurate record of all that went on, as far as I know."

But the truth, Domenic, does it contain that? Shepherd's look seemed to ask. "So there will be nothing coming back to bite us? They were tense times, Domenic, a lapse here or there would be understandable."

Jejeune let his silence stand as his answer.

"Very well, then. But just remember. There'd still be a fair reservoir of goodwill, if it ever became necessary to call upon it."

If anybody was to fill in some of those empty spaces between the facts, you mean, thought Jejeune. He stared around the room. The sunlight seemed to have reached every corner, even those that were normally in shadow.

His mind went back to a conversation of a few weeks earlier, in this very office, when frost still rimed the fields beyond the window and the light outside was pale and flat: "It's to be a new start between us, Domenic." Shepherd had a knack of making such pronouncements sound like the consensus of a long-debated position. She'd looked over her glasses at this point, pausing as if to consider how far she wanted to take her explanation. "I'm aware of all that's gone on, why you were chasing around Elvery when you should have been backing up the team on a gun call." She'd smiled at him. "No one came to me, in case you were wondering. I made it my business to find out. I was actually quite a good copper at one time, believe it or not."

She'd been referring to the breach of duty for which she had transferred Jejeune, a decision she had only rescinded at the last moment. At that early stage in their reconciliation, it had still been difficult ground for both of them. But he hadn't been surprised when she brought it up. It needed to be covered if they were to repair the damage between them. "I understand your need to protect Lindy from what you perceived to be a genuine threat, but since it wasn't Ray Hayes in Elvery, I'm suggesting we draw a line under this incident and move on. However, there are to be no more secrets between us, Domenic. Everything out in the open from this point on. Agreed?"

Jejeune remembered looking at the barren fields outside, stretching to the horizon beneath the low winter sky. "No more secrets," he had repeated at the time, hoping it would be true.

7

Jejeune turned his head quickly, just in time to see a family of Grey Partridges scuttle away under a hedgerow. The passenger seat of Danny Maik's Mini would never be one of his favourite spots anyway, but with the way the car was agonizing over every bump in the road, and its right-drifting tendency requiring Maik's constant correction, the vehicle was inspiring no great confidence today. Like many accomplished drivers, Jejeune wasn't the best of passengers, and the cramped quarters, plus the inevitable barrage of dated music, such as this particularly angst-ridden offering called "Why When Love Has Gone," meant he often spent long portions of their drives regretting his decision to leave the Range Rover behind. In fact, about the only upside to having Maik drive him like this was the opportunity to do some risk-free birding from a car. And in that regard, he conceded, a covey of partridges wasn't a bad way to start the day.

Maik's expression was set somewhere in the space between contemplation and resolve. How many times had he made journeys like this, wondered Jejeune, knowing what was to follow once they delivered their news? And for what, in this case? They could not ask about enemies or potential motives in a son's death they could not yet even confirm. They could bring only the possibility of loss, an uncertainty that was a pain all of its own, beyond sadness, beyond grief. He sighed. He was not looking forward to the next half-hour or so, though he conceded it would have been immeasurably worse without Danny's reassuring presence.

Maik wheeled the Mini into a narrow driveway off the lane and shut off the car engine, simultaneously putting both Domenic Jejeune and The Isley Brothers out of their misery. Patches of once-white plaster showed through on the front of the house where the stucco covering had fallen away. Alongside the drive lay a scruffy patch of dirt partitioned into rows. A vegetable garden, Jejeune guessed, awaiting the arrival of planting weather. Despite the age and disrepair, there were signs of pride in the home: a neatly brushed front step, crisp white lace curtains in the bay window, even the row of bricks neatly outlining the garden's perimeter.

A woman was standing in the open doorway. She looked like she had been there a long time, even though they had not called ahead to tell her they were on their way. Perhaps she stood here every day, holding a vigil for her missing son.

As they got out of the car, the strains of a wheezy birdsong reached them from a nearby hedgerow; Greenfinches, celebrating the imminent arrival of spring; a new chance to breed and raise young, to nurture them, watch them grow. Jejeune hoped he and Mrs. Kowalski were not tuned to the same wavelength.

"You are police?" she asked, not raising herself from the door jamb as the two men approached. "You have come with news of my Jakub?" Her question was not elevated with hope.

"Should we go inside?"

"It is a nice day here," she said, turning her head to indicate the garden. "Here is where I wish to hear your news." She was pale and gaunt, almost to the point of looking malnourished. But she brushed her straw-coloured hair back from her brow with a dignified gesture, and Jejeune saw strength in the hollow features.

"The body of a man was discovered two days ago," said Jejeune. "It has not been possible to identify him yet, but a weapon was found beside the body. The gun is registered to your son."

"This body, this person, it is the one discovered at construction site? The one who was burned?" A stab of pain flashed across her features. "My poor Jakub," she said mechanically.

"As the inspector said, ma'am, we have not established the identity of this person at this time. We are trying to …"

"It is him. I have known this since he disappeared. We can go inside. I have no wish to see this day anymore."

She led them indoors to the small, sparsely furnished living room and sat down in a threadbare armchair. She leaned forward slightly, clasping her hands in front of her and resting her forearms on her knees. Sorrow etched itself into the lines on her face. But there were no tears.

Jejeune had taken a seat on the sofa opposite the woman in the cool, shadowy room, but Maik remained standing. From his vantage point, he could see the sunlit garden outside. It seemed to belong to a different world.

"Does Jakub's father live here?" asked the inspector.

"Jakub had no father — only a man who made a girl pregnant and then ran away. *Tchórz*," she said, "Coward. Jakub was raised by his grandfather. As a girl, I was a disappointment to my father, but he loved my boy with his whole heart." A shadow of sadness swept over her face, and again her lean features tightened with pain.

"Your father is not here with you both?"

"Gone," she said. "Many years now. In Poland. He never came here. Jakub and I had only each other in this place." She waved a hand around to embrace the house, perhaps all of the world. "This is why I know he would never go away without telling me. He would never leave me."

"When was the last time you saw Jakub —?" Jejeune's question stopped abruptly and Maik knew the DCI had barely prevented himself from adding "alive."

"He left this house on Tuesday. It was late afternoon. He was going to Tidewater Marsh. He said he may be able to make money there."

"What is your son's job?"

Maik noticed Jejeune wasn't prepared to yield to the past tense yet. The woman had hope, and even if she didn't hold onto it herself, it was not the DCI's place to take it away from her.

"Many jobs," said the woman, shaking her head sadly. "Jakub had a good mind as a child. He could make plans. His grandfather and I thought he might become an engineer one day. But he did not want to follow this path. He liked money. He would work for it if he had to, but he liked it best when he could get it easy ways. There are many people in our society like this, I think."

"Why does your son own a gun, Mrs. Kowalski?" Maik's tone found the perfect pitch, as always, compassion balanced with an efficiency that suggested he required this information to help locate the missing man.

"He was a hunter. Birds. He was an excellent shot. Licensed even by the government."

Jejeune seemed to stiffen slightly at this information, but a flicker of something outside drew Maik's attention away. He crossed to the window and peered out into the garden. He saw nothing, but when he returned his attention to the room, he could tell that something had changed. His DCI wasn't ready to ask his questions yet, though. He was still letting the pieces fall into place. Maik recognized the need to step in for the moment.

"How did your son become such a good marksman? Was he in the army?"

She shook her head, lowering her eyes into her lap to stare at her hands. "We lived on a farm, far from the city. Vegetables we could grow, but the only meat we ate were the birds Jakub and my father brought home. My father taught Jakub to shoot. He taught him everything. And then he sent his precious grandson away, to England, to a better life." She cast her dark eyes up and looked at Maik. "Do you know how much you must love someone to say goodbye to them forever, because you believe it is better for them? But we would lay down our lives for those we love. Surely to sacrifice our happiness is nothing."

"Does your son hunt for bounty, Mrs. Kowalski?"

Maik spun his head and looked at his DCI. Even after all this time working with Jejeune, the DCI still had the ability to come up with questions for which there seemed to be no point of reference at all.

Paulina Kowalski nodded. "Ducks, the foreign ones. When he heard the government was paying hunters to kill them, Jakub applied for a licence. He was a good shot," she said emphatically. "Always at the head. No suffering for the birds. No wounding, no dying from injuries." She paused. "It is better this way."

Maik nodded in understanding; a man who recognized that there were different ways of killing, even if the result was always the same. But why would the government sponsor the killing of any birds, humanely or otherwise? Jejeune apparently had no need to ask.

"And this was at Tidewater Marsh?" he confirmed.

Paulina Kowalski nodded again. "A pair of these ducks had been reported there. He went to find them." She paused and drew in a breath. "This was the last time I saw him."

Maik's attention had been drawn to the window again, to faint shadows outside that seemed to be changing for no reason. Behind him, he heard his DCI's delicate preparation for another inquiry, the most important one they would need to make today.

"We were wondering about your son's health," began Jejeune, slowly. "If you have the name of Jakub's doctor and his dentist, that would be very helpful."

Though the DCI had couched the matter as delicately as possible, there was slight tightening around Mrs. Kowalski's lips that suggested she may have detected the real reason for the request. She reached across to a small address book on a table and withdrew two business cards. "Jakub had the same doctor as me, but not the same dentist. I must see a specialist now. I have many problems. My doctor says my diet lacked nutrition when I was young." She gave a bitter smile. "I lacked many things when I was young."

"Gun!"

Maik's shout froze Jejeune for a heartbeat, and then he and the sergeant simultaneously burst into action. Jejeune dived towards Mrs. Kowalski, catching her in the chest with his shoulder, flipping the armchair back towards the wall. Maik had already dropped, and was rolling across the floor. But not towards the cover of the upturned chair, behind which Jejeune and Mrs. Kowalski now lay. Maik was moving in the other direction, away from safety, in the direction of the door.

"Sergeant!" called Jejeune. But it was too late.

Police safety protocols stood no chance against Maik's instincts, which were to face the line of fire, drive out into it, attack it. He drew himself up into a crouch and burst through the doorway into the garden, spinning into a low roll as he emerged. Jejeune braced himself for the sound of gunshots, but none came. Leaving Mrs. Kowalski huddled behind the chair, he began inching across the floor. He squatted low and pressed his back against the wall beneath the window. He was breathing heavily and he inhaled sharply to give himself the chance to listen for sounds outside. Silence. Turning, he cautiously raised his eye level up to the window and peered out. He was still hunched against the explosion of activity he expected at any moment. But there was only stillness. The sunlit garden was empty, the shadows undisturbed. On the driveway beside the Mini, he could see the bulky, unwounded form of Danny Maik getting up slowly and bending to pick something up.

Maik returned to the room as Jejeune was helping Mrs. Kowalski to her feet. A photograph had been knocked from a wall in the commotion, but there were no other signs of damage in the tiny living room. Maik hefted the chair to its upright position and eased the woman once more into her seat. "Sorry, ma'am," he said gruffly. "False alarm. All this talk of guns, I suppose. Made me a bit jittery. But the coast is clear. There's nothing to worry about. Can I get you a cup of tea? Help settle the nerves? I know I could use one myself."

Jejeune looked for a long moment at the man made so jittery by all this talk of guns. But he said nothing. He set the broken photograph on a side table and continued to reassure Mrs. Kowalski in low, measured tones until Maik returned with the tea. As he handed her a cup, Jejeune asked again whether she had been hurt by his rugby tackle, but she assured him she had not and brusquely brushed off further questions. She seemed impatient now and keen to have them gone. Perhaps this shock had opened up her defences, and she was ready to disappear into grief over the fate of her son, of which she seemed so certain. The men bowed to her wishes and left.

Outside, Maik took a moment to look up and down the quiet country lane before the two men climbed into the Mini. The sergeant unfurled his hand to reveal the soft black sponge cap he had retrieved from the driveway. "Off a mic. One of those with a long arm."

One that could look like a rifle at first glance, thought Jejeune. "Media?"

Maik shrugged. "Can't think of anybody else who might be interested. I heard a motorbike leaving in a hurry on the far side of the hedge, but I didn't get a look at it."

"Worth checking CCTV, you think?"

"Possibly, but if they know the area well, there are plenty of lanes and back alleys where a bike could avoid cameras. I'll tell uniforms to be on the lookout, but my guess is that they're long gone by now."

Jejeune looked at the foam mic cover carefully. The media may well have an interest in a police visit with a woman who had almost certainly just lost her son, but how had they found out about it so quickly?

The same question played on Danny Maik's mind, as they drove back to the station. It was only much later that afternoon that he thought about the other question that had interested him. The one that concerned the licensed killing of foreign ducks.

8

Jejeune was leaning on the railing, staring up at the heavens, when Lindy rounded the corner at the rear of their cottage. She paused, unwilling to trespass upon his meditations. The flawless marble moon hung suspended over the dark sea, its reflection shimmering like a half-forgotten memory.

Jejeune sensed her presence and turned. She handed him a glass of wine and joined him at the railing. *"Then on the shore of the wide world I stand alone, and think. Till Love and Fame to nothingness do sink,"* she quoted. "I don't suppose your paltry Canadian education covered Keats, did it?"

"What's a Keat?" asked Jejeune, playing along. "I was just thinking about those lunar features you were mentioning; the Sea of Tranquility, and the other one ..."

"The Bay of Rainbows. There's the Island of Winds, too, and the Sea of Serenity, the Lake of Solitude, and dozens of others. Incredible, aren't they? I always imagined they were named by somebody staring up at the night sky like this, armed with a glass of Chablis and an imagination as wide as the universe itself. In reality, it was probably some spotty wonk in the bowels of a lab somewhere. I suppose I've never bothered to find out because I've always preferred my version.

If the truth is going to disappoint you, I say why bother with it. Just make up one of your own."

A light wind came in off the water, rustling the pampas grasses Lindy had arranged in the huge planters at either end of the patio. *Non-native vegetation*, thought Jejeune, *or perhaps merely exotic*. A ribbon of low clouds drifted gently across the horizon, skirting beneath the moon. They stood side by side, sipping their wine, looking out over the sea and the night sky, united in their silent awe of the world and its wonders.

"Still no news, then?"

Jejeune shook his head. It was the code they used for Damian's situation; the shorthand they had settled on as the indecision had dragged on from days to weeks, and now to months.

"Shepherd offered to make some semi-official inquiries, but ..." He let his point fade away on the evening breeze. The Colombian authorities wouldn't be hurried into a verdict just because a DCS with the North Norfolk Constabulary was now making it her business to get involved, not even a DCS as formidable as Colleen Shepherd. The Colombian judiciary had been deliberating Damian's case for this long, and even if Jejeune still chose to interpret that as an encouraging sign, there was no reason to believe they were in any hurry to come to a decision.

"If it ever gets sorted, do you think a family reunion would be on the cards? After all, you think he's already back in Canada somewhere, right?"

Jejeune nodded. The Northwest Territories, he would have guessed, or the Yukon. Somewhere that still retained vestiges of that frontier mentality, where people didn't ask too many questions and were prepared to accept you for who you are, not who you may have been or might be in the future.

"Only, I was thinking, if you were going home to Ontario, perhaps I could come, too. You know, see those places you're always banging on about: Presqu'ile, Carden Alvar, Point Pelee.

I could meet the family, do a bit of sightseeing. I've always wanted to see Niagara Falls."

"Sounds good," said Jejeune absently.

Lindy wasn't fooled. Domenic was always comfortable tacitly agreeing to plans with no timetable. But she'd leave it there for now. She'd broached the subject, and that was enough. She wasn't sure she'd ever had a picture of where their relationship would finally settle. Perhaps it was marriage, perhaps something else. All she knew was she wasn't ready to accept that where they were now was the final stage; all there was and all there ever would be. Try as she might to convince herself, it wasn't enough. She had long known that any further developments would be on hold until this business with Damian was resolved. But they were on the cusp of that now, and whatever the result, beyond it, new horizons would open for them. She felt emboldened to think about the possibility of something lasting, something permanent, but part of that future must involve travelling to Domenic's homeland, to meet his family, to know his past. She was sure Dom would welcome the idea, but he would need time to come to terms with it. All she was doing, she told herself, was beginning that process. The long game, the strategists called it. Plant the seed and move on.

"Since you're in a poetic mood," said Jejeune, still looking at the moon, "Danny Maik quoted me an old poem the other day."

"That doesn't sound like any Danny Maik I know," said Lindy. "Not unless some Motown artist set it to music."

"About Magpies. *One for sorrow, two for joy*. Do you know how the rest of it goes?"

"Wow, Dom, it's been a long time. Let's see:
One for sorrow, two for joy,
Three for a girl, four for a boy,
Five for silver, six for gold,

Seven for a secret, never to be told.
Eight's a wish, nine a kiss …"

She paused and turned to him. "Ah, ten. That's the one for you. *Ten is a bird you must not miss.* Speaking of which, is there any chance I'll be able to tell Eric about Donald and Daisy soon?"

Still immersed in the mist of thoughts about the first time he'd heard the rhyme, Jejeune stared uncomprehendingly at Lindy.

"The ducks. Eric asked me today, point blank: 'Domenic seen anything interesting recently?' Completely out of the blue. I mean, we go days and days without his ever mentioning birding, and the one day I'd like to avoid the subject at all costs, up it pops. Amazing how often things like that happen, isn't it?" Lindy stared at the heavens for a long moment. "Makes you wonder whether there really is some force out there, after all, zipping around the cosmos, making connections, joining dots, knitting together loose ends. I mean, it can't all be coincidence, surely." She paused and looked at Domenic in case he wanted to contribute anything. Apparently not. "So exactly what is it about these ducks that means I can't discuss them with the only other person I know who might conceivably have some interest in them?"

"Ruddy Ducks are subject to an eradication policy," said Jejeune. "Anyone who sees one is supposed to report it immediately. DEFRA will dispatch one of a team of hired marksmen to track it down and kill it."

"The government has put out a contract on ducks?" Lindy shook her head incredulously and her long blonde hair danced on the breeze. "Oh, Dom, this is priceless. Assuming this is not a windup," she cast him a sidelong glance, "why on earth would they want to do that? What could these ducks have done to cause the government to hire hit men to bump them off?"

Lindy recognized Jejeune's sigh as the prelude to a convoluted explanation. *About ducks?* She almost regretted asking, but if she was going to be forced to listen, standing here under a canopy of stars with a soft breeze playing around her shoulders was about as pleasant a setting as any she could imagine.

"Ruddy Ducks are non-natives. They're from North America originally."

"*Vagrant* was the term I saw, I believe," said Lindy. "Sounds a bit prejudicial, if I'm being honest."

Jejeune nodded. "Though no more so than *invasive*, which is another word people use to describe them. The thing is, a few years ago, Ruddy Ducks were found to be interbreeding with White-headed Ducks in Spain, to the extent that it was feared the genetically pure White-headed Duck population would eventually disappear. So a decision was made to eradicate the entire U.K. population of Ruddy Ducks."

"But that's awful," said Lindy, suddenly becoming serious. "It amounts to nothing more than a government-sanctioned slaughter. Surely people in this country wouldn't stand for that?"

"It was certainly controversial, but there are some genuine arguments in its favour. The U.K. has signed on to numerous treaties to protect biodiversity. I'm betting there wasn't an environmentalist in the country who thought it was a bad idea at the time, but it means when a genuine threat to species survival has been identified, you're duty-bound to deal with it."

"But there has to be another way. Besides, ducks fly, don't they? They're migratory. I mean, how realistic is it to think you could kill them all?"

"They've just about managed it. As of a couple of years ago, some six and a half thousand birds had been killed, and now there are only a handful left in the U.K. The cull is all but over, but if anyone becomes aware there are Ruddy Ducks around, the government will pay to have them killed."

"And this has been going on for years? Why haven't I heard about it before now?"

"I don't think anybody has been too keen on broadcasting it. The authorities realize it's a deeply divisive issue. There are arguments on both sides, and not everybody understands, or wants to understand, the complexities. The lower-profile it was allowed to remain, the less chance of concerted opposition or open hostility. It's safe to say, though, the cull remains deeply unpopular with some."

"Not least the ducks, I would imagine," said Lindy. "So you're trying to decide if you should do the required thing and report them, or keep mum and hope they fly away to become somebody else's ethical dilemma." He turned from the railing to answer her, but she held up a hand. "I'm not criticizing. It's probably what I'd do. But I think it wouldn't hurt for you to talk to Eric about this; the sooner, the better."

She stared out into the night. Above the moon, a causeway of stars stretched across the endless black canvas like the trail from a vanished comet. On another night, they might have simply locked arms and sipped their wine and watched the moon's progress up the sky. But she knew his heart would not be in it tonight.

"I'm going in," she said. "I have a couple of things to finish before bed."

"I'll be there soon," he told her, without turning.

After she left, he looked up at the moon, at the shadowy lines traced over its yellow surface. Perhaps with his bins he might have located those lyrically named features. The labels were undeniably beautiful, but he wondered about the darker impulses they revealed. What right had humans to impose names, even such wonderfully poetic ones, on areas of a world so remote and distant from our own? To name something is to take away part of its wildness, to tame it. It's what we do, he thought sadly, we claim things, draw them into our human world and make them a part of it. Even the moon, a place that should remain as free and unconquered as our own souls, even to this we had laid our proprietary claims. We did it with so many things. Places, birds, even people.

He looked up again into the vast black emptiness of the sky around the moon, beyond the stars, between them. *The eternal silence of these infinite spaces terrifies me.* Blaise Pascal wasn't known for his verse, but when Jejeune thought about facts, and the truths that lay between them, he realized the French philosopher understood the universe every bit as well as Lindy's romantic poets.

9

The music wasn't reaching Tony Holland over in the far corner, but he was aware that it was on. When Danny Maik was working on one of his handwritten reports, music was always on. Holland knew Maik was struggling with his account of the previous day's events. "Storm in a tea-cup," he'd announced curtly when Holland had broached the subject. The constable had let the matter drop. Despite his well honed sense of mischief, even Holland recognized when the sergeant's tolerance had reached its limits. Maik wouldn't have enjoyed embarrassing himself at the Kowalski woman's house. He would enjoy even less being reminded about it.

Both men looked up at the confident knock on the door. To Holland's eye, the young woman who entered carried her-self with a good deal more authority than might have been expected from a young person with such a diminutive frame. She seemed dwarfed by the doorway. In his view, her dark business suit and neat, bobbed hairstyle belonged on some-one much older. The woman had large, dark eyes and high cheekbones that seemed to ease the corners of her mouth into a perpetual promise of a smile. It was an attractive feature, but it did nothing to add any years to her appearance.

"Sergeant Maik?" she asked, crossing the room and extending her hand. "DC Desdemona Gill. Des. I'm an Empowered Investigator for the Met's Department of Professional Standards. DCS Shepherd said you might be able to find me a place where I could set up. It'd be brill if there was a spare desk in here."

"You're an Empowered Investigator?" Maik wasn't sure quite what image the title conjured up for him, but somebody who looked like they'd just dodged out of a school trip to the police station certainly wasn't it. He realized too late his tone and his expression had conveyed that message all too clearly.

Gill smiled to show there were no hard feelings. "No prob. I get it a lot. But I assure you, I am of age for vice. To investigate it, I mean."

Maik gave her an apologetic grin. "Welcome to Saltmarsh, Constable Gill."

Tony Holland crossed the room to give Gill one of his fit-for-purpose smiles. "That your bit of retro out in the car park?"

"Nineteen seventy-nine MGB," she said. "It's a family heirloom. Original paint job, even. Pageant blue."

Holland nodded approvingly. "Very nice, I'd definitely let you take me for a spin in that. DC Holland, by the way. You can call me Tony."

"From what I hear," said Gill, "you've already got enough on your plate with the female officers in Traffic Division."

"Ah, the girls in Traffic," said Holland, faux-wistfully. "Who knows why they seem to find me so irresistible?"

"Perhaps it's all those petrol fumes they breathe," offered Maik, who'd gone back to studiously scrawling on his form.

"So you're an Empowered Investigator," said Holland, ignoring the comment. "What does that mean, exactly?"

"Well, let's just say I'm a person whose questions you'd be required by law to answer," she said with a flat smile. "*Actch*, I probably won't have any questions for you. I'm just here to do a straightforward, run-of-the-mill audit on an old case."

"The one involving the kidnapping of the Home Secretary's daughter," said Holland, who had never quite seen the value of circumspection when it came to impressing the ladies. "So what exactly is your remit, then, if you don't mind my asking?"

Tony Holland could do engaged interest as well as anybody when he put his mind to it. But there was always a suggestion it might not be entirely sincere. After a long look at him, Des Gill decided to give him the benefit of the doubt. "I simply need to go over the case notes with an officer who was involved at the time; to verify statements, fill in any blanks, correct any oversights."

"Surely, there are oversights in all case notes."

"Not after I've finished with them," said Gill. She set down her bag and encompassed both men with her look, to make sure they didn't miss the point she was about to make. "Okay, there's no point pretending we don't all know what this is about. But you need to understand I haven't come here looking to ruin anybody's rep or anything. Far from. Truth be told, I'm a big admirer of the DCI's work."

"You don't have to explain anything to us," said Holland. "It's understandable you'd want to have a look into his conduct. I heard there were inconsistencies in his reports, which is hardly surprising, considering the way he operates."

Des Gill shook her head. "No," she said. "Look, I don't intend talking about this much, but I've never been a fan of letting false rumours go unchallenged. I've read the inspector's reports, or more accurately, the sergeant's, as he was then, and I can tell you there were no discrepancies in them. None at all. They were entirely consistent throughout."

Which was not to say there weren't discrepancies between his accounts and those of other officers, thought Maik. But since

Desdemona Gill didn't seem interested in pointing out the distinction to Holland, he saw no reason to, either.

"So, you're just here to get the Saltmarsh Superman to admit to any mistakes he might have made in the way he went about his investigation? Good luck with that."

"You seem to have an interesting opinion of the DCI, Constable Holland," said Gill. "Perhaps I could make it part of my report. I imagine the top brass would find your perspective fascinating. As far as I know, they are just about unanimous in the idea that Domenic Jejeune is a very good police officer. I'm sure they'd be interested to hear otherwise from somebody who works so closely with him. Would you mind going on record with your views?"

"No, wait," said Holland hurriedly. "Look, I can assure you, no one round here is a bigger admirer of the DCI than me. I've learned so much simply by observing his methods, and I know I'm a better detective for having been around him." He nodded emphatically. "Greatness like that, it just seems to rub off on you."

Gill was thoughtful for a moment. "You know," she said quietly, "I'm sure many women might not see it this way, but looking younger than your age does have its drawbacks."

"Really? Like what?"

"Like people tend to think you're going to believe any old horseshit they tell you," she said, staring at Holland frankly.

Maik suppressed a slight smile as he looked up to see the constable raising his hands in protest. "Point taken," said Holland affably, backing away towards his own desk with his hands still aloft. "I can already tell it would be a big mistake to misunderestimate you."

"I couldn't misagree with you more," said Gill.

"Why don't you set up at Lauren's … Constable Salter's desk," said Maik, whose tolerance for blood sports was never very high, even when the quarry was Tony Holland. "If you're only intending on being here for a few days, it shouldn't be a problem. It's that one over there."

Maik watched Gill approach the vacant desk and picked up his pen to continue with his report. He paused when he sensed her staring at him.

"Sorry, I was just thinking how fab it is to see somebody writing a report out by hand. With a fountain pen, no less." She held up a hand. "No, really, I think it's brill. I take longhand notes, too, though I always end up transcribing them onto the comp, natch."

Maik realized time was likely to be in short supply in the life of a dynamic young Empowered Investigator, but he found himself wondering if Des Gill really couldn't spare enough of it to use entire words. She began carefully easing Salter's own items to the periphery of the desk as Maik watched.

"I'll try not to disturb Constable Salter's things too much," she said. "It's a pity I won't be here long enough to meet her. She has an excellent rep. I imagine you must be looking forward to her coming back soon."

"I can't say I am," said Holland from the other side of the room. "She'll be a sergeant when she returns, which I suppose means all the fetching and carrying will be down to me. I can't see Lauren Salter being willing to do any of the donkey work once she has her stripes."

"Perhaps if you called it zebra work?" offered Gill.

Desdemona Gill would probably turn out to be decent company, thought Maik, as soon as she learned to finish her words.

Holland, for whom rapid recovery had long been a trademark, took the humour as a signal that Gill's mood had softened. "Desdemona," he said. "It's a nice name. Does it mean something?"

"It means English professors should never be allowed to choose names for their baby daughters. Did you want something, Constable Holland? Only, I have a lot of work to be getting on with."

"Listen," said Holland, straining for a conciliatory tone which he very nearly reached, "we seem to have got off on the wrong foot, you and me. How about we start again? If you want a local guide to show you around while you're here, I'd be happy to offer my services."

Gill, to her credit, met him halfway. "Fair enough. I know a lot of these small villages have their own little rituals and ceremonies. If there was one of them going on, I might be interested in seeing something like that."

"Yeah, absolutely. In fact there's a special ritual going on here in Saltmarsh tonight, as it happens."

"There is?" The comment came from Gill, but it could have been Maik's, such was the sergeant's own surprise. He laid down his pen and looked at Holland.

"This evening," said Holland, painting a picture in the air with his hand, "as the light fades and the moon begins to rise, the locals will leave their homes and make their way down long-established routes, coming from all directions to one special gathering place. It's a time-honoured tradition we here in Saltmarsh like to call *going down the pub*."

"Sounds terrif," said Des, smiling. "Pity I'll have to miss it. I need to make a start on all this tonight. There's a lot more material to go through than I normally have."

And perhaps there was just something in her tone, thought Maik, that suggested the Empowered Investigator might already have her doubts about just how straightforward and run-of-the-mill this audit of Jejeune's old case was going to be.

10

Jejeune and Maik had been met in the lobby of the Whitehaven Golf Club by a timid receptionist who seemed to expect her every sentence would be met by a rebuke. Though neither man was happy with what she told them, they were careful not to imply she was to blame, offering only smiles of gratitude as she guided them along the maze of short corridors. They had been summoned here on the premise of meeting a golf pro who claimed to have information about an open murder case. There was currently only one open murder case on the Saltmarsh Division docket. But the man in question had apparently developed a sudden illness, and while second thoughts were not unusual with witnesses, or informants, the detectives were being ushered to the executive suite with a speed and efficiency that suggested prior planning. Neither detective now believed there was ever a possibility that the golf pro would have been providing them with information about an open murder case, or anything else.

They were shown in to the lavishly appointed corner office and stood side by side, just inside the doorway. Light poured into the room through banks of floor-to-ceiling windows that ran along the two outside walls. Beyond them, Jejeune could see the immaculately manicured greens and fairways of the golf course, fringed along the far edge by a stand of trees. The sight seemed to fascinate him, and he stood for a long time looking out while Maik took a survey of the room. It was redolent of the Empire: a glass-encased Union Jack hung behind an expansive oak desk, while a picture of the reigning monarch, in full regalia, adorned the remaining wall.

Both men turned at the sound of a side door opening. Jejeune did not recognize the man, but judging from Maik's reaction, this was someone in whom he might need to take a professional interest.

"Welcome to Whitehaven, gentlemen. Can I get you anything? A nice pre-lunch G&T, perhaps? I can offer you Gordon's. It's English."

"I didn't know you ran this place," said Maik guardedly. "Or is this just another one of your property development deals?"

"Develop a pretty little corner of England like this? Perish the thought, Sergeant. I own it. I have others to do the day-to-day, but I take an active interest in the goings-on here. Active," the man repeated. He crossed to Jejeune with a hand extended. "Since the sergeant here obviously isn't going to introduce us, I'll do it myself. Curtis Angeren. And you, I know to be Inspector Jejeune."

The DCI understood Maik's reaction now. And his comment. Jejeune, too, would not have expected a leading activist in one of the country's most radical nationalist groups to be running a golf club. Perhaps it was Angeren's reputation that had led Jejeune to expect someone with a greater physical presence, more robust, more overtly threatening. But the man before him, neatly attired in dark trousers and a restrained sweater, was unremarkable in build and appearance. Only the luxuriant waves in the neatly cut grey-blond hair were of particular note.

Jejeune turned back to the window and looked out at a foursome that was getting ready to tee off. "Is this a private course?"

"Private and very exclusive, Inspector. A lot of people felt the Saltmarsh Club had let its standards drop over the years. Letting all sorts in there now." He shook his head in what might have passed for regret. "Still, it did provide a niche in the market my associates and I were only too happy to fill. Here, our members get to choose the kind of people they share the clubhouse with." He joined the detective at the window. "Nice set of clubs that bloke has. All made in Asia, of course. I sometimes wonder if we'll have any industry left at all on this side of the world in a few years."

He looked across to see if Jejeune would react, but the detective was now scanning the trees on the far side of the fairway. Angeren crossed to his desk and opened an elaborately carved wooden box. "Care for a cigar?" he asked. "Cuban. Couldn't find any English ones." He flicked a brief smile at the men as they declined. He withdrew a cigar and clipped the end carefully before lighting it. He puckered it to life and gazed at the glowing tip for a moment before turning again to the detectives.

"So I suppose you're wondering why you were asked to come here."

"We know why," said Maik. He seemed particulary keen to take the lead, and since he clearly had more experience with Angeren, Jejeune was happy to let him. "We were going to be interviewing a golf pro, who may have information pertinent to a case we're working on. Except he seems to have had an attack of the vapours."

Angeren nodded. "Ah yes, Nigel. Finished nine holes this morning but then came over a bit strange. Said he wasn't quite himself."

"Feeling a bit above par, was he?"

The quip earned a couple of appreciative jabs from the end of Angeren's cigar. Even Jejeune managed a smile. Maik's humour was usually worth waiting for, even if it generally had a message. This comment was delivered in a tone that suggested he wanted to get on with things, as if he didn't expect he was going to enjoy Angeren's company very much. Jejeune concurred, but it was clear this meeting was going to proceed according to Angeren's schedule. And people didn't often go through the elaborate ritual of lighting up a cigar unless they had time on their hands.

Angeren inclined his head slightly. "I thought a bit of discretion might be in order. A person of my known political affiliations, and a high-profile detective … a couple of them —" a smile in Maik's direction here "— you know what the gossip is like around these parts. Which is partly what I wanted to talk to you about. After all, Inspector, if you're as good as they say you are, you're going to come across the rumours soon enough."

He pulled on his cigar, providing a pause long enough to check whether any rumours had yet come to light. If they had, neither detective was saying.

"I understand that body they found on the construction site has been identified as Jakub Kowalski." He shook his head. "Must be awful for the mother, losing her only child like that. The grief, you can't imagine it, can you?"

Maik was inclined to ask where he might have learned about the tentative identification of the body, but since his DCI seemed uninterested in pursuing the point at the moment, he let it go.

Angeren took another deep draw on his cigar as a prelude to continuing. "The thing is, you might come across some talk that I was not best pleased with Mr. Kowalski. I may have said a few things that, taken out of context, could be misinterpreted."

"And what might someone have misinterpreted them to say?" asked Maik warily.

The developer walked to the window again and looked out at the first tee, where another party of four were readying themselves to begin their round. "Look at that. 11:40 bang on the dot. That's another thing our members get to enjoy here: properly observed tee-off times. I mean, it's not really what you'd call a strength of your average foreigner, is it, punctuality?"

"The Swiss seem to have got the knack of it," said Maik. "We were talking about misinterpretation."

Angeren turned slowly from the window. "I see now, with the benefit of hindsight, that my comments could be interpreted as wishing Mr. Kowalski might come to some harm. That's the trouble with words, isn't it? Once they're out there, there's really no way of retracting them." He flashed a short smile, asking for understanding, but receiving none.

"Are you telling us you put out a contract on Jakub Kowalski?" asked Jejeune with surprise.

"No, I'm saying I can understand how my outburst could have been interpreted that way. Figures of speech, you see; you can never tell when somebody's going to take them literally, can you? A keen bunch, the rank and file in our organization, but I don't imagine any of them have ever been accused of over-thinking anything, if you get my drift."

"Even if what you say is true," Maik's pause left plenty of room for an alternative point of view, "if somebody decided to kill Jakub Kowalski directly as a result of your comments, you'd still be criminally responsible."

A faint smile softened Angeren's features. "And that's why I've gone to all this trouble of inviting you gentlemen here," he said indulgently. "To assure you with absolute certainty," he paused, "absolute certainty, you understand, that Jakub Kowalski was not killed by anyone in my organization, or by anyone associated with me."

"How can you be so sure?" asked Jejeune.

Angeren shared a knowing look with Maik. "Because I've asked them." He looked out the window again. "You should have bought your binoculars, Inspector. We get some lovely birds out here. Got all the kit, I suppose — binoculars, digiscope, spotting scope? All made in Asia, no doubt."

"Some of the finest optics in the world come from Asia," said Jejeune flatly.

"That's not what I hear. I hear they tend to lose crispness over long distances, they're subject to image instability, definition's a bit suspect. Lot of tat from that part of the world. Have to be very careful about the quality." He regarded the detective closely. Curtis Angeren had spent a lifetime detecting the tiniest sparks of complicity in like-minded souls; a look, a subtle inclination of the head, a glint in the eyes, anything that might suggest the person did not entirely disapprove of Angeren's point of view, even if they weren't ready to voice it in polite conversation. That didn't matter; a spark could be nurtured later, fanned into flames of indignation, of anger, in any number of ways. It was the initial sentiment that was important. He waited a moment longer but there was no reaction from the detective.

"The thing is, gentlemen, it would be very useful to me to know just who was responsible for Jakub Kowalski's death. In my world, you see, if somebody hears you want something done and they do it, they believe you owe them. And they expect repayment — in one form or another."

"Only you didn't, did you?"

Maik's remark seemed to puzzle Angeren.

"Want something done to Jakub Kowalski. So as I see it, you'd be in the clear with these people, even if they did think they were doing you a favour."

Angeren turned his gaze from the speaker to his boss. "I was hoping you could do me the courtesy of keeping me apprised of your progress in this case."

"You know we can't do that."

"Yes, but in this case, I thought you might be able to make an exception?"

Maik was about to reiterate their position in terms Curtis Angeren would understand quite clearly, but Jejeune stepped in. "Why might we want to do that, Mr. Angeren?"

"Because I happen to know that an old acquaintance of yours was in town a short while ago," he said. "A man named Ray Hayes. Apparently, he was asking around about some girl."

Jejeune had not moved, not blinked, not allowed any expression to cross his face. But he had turned to the window now, to look out over the fairway. If his action seemed abrupt to Maik, the sergeant understood why. Jejeune would be reeling from the news, possibly physically sickened by the shock of it. At the very least, he needed a moment to compose himself. Maik locked his eyes on the developer.

"What do you know about Hayes?" he asked sharply.

Angeren shrugged. "Just that he was making some inquiries about a local journalist. Something of a looker, by all accounts." Angeren took a long, slow draw on his cigar.

"If you know Ray Hayes's whereabouts, I suggest you share that information with us immediately," Maik said in a tone that seemed to reduce the light in the room.

"Why would I want to do that?" asked Angeren pleasantly. "There's no warrant out for him, is there? He's not committed any crime. It'd be a breach of his rights for me to be telling the police his personal business. I assume English people do still have some rights in this country."

Jejeune still hadn't turned to face them. An electronic silence seemed to buzz through the room. From somewhere outside came the faint sound of applause for a well-hit drive.

Maik leaned in, close enough for the other man to see the tiny blood vessels the sergeant's sleepless nights left in the corners of his eyes. "It's a bit noisy in here," said Maik, the menacing irony dropping his voice a further notch, "so just in case you misheard, I asked if you'd mind volunteering information as to the whereabouts of Ray Hayes."

Angeren drew deeply on his cigar again and let the smoke dribble slowly from his lips into the narrow gap between them. "See, Sergeant. I ask you people for something, you say no. And then you turn around and expect a favour from me in return." He paused for a couple of heartbeats to look directly into Maik's eyes before breaking the spell, wheeling away and rounding the desk. "But I'll tell you what I'll do, just as a show of good faith. I'll tell you the exact location of Ray Hayes at this moment in time. He's in Cambridge."

"Cambridge? What's he doing there?"

Jejeune turned to hear the answer, and he watched as Angeren drew an expensive watch up to his eye line. "Almost certainly sleeping, I should think. It's the middle of the night. Cambridge, Australia — did I forget to mention that? It's near Perth, I believe. His uncle has some land out there. He's not doing well, apparently, and Hayes has gone to pay his last respects. I imagine he'll be back soon, though." Angeren made a point of looking at his watch again. "Well, gentlemen, I'm sure we all have things to do. I appreciate you dropping by so we could clear up that misunderstanding about poor Mr. Kowalski."

Maik had not expected his DCI to be in any condition to contribute anything further, but as Angeren's hand reached for the door, Jejeune spoke, his voice steady and firm.

"What did he do?"

"I'm sorry?"

"Jakub Kowalski. What was it he did that upset you in the first place?"

Angeren turned back to face the room and shook his head ruefully. "You know, I can't even remember. I'm like that, see. Impulsive. Fireworks one minute, but the next it's all blown over and I'm back to my usual affable self." He nodded slightly. "I have struggled with my anger issues in the past, I don't mind admitting it. But no harm done, in this case." He looked at Jejeune one final time. "I trust you'll have a think about my request, Inspector. See what you can do. Good day, gentlemen."

Angeren exited through the side door, leaving the men to find their own way out.

11

At first glance, the shapes in the distance looked like animals, grazing cattle, perhaps, or even deer. But one by one, the tawny backs straightened and several humans stretched to their full height. Behind them, the pale afternoon sun threaded its way through a veil of mist hanging above the wetland. Pools of silver light flashed among the reeds, and the stands of tall grass fringing the marsh tilted lightly in the breeze. No sound disturbed the ethereal silence that hung over the landscape. The people stood, as quiet and still as the land of which they were a part, watching as the detectives approached.

The two men had been subdued on the drive out. Maik had not insulted Jejeune's intelligence by suggesting there was still no firm evidence to connect Hayes to the explosion that had hospitalized Lindy some months earlier. Jejeune had been convinced at the time that Hayes was involved. They had both been willing to believe he was wrong, based on later events, but now that Hayes had re-entered the picture, it was all the confirmation either of them needed, firm evidence or not.

"I'll put out an alert for us to be notified when Hayes returns from Australia. I can be his welcome home committee, if you like."

Jejeune had given his head a short shake. "Angeren is well-connected enough to hear about any official request from us to the Border Force, and he'll make sure Hayes finds out about it. As he pointed out, there is no legal reason for us to be paying any special attention to Hayes. A harassment suit would effectively tie our hands from now on. Besides, I'm fairly sure Angeren will still be willing to let us know when Hayes is scheduled to return."

For a price, he didn't say. A price Maik was certain his DCI had no intention of paying. But they both knew as long as Hayes was out of the country, Lindy was in no danger, which meant Jejeune still had some time to work on ways of keeping his girlfriend safe. They had let the subject drop and completed the rest of their journey in silence. Now they were ready to concentrate on matters at hand. Namely, interviewing this tall, distinguished individual who was striding toward them over the marshy ground with such purpose.

"Good morning. I must inform you that this is Crown land, access is restricted. Signs are posted at the road entrance. But perhaps you did not see them?" Even in these rustic surroundings, the man's elegant bearing was undiminished. He held his tall body upright with the kind of rigour that suggested a military background. But there was more here than simple discipline. His finely carved features spoke of a noble heritage and were carried with the confidence of the high-born. His white hair was worn in a longish cut, and his clothes betrayed the faint vanity of those for whom appearances are a kind of silent testimony to character. Rather than the same tawny colour as the others' jackets, this man's yellow coat took on almost a golden hue against the soft, diffused light that rested over the wetlands behind him.

Maik flashed his ID, and the man inclined his immaculately coiffed head. "Ah, to the police, of course, no access is restricted. Welcome to Tidewater Marsh," he said.

"We'd like to speak with Teodor Sikorski," said Jejeune.

Another slight incline of the head accompanied his smile. "At your service."

The men introduced themselves and Sikorski's face brightened. "Inspector Jejeune! Our paths have never crossed, but I know of your reputation. An Iberian Azure-winged Magpie. A first British record," he said with a broad smile.

Maik sighed inwardly. For such an elite group, there sometimes seemed to be a birder in every crowd. He realized the longer he left it before bringing the conversation round to the topic at hand, the harder it was going to be to prevent the visit from sliding off into a session of record-swapping. Though it might be easier today than usual since, for once, the DCI seemed to have no particular appetite for pursuing the subject.

"May I ask what it is you're doing out here?" said Jejeune.

"Controlling invasive species. Sadly, this area has become colonized by one particularly disturbing interloper. Even the scientific researchers are calling it *Frankenweed.*"

Maik's stare had a way of conveying many things, impatience with fools among them. Sikorski was the essence of courtesy, however.

"You have heard of Japanese knotweed, of course," he said, "the invasive weed that has caused such well-publicized problems for unfortunate homeowners."

They had. The litany of issues was long: catastrophic declines in house prices, buildings abandoned, mortgages being refused; all directly linked to the presence of the species on or near a property. Efforts to remove it were exorbitantly expensive and time-consuming. Some estimates put the total cost to the national economy in the region of two hundred million pounds per year.

"At a place called Haringey, this weed hybridized, naturally as far as anyone can tell, with Russian vine. Imagine, please, the devastating potential of the aggressive spread and root tenacity of Japanese knotweed combined with the rapid growth rate and tensile strength of Russian vine."

Jejeune's eyes opened wide. *Frankenweed* suddenly made a lot more sense.

"It was thought to be restricted only to this one site in the U.K.," said Sikorski. "Unfortunately, it was recently discovered in Tidewater Marsh. We have no idea how it came to be here. As a restricted area it is not often visited. But the length of some of these vines suggests it must have been growing here for a long time. It does not yet appear to have spread to other areas, but it could be just a matter of time if we allow it to become any further established. The government wishes to ensure its complete eradication. So we must dig it out by the roots."

"Wouldn't it be easier just to pull it out by hand? Presumably such a strong vine wouldn't give way."

"Indeed, the vine itself is as robust as rope, but the root base of Japanese knotweed is incredibly well-anchored. Digging it out is the only way of removing it effectively. It is why the cost of clearing the species from one's property is so expensive."

"Still," said Maik, "it looks like back-breaking work. Couldn't the government just get a mechanical digger in?"

"They could, but this would remove all species." Sikorski gave another charming smile. "Do no harm, Sergeant; it is an important principle of conservation. We must take care not to destroy the beneficial native species. Sometimes, the hardest work of all is to protect the innocent, is it not?"

As far as Maik was concerned, doing no harm was a handy principle to live by, conservation-related or not. Unfortunately, in his line of work, it wasn't always possible.

"Did these people work on invasive species control back home, then?" he asked. "Only, I wouldn't know a Haringey knotweed from a sprig of Saltmarsh samphire."

"This is my role." Sikorski gave the smile of a man who'd held positions of authority and was used to the respect they brought. Neither detective sensed any notion of self-importance. "I have expertise in this area. Many invasive species bear a strong resemblance to native ones. For now, identification of the Frankenweed by sight and removal by hand is the only foolproof method."

Jejeune gazed back at the group of workers, perhaps a dozen or so, who were still standing and looking at the men. Some held bunches of vegetation in their hands, others had shovels. Behind them, the flat sunlight glinted off the water like a mirror.

"Are all these workers Polish?" he asked.

"They are seasonal farm workers. They are awaiting the planting season. Until then, they will do this work."

"If they work on the farms in the area, I take it your associates all speak English," said Jejeune. He wondered why they remained so silent, content to let Sikorski act as their spokesman. That said, you could do worse than have such an eloquent and charismatic representative.

Sikorski inclined his magnificent white head once more. "They speak the language well enough, but sometime a little Polish helps. A description here, an explanation there ..." Sikorski gave them a frank look. "Perhaps either may help you with what you came here to find today."

"We are wondering if you know a family named Kowalski?" said Jejeune.

"I know many people with this name. It is a common Polish name, perhaps the most common."

"The ones we are interested in are a woman and her son: Paulina and Jakub."

"Again, not unusual names. But yes, I know this family. Are they in difficulties?"

"We would appreciate any background you could give us on them," said Jejeune. Like all good police officers, he'd mastered the deft deflection of inquiries he didn't want to answer.

Sikorski bowed his head in thought for a moment. "Sadly, neither is as community-minded as we would wish. The mother, Paulina, does some record keeping for us at our community centre. The large hall at the end of the track from the main road," he explained. "You would have parked beside it, I imagine. On the edge of the raised berm?"

The men confirmed they had, though neither had known what the building was at the time. They had taken it for a dilapidated old barn.

"She deals with records to do with employment like this?" asked Jejeune.

Sikorski nodded. "She assists with filling out applications for various services. Legal documents, medical files, immigration records. It is valuable work, but her skills are offered grudgingly. To those who are dependent on the help of others, such things are noticed. It is important to them that such assistance is also given willingly."

"And does the son, Jakub, help at the centre also?"

A sad smile crossed Sikorski's face. "Unfortunately, Jakub Sikorski wishes no connection with our group at all. A sense of togetherness, of belonging, is so important for a small community like ours. We have all come here from the same place, and we now find ourselves in the same circumstances. People believe it is important to remember that you share your background with everyone else."

"So, would you say Jakub Kowalski is unpopular with members of the local Polish community?" asked Maik.

Sikorski considered the sergeant's question, seeming, somehow, to appreciate the importance of it. "I would not use this word. Perhaps his desire to isolate himself is just not well understood."

The two detectives regarded the group carefully. They had not moved from their stations at the edge of the marshland. They stood still, the afternoon sun at their backs, cutting tools and bundles of vegetation dangling from their lowered hands. Only their eyes moved. Warily. Guardedly.

"Forgive them, gentlemen. Their distrust is not of you, but of life itself. They have suffered many hardships in the past. They are hopeful that you will not bring them more."

"Thank you for your time, Mr. Sikorski," said Jejeune. "We'll leave you to get on with your important work."

Maik turned to accompany his DCI back along the track to where they had parked the Mini. *Do no harm.* If they'd learned nothing else from this visit, at least they could now be fairly sure that Jakub Kowalski's killer was no conservationist.

12

"Well, that went well," said Lindy, with the kind of heavy irony that suggested she would want an audience for her grievances. Jejeune shut down the document he was working on and closed his laptop, watching as she crossed the living room. She tossed her bag onto a vacant chair and slumped heavily into another, on the far side of the fireplace. He had not been sure which Lindy would return, one aglow with victory in a spirited intellectual battle, or the chastened victim of a coordinated ambush. She had written an article which hearkened back to the previous summer's Saltmarsh Festival, and made a series of dire predictions about the forthcoming one. *A Fête Worse than Death* had been intended as little more than tongue-in-cheek filler for the magazine, but it had generated a surprising amount of feedback and public discussion. As so often, Lindy had tapped into an undercurrent of sentiment in the community. But the piece had also caught the attention of the fête's organizing committee, and Lindy had been invited to defend her criticisms in person. Never one to shy away from the chance to justify her position, Lindy had accepted the invitation and marched out of the cottage earlier with a clear-eyed determination. Whatever she had now returned with, Jejeune sensed it wasn't the glow of victory.

No matter what he chose as his opening gambit, it was unlikely to change the direction of the conversation. Innocent misinterpretation seemed as safe a route as any. "So it went well, you said?"

"No, Domenic, it did not go well. I have seen the Face of Evil, and its name is Calista Hyde. Have you met her?"

Jejeune shook his head slowly. "I don't think so."

"Well, if you ever do, beware. She's one of those devious, manipulative types who can get you to do whatever they want."

"A woman, you mean?"

Lindy gave him one of her special glances, but there was no real malevolence in it. Nevertheless, Jejeune decided to make amends by going to the kitchen and returning with two glasses of wine. "What did she get you to agree to?" he asked, handing one to Lindy and moving her bag so he could settle into the chair opposite her.

"I've been forced to accept a place on the planning committee for this year's fête. I could hardly refuse, could I?" said Lindy, shifting position in the chair. "Unless you're prepared to contribute towards putting something right, criticizing it seems like a fairly pointless exercise."

She looked so frustrated and helpless. The urge to protect her from Ray Hayes welled up inside him like a physical force. But protect her how? At the moment, Hayes was an invisible threat, thousands of miles away. For an undetermined amount of time, it seemed he would remain so. But if they were to continue to enjoy moments like this, shared, intimate evenings over a glass of wine, he would have to act at some point. He didn't know how yet, or when. All he could be sure of was that the time was coming.

"Danny Maik was asking how you like your new car," said Jejeune, as if to emphasize to himself the value of such unguarded casual conversation, of all they stood to lose.

Lindy came back from her thoughts. "The Nissan Leaf? It's fine, great." She wasn't a person who fell head over heels in love with material things, as a rule. She saved her overwhelming passions for moments in time, special occasions. Or people. "Why is he asking? The Mini playing up again?"

"It hasn't been right since that accident last year. I get the feeling it should have been written off, but I'm sure the suggestion didn't go over well."

"It's his sense of loyalty, I suppose," said Lindy. "He's very fond of that car, and I'm sure he feels he owes it something. You know Danny."

"Still, there has to be a time to let go if a thing's no longer working."

"Do you think so?" Lindy sat forward earnestly and set her glass of wine beside her. "You don't think it's worth trying to put things right if problems occur? Surely, it's worth having a go at fixing something, rather than just abandoning it."

Jejeune looked at her with genuine puzzlement. "The suspension is shot," he said, "and the alignment is off, too. I'm pretty sure the frame got twisted in the crash. One of these days he's going to get pulled over by Traffic for operating an unsafe vehicle."

That's the trouble with writers, thought Lindy, *we see metaphors everywhere.* But as long as Domenic was going to limit his throwaway attitude to cars, rather than relationships, she would be content to let his comments go without further challenge. "That traffic cop would have to be pretty desperate to meet his quota," she said. "It would take some courage to walk up to the formidable Danny Maik and hand him a ticket." She picked up her glass again and seemed surprised to find it empty. "Want another?"

She took Jejeune's glass and padded past him into the kitchen. "Anyway," she called over her shoulder, "tell him if he'd like to take my Leaf out for a test drive, he's welcome."

From the kitchen, Jejeune could hear the resonating gurgle of the wine tumbling into the glasses. They had recently agreed to cut down on their drinking at home, but the resolve had softened to apply only indoors, because their patio was such a glorious place to watch the sunsets and look out over the sea, and a glass of wine just seemed like the perfect complement to that. And exceptions could obviously be made for significant moments indoors, too — times of celebration, or consolation, or of undefined but agreeably apt momentousness. The parameters seemed to shift on any given day, but a gruelling encounter with the manipulative Face of Evil surely qualified. Still, though, it made Jejeune begin to wonder if they shouldn't just limit their new resolution to not drinking at home on dull days when nothing really happened. Except those were exactly the kinds of days they felt most like a drink. In all honesty, he couldn't see this resolution lasting much longer than those Lindy made so faithfully every New Year's Day and abandoned so brazenly a few days later.

She returned and handed Domenic his wine, sliding back into her own chair and snuggling in luxuriously. She swirled the wine around in her glass and peered through it into the fireplace. "I really shouldn't be doing this," she said. "I need to get going on some notes for the next meeting of the Fête Committee. I get the feeling Calista's the kind of taskmaster who's going to make Eric look reasonable by comparison. She's a pretty formidable character, that one."

"It is a pity Danny prefers to be alone," said Jejeune, smiling, "or you could try hooking the formidable twosome up."

"I'm not sure anyone prefers being alone, Dom." Lindy leaned towards him, forearms resting on her knees, the wine glass cradled between her hands. "They might prefer being on their own to being with the person they're currently with, but I'm not at all sure that's the same thing. Love can break your heart, but only loneliness can ache like it does."

Domenic looked slightly dubious, as if he thought perhaps she'd already had enough wine, and she wondered whether she'd overplayed her hand. But she had seen too many relationships flounder on the rocks of apathy, too many people wait too long, assuming something would always be there, until one day it wasn't anymore and it was too late to do anything about it. She wasn't thrilled she'd taken the conversation down this road, but she didn't entirely regret it, either. Nevertheless, it was probably time to give them both some breathing space. Besides, she had other tricky waters to navigate tonight.

"Well, I suppose I'd better get to work," she announced. She stood up, but made no effort to walk towards their office. Instead she lingered, looking around her. Jejeune sensed it was going to be an awkward topic by the way Lindy seemed to be working up to it. He stood up, facing her.

"Erm, I think I forgot to tell you. Eric said to tell you there'd been a report of a possible sighting of a Ruddy Duck."

"Ah. Did he say which one?"

"No, but it was a male. He started to tell me about the lovely blue beak."

"Started to?"

Lindy gave him a guilty look. "I couldn't keep him in the dark any longer, Dom. It didn't seem right."

"You told him about the female we saw, too?"

She looked crestfallen. "He says a pair together at this time of the year might mean they're setting up a breeding site. That's what you're afraid of, isn't it, Dom? That they'll be on territory, easy to find, if you report them."

Jejeune gave her a sad smile. "What does Eric say?"

"He thinks you have a responsibility to report them, but

he's agreed to leave the decision up to you."

"He's correct," said Jejeune quietly. "It's the right thing to do. The fate of a species shouldn't be put in jeopardy because of concerns about a couple of individual birds."

"Well, yes, obviously, in theory," said Lindy, waving her wine glass slightly. "It seems a perfectly reasonable position when you're talking about ducks in the abstract. But Donald and Daisy are individuals. I know them. It's personal with those two now."

"And you weren't able to sway Eric with that logic?" asked Jejeune with an ironic smile.

"He says naming them was a mistake. But it's not really anthropomorphism, is it? I mean, I'm not assigning human traits to them, just cartoon names. At worst, it's only a halfway step."

"You discussed all this at work?"

"Oh, don't worry. There was only the two of us left by that point. It's amazing how quickly you can clear a room just by turning the talk to birding."

It's probably just as well, thought Jejeune. A discussion about giving cartoon names to real birds might just have lacked the intellectual cut and thrust the staff had come to expect from Lindy's exchanges with her boss.

"Couldn't you report these ducks to the relevant authorities, but say you needed them to be kept alive? Imply they were important to your investigation, perhaps?" Lindy tilted her head in a way that had sometimes proved to be the clincher in past requests.

"Claim they were ducks of interest, you mean?" Jejeune paused a moment, looking into Lindy's innocently wide eyes, pretending to consider the idea. "Possibly, but I'd still have to let them go as soon as I'd interviewed them."

Lindy tilted her head back to an upright position, mission unaccomplished. "I thought you liked birds," she said tartly.

"Why do they have to be killed, anyway? Can't they just be captured and sent to a sanctuary somewhere, even if they're kept in separate facilities? No, I suppose not," she admitted sadly. "It would be an awful life for them. Wings clipped, no mating, facing the same boring existence every day."

"They might as well be married," said Jejeune with a smile.

Lindy lay a palm against Jejeune's chest in lieu of the words she was having trouble finding. Eventually, she managed to raise lightness from somewhere. "Talk about anthropomorphism! And poor old Daisy wouldn't even get a ring."

13

Des Gill clearly hadn't expected Detective Chief Inspector Domenic Jejeune to be standing at the front of the Incident Room as she entered. Perhaps her research had prepared her to look for him at the back, perched on a desktop somewhere, his feet resting on a chair in front of him. She seemed taken aback to find herself standing directly opposite him.

"Oh, sir … Inspector Jejeune." She extended a tiny hand. "Great to meet you. Really. I mean, terrif. I can't tell you how much I've been looking forward to this." She shook her head. "Sorry, that doesn't sound right. I mean your work, sir; they had us review some of it as case studies when I was in training. Sorry, I don't mean to embarrass you."

"I wouldn't worry about it," said DCS Shepherd, who was standing beside Jejeune. "He's heard it all before, haven't you, Domenic?"

If he had, Jejeune's expression suggested he was no more comfortable with hearing it this time around.

"Well, I'm sure Domenic will give you his full co-operation, Constable Gill, as long as we remember he is working on an open murder inquiry at the moment." She gave the Empowered Investigator a short smile that contained no discernible message. "Shall we begin?" she asked Jejeune, ending the awkward staring contest that had ensued between the inspector and his admirer.

The attendees settled quickly as the trio at the front of the room broke up, and Shepherd took it upon herself to get the ball rolling.

"Sergeant, I haven't seen any paperwork yet from Dr. Jones officially declaring cause of death. You were down there. Is he prepared to agree it was the gunshot to the back of the head?"

"Perhaps." Maik raised his eyebrows at the roomful of people looking at him. "He can't rule out the gunshot being post-mortem."

"He's seriously suggesting the victim could have been killed by a method yet to be determined, *then* shot, *then* burned?" asked Holland incredulously. "Just how dead does he think the killer wanted this bloke to be?"

"There's no chance he might want to change his mind?" Shepherd asked the sergeant.

"Unfortunately, I think he's happy with the one he's got. We are getting closer to an ID, though," he said, mainly because Shepherd was distinctly looking as if she needed some good news. "Dr. Jones requisitioned the dental records as soon as we gave him the name of Kowalski's dentist. He says the dental work is an exact match, but he wants to check something else before he signs off."

"What on earth does he want to check?" asked Shepherd with exasperation. "If the dental records match, there can be no other interpretation of the facts, surely." She set her fists on her hips like a gunslinger. "The bloody man's impossible. I take it he knows that, in the absence of witnesses, his findings are likely to be the best leads we're going to get on this case?"

"I did point that out," said Maik testily. "He seems to have taken this to mean he needs to scrutinize the evidence even more carefully than usual."

Shepherd drew in a breath. "Domenic, please tell us you're at least following some leads that don't require Dr. Jones's seal of approval." She looked at him, not so much to elicit some details, but almost as if to ensure he didn't offer one lead in particular. At least, not yet. She fed him an opening, to guide him in the right direction. "You went to see Curtis Angeren. Anything there?"

From Maik's vantage point, he could see how Jejeune's uneasy shuffle could have been taken as mere preparation to address the DCS's question. The only person who knew differently watched with interest as Jejeune turned to ask the room a question. "As I understand it, we had no family history on Paulina Kowalski, just the basics: address, driver's licence, national insurance number?"

Maik saw a couple of smirks in the room at the inspector's reference to the card's formal name, which no native would be likely to use.

"That's correct, sir," confirmed the sergeant. "With itinerant EU citizens who move here, it's often a case of back-filling the record whenever one of the agencies comes across new information. It can leave a lot of holes."

"So, I wonder where Mr. Angeren found out that Jakub was Mrs. Kowalski's only child." Jejeune raised his eyebrows in Maik's direction, but everyone in the room knew there was only one explanation that made sense. Angeren found out at the same time Jejeune and Maik did — when Mrs. Kowalski told them, at her house, on the day a person with a boom mic came to visit.

"If we are thinking it was Angeren who was behind that attempt to listen in," said Shepherd, "that would certainly tie him in after the fact, but I don't see that it connects him to the murder itself."

"He made the connection for us," said Holland. "He's the one who denied it, before we even knew which way was up on this case. Now I ask you, is that the action of an innocent man?" Holland flicked a look in Des's direction, but she was making a note in her Moleskine journal, so it was impossible to tell if she'd registered Holland's detective wizardry or not.

"The problem is," said Shepherd, "if we're taking him at face value, he says nobody collected on his contract to kill Kowalski."

"If we're taking him at face value, he says he didn't offer one," observed Maik.

Shepherd's look towards the sergeant wasn't one of gratitude. But other challenges awaited her. She drew the deep breath of someone aware that once she'd plunged in, she might not be surfacing for a very long time. "Now, the inspector has a theory," she told the room, "that this may be something to do with the bounty hunting of some birds." She turned to Jejeune. "Have I got that right, Domenic?" she asked with just enough dubiousness to assure the rank and file she hadn't completely taken leave of her senses.

She hadn't got it right, but it was close enough to offer Jejeune a springboard for his explanation. "The person we believe to be Jakub Kowalski was found with a weapon beside him that he used to hunt ducks under government licence. Ruddy Ducks," he added, though he didn't know quite why. He doubted anyone else in the room would have the slightest interest in the birds' identity. "They are an invasive species and a decision was taken to eradicate the population."

"Not a shoot-on-sight policy, though, is it, Domenic?" prompted Shepherd.

"The government has licensed a small number of highly skilled hunters to kill any birds reported to the hotline. They pay a bounty on a per-bird basis. Jakub Kowalski was one of the hunters licensed to kill these birds."

"Sorry, sir, but this connects to the murder how, exactly?" If Holland's respectful tone came as something of a surprise, most people in the room recognized its cause. It was sitting right next to him, still making notes in her Moleskine.

"Among the very few things Mansfield Jones is prepared to concede," said Danny Maik, "is that the wound in the skull could have been made by a hollow-point .22."

Shepherd looked across at Jejeune, but it was clear he wasn't going to raise any objection. Nor, it seemed, was Tony Holland, who was still engaged in trying to prise Gill's attention from her note-taking. The DCS had decided on a discreet distance, as she often did with Jejeune's more obtuse theories. But her natural policing instincts wouldn't permit her to stay silent when such an obvious point needed to be raised. "That's a large calibre to kill a duck, Sergeant. Surely, a .17 would be enough to get the job done. I'm assuming the only reason these hunters are using bullets at all is because the spread of pellets from a shotgun might indiscriminately kill other birds if one of these ducks was in amongst them."

Maik nodded. *Do no harm*, he thought. Even when killing. "There are some new .22s out there that are very quiet," he said matter-of-factly. "A hunter might use one if he didn't want to scare away other birds, perhaps if there was another one in the same flock he also needed to kill."

"I could accept the use of the same ammunition as a viable connection between the murder and this duck cull," said Holland magnanimously. "But I'm afraid I'm still missing the connection as to how this might have got him killed."

The thought of what Lauren Salter might have made of Holland's newly-acquired public school etiquette almost made Maik smile. At this rate he was going to have to consider banning Des Gill from future briefings, just so they could all get back to some semblance of normalcy. Predictably, however, Jejeune handled Holland's question with his usual quiet courtesy.

"It was a very controversial scheme on a number of levels. Not only were scientists in disagreement over its effectiveness, people were opposed on ethical grounds. And then, of course, there's the cost involved."

"To kill a few ducks, Domenic?" said Shepherd from the sidelines. "Really?"

"In the early phase of the project, tracking and killing the birds was easier, but even then it cost the government over four and a half million pounds to kill the first six thousand."

Shackled by decorum for so long, Holland's natural instincts suddenly burst forth. "Bloody hell, that's seven hundred and fifty quid a bird!" he said. "I'm in the wrong business."

"The problem is," continued Jejeune, "as the number decreases, the cost of tracking individual birds goes up incrementally. Now that they are down to the last few, it's costing the government around three thousand pounds per bird."

"Three grand to kill a single duck?" said Holland. "That's ridiculous." A thought seemed to occur to him. "Hey, perhaps the killer was just somebody who was upset about the size of the duck bill?" He gave a wide grin and spread his hands to the room. "What can I say, it's a gift."

Maik's expression suggested that if so, it was one better kept wrapped. "Kowalski had been granted permission to enter a site called Tidewater Marsh to hunt for the birds," he said. "We can't be sure whether he found them or not, but he never put in a claim, which suggests he either didn't locate them, or he was dead before he could apply for his bounty. Either way, that seems to be the last time anyone saw him. So for now, that's where we'll be concentrating our efforts."

"Well," said Shepherd, encompassing everybody in the room with her gaze, Des Gill included. "I suppose this represents progress of a kind. To reiterate, then, we can let the inspector have a look at this duck business, but Curtis Angeren remains very much our main focus. We tread carefully, however. A lot of good people have tried to take on Angeren over the years, my predecessor included. There's a reason only one of them is still around these parts. Angeren is intelligent, vindictive, and relentless. Once you've made an enemy of him, he'll make it his business to destroy you. So we wait until we have good cause — very good cause — before we make any moves in his direction." She turned to look at Maik. "And let's get somebody downstairs to have a chat with Dr. Jones, see if we can hurry him along a bit."

Maik's look had barely made its way across to Holland when the constable held up his hands. "Ah, might be a problem there, Sarge. Me and the doc had a bit of a run-in a while ago. He insisted on giving me details about what would have been happening to Darla's body as she died. He wanted to reassure me she wouldn't have suffered any pain. I imagine he thought it might help, but I wasn't ready for it at the time and I let him know it." He shrugged. "I'll get around to apologizing at some point, but in the meantime, I doubt he'd be best pleased to see my grinning mug down there."

Maik recognized that Holland's ability to talk about the death of his former girlfriend in such matter-of-fact terms was an important step towards his recovery. His compassionate leave had given him the time to reconcile himself once again to the world and to find a way to function in it. Maik knew it was now just a matter of constantly moving forward, day by day, one foot in front of the other. In time, the loss would settle into the dust of Holland's past, become a part of it; never forgotten, but no longer the debilitating morass of darkness it had been before his leave. In the meantime, in an effort to insulate himself from any genuine emotions, he had wrapped himself once again in his carefree playboy persona, albeit a more brittle and transparent version than before.

Maik didn't doubt, though, that Holland was right about his present relationship with Jones. The well-meaning M.E. would have been bewildered and wounded in equal parts by Holland's angry response, and now he would almost certainly want to avoid anything to do with the constable. Maik realized that the job of visiting Jones had fallen to the only other person available. He drew in a resigned breath. "I don't suppose anybody's got any aspirin."

Shepherd shook her head. "Perhaps there's some in Lauren Salter's desk. Have you got a headache, Sergeant?"

"Not yet."

Shepherd sighed with exasperation. "Oh, for God's sake. Leave it to us. The DCI and I will go down there and see what Jones is playing at. Come on, Domenic."

As they left, Maik wondered if Jejeune might find the opportunity while the two of them were together to tell the DCS the one other thing that had come up during the Angeren interview. Namely, that Ray Hayes was now back in the picture.

14

"We'll take the stairs," announced Shepherd. "Do us good to get a bit of exercise." The DCS was never shy about including others in her initiatives. It was part of her leadership skill set, Jejeune supposed. It was harder to opt out of something when you weren't given a choice. She pushed open a door leading from the corridor and began descending the narrow stairwell, the clacking of her high heels echoing overloud off the walls. Jejeune fell into step behind her.

"So what do you make of Our Lady of the Abbreviations?" asked Shepherd over her shoulder. Jejeune was surprised by the question. From his perspective, Shepherd seemed to be doing all she could to keep Constable Gill out of his orbit; this most recent intervention a case in point.

"I haven't had the chance to form much of an impression yet," he said guardedly. "She has a reputation for thoroughness, though." If he was sending Shepherd the message that he'd done some research on Gill since her arrival, it would be no more than the DCS would have expected.

"You know, the more I think about this review, the more I wonder if I'm missing something. The thing is, Domenic, for the life of me, I can't see who this is meant to serve. I'll accept that a deathbed confession wasn't the most satisfactory of resolutions. But since a confession precluded the presentation of any evidence, an unsafe verdict doesn't come into it. So again, just who is this review hoping to satisfy?"

Behind his DCS, Jejeune said nothing. He wasn't ready to let his own misgivings about the case see the light of day. But Shepherd detected their existence anyway. She stopped on the landing and turned to look at him. "Tell me honestly, Domenic," she said, fixing him with the kind of stare that would give him no alternative, "is there any reason to suspect Gill will uncover something?" She searched his face carefully. He could be maddeningly inscrutable at times, and she'd never entirely worked out to what extent it was intentional. Even his normal expression was disconcertingly blank. When it became clear he was waiting for more from her, she continued. "I understand why everybody was in such a hurry to draw a line under the case," she said reasonably. "The Home Secretary's daughter had been through a lot, the entire family had. Nobody wanted this thing dragging on. As soon as they had their confession, it was inevitable they'd want to roll it up as quickly as possible. But that's how things get missed." She examined him with the same stare as before.

Jejeune looked around, at bare whitewashed walls, the concrete steps, the metal railing. Whether by design or not, Shepherd had chosen her territory well. Surrounded by the ambient noise of office commerce, or other human traffic, he might have kept his silence. But here in the cold, stark emptiness of this stairwell, suspended between the vague uncertainties of the Incident Room above and the world of Mansfield Jones's irrefutable facts below, there no longer seemed to be anywhere for Jejeune to hide his doubts.

"It always seemed to me the investigators didn't have much interest in probing too deeply. If they found an explanation that fit, they settled for it."

"I presume you're talking about that business with the bird? The Magpie." She nodded shortly. "I remember that. To tell you the truth, I'd half expect you to have been the one proposing it."

"I wasn't involved in closing out the case. As soon as Carolyn Gresham was returned to her family, I was moved...."

Yes, she thought, *and if you would hesitate to use the word 'up,' no one else would. Moved ... to a DCI posting with the North Norfolk Constabulary, where you have consistently and spectacularly proved your worth ever since.*

"But the Magpie had been coming to the property on a regular basis, though, hadn't it? It was a plausible enough explanation, that it would have taken the pin." She made a face. "Never been much of a fan of Magpies, if I'm being honest," she said. "They've always seemed a bit shifty to me, all that thievery and such. The criminal class of the bird world, I suppose."

But Jejeune had retreated into silence. And perhaps now, she shared his unease that, as insignificant as the disappearance of the pin itself undoubtedly was, the cavalier manner in which it had been handled could be a troubling indicator of the way the investigation was wrapped up. Including one aspect in particular.

"How about the confession, Domenic?" she asked. "Ever any doubts there?"

The sudden introduction of the topic took Jejeune off-guard. It crossed his mind that perhaps this was Shepherd's intention. He shrugged. "Any time a case is closed on a deathbed confession, there are bound to be questions left unanswered. But nothing that stood out. As I say, though, I wasn't involved by that time. DI Laraby handled it. He insisted. He —"

"Needed a victory. Yes I know." Shepherd nodded absently, and Jejeune wondered again about her choice of location for this conversation. There had been something about her previous question; a hesitation, even a certain tentativeness. At first, he put it down to the awkwardness of their positioning, with him towering two steps above her, as she twisted her neck up and backwards to look at him. But he knew now there was more to it. Because it was present again in her next question.

"So you never heard anything about a payment for the confession?"

"To a man with hours to live?"

"Or his family? You can see how it might raise questions, even at this late date, if any money had changed hands prior to Vincent Canby offering his dying declaration."

Jejeune nodded, although why Shepherd might be bringing it up now also raised a few questions.

The DCS bowed her head in what might have been deep thought. "The family's bank account," she said. "I suppose that would be where somebody would start. Our intrepid Empowered Investigator, for example, if she ever got wind of a rumour like that."

The abruptness with which Shepherd turned to continue descending the stairs did more than declare an end to the conversation. It also told Jejeune she wasn't going to wait around for him to dwell on exactly why she might have spoon-fed him such an obvious line of inquiry.

She was waiting for him at the bottom of the stairs, and turned to him as he arrived. Considering the close confines of the stairwell, she had managed to put an ocean of distance between herself and their previous conversation. "I always hate this part," she said. "But it's what we do, isn't it, Domenic. It's the role we've chosen for ourselves. We deal with the unpleasant things, so others don't have to." She pushed through the door into the world of Mansfield Jones without waiting for her DCI's response.

* * *

Jejeune and Shepherd entered the over-bright room and heard Jones whispering to the body on the table. He stopped and straightened at their approach. Despite having dismembered the torso at various points, the M.E. had rearranged it on the slab so that it appeared intact. He noticed their looks. "There seemed to be no reason not to," he said simply. He looked down at the body again and shook his head. "How does a person take that final step?" he asked. "I can imagine the rage that could bring you to the precipice." He looked up and gave them a thin smile. "Yes, even in someone as phlegmatic as a medical examiner there can be rage. But to preplan a murder? To look at another human being and know beforehand that you are going to cross that final line, to take this person's life? That should surely be beyond any of us."

"Can I ask, Dr. Jones, what was it you were saying to … Mr. Kowalski as we came in?"

Shepherd looked slightly taken aback that Jejeune would ask such a brazen question, but far from seeming embarrassed, Jones answered immediately and openly. "A simple explanation of a forthcoming procedure and the necessity for it. It's a way of reminding myself who I am dealing with, regardless of outward appearances. In some ways, I think it helps me, to continue to see a complete human being there. It reminds me of what is at stake, the enormity of getting things right."

"Indeed, Doctor Jones." Shepherd had summoned the officious voice she used when an obstacle was about to be mown down. "And we all appreciate your thoroughness. However, I do think at some point it's necessary to accept that you have done enough." She paused and looked at him over her steel-rimmed glasses. "We have reached that point. I have a man here capable of solving this murder and bringing someone to justice for this horrific act. But he needs to know in which direction he should proceed."

"As I believe Sergeant Maik has already told you," said Jejeune, "we're working on the theory that the victim was not shot at the site. It would be helpful if we could confirm any aspects of this line of inquiry."

"Until I've had the time to eliminate all other possibilities, all I could offer would be merely guesses, educated ones perhaps, but guesses nevertheless, based on the most plausible of the explanations. It seems like a monumental waste of police resources if a few idle musings set you off running in the wrong direction."

"I take your point," said Shepherd, with an empathy Jejeune suspected owed more to training seminars than heartfelt sentiment. "The thing is, Dr. Jones, these educated guesses, musings, call them what you will, are a vital part of this investigation."

"Your own, yes, I can see that, but relying on the speculation of others? It seems to me a shockingly unreliable way of conducting an investigation. Not you personally, you understand, Inspector, just as an operating principle in general." Jones bent his over-tall frame forward slightly to close the gap across the table as he addressed them both. "You do understand, I hope, that I'm not being difficult."

Jejeune thought he detected a short intake of breath from Shepherd. He wondered if he should point out to a man so consumed with precision that "not trying to be difficult" was perhaps the more accurate phrase. But it seemed that Shepherd had managed to conceal her astonishment anyway, so he decided to let it go.

The M.E. shook his head slowly. "Taking whatever findings you need, ignoring the ones that don't fit. Interpreting facts in whatever way you need to, in order to conveniently arrive at a conclusion which matches up with some preconceived notion of the truth." Jones shook his long head sadly. "There's just too much of it these days. It's simply wrong. It has no part in a legitimate criminal investigation. Does my desire to be so certain of everything make me remiss in my professional duties? Quite possibly. But once I have presented findings I know to be accurate, I can at least have a clear conscience."

"I understand your reluctance to give out any incomplete information that might be manipulated to suit a need," said Jejeune. "But I can assure you, doctor, I need your conclusions only for the truths they hold."

Jones nodded in appreciation of Jejeune's comment. They were a strange pair to get on so well, thought Shepherd; Jones, who remained so unsure about the things he could see, and Jejeune, who always seemed so certain about those he could not. "Doctor Jones," she said. "Regardless of your reservations, I can't have you holding onto this any longer. A poor woman, a mother, is hanging in a state of limbo, not knowing whether her son is alive or … not. She needs to know definitively that he's gone, so she can begin the process of grieving for him properly. I need you to sign off on cause of death and the identity of the victim unequivocally. So I will ask you one more time to formally confirm the identity of this victim."

Jones nodded slowly. "The teeth have not been tampered with to make them match the dental charts. The work is as old as the dates indicate. Based on dental records, I am prepared to concede that this is the body of Jakub Kowalski."

Shepherd sighed. "And the cause of death. Have you found anything to suggest he survived the gunshot wounds? Anything at all?"

"No, Superintendent," said Jones. "I have not."

She turned to Jejeune. "Very well, then. Jakub Kowalski. Killed by a rifle shot to the back of the head. Let's get back upstairs and start putting together a line of inquiry based on that."

As she and Jejeune reached the doors to the stairway, Shepherd turned to look back at the M.E. He was bent over the torso again, performing some meticulous examination with a scalpel. *What it must cost him*, thought Shepherd, *to look upon a charred form like that in terms of the person it once was, even as he prepared to do what must be done to it.* It wasn't always easy to put up with Mansfield Jones, but it was certainly possible to admire a man who was willing to sacrifice so much of himself simply to afford a dead person some dignity.

"Thank you, Doctor Jones," she said from the doorway. "You've been most helpful." And for once, she meant it.

15

Tony Holland sat at his desk leafing through an extraordinarily thin file. "This is useless," he said with exasperation. "All it tells us about the victim is that he was Polish, and his name was Kowalski. I mean, aren't they all?"

He saw Maik and Gill looking up at him and held up his hands. "Oh, wait, no, listen. I just meant there are a lot of Polish people called Kowalski, that's all. Like Smiths in England, right? I didn't mean anything by it."

He looked genuinely upset that his comment may have been seen as a sign of some deeper prejudice. But it didn't take long to detect those kinds of undercurrents in police officers, and Maik knew the real Tony Holland. He had seen him in action any number of times, and he was always the same, regardless of the villain's cultural background: irreverent, perhaps a touch too gleeful at having nicked somebody. But as far as Maik could remember, Holland had never exhibited any bigotry toward anyone — except, perhaps, birders.

Gill, too, seemed willing to accept Holland's explanation at face value. "That was the first time I've ever seen DCI Jejeune in action," she said from her station at Salter's desk. "Is he always that low key?"

"You should see him when he hasn't had any coffee," said Holland with evident relief that the conversation had moved on. "I feel like checking for a pulse sometimes."

"Still, the way he picked up on Angeren knowing about the only child, that was just brill."

Holland rolled his eyes. "I'm sure he'd be willing to sign your chest if you asked him nicely."

"Really? Do you think I'd have to empty the tea out of it first? All I'm saying is it's not the first time he's picked up on things other people have missed."

Holland looked unimpressed. "Just because he's the one pointing things out all the time, it doesn't mean he's the only one who's noticed them. Perhaps I just have other ways besides words to show how clever I am."

"Like one of those sign language gorillas, you mean?" said Des. She reached for a set of headphones on her desk and plugged them into her laptop. "Okay, enough chit-chat. If you'll excuse me, I have some listening to do."

The men watched as she adjusted her headphones and cued the audio file on her laptop. Once ready, she opened the paper transcript and arranged the pages in a way that would allow her to flip them over easily as she followed the progress of the recording. Finally, she placed her notepad close to hand and set a pen beside it. The meticulous way Gill went about her preparations suggested she was unlikely to miss anything of significance through frantic scrabbling around for somewhere to jot down a note. And they had already seen enough of her approach to suspect she wouldn't miss much through any other oversight, either.

Saturday November 20th, 12:31 p.m. Call duration: 2 minutes 27 seconds

Laraby: *This is DI Marvin Laraby. Who am I speaking with?*
Caller: *Somebody who's not an idiot. I have information about the whereabouts of the Home Secretary's daughter and her boyfriend. I want paying for this information.*
(Muffled sounds; eight-second silence)

The sound would be Laraby's hand over microphone, thought Des. The demand would have thrown them, but it was clever. The authorities couldn't be on record negotiating with kidnappers. But the police paid for information all the time. Only, Laraby wasn't buying it.

Laraby: *Okay, son. Now I don't know if you realize it, but you've got yourself in a world of trouble here. Fortunately for you, it's not too late to get yourself out of it. And I'm here to help you.*
Caller: *So they go free and you're just gonna make all my troubles go away, are you?*
Laraby: *That's all we want, and it will all be over. You have my word.*
Caller: *Really, no charges or anything? Like I said, I'm not an idiot. You start treating me like one and we're not going to get very far. Now, I want a hundred thousand pounds for my information.*
Laraby: *That's an awful lot of money. But before we even get to discussing any of that, we*

have to know Carolyn is safe. Unharmed. We can only start talking about paying for your information when we know this for certain.

Unidentified Voice: *Are they both safe?*

Laraby: *And the boy, too. Is he okay? Are they both okay?*

Caller: *Yeah. For now. Who's that?*

Laraby: *Another officer. He's in the room with me.*

Caller: *Put him on.*

Laraby: *I'll be negotiating with you on this. My name's Marvin. Marvin Laraby.*

Caller: *Put the other bloke on, Marvin. Now.*

(Shuffling sounds; inaudible conversation in background)

Jejeune: *This is Sergeant Jejeune. Domenic.*

Caller: *You don't sound English, Domenic.*

Jejeune: *I'm Canadian. So they're both safe?*

Caller: *Yes.*

Jejeune: *That's good. What about you?*

(Inaudible conversation in background)

Caller: *Me?*

Jejeune: *You're going to be handling these negotiations. It's a big responsibility, to make sure everybody gets what they want, everybody gets home safe. You're going to need to be at your best. You'll need to take care of yourself, too.*

(Shuffling sounds)

Laraby: *DI Laraby, again. Marvin. Now listen to me, what we need you to do first …*

Caller: *Put the other bloke on again. The Canadian. From now on I deal with him.*

Laraby: *Not possible I'm afraid. As the senior officer here, I'll need to be the one handling this.*
Caller: *Get him, now, or we're done. I ring off, you don't hear from me again. Ever. You got it?*
(Shuffling sounds)
Jejeune: *It's okay. I'm here, I'm here. Don't ring off.*
Caller: *Okay, it's you and me from now on, Domenic the Canadian. Nobody else. We're going to handle the negotiations between us two.*
Jejeune: *I'm not the senior officer on this case. If there are decisions to be made …*
Caller: *There's really only one decision to be made here, Domenic. Whether or not you want those kids back safe and sound. I don't think you need to be any particular rank to answer that one, do you? I'll be in touch.*
Call ends.

But not the fallout, thought Des. She could imagine the chaotic scene in the room, the senior officers rounding on Jejeune, asking what the hell he thought he was playing at, asking after the well-being of the kidnapper, telling him to take care of himself. Without the presence in the room of the Home Secretary's man — she riffled through her notes to look up the name, somebody called Giles — Jejeune would likely have never seen another investigative case in his career. But Giles had recognized immediately what all the others undoubtedly had been trying to disguise from him: Jejeune was the one who had established the line of communication with the kidnapper. He was now the lifeline to Carolyn Gresham. And that was all that really mattered. From that moment on, Domenic Jejeune would be point-of-contact on this operation; at the

Home Secretary's personal behest. And it would stay that way until the case was resolved.

Gill considered what else she had heard on the tape. *Even then, Monte Harrison was just as important to you, wasn't he, Sergeant Jejeune? And I think the kidnapper knew that, right from the beginning. Even if perhaps some of your fellow officers didn't.*

She peeled off her headphones and looked at the two men, one hard at work with his head down, the other trying to disguise the fact that he had been watching her.

"I was wondering, does the inspector ever talk about what went on around that time?"

"It's not generally the way he goes about things," said Maik.

"To tell you the truth, I think the main reason he keeps quiet about it all is because he's embarrassed." Holland shook his head derisively. "I mean, it's one thing for the Home Sec. to be grateful, we all get that, but to give him a DCI as a thank you, well, it's just not on, is it, really?"

"I think there's more to Inspector Jejeune's success than just having the Home Secretary's blessing, Tony. I mean, you don't rise through the ranks like he did unless you've got something really special."

Holland tilted his head. "All I'm saying is anybody could have made DCI with the kind of backing he got from upstairs. Well, not anybody, obviously, but those of us with a bit of talent. I mean, it stands to reason nobody's going to tell the Home Sec. he's got it wrong, but I don't think anybody's kidding themselves that Jejeune has got to where he is strictly on merit."

Gill raised an eyebrow. "You don't think so, Tony? You think you could have come up with the fingerprint trick he used to narrow down the location of the kidnap victims?"

"Fingerprint trick?" Holland turned to Maik. "Has he ever told you about this?"

Maik shook his head.

No, thought Gill, looking at Maik carefully. *But that doesn't mean you don't know about it, does it, Sergeant? You've already done your homework on Domenic Jejeune. And you were as impressed by what you found as the rest of us.*

"Read up on it, Tony," said Gill. "And then when you have, come back and tell me you could have come up with an idea like that."

Maik watched as Desdemona Gill went back to her review of the audio files. As much as she clearly admired the DCI, she was going to go over this material in minute detail, assuming nothing, taking nothing for granted. He looked at her now, her tiny frame hunched over the desk, her dark hair falling forward over the childlike features. She'd already alluded to her youthful appearance, and the challenges it presented, but the fact that she had worked her way up to her current position told you something about her, and the fact the Met had trusted her with this review told you plenty more. Maik suspected that if you asked where DC Desdemona Gill saw herself in five years, there wouldn't be much flailing around for vague answers in which the word *hope* appeared. This review of the Carolyn Gresham kidnapping was one giant step on her climb to the top. And Maik suspected that meant DC Gill wasn't likely to let her admiration for the inspector, or anything else, *actch*, stand in the way of finding the truth.

16

Domenic Jejeune strolled out to Blakeney Point, enjoying the slow unfurling of spring along the coastal path. The breeding season for the seal colony at the point had already passed, but the Sandwich Terns had not yet established their nests. The detective found himself in a landscape during that rarest of times, a gap in nature's cycles.

The late afternoon light rested easily on the undulating surface of the sea. Silhouetted seabirds circled lazily against the sky, their occasional plaintive call no more than a comment on the peacefulness that had settled over this part of the north Norfolk coast. Jejeune checked his watch. He was always conscious of being out of cellphone range. It was a legacy of an earlier event, one that would never leave him. He would still allow himself these pockets of time, to wander, to explore, to bird, but his first act on reacquiring a signal would always be to check his messages. It was too late to correct the errors of the past, but he would do whatever he could to make sure they were never repeated.

He walked out almost as far as the point, where even on a becalmed afternoon such as this, a faint breeze tousled the vegetation and sent foamy white wave breaks fussing over the shoreline. In the distance, a parcel of Oystercatchers were being disrupted from their pursuit of cockles by one individual flitting and fluttering amongst them. *A widowed bird*, thought Jejeune, *searching this group of committed monogamists for another lonely soul to be its partner for the upcoming breeding season*. The detective didn't bother raising his bins, enjoying instead the wider spectacle of this group of black and white shorebirds against the backdrop of the pale blue sea.

As he made his way back along the far side of the point, he noticed a small stand of scrubby trees, and he realized what it was that had drawn him out here; the ghost of birding past. On a September day a few years earlier, an *Empidonax* flycatcher had shown up in this place. The North American native was considered a mega rarity in Britain, and this one's appearance had been greeted by local birders with equal parts delight and disbelief. He remembered the long walk out here, and the weather, almost impossible to imagine on a soft day like today; a cold, horizontal grey rain that drove onshore in ragged, wind-driven torrents. The noise, too, had been a world away from the balmy quiet of this shoreline now. Sound swirled around then with such force it was like a physical presence; winds roaring like a steam train, waves crashing in shuddering explosions against the shore. It was hard to believe any bird could survive in such conditions, let alone such a fragile visitor. But eventually someone in the group had located the little *Empid*, huddled low in a sycamore. He smiled now at the thought of what Lindy had said about the relative intelligence quotients of the small bird seeking shelter from the weather, and the group of fifty-odd birders standing out in the teeth of it, bundled up in waterproofs and bulky clothing, vying for the chance to peer at the rare arrival.

He played his bins over the branches of the tree where the bird had been. Jejeune had no idea why he had come to see the flycatcher that day. Perhaps it was some attempt to fit in, to become part of the local birding community. Certainly it wasn't the bird itself. He had seen plenty of *Empids* back home. And besides, no one had even been able to definitively identify this one. The *Empidonax* flycatchers were a notoriously difficult genus to differentiate. Habitat was one method, but since this bird was thousands of miles from its home territory, that hardly helped. Song was the best clue, but, not surprisingly, the bird was finding little to sing about in the midst of a north Norfolk storm. On field marks alone, it could have been any one of three species. Later, Jejeune had heard some people had settled on Willow Flycatcher while others had plumped for Alder. They had taken whatever facts they needed, and from them, fashioned a truth that suited them. *Perhaps Mansfield Jones had a point, after all,* thought the detective.

Further out to sea, a raft of ducks bobbed in and out of his view as they rode the gentle swells. Likely Common Eiders, down from the colder northern waters to breed, but he needed better looks to be sure. He went down to the waterline and tried to fix his binoculars on the birds, but they were drifting further out to sea now, disappearing behind the swells with increasing frequency. Without a scope it was impossible to make a definitive identification.

His feet felt suddenly wet, and he looked down to find water lapping over his shoes. A cold rush of memory welled up inside him: another day, another time the water had swept over his shoes. And with the memories came the feeling again; fear, not for his own safety but that of someone else. Only, things were different this time. He was directly responsible for the danger that now threatened Lindy. He had brought her into his world, where vengeful criminals and violent reprisals were always a possibility. He had done so because he wanted her by his side, sharing his life. They had never discussed the dangers, never weighed the risks. There had been no conditional offer, no exit clause. Now, the threat he had always dreaded was coming for her, and he was to blame. He knew it was his responsibility to protect Lindy, but he had no idea how to do it, and he was afraid that he would not be able to.

Along the shoreline in the distance, three small brown birds dropped in. Jejeune raised his bins and studied the new arrivals closely until he could be sure; Shore Larks, huddled on the shingle ridge, the wind tousling up their soft brown plumage into feathery cowls. Horned Larks, they had been to him once, in a past life. It was a good sighting, but despite it, and the low, saffron light of the late afternoon sun and the soft sea breeze and the calls of the circling gulls overhead, his troubling thoughts refused to leave him. This place was now beyond redemption for him today. Only another visit, at another time, would bring back its joy. He turned to make his way back to the car.

Back at the Range Rover, he dug out a spare pair of dry socks and changed into them. He climbed into the driver's seat and checked his phone. There was one text, from Danny Maik. *Incident at Kowalski residence. On my way.*

17

The shadows of evening were encroaching when Jejeune arrived, but he noticed the gaunt form of Paulina Kowalski immediately. She was hunched down beside a hedgerow on the far side of the road, about fifty metres from her house. Jejeune pulled over the Range Rover nearby and got out. Maik's Mini was parked in a small lane just behind him.

As the detective approached, Paulina Kowalski motioned him over with an urgent gesture. "Two men. They came to my door. They said they were policemen." Her face twisted slightly. "Pah, I have seen this kind of policemen before. They said they must take all my son's belongings away. They told me a list: laptop, phone, other things. They said, when a foreigner disappears, they must take all his belongings to the police station. Do policemen talk like this — *a foreigner?* I told them my son and I have been here for seventeen years. We are not foreigners."

"Did you let them in?" Though Jejeune was listening carefully, his eyes had not left the front door of the house since he arrived. Neither had Paulina Kowalski's.

"I would not let such men into my home. I said I was going out. They went away, but I was afraid, so I called Sergeant Maik. He told me to leave the house and stay away until he arrived. I walked to this place and watched. The men returned and put something in the lock, a metal bar, I think."

"They went inside? Where is Sergeant Maik now?" Despite his whispered tone, the alarm in Jejeune's voice was clear.

"He went into the house also. He asked me to stay here until you arrived, and tell you what had happened. He said if I heard any noise from the house, I should call the police emergency number." She paused for a second. "I have heard no noise."

Jejeune reached for his phone but hesitated. A call to the station now would likely result in questions about why a senior police officer believed the established hostile entry procedures didn't apply to him.

"How long ago did he go in?" he asked.

"A few minutes, no more."

Jejeune regarded the house carefully. If Maik hadn't encountered any resistance by now, perhaps he wasn't going to. But there was no guarantee. "I'll go over. Please stay here until one of us comes to get you," he said to the woman. "And as the sergeant said, if you hear any noise, please call that number."

There are sounds an empty house makes; ticks and hushed whisperings. They seep from the floors and walls and ceilings in the absence of human habitation. But there are other sounds — a creaking floor, the rustle of a window curtain — that could be the telltale signs of a house that only appears to be empty. The trick is in knowing the difference. Jejeune eased the front door back carefully and sidled into the narrow hallway. He paused for a moment, straining to listen beyond the silence, beneath it. He heard nothing. He cast a glance at the staircase as he passed, watching for moving shadows. He saw none. Jejeune tightened his grip on the knob of the door leading off the hallway and drew in his breath. He felt the tension that leached the resilience out of so many police officers eventually; not the adrenaline jolt of action, of confrontation, of a weapons threat even, but the taut, nerve-twisting anxiety, the edgy racing pulse and elevated heartbeat that comes from knowing that danger could lie behind any door, and wondering whether this was the one.

He opened the door slowly and peered in. Beyond the window on the far wall lay the street, but in the darkened glass he could see only the reflection of the interior of the room. He waited for his eyes to adjust to the low light and peered into the shadows. Again, nothing. He withdrew and padded softly along the narrow hallway, heading for the kitchen. He heard a sound that might have been a faint creak and froze. In the stillness, the silence seemed to hang around him menacingly. Behind him, the staircase receded into a pocket of deep shadow. He had already begun a slow turn when he caught a flicker of movement from the corner of his eye. He spun in a half crouch, forearm cocked, ready to deliver a strike.

"All clear," said Maik from the lowest stair. "They went out through the back garden, by the looks of it. The gate is unlatched." He had affected to look elsewhere while his DCI straightened to his full height and brought his breathing back under control. But now it was time to look at him directly. Or as directly as the shadowy light in the hallway would allow. "They've had a bit of a look around in what I assume was the son's bedroom, but it was careful. Not much disturbed, nothing broken."

Jejeune nodded. He knew the sergeant's survey would have been thorough. Maik knew how to look *at* a room rather than *in* it. To concentrate on looking for something specific meant it was easier to miss something else of importance. "Mrs. Kowalski is waiting to come back in," said Jejeune. It was clear he wasn't going to dwell on his scare. "We can ask her to check if anything's been taken."

Jejeune watched Maik leave and found light switches for the hallway and living room. He sat on the staircase for a moment, letting his heart rate retreat towards normal. He knew he would have to address Maik's newfound penchant for solo heroics. But now was not the time.

Paulina Kowalski hesitated for a moment in the doorway. On the step behind her, Maik waited patiently. He recognized the signs; a homeowner reluctant to enter a house from which the sense of security had been stripped. A home was supposed to be a place of refuge, a place where you felt protected and safe. With the previous incident and now this one, this house no longer offered Paulina Kowalski sanctuary. Now it was a place of uncertainty, of danger, even. Maik leaned forward slightly, addressing her back in a low murmur. "As I say, ma'am, we've checked everywhere. However, if you'd be more comfortable staying somewhere else tonight —"

"This is my home," she said, striving for defiance even as her voice faltered slightly. "I will not let these men of the *Agencja Bezpieczeństwa Wewnętrznego* force me from it."

"They were not Polish secret police," said Maik. "They were not policemen of any kind."

With an effort of will that was almost visible, she forced herself to step across the threshold. It changed things, and she began to settle a little.

"I will make tea," she said, shrugging off her coat and heading to the kitchen.

Maik's reflex was to stop her, but Jejeune held up a hand and the sergeant nodded his understanding. She needed to do the small things again, the routines, the little rituals of domestic life. They would help her regain possession of her home. And it was a fair bet the intruders hadn't stopped to make tea while they were here; if the fingerprint team was going to recover any usable prints when they arrived tomorrow, they wouldn't be from sugar tongs or a teapot.

The two detectives were sitting in the living room, each deep in his own thoughts, when Mrs. Kowalski entered with a tea tray. She set the items out on the table meticulously and poured three cups of tea with the same careful attention, as if observing the rules of some exacting ritual.

"Do you mind if we go up and check whether anything was taken from your son's room?" asked Maik, cradling the cup in his large hand as he stood.

The woman nodded silently. Maik guided her to the stairs while Jejeune stayed in the living room. He was sitting in the same chair as on his previous visit. The cracked photograph had been repaired roughly with a piece of tape and had been re-hung on the wall. It was the only sign of the turmoil that had erupted the last time they were in this room. He sipped his tea and looked around him. *A normal living room in a normal house*, thought Jejeune. Quiet, modestly furnished, unremarkable. And yet what kind of normal house witnessed talk of guns and break-ins and Polish secret police. He looked at his hands and listened to the emptiness of the room.

Paulina Kowalski re-entered and took a seat. Maik followed. He shook his head. "Nothing obvious anyway. Once the fingerprint team has been in, we should be able to tell where they were concentrating their efforts. It might give us a bit more of an idea if they were looking for anything in particular."

"The list of belongings they asked you for," said Jejeune, "can you remember it?"

Paulina Kowalski nodded. "Laptop computer, phone, digi-scope, external drives, iPad."

"And these men wouldn't have found any of these in Jakub's room?"

She shook her head firmly. "I do not know where they are."

"Could they be in his locker at Wawel?"

Again she shook her head decisively. "Jakub would not store anything like this there. He used this locker only for his hunting clothes and his rifle. His ammunition he kept here. Beneath the sink. It is here still. I checked."

"They didn't ask about his rifle?" said Maik.

"No, they did not ask about this," said Mrs. Kowalski firmly. The detectives exchanged a glance. There would be no need to ask about the rifle if you already knew where it was.

Jejeune shifted to face Paulina Kowalski directly and Maik knew he had steeled himself for this moment while they were away. "Mrs. Kowalski," said the DCI softly, "I'm very sorry to have to tell you the dental records have confirmed the body we recovered was Jakub."

The teaspoon chinked softly against her cup as she set it down; a tiny chime to accompany the passing of all hope.

"Yes," she said simply. But there was something else in her face, just for a moment, the same disconcerting look in the woman's eyes that Jejeune had seen the first time he sat in this room. As before, it was gone before he could identify it. His brief glimpse over at Maik told him the sergeant had not seen it.

"I can arrange for a police officer to come here tonight, if you would like," said Maik, "perhaps even just for the company."

"The only company I wish is that of my son," she said quietly. "And this I can never have again." Her sigh was a deep, wretched sound, and she seemed to teeter for a moment between this tiny, sparse living room and an abyss of sorrow waiting to swallow her. Finally, she returned from the precipice and looked at Jejeune intently. "It is our duty to protect our loved ones from the dangers in the world, Inspector. But no matter how hard we try, or how much we wish to, we cannot always save the ones we love." She looked around the room, at the heavy, dark curtains, at the washed-out wallpaper and the threadbare furniture. "Jakub was my only treasure on this Earth," she said. "And now he is gone."

18

The Polish Community Centre was situated on the far end of a berm, an earthen barrier that rose six metres above the surrounding landscape, separating farmland on one side from the watery expanses of Tidewater Marsh on the other. The track that led from the coast road described a wide, sweeping curve across the flat terrain, with a short, sharp incline at the end that climbed up to the berm itself. Once on the top, there was enough room to drive along the berm and park, but turning a car around to leave again didn't allow much room for error. It was a steep drop on either side, to the water in one direction and the soft brown earth of the fields in the other. As they parked and got out, for once Jejeune was glad they had chosen to make the journey in Maik's protesting Mini.

At the side of the building were several large piles of vegetation. It was the Frankenweed that the workers had dug from the marsh, being left to dry before being incinerated. The long vines dangled limply from densely-tangled, interwoven mats of roots that bore the scars of having been ruthlessly hacked out of the earth. Jejeune was still staring at the mounds when a young woman opened the front door. He recognized her as one of the workers from the marsh. "The Count offers his

apologies," she said. "He will be with you soon. He has asked if
you would be kind enough to wait."

"Sikorski is a Count?"

The woman offered Maik a shy smile. "This is how the
people of our community refer to him," she said. "He does not
use the title himself."

The sergeant let his gaze linger on the heavy metal grille,
now folded back from the doorway, as they entered the building. The detectives exchanged impressed glances as they were
led through a large central hall. From the outside, the building
had the rough, careworn look of many old structures along
the north Norfolk coast. Neither paint nor shingles fared well
in the face of the fierce storms that pounded the area, and
the elements seemed to save a special kind of fury for places
that dared to sit on high, exposed ground, as this one did.
But the peeling, cracked skin of this building gave no clue to
the impressive interior that awaited visitors. Throughout the
length and breadth of the hall, white-plastered walls were
half-timbered with rich, dark panelling. Beneath the men's
feet, an immaculate hardwood floor glistened. Around its
outer edge, the floor had been expertly dressed with an intricate herringbone pattern.

Jejeune nodded approvingly. "The members of your community did all this?"

"The materials, paint, window glass, wood, these were all
provided by an anonymous donor." Her smile left the men in
no doubt about her own suspicions. "But the labour and the
decoration, yes, this was all done by them."

People milled around the building freely, giving it an air of
quiet industry. The detectives recognized most of them from
the marshes. They were gathering beside a set of lockers lin-
ing a corridor, busily kitting themselves up for another day
of removing the Frankenweed from Tidewater Marsh. The

girl led the men into a comfortable room at the front of the building. A tray of tea was waiting, but before they could pour, Sikorski appeared in the doorway. "My sincere apologies for making you wait, gentlemen," he said. "There are many ways to help people, but so little time to do so. Anyway, welcome to Wawel. This is the name the people have given this place. It is named after a castle of great importance in Poland's history. Come, let me show you around." He led the way to the entrance of the large hall and spread his arms proudly.

"Behold the work of our family. The carpentry, the plumbing, electrical. Everything. The local Polish community has over a thousand years of combined life experience. Among these people we have tradesmen, builders, artisans of the finest kind."

"Any of them know how to use a firearm?" asked Maik.

"Some," admitted Sikorski unguardedly. "A couple have served in the army. Others were hunters. Even I did some hunting as a youth, until I discovered where my heart lay in this world. Often it is this way, is it not? We begin on one path and find ourselves going in the opposite direction later on."

They passed a stack of thin mattresses propped against the wall of the corridor. "In the farming season, some of our members find it more convenient to sleep here, rather than return to their homes each night," Sikorski explained. A man approached the Count and spoke to him briefly. Sikorski unlocked a wooden cabinet on the wall, taking a key from a hook and handing it to the man. "We keep a spare set of keys to the padlocks for the lockers," he told the detectives, "but this is only in case they forget their own. We consider these lockers to be their property. We have no right to enter them."

Maik looked at the group, readying themselves for another day of back-breaking manual labour. "I thought I read somewhere they were trying to find a natural predator of some kind to control invasive weeds," said Maik.

"Ah, yes, sergeant, but my own studies have given me a healthy skepticism about the wisdom of introducing such non-native predators. The question too often becomes *Quis custodiet ipsos custodes*?"

"Who polices the police?" Maik translated to the surprise of everyone, himself included. "I had an old CO who was fond of a Latin quote or two," he explained meekly. "We found a couple of military police stealing supplies from the NAAFI one time." He still seemed slightly stunned to discover the phrase had stuck with him.

Sikorski nodded. "You are exactly right, Sergeant," he said, without a hint of condescension. "It may be possible to bring in natural controls, but who will control them? If we do not consider how we will restrict the spread of the introduced predator, police them, as you say, we may face an even greater ecological catastrophe."

Jejeune nodded sadly. "I hear the cane toads in Australia now number one and a half billion."

"From an initial cohort of one hundred and one," said Sikorski sadly. "And expanding their range across northern Australia at a rate of sixty kilometres per year. We have learned lessons from disasters like this, but my concern is that we have not learned them all. Until we have, the safest approach is to dig out the invasive weed by hand."

He led the men along the corridor and they entered a narrow alcove with a single wooden bench running around the three sides. High in the wall opposite was a single stained-glass window. Beneath it a small altar had been set up. The entire room was painted bright white, except for the red pilasters in the corners. Although they were only decorative, they gave the space a grandeur far beyond its size.

"Our chapel," said Sikorski. He indicated a small alcove in each side wall, in which there were statues. "Two of Poland's five patron saints," explained Sikorski. "Saint Stanislaus is the saint of community. St. Adalbert is the saint of charity."

"Are these statues particularly expensive, sir?" asked Maik. "Only that's a fairly impressive metal grille you have on the door. Same with the larger windows, I notice."

Sikorski looked at Maik with genuine regret. "I would leave Wawel open for all to enjoy. But some members of our community store valuables in their lockers. So when there is no one here, we must bar the doors."

"Jakub Kowalski had a locker here, didn't he?" asked Maik.

Sikorski's eyes dimmed slightly. "Your tense confirms what I had suspected. He was the man found at the construction site?"

"His mother didn't tell you?"

"It is not the way of this family. And she has not been in to help with the record keeping for many days." Sikorski shook his great white head slowly. "Her son chose not to be of this community, but he was from our homeland. He will not be mourned, but there will be sadness for the family."

"Can I ask when was the last time you saw him?" inquired Jejeune.

"Here, at the marsh. It was on a Tuesday afternoon, two weeks ago. He came to take his rifle. You know about his role in the Ruddy Duck eradication programme." Sikorski had not phrased it as a question. "He came here hunting a pair of them."

"Did he find them?" asked Maik.

Sikorski lifted his hand. "There are many small backwaters here. He had not located them by the time the rest of us left for the day."

"There is restricted access to this land," said Jejeune, "so someone from the group here must have told him about the ducks."

"This seems likely," said the Count. He smiled. "The last thing I said to him was at least he was following the old ways, hunting during the new moon. The rural people in Poland believe it is always better to hunt ducks then. When the moon is full, the birds are too active at night. They sleep during the day and you cannot find them." He smiled again. "It was a joke, but Jakub Kowalski had no time for *babskie gadanie* from the Polish countryside. Old wives' tales. Like here, they are the repository of the nation's superstitions."

Possibly, thought Maik, *but that isn't to say you couldn't find a few truths amongst them.*

"May we take a look in Jakub Kowalski's locker?"

"If his mother will permit this. But you will have to ask her which one it is. I don't know. I hope you will allow me to preserve the privacy of the others by not checking all of them to find out."

Maik nodded. "Fair enough. But if she returns to work before we speak with her, perhaps you could ask her yourself."

He looked across at his DCI to see if he had any more questions. He did, but not about the locker. "If Jakub Kowalski didn't find the Ruddy Ducks, they could still be around. Perhaps one of the workers has seen them." Jejeune pulled a phone from his pocket and approached the group at the lockers. "This is a Ruddy Duck," he told them. "I'm wondering if any of you have seen one here recently?"

They gathered round and peered in at an image on his phone. In turn, each offered a regretful shake of the head. Maik and Sikorski drew up to the group. When Jejeune finally swivelled the phone around in their direction, Sikorski gave a hearty laugh. "This is not a female Ruddy Duck. It is a Common Scoter. Look, there is no eye stripe."

Jejeune smiled sheepishly and tucked the phone away. He thanked the workers and turned to Sikorski. "We'll leave you to get on with your work," he said. "Thank you for the tour. It's an impressive set-up you have here."

"You were not expecting this, I imagine, from our modest exterior. We keep it this way deliberately. It is not the Polish way to flaunt our presence. But to see Wawel in all its glory, you must return here in two days' time," Sikorski told them sincerely. "You shall be my guests when we celebrate the feast day of Saint Stanislaus. There will be music, dancing, food. You have seen the bones of this building. Then you will see its soul."

The men promised to make it if they could.

As they passed the mounds of harvested Frankenweed on their way out to the Mini, Maik noticed Jejeune checking his phone. "Might want to think about getting a new app, sir, if that one's going to make mistakes like that."

"I think this app's fine, Sergeant," said Jejeune. His faint smile told Maik all he needed to know. The sergeant had never met a birder yet who could have resisted correcting Jejeune's mistaken identification. But only Sikorski had risen to the bait. Which meant only Sikorski could have alerted Jakub Kowalski to the presence of the ducks here. As the two men walked along side by side, another Latin phrase from Maik's classically educated CO came to mind: *Si tacuisses, philosophus mansisses*, thought the sergeant ruefully. *If you want people to think you're clever, it's better to keep your mouth shut.*

19

The stationary figure stood out against the great downhill sweep of the empty fairway like a buoy in a green sea. Maik and Jejeune made their way down the edge of the fairway. From the tangle of leafless bushes and trees, thin trills of native birdsong floated towards them: Wrens, Blackbirds, Chaffinches. Jejeune could identify no spring visitors among the calls yet, though he expected to hear them any day now.

Curtis Angeren turned as the two men approached. He seemed to have been contemplating something in the fringe of trees, and turned to do so again now. "Just imagining the changes this old elm must have seen over the years," he said as the detectives came alongside. They stood beside him, regarding the large tree at the edge of the rough. The bark was deep-grooved and gnarled with age, but the bare branches rose into an impressive crown and the mass of healthy-looking buds suggested it would soon be out in its full, spreading splendour. "They tell me a stand of these used to line the driveway coming up to the club at one time. Of course, we lost them to that disease, didn't we? I hear you're having the same trouble with the ash trees in your country, Inspector."

"Yes, with the emerald ash borer," said Jejeune.

Angeren nodded thoughtfully. "From Asia, am I right? Like that birdwatching kit of yours." He flashed a mirthless grin at the detective. "I was just about to have a stroll up to the clubhouse. Perhaps we can discuss whatever it is you came to see me about on the way."

Jejeune walked beside Angeren, while the sergeant stayed a couple of paces behind. From his vantage point, Maik eyed the man carefully. About the time that beautiful stand of elm trees was disappearing, Curtis Angeren was making a name for himself as a rising star of the far right on university campuses across the country. After a series of run-ins with various police forces, he gradually morphed into that most dangerous of enemies: the one clothed in respectability. Curtis Angeren may have long since reinvented himself as a legitimate property developer, but both his political affiliations and his radical views had survived the transition intact. And now here he was, full circle, once again helping the police with their inquiries.

"We'd like to talk to you about a break-in at Paulina Kowalski's," said Jejeune.

The developer offered a sad head shake. "The mother of the dead man? Never rains but it pours for some people, doesn't it? I do hope she wasn't home at the time."

Maik came up to walk beside them. "There's a line of thought that it might have been a couple of men from your organization," he said.

"There are a lot of men in my organization, Sergeant. I don't condone any illegal action, as I'm sure you know. But if I'm to have a word with them, I'm afraid you'll have to identify them to me first."

"If we identify them, it won't be you having a word with them. Impersonating a police officer is a custodial offence."

Angeren stopped and they waited while he went through his elaborate cigar-lighting ritual again. They noticed he hadn't bothered to offer them one this time. He still had all the time in the world, he was telling the detectives, but he didn't intend on spending it with them.

He looked along the fairway and puffed on his cigar. "It's a lot of work, this place," he said. "But I'm proud to be doing my little bit toward preserving what's left of the English countryside."

Jejeune wasn't sure if overlaying pristine habitat with sand traps and half-kilometre swaths of what Lindy called green concrete would be most people's idea of conservation, but he suspected it wasn't the countryside part of things Angeren was most interested in preserving anyway.

The developer began walking again and Jejeune fell into step beside him. As before, Maik hung back a couple of steps. He seemed to prefer putting a bit of distance between himself and Curtis Angeren. The scent of freshly mown grass carried to Maik on the light spring breeze, and the gentle sun warmed his shoulders. It occurred to him what a pleasant walk this could have been, under other circumstances. "Those men who forcibly entered Mrs. Kowalski's house," he said from behind them, "they had a good rummage round. Any idea what they might have been looking for?"

"None at all. Did he have anything worth stealing?"

Maik saw Jejeune look across at Angeren and leave his eyes on him for a long time, as if deciding whether to pursue something. The developer kept looking straight ahead as they walked. In the end, the DCI decided against it.

Angeren took an exaggerated draw on his cigar. "One of the great English traditions, a round of golf. At least it used to be. God knows what the game'll look like in a few years, if people like those at the Saltmarsh Club have their way. Not enough we're losing our jobs to foreigners. Now they've got to take over our hobbies, too." He cast a glance in Jejeune's direction. "A look of disapproval, Inspector? From what I've seen, your own pastime doesn't seem to draw a particularly diverse crowd, if you get my drift."

"Not diverse enough, no, but there are encouraging signs. The numbers are building slowly."

"Ah, that's how it starts, see. The numbers build, and then one day you look around and you realize there's no room left for the ones who were here in the first place, people like us, the ones who belong here."

"I'm Canadian," he reminded Angeren.

"Indeed you are, Inspector. But your situation is hardly typical, is it? I mean, it'd be hard to make a case that you're over here keeping somebody out of a job. I can't see any of those lead-arsed halfwits down the Met filling your shoes, can you? No, I'm all for bringing in overseas talent, as long as it's merited. I'd go so far as to say you're an asset to this country, you and your type."

The clubhouse came into view at the top of the rise. Angeren paused again to look back down the pristine expanse of green they had just come along. "Know what I think of when I see this? Jerusalem. *And did those feet in ancient time, walk upon England's green and pleasant land?*"

It was perhaps to be expected that Angeren would cobble together the parts of Blake's poem that suited him. Jejeune wondered what sort of reception the Holy Lamb of God would really have received if Angeren and his associates had been there to witness the arrival of another foreigner on their shores.

From their vantage point, they could see the elm, standing tall at the edge of the fairway. Angeren indicated it with the butt of his cigar. "It was a foreign species that killed off our elms, wasn't it? Heavy price we pay, sometimes, for not protecting ourselves against those from other parts."

"Invasive species are a problem for all countries, Mr. Angeren," said Jejeune reasonably. "The British Isles has exported its fair share."

"You're talking about the Acclimation Societies. That was during the colonial period, when people were immigrating to new places. There were sound economic reasons for those introductions."

"I'm not sure what economic benefits Eurasian Starlings offer," said Jejeune. "A man named Eugene Schieffelin released one hundred of them into New York's Central Park in the early 1890's, solely because starlings are mentioned in Henry IV, Part I. It was part of a plan to introduce all the birds that appear in Shakespeare's plays. Far from benefitting from that introduction, North America is now dealing with a starling population well in excess of two hundred million birds."

"There's nothing wrong with starlings," said Angeren defensively. "Lovely little birds. The Americans should be glad to have them."

Behind the men, Maik shook his head slowly. It was a waste of time trying to reason with people like Angeren. They always had the facts at hand to support their worldview. Like his list of shortcomings in Asian optics, all carefully researched and ready to be trotted out at a moment's notice.

"I've got to be on my way," said Angeren, "but it's always a pleasure exchanging ideas with a man of intelligence, Inspector, even if we can't see eye to eye on things." Angeren extended a hand to Jejeune. The DCI suspected it was no accident Maik found himself just too far away for a handshake of his own. As the developer turned to leave, a final thought seemed to strike him. "Nothing further to tell me about who killed Jakub Kowalski, I suppose?"

"Your request to be informed about developments in the case has already been denied, Mr. Angeren," said Jejeune formally. "We won't be revisiting that decision." He was slightly puzzled that the man had returned to the subject. He didn't seem the type given to chasing lost causes.

"That is disappointing," said Angeren, "especially with the news."

Maik had closed the distance before Jejeune had time to respond. The sergeant now stood less than a foot from Angeren. In the trees along the fairway, the birdsong had fallen silent. "What news?"

"Oh, that's right, you won't have heard," Angeren said pleasantly, taking time to draw on his cigar. He looked from Maik to Jejeune and back again, enjoying the moment. "According to the grapevine, Ray Hayes is back. And he's on his way to Saltmarsh."

20

Maik had wanted to press, out there on the golf course, with nothing but green, open spaces around them and the nearest sets of ears on the next tee, hundreds of metres away. He felt he might have been able to make an effective pitch for Angeren's co-operation. But the chances were good that Angeren wouldn't know Hayes's exact location anyway, and Jejeune didn't want to give him the opportunity to delay them any longer. The two officers sprinted up the fairway and raced back to the Range Rover. Jejeune had it in gear and moving before Maik's door was shut.

As they sped towards town along the narrow lanes, Maik dialled a number and asked for Lindy. He listened carefully and switched off his phone, letting it rest in his hand. "She's gone to Saltmarsh Square to meet someone. At the café there. The receptionist doesn't know who, but it wasn't in Lindy's diary this morning. She's guessing the call hasn't long come in, but she doesn't recall putting it through herself."

Jejeune risked taking his eyes off the road long enough to flash a quick look in Danny's direction. "It's market day."

Maik nodded. Pedestrian access only. They'd have to park on the perimeter of the square and go in on foot, between the market stalls and through crowds of vendors and shoppers packed in so tightly that running was impossible. The big Range Rover sped forward as Jejeune poured on the power, rocking slightly as it emerged from a high-speed corner. If they met anything coming the other way on these narrow lanes, Maik suspected the customary north Norfolk road courtesies wouldn't be applying today.

The Beast skidded to a stop at the corner of the nearest open road on Saltmarsh High Street and the two men jumped out hurriedly. The entire length of the High Street had been barricaded off into a pedestrian-only area, and it was teeming with bodies. The Saltmarsh Market was a popular destination anyway, and the early spring sunshine had brought the shoppers out in numbers. From the edge of the low metal barrier, Jejeune craned his head, frantically looking for Lindy in the milling crowds. It was a hopeless task. Heads bobbed everywhere. He knew, too, Lindy's penchant for punctuality meant she would almost certainly already be at the café by now, sitting in the sunshine, working on her laptop as she waited for her guest to arrive. He knew Lindy always switched off her phone for meetings. It was a courtesy Jejeune had often praised, but he cursed it now. The Market Café was equidistant from any entry points the two policemen could have accessed, but it was tucked back off the main square, not visible from where they stood. Their only option was to go in on foot.

"I'll make my way from this end," said Maik, forcing his way between the barriers. "You go along New Lane and come in from the other end." The sergeant eased his way into the flow of the crowd and in seconds even his imposing frame had been swallowed by it. Jejeune turned and ran to the road parallel to the High Street, unfettered by barriers and open to traffic as an alternative route through town on market days.

He sprinted along the street, choosing the edge of the roadway in an effort to avoid the window shoppers and placards that littered the pavement. Heads turned to watch as he raced past, jacket flailing, arms pumping. This was not a man trying to catch a bus; it was someone going full out, running for his life. Or somebody else's. At the far end of the street, where it bent towards the enclosed market area, Jejeune skidded around the corner and vaulted over the barrier. It rocked under his weight but held firm, and he landed on the other side safely. He was panting heavily now, but he didn't wait to catch his breath. Instead, he began squirming, side on, into the flow of the oncoming crowd. He turned his head back and forth, his eyes in constant motion, but he took in the colour and noise and smells of the marketplace only as a background blur. He was looking for Lindy, still hoping to find her, late and flustered, hurrying to her meeting. He was looking for Hayes, too, a small skulking figure who habitually wore a hoodie to disguise the shaved head and prison tattoos. But anyone that small wouldn't show up in this sea of heads that Jejeune now found all around him.

He noticed a gap between the rows of vendors' stalls where they had arranged them back-to-back along the centre of the main street and he headed for it. It was unpeopled, but cluttered with crates and cartons and coils of thick black power cable. Progress was faster than swimming against the tide of humanity in the crowded street, but not by much. It was hotter in here, too, and he began to sweat as he clambered between the obstacles, earning the occasional shout from the vendors who noticed him scrambling past. He emerged from the end of the row of stalls to find he had veered off somehow into one of the side streets. He didn't know where he was, and panic gripped him as he felt time slipping away. He leaped onto one of the old metal lamp posts that lined the streets of this historic quarter and found a foothold on a moulding. With his arm wrapped around the post and passersby staring at him quizzically, he surveyed the marketplace from his perch. He could see the white lights trailing around the perimeter of the café courtyard. It seemed impossibly far away, a land-mass separated from him by a seething, swirling ocean of tightly-packed human bodies. He knew he couldn't get there in time. Danny Maik was his only hope now. The sergeant's formidable presence would have parted the oncoming crowds like a freight liner and he would have made better progress than Jejeune had. He was about to jump down to renew his own push through the crowds when he saw a small form, grey-hooded and moving with a nimbleness that allowed it to slide easily through the momentary gaps between the people. Grey Hoodie was probably fifty metres ahead of Jejeune's position, heading directly for the café.

Jejeune jumped into the crowd and began forcing his way through, ignoring the protests and angry shoves of the shoppers as he passed. The sweat was dripping into his eyes, stinging them, making them blur. He blinked it away and pushed on. Perhaps he was closing the gap, but he had lost sight of the hoodie now and couldn't tell. All he knew was they were both heading for the same destination, And he had to get there first.

The Market Café was housed in an old building flanked on either side by a narrow alleyway. A small open-air patio had been set up in front, enclosed by a low metal barrier on three sides to protect the patrons from the crowds of shop-pers streaming by. The single entrance to the patio was from the street. The side barrier caused a chicane, with the crowds bending towards the centre of the street to get past. It cleared the sightlines slightly, and from his position Jejeune could see all the way up to the patio. His heart lurched as he caught sight of a shock of corn-blonde hair. Lindy was sitting at a table beside the railing, with her back to him. If Hayes decided on a simple knife swipe in passing, she was in direct line. From the corner of his eye, Jejeune saw the grey hoodie, veering in towards the café. Hayes was ten metres in front of him, the same distance from Lindy. Jejeune frantically scrabbled past the bodies in front of him and surged up behind the figure. He was within striking distance now, and drew back to whip an arm around Hayes's neck and wrestle him to the ground. He never got the chance. From somewhere in the crowd a figure materialized and hauled Jejeune into the alleyway beside the café. A number of passing shoppers momentarily turned their heads in surprise. But Lindy didn't. Nor did the hoodie. Both were still facing away from Jejeune. Grey Hoodie rounded the barrier into the patio and approached Lindy's table.

With his shoulder blades pinned against the rough brick of the alley wall, Jejeune found himself looking into a face he recognized. From the café table, he heard a voice. It was familiar, too.

"Hi, I'm Lindy." Jejeune heard the scraping of a chair being drawn back. "And you must be Des."

21

"Nice of you to join us this morning, Sarge."

"I had to walk in," said Maik tersely. "Car trouble."

"You know, the kindest thing might be to have it put down," said Holland. "They do it humanely now. It won't feel a thing. I promise." Holland decided not to push it any further. Apart from anything else, Maik prized punctuality highly, and he wouldn't be best pleased about showing up late, regardless of the circumstances. The constable switched his attention to the other occupant of the workroom. "So, where'd you get to yesterday?" he asked Des Gill.

"Oh, you know, around. I went down to the market," she said. "I thought I'd take in a bit of that local colour you were talking about."

"Must be nice; get a bit of shopping in while the sergeant and our intrepid DCI were off having a stroll around the links. Meanwhile, I was stuck here, slogging my way through this useless background stuff on the Polish community. Did you get anything of interest from Angeren, by the way, Sarge?"

Maik looked at Holland for a long moment, trying to determine whether the constable had any special motive for asking. But Holland wasn't fixing Maik with a stare, as you might if you wanted to detect evasion about something you already knew, like the fact that Ray Hayes was now back in the picture. In fact, the constable's attention was being drawn more in the direction of Empowered Investigator Gill as she bent over the desk to plug in her laptop. If Holland hadn't returned his gaze to the sergeant, Maik might not have bothered answering at all. As it was, he gave a small shrug. "Not really. Other than the fact he did confirm he was behind the break-in at Paulina Kowalski's house, so it seems a pretty safe bet now that he was the one who sent the eavesdropper the first time we were there."

Gill, who had been half-listening, turned to Danny as she straightened up. "He really had the audacity to confirm that he was behind the break-in?"

Maik tilted his head slightly. "When we inquired whether they'd found what they were after, Angeren asked if 'he' had anything worth taking. The only room the burglars paid any attention to was the son's."

"Could be just a slip-up, though, surely," said Holland.

Maik shook his head. "The Curtis Angerens of the world don't stay on top very long if they make mistakes like that. He wants us to know he's involved now because he thinks it'll only serve to show he had nothing to do with the murder."

"And we're buying that, are we?"

"We are," said Maik. "For now."

He stopped and looked at Gill. She was watching the two men, but with a different kind of interest now, as if she might gain some insight into them, rather than the case they were discussing.

"All in order, DC Gill?" asked Maik pleasantly. "Got everything you need?"

"All in order, Sergeant," she told him in a semi-official tone. Nestling on her headphones, she flipped open her laptop and clicked on the audio file.

Sunday November 21st, 10:38 a.m. Call duration: 1 minute 38 seconds

Caller: *So, you all set to listen to what's going to happen, Domenic the Canadian?*
Jejeune: *I'm all set. How are Carolyn and Monte coping?*
Caller: *Let's get this deal done and you'll be able to see for yourself, won't you? Now the way this is going to work is —*
Jejeune: *The authorities will need proof of life before we enter into any negotiations.*
Caller: *We'll do things the way I say we do them. You pay, they get released. End of.*
Jejeune: *There will be no payment without prior proof of life. I don't want this to seem like it's something between us. I'm simply telling you, nobody is going to sanction a payment unless that condition is met.*
(Muffled sounds; eight-second silence)
Caller: *I'm listening. Not agreeing. Just listening.*
Jejeune: *A phone call, to each of them in turn. I will ask them each one question. No tricks, but it will be a question to which only they will know the answer. When we're sure it's them, we can move on to the terms of the exchange.*
Caller: *No calls. I'll send you a photo of each of them. Separate. Holding today's paper.*
Jejeune: *That won't work. It's too easy to Photoshop photographs, and it will take us too long to verify them. It has to be a phone conversation. I have to have proof they are still alive and unharmed.*

Caller: I told you, no phone calls. It's photos or nothing. Don't make this difficult for everybody, Domenic.
(Seven-second silence)
Jejeune: Okay, a compromise. You get one fingerprint from each of them, and you send it to us.
(Six-second silence)
Caller: I could do that. I'll get some prints on a glass.
Jejeune: No, it has to be something you buy, something you couldn't possibly have lying around there already, that might have picked up their prints beforehand. I want to know you've been able to get fresh prints, since we spoke.
Caller: Like I said before, I'm listening. Only.
(Five-second pause)
Jejeune: Do you have any medication with you in case either of them goes into shock?
Caller: What? She's fine, Domenic. They both are. Are we going to talk about proof of life or not?
Jejeune: It could happen. You need something on hand, just in case. A person in shock can go downhill quickly without treatment. Here's what you need to do …

Holland's tap on the shoulder startled Des. She peeled off the headphones and looked at him. "So what is it today, more of His Birdship's greatest hits?"

"Just the section of the negotiations where Jejeune asked the kidnapper for proof of life."

"As you would," said Holland. He set a mug down on the desk in front of her. "Coffee, black and strong, according to your mates down at the Met." He gave her a wink and she smiled. Holland parked himself on the corner of her desk, but to the watching Danny Maik there was a less predatory feel to the approach than other times he'd seen Holland operate. Perhaps DC Des Gill had already set some boundaries with their earlier encounters.

"Always a bit dodgy, that proof of life thing," said Holland pensively. "Stands to reason these kidnappers are going to be sadistic bastards anyway. You don't want them sawing off any body parts and sending them to you through the post, just to make a point."

Des shook her head. "I get the impression Jejeune knew right from the very beginning this one wasn't going to be like that. He seemed to sense the kidnapper really did want to let them go unharmed."

"So what did he ask for? Video?"

"Not even. Just a call." Des sipped her coffee and started back from it a little. *Hot*, they would have told Holland down at the Met, too. He'd obviously taken the instructions to heart. "But the kidnapper refused. No phone contact of any kind. Instead he agreed to provide fingerprints, on an object Jejeune would designate. One he would have to go out and buy."

Holland looked down at Gill and nodded slowly. "So he refuses a simple phone call, the easiest proof of life there is, but agrees to one that's going to cause him a lot more trouble." He smiled at her. "If it was me, I'd have to wonder if that wasn't telling me something else. Like maybe no phone signal at the place where the kids were being held."

Des flashed a look at Maik, who was watching the exchange with interest from his desk. "You'd have fit right in on the kidnapping detail, Tony," said Des with a smile. "Because that's exactly what they thought."

"How about that?" he said, easing himself off the desk, "Well, I'll leave you to your listening."

"I need a break. I can't wear those 'phones for too long. They make my ears ache."

"I have that problem with Sarge's Motown," said Holland with a wink in Maik's direction. He returned to his desk and Des reached for a folder of case notes.

"What? That can't be right, Sergeant."

The comment startled Maik. He'd been immersed in The Marvelettes' radical solution to love's disappointments, letting the harmonies of "Locking Up My Heart" swirl around him. It took him a few seconds to realize Gill was not speaking to him. She was studying a file, a hefty set of curling pages in a battered folder yellowed with age. Her elbows rested on the desk, fingertips pressed against her temples as she read, oblivious to the world. She seemed unaware she'd spoken out loud.

Holland had looked up at the comment, too. Like Maik, he had expected to find Gill staring in the sergeant's direction. But her eyes were still on the notes before her and both men realized the sergeant she was addressing was not the one sitting across the room from her now, but one who had been stationed in an office at the Met, a long time ago. Together, the men watched as she flipped back and forth through the sheets, checking and rechecking. Her frown suggested a second reading had done nothing to make Sergeant Jejeune's statements any clearer. She brought up a map on the computer screen and peered at it for a few moments, one-handing a few searches into Google. Then she took out her phone, jabbed a series of numbers into the calculator function and jotted down a few more notes. She twisted her mouth from its default smile and tried the calculations again. Doubt etched lines into her flawless, child-smooth skin. She'd found something, and despite her best efforts to calculate it away, it was still troubling her.

Gill sat staring at the case folder for a long moment before fixing her upbeat persona back into place. By the time she finally looked up at the room again, both men had managed to avert their gaze.

"Can I ask, did the inspector ever talk to you about the rare bird he spotted around that time, a kind of Magpie?"

Holland had a surprisingly engaging laugh when he wasn't trying to use it as a weapon. "Erm, I suspect he might have realized he wouldn't find the most rapt of audiences in here. It's probably the way our eyes glaze over whenever he starts banging on about birds."

"I know there was a mention of a Magpie in the case at the time," said Maik, "but the DCI has never made any reference to it since, not to my knowledge anyway. If you needed to know anything about that bird, it'd probably be best if you went directly to him."

Delivered in a different tone, it could have been a warning. But Gill took it for what it was; helpful advice. She shook her head. "Thanks, but that was a different species of Magpie," she said. "That one took off with a piece of evidence from the kidnap scene. But it was just your common or garden-variety Magpie, the ones we see in the U.K. all the time. This other bird was special. Iberian Azure-winged Magpies live in Southern Europe. This was the first time a wild one had ever been recorded in the U.K. And Domenic Jejeune was credited with the find."

"So there were two Magpies about," said Holland thoughtfully. "What would they call that, I wonder?"

"Joy?" offered Maik.

"A group of Magpies is called a tiding," said Gill, with the kind of authority that suggested she'd made a point of finding out. "So he never said anything about this sighting then?" She tapped her teeth with a pencil in thought. "Okay, thanks."

"You know, one of my earliest cases in uniform involved a Magpie," said Holland, smiling now at the memory. "A woman called to say her engagement ring had been nicked by one. I went round to take her statement for the insurance. I remember she had a right shiner, and I wondered if her boyfriend had given it to her for losing the ring."

"And I suppose you comforted her," said Gill, pulling a face.

"Preying on the vulnerable? I can see you share the same high opinion of me as some other people round here." He looked across to where Maik was still staring at the pair of them. There was lightness in Holland's tone, but it still made Gill feel slightly ashamed of her comment.

"Anyway," continued Holland, "she said the bird took the ring right off the kitchen windowsill while she was doing the washing-up."

"Magpies are known to be very quick-witted," offered Gill eagerly.

Holland nodded. "This one must have been. It took the ring to a pawnbroker. I saw it there a couple of months later. When I went back to confront the woman, she'd gone. The boyfriend said she'd taken the insurance payout with her when she left. He wanted to file a complaint, but I said she'd mentioned something about domestic abuse when I was round there before. She hadn't, but it made him think twice. In the end, he decided to let it drop."

Des was staring at Holland now, her head tilted slightly to one side, as if she was unsure quite what to make of his story. Or of him. But for now she had other things on her mind. And they were more pressing.

22

By the time he parked the Mini and opened the door, Danny Maik could hear the music; a cacophony of dulcimers, mandolins, and drums. He hoped the doors weren't locked; the people inside would have a hard time hearing him, and his chances of forcing his way past that formidable-looking iron grille on the door were non-existent.

Despite Sikorski's effusive invitation, the Feast of Saint Stanislaus was not an event Danny would normally have attended without pressure from above. But he had some information he thought Jejeune would want to hear sooner rather than later. He knew the DCI would be here, whether he shared Maik's reluctance about such gatherings or not. Lindy would not want to miss an event like this.

He needn't have worried about the grille. The doors were wide open, spilling out noise and people and bright lights onto the ground outside the building. Maik made his way inside and stood self-consciously in the doorway of the large central hall. It was packed with people, all milling about in a state of high revelry, laughing and shouting to each other over the sounds of the music and the din of other conversations. It was hard to reconcile this riot of colour and noise with the dignified, restrained space he had seen on his last visit. The walls, formerly so stark and pristine, had been transformed into a festival of colour with hand-woven doilies and painted icons. The iron bars on the windows were hidden behind exquisitely crafted lace curtains. In the far corner of the room, a five-piece band was playing for all they were worth, compensating for any deficiencies in technique with an enthusiasm that was clearly infectious. Along the side wall ran a series of long tables dressed in crisp white cloths embroidered with red and gold. On them sat one of the most astonishing arrays of food Maik had ever seen. Platter upon platter was piled high with kielbasa, potatoes, chałka bread, cabbage rolls, and a large selection of babka and other sweets.

With all the distractions on offer, it was no surprise someone could approach Danny undetected on his blind side, "Dom's over there," said Lindy. "Something tells me he's going to be glad to have somebody to share his misery."

To Maik, Jejeune looked as lost in this crowded room as a man on a desert island. It would have been a stretch to say he looked happy to see Maik, but relief was not far off the mark. He made his way over hurriedly.

"Des is here, too," said Lindy as Jejeune approached. "We met at the market yesterday for coffee, so I invited her. Might not be a typical night out in Saltmarsh, but at least she gets to see a local community event. We came together in her car." She looked at Jejeune. "I'm DD-ing tonight."

Maik looked over to where Des was standing in front of an older woman. She was pitched forward on her toes, bellowing a comment to the woman, who was leaning forward to hear her.

"I'm not surprised to see Calista Hyde here," said Maik, indicating the older woman. "She's involved in just about every community event around here in some capacity."

Jejeune regarded the woman carefully. She was of modest height and generous build. With her kindly face and loose grey curls, she reminded him a little of his grandmother. In truth, she reminded him of just about everybody's grandmother. "So that's Fêtezilla? Perhaps I should go over and say hello."

"She'll be busy," said Lindy hurriedly. "I'm sure organizing this event means she's got loads of things to do. Oh, look, they're setting up some sort of folk dance. I'll bet Des and I could do that. Hey, Des," she shouted over, indicating the dance floor, "fancy a go? Come on, let's give it a bash."

Jejeune let his gaze follow Lindy as she led Des onto the dance floor, weaving between the tightly-packed bodies to find a space. He watched the women sharing peals of laughter as they misstepped their way through the intricate patterns of the oberek.

"Not as easy as it looks, apparently," Jejeune said to Maik. He seemed unable to take his eyes off Lindy. Her vivacity seemed to linger around her like a trail of glitter as she moved. But for once, it did not bring a smile to Jejeune's face, only a faint shadow of concern.

"I paid Curtis Angeren a visit today," said Maik, without taking his own eyes off the dancers, even as Jejeune snapped his head round to look at him. "Turns out the report of Hayes's return was a bit premature. He's still in Australia. I told Angeren any more false alarms and I might take up an interest in golf."

Jejeune could imagine the scene Maik's words would have painted in the developer's mind: a menacing colossus standing splay-legged in the foyer of the clubhouse, glowering at members as he quizzed them about some person named Ray Hayes. News of a plutonium leak would not clear the building any more rapidly.

Jejeune had not realized what had been trapped within him until it had been released. It felt like a captive bird had fluttered from his heart and left behind only the soothing stillness of relief. He started to speak, but paused, as if perhaps he didn't quite trust his voice yet.

Maik misinterpreted Jejeune's silence. "I think we'll be able to rely on any information we get from him from now on, sir. Whatever Angeren wants from us, news about Hayes's return would be a decent bargaining chip."

The breathless return of Lindy and Des from the dance floor saved Jejeune from having to respond. "Blimey, you're in good shape," said Des breathlessly. "It was all I could do to keep up with you."

"Really, I didn't find it that bad," said Lindy, between gasps. "To be honest, I'm surprised you know how to dance at all. I thought it was all video games and social media with you young 'uns. Staying indoors all day, never getting any exercise."

"Not me. Tennis is my thing, *actch*. I play a couple of times a week when I'm home. You?"

"Tennis? God no, I've always thought of tennis as basically golf for fit people. I run — 5Ks. Quite regularly, as a matter of fact." Lindy made a point of avoiding Jejeune's stare.

Teodor Sikorski approached the group, his eyes shining with alcohol, cheeks flushed with high colour. "Ah, the inspector of the rare birds, and the sergeant of the Latin phrases." Maik looked slightly abashed. "I'm very happy you have chosen to join us tonight. And your delightful companions, too." He clipped his heels together and gave a slight formal bow.

"It's wonderful," said Lindy, looking around the room, still recovering her breath. "I should think the entire Polish community of Saltmarsh must be here."

Not quite, thought Jejeune. There was one very conspicuous female absence — plus, of course, a young man who would never be attending gatherings ever again.

Des excused herself to go off in search of a cool corner and Maik's sense of chivalry led him to accompany her.

"Dom tells me you're heading a project to remove some invasive species out here," said Lindy.

Sikorski offered her a charming smile. "Perhaps some people think we wish only to come here to play chess and drink tea and talk about the old country. No, we have chosen to do something useful, to remove unsightliness from the English countryside."

"But surely you've not been asked to remove this Frankenweed just because it's ugly," said Lindy.

"No? If we were truly committed to removing invasive species, we should treat them all equally. Instead, it is only the unattractive ones we target. Think of the Mute Swan in your own country, Inspector. This is an invasive species, is it not? Before 1800 there were none in Canada. Now ..." Vodka sloshed over the side of Sikorski's glass as he made a wide, sweeping gesture to emphasize his point, "it is far more familiar to most Canadians than any of the native swans. Why has there been no effort to remove it? Because it is beautiful. No other reason. But I ask you, Ms. Hey, what is beauty, after all, other than one person's opinion?"

"John Keats said beauty is truth," she offered.

"And truth beauty." Sikorski shook his head. "Pah, he was twenty-three years old when he wrote this. What does an innocent boy like this know of the real world? Beauty is not so pure. She corrupts our ideals." He nodded slowly. "To rid the landscape of an unattractive weed, yes, everybody wants this. But other species are allowed to remain here, to thrive even. They do not ask us to remove rhododendrons from the English landscape. I wonder, if this Japanese knotweed hybrid, this *Frankenweed*, was a beautiful flowering plant, would they still ask us to eradicate it? Or would its beauty save it?"

Sikorski extended an arm to corral someone as she passed by. "But we must now speak of other things, of a person who has contributed so much of her time to tonight's event." He placed a hand on his heart. "Calista, to you we are truly indebted. Forgive me, but I must greet some other guests. I shall return soon, Inspector, and we shall drink to life."

Sikorski melted into the crowd as Calista extended her hand. "You must be Domenic. I have to say, we can't thank you enough for insisting Lindy come out to join our committee."

Jejeune simply smiled and raised his eyebrows, as was his custom when he hadn't understood a comment.

"We're quite aware that Lindy would never have joined without your constant encouragement, but we're so delighted you persevered with her. We're certain she's going to be a wonderful addition to the committee, despite having been cajoled into it by you, against her better judgment." Calista gave a kindly smile.

Jejeune looked across at Lindy, who appeared to have found some speck of dust in her eye, to which she was now attending with a delicate fingertip.

"Well, she tends to lack confidence," Jejeune told Calista, leaning in confidentially, "but once she gets started, there's no holding her back. I'm sure if there were any vacancies elsewhere — the lawn bowling committee, say, or the shuffleboard club she'd be delighted to take on those, too."

Calista looked uncertainly at Lindy, who had stopped fiddling with her eye and was now offering Domenic a strange smile. "Well, if I hear of anything, I'll certainly let you know, Lindy. But I must get on. I still have more food to prepare. The Count will not be satisfied until everyone has had their fill tonight. He sees it as his duty to bring as much joy and comfort into these people's lives as he can."

"Polish culture obviously agrees with you," Lindy told Jejeune as they watched Calista leave. "You certainly weren't this frisky earlier today. It's like you've suddenly had the weight of the world lifted off your shoulders."

If he had, the reason for it was approaching them now. As Maik and Des rejoined them, Sikorski emerged from the centre of a crowd. "Ah, Inspector. Please, all of you, a drink. A special drink!"

"My night to be DD," said Lindy. "Designated driver."

Sikorski bowed his head. "A noble gesture indeed. I trust the inspector will honour your sacrifice by drinking to it."

He waved over the young woman who had greeted the detectives on their previous visit to Wawel. "Please bring Goldwasser, for my special guests."

He turned to them. "Polish vodka. The best. None of that Russian *płyn do płukania ust*."

A group nearby roared with approval as the woman offered the translation. "Mouthwash," she said. "The Count does not use bad words — in English or in Polish. He has only good words, for all people."

She disappeared and returned with a tray holding four glasses and a bottle of clear liquid with what looked like gold flakes suspended in it. "You are very fortunate," she confided as she filled the glasses and handed them out. "The invitation to drink personally with the Count is seen as a great honour among the people here."

"Come, drink," urged Sikorski amiably. "*Zdrowie wasze w gardła nasze*. To your health, down our throats."

They tipped up their glasses together. Des choked at the liquid's burn and waved away the offer of another, but the men had their newly replenished glasses thrust into their hands once more. "And now, Inspector, the man who will shield our community from the evils of the outside world, the toast is yours."

Jejeune looked across at Danny Maik and smiled. "To those who would protect the innocent."

The nearby group applauded loudly as the men tossed back the drinks. The glasses were filled for a third time as if by magic. It crossed Lindy's mind that this ritual might go on indefinitely unless somebody intervened.

"So, I'm wondering, Count Sikorski," she said in her best investigative journalist tone, "based on our earlier conversation, would you expect someone to report a pair of Ruddy Ducks if they saw them? After all, they're very attractive."

Sikorski rocked slightly on his heels and turned his bleary eyes upon her. His courteous smile remained undimmed. "People want to protect this bird, with its pretty blue beak and its chestnut feathers and its turned-up tail," he said. "Our ideology will always be compromised by our emotions, you see; our hopes, our wishes, our personal feelings."

The crowd around them had grown as people gathered in to hear Sikorski hold court, and he turned to them now, seeming to mesmerize them with his talismanic charm. "Take these beautiful Polish girls," he said, thrusting his arm out unsteadily to indicate a group of young women gathered nearby, "these women with their long blonde hair, their skin like white satin, their eyes the colour of glaciers. Do you think these are the ones people want to send back to their own country?" He shook his head, his eyes alive with fervour and alcohol. "No, even Curtis Angeren would allow beauty like this to remain here." He slapped his chest with his palm and wagged an unsteady finger in Lindy's direction. "Our hearts, you see, Ms. Hey. They will make traitors of us all!"

Jejeune and Maik stood side by side in the soft evening air. When the festivities started, the dying sun in the west was a blinding orange disc, but now around them was only darkness, an emptiness in which they knew a vast, quiet marshland lurked. Behind them, the last of the departing guests were spilling out of the centre and Calista was waiting to secure the metal grille over the door. After she got in her car and left, only three cars remained parked beside the building: The Beast,

Maik's Mini, and an MGB with the motor running and the two women inside.

"Don't go wandering off," Lindy called to them as she pulled away. "Remember, there's a steep embankment on either side of this berm. In the dark it would be easy for one of you to end up in the drink."

She waved an arm through the open top of the MGB as she drove off. Having piled the sports car's worse-for-wear owner into the passenger seat, Lindy was on her way to drop Des off at her B&B, where she would pick up her own car before returning to collect the two vodka-shot detectives. She would load Domenic into the back of the Nissan Leaf and deliver Danny safely to his house on their way home.

The men watched the red tail lights disappear into the night. A three-quarter moon was casting a pale, silvery light over the fields in the distance. Jejeune wanted to say something, to thank Maik for caring enough about Lindy to pay that visit to Angeren. But he knew neither man was in the right condition for him to attempt something like that. At best it would be inadequate; at worst it would end up embarrassing them both. Maik had done what he'd done, he'd told Jejeune about it, and Jejeune had acknowledged his gratitude with a toast. It was enough.

Maik looked around, taking in the night. Beside them, the vast piles of drying Frankenweed looked like dark shrubs.

"Sounds to me like they'll be needing another niche in that saints' chapel soon."

Jejeune smiled, taking Maik's point. "When a person of faith has nothing, an anonymous benefactor must seem like a gift from Heaven."

But how much devotion would such an earthy saint command? Would gratitude for a few painted icons and a place to hold Polish folk dances be enough for someone to commit murder on a saint's behalf? Or even on his orders? Perhaps, if your faith was strong enough, or your humanity weak enough. But even if not, there were other possibilities. *A thousand years' worth of life experience*, thought Jejeune. If Jakub Kowalski was as unpopular among the local Polish community as Sikorski said, that also meant a thousand years' worth of motives. The night had been an enjoyable one, but it hadn't done much to narrow down the pool of suspects.

23

Jejeune leaned against the Range Rover and watched the dust trail swirl in the morning air in the wake of Lindy's departure. Maik had left moments before, the little Mini trundling across the berm with such effort Jejeune half-expected Lindy would come across it broken down on the dirt track before she even reached the main road.

The detective drew a breath and slowly took in the view, listening to the sound of no sounds. Beneath a wide, low sky filled with clouds, the estuary lay in silvery silence. All around him, nature awaited the coming of a new day with its eternal patience. Along the narrow channel at the base of the berm, tall reeds nodded gently in mute tribute to a passing breeze, while a solitary Coot drifted through its watery domain without making a sound. Even before the unwelcome reappearance of Ray Hayes on his horizon, there had been a constant background noise in Jejeune's world: a murder case that was beginning to raise warning flags in his mind, an Empowered Investigator from the Met delving into areas of his past he had long thought buried. But perhaps the peace that had settled over this place would also settle over him.

Beside him, set against the wide open spaces of the flanking marsh, Wawel seemed smaller this morning, diminished by its emptiness. To Jejeune's fanciful imagination, it seemed almost to be hunching into the landscape, ashamed of its role in last night's revelries. He smiled at the thought. Nights like the previous one saw Lindy at her vibrant, audacious best, embracing every new experience and hugging it to her soul. She seemed to charge the air around her with her enthusiasm, the life force coursing through her like an inner light. He tracked the dust trail as her car followed the wide, sweeping arc back up onto the road. And now she was off to look the world in the eye for another day, to meet its challenges head on, as fearless and confident as always.

From up here, he could see the coast road, less than a quarter of a mile away across the dark rubble of the unploughed field in front of him. He wondered who had decided the roadway from the berm should follow the route it did. Who had drawn the plans that saw the track sweep down in its massive half-mile loop, marsh on one side, farmland on the other, before linking up with the coast road so far away, instead of simply cutting a much shorter route directly across this field? Like so many of north Norfolk's secrets, it was a story that had been written into the landscape long before he arrived.

From a nearby shrub, a male Stonechat swooped down to take an insect, returning in a single graceful loop to his perch on the same branch, just as Jejeune had seen those cryptic *Empid* flycatchers do back in Canada — the Acadian, the Willow, the Alder. He wondered idly if there was a collective noun for flycatchers. A spiderweb, perhaps? How about an outfield? He smiled at his joke, even as he accepted there was likely not a single other person in Saltmarsh who would have understood it. Even Lindy would have to put it under the microscope. *Okay, Dom, I get the baseball thing, the outfield, but why are the high balls the fielders catch called flys?* He sighed to himself. Maybe he could draw stick men diagrams to accompany the joke. Better still, perhaps he'd simply keep it to himself. There were times when he missed having someone who could pick up on his Canadian references at face value. No matter how long you lived somewhere, he supposed there were always going to be little reminders that a part of you belonged somewhere else.

And yet he really felt he belonged here now. He rarely reflected these days on how much he loved this landscape, with its unpredictable weather and its shifting light and its wide open spaces. But it was here among the coastal marshes, like nowhere else, that Jejeune understood the world. His senses brought the world to him here, what it looked like, felt like, smelled like. They told him of its moods, its promises. The hint of purple in the cloud cover, the dry-dust smell carrying to him on the winds, the uneasy swaying of the reed beds; they all whispered to him of coming rain. How could he say he was not from here, not a part of this place, when he could read it like this? Saltmarsh was in him now. It would be with him always.

On a far mudbank, a dispute between a pair of Mute Swans flared into a noisy squabble. For a moment, their angry hisses and agitated flapping tore the peace asunder, an unwelcome intrusion on this soundless landscape. But the thrusts and parries subsided as quickly as they had begun, and the birds settled again to their tranquil co-existence. Jejeune watched as they smoothed their ruffled feathers around themselves and tucked their heads beneath their wings, nestling once more into the still morning air. *Silence. It is the final resting place of all disputes*, thought Jejeune, *of all conflicts.* So much good came from silence. It was where feelings could float to the surface, where we could reach our emotions, where our thoughts found a safe haven. But silence had its dangers, too. It could lead to misunderstandings. And it could destroy relationships. Because silence was the enemy of trust.

There are to be no more secrets between us, Domenic.

No more secrets. And he had agreed. But what of Shepherd's own secrets? He thought about her word. *Us,* she'd said. Nothing for *us* to worry about. Nothing coming back to bite *us*? As far as Jejeune was concerned, even if there was any fallout from the Carolyn Gresham kidnapping case, it couldn't possibly compromise Shepherd. She'd had nothing whatsoever to do with the original investigation. Everything had been signed off long before the DCI made his transfer to her jurisdiction. So why was she so concerned that Des Gill's investigation would reflect badly on her and the Saltmarsh team?

A shaft of sunlight had broken through the cloud cover at a low angle, lighting a patch of reeds on the far side of the water with its ethereal glow. In a heartbeat, the scene had been transformed. But even as he looked out over this new landscape, shot through with silken threads of golden light, Jejeune's peace refused to come. The approaching threat to Lindy rose up out of the silence and engulfed him. Whatever information Angeren needed about the Kowalski murder, while he still felt there was a chance he could persuade the detectives to provide it, he would keep tabs on Ray Hayes. The danger would come when the developer finally accepted that Jejeune wasn't going to co-operate. Then there would be the possibility that Hayes could strike without warning. And he would not be able to protect Lindy.

Perhaps they could escape back to London, lose themselves in The Smoke, where Lindy wouldn't be as exposed, as vulnerable as she seemed out here on this wide-open north Norfolk coast. But their life was here now, in this community, and Lindy wouldn't want to give that up. Despite the wiles of the formidable Calista, Jejeune knew his partner would have never agreed to work with a group of people she had so recently called *some of the finest minds of the nineteenth century* unless she wanted to. Lindy was making an emotional investment in Saltmarsh, wanting to contribute, to be part of the community's beating heart.

Besides, Jejeune would have to tell Lindy why they were leaving. Could she still face the world with the same confident glint in her eye, still greet it head on, knowing she was the target of a killer, a madman Jejeune had yet to come up with a plan for capturing? He knew she could not. But she was innocent in all this. She deserved her peace of mind, and her joyous, boundless love of life. It was his duty to preserve it. He knew the time was approaching when he would have to confide in Shepherd. Silence had always been a part of his personality, part of what made him so successful in his work. It was his realm, where he developed his theories, where he stalked his prey. But what kind of person would risk the safety of another simply to satisfy his own vanities? In the end, his silence could only put Lindy in more danger. So yes, Colleen Shepherd would have to be told about Hayes at some point. But not yet.

He drew another deep breath and sighed again into the quietness. He knew he should leave, climb in The Beast and head out to confront the day's challenges. There were many. But troubled thoughts had robbed him of his enjoyment of Blakeney Point. He would not allow them a second victory. He would stay a few moments more, leaning against his Range Rover, drinking in the soft beauty of this place, its iridescent light, its unpeopled wildness. And its silence.

24

*T uesday November 23rd, 9:28 a.m. Call
duration: 2 minutes 44 seconds*

Caller: *You got the prints? They wouldn't sell
me two one-hundred-milligram containers.
Only fifties. But the other stuff, cleaning the
surfaces with rubbing alcohol, wiping them
down with a lint-free cloth, that was all done
just like you said.*

Jejeune: *We received the containers. The fingerprints have already been verified.*

Caller: *The thing I can't work out, Domenic, is
how a fingerprint is proof of life?*

Jejeune: *By agreeing to meet the conditions,
you've shown you want this to work. It's
unlikely you'd let them come to any harm now
you've come this far.*

Caller: *I'm not following your logic here,
Domenic. And that's not good for either of us.*
(Five-second pause)

Jejeune: *It's also proof you still had access to
both people very recently. I doubt you'd have*

wanted to stay that close if any harm had already come to them.

(Eight-second pause)

Caller: *Okay, for now, you get the benefit of the doubt. But just so we're clear, no more proof, no more anything. From this point on, I say, you do. Anything happens that I don't like, and things fall apart fast.*

Jejeune: *Nobody wants that. We're ready to work with you to make sure everybody gets what they want.*

Caller: *That's good to know. You know the fee. The girl gets released on delivery. Then, when it's clear there's nobody coming after the money, the boy follows. A day later, tops.*

Jejeune: *Monte. That's the boy's name. The girl is Carolyn. They have to be released together.*

Caller: *Perhaps you weren't listening, Domenic. I tell you what's going to happen. I hang up now, you don't hear from me again. You understand what I'm saying?*

(Muffled sounds)

Jejeune: *Wait, no, don't hang up. You're in control. Everybody knows that. But you're going to need to make decisions based on what's possible. I know you want these people returned safely. I know you want that. But there can't be any deal just for one of them. It has to be both.*

Caller: *You tell them, Domenic. They'll listen to you. You tell them this is the way it's going to be. This is the arrangement and they have to take it.*

Jejeune: *I can't do that.*

*Caller: That's not what I need to hear. I need to
hear it's going to happen or I walk away.
Jejeune: It won't happen. Both must get released
at the same time. It's the only way …*
Call ends

Gill expelled a long, low breath and peeled off her headphones. There was sweat at her temples and around her
hairline. She found she was trembling slightly. But she'd heard
what she knew she would.

*There's no way you'd have sacrificed that boy to get Carolyn
Gresham back, was there, Sergeant Jejeune? It was only ever
going to be a package deal. The two of them. No negotiation.
And you knew he'd agree, didn't you? Something you heard in
his voice, perhaps in his words; I have no idea what it was, but it
told you he'd come around to the terms you asked for in the end.
So how do we go from that to the part where Carolyn Gresham
gets reunited with her family and the boy never gets to see his
parents again? What's the missing piece, Sergeant Jejeune?*

She folded away her concerns as she had on the previous
occasion, and dug deep for another untroubled expression. It
didn't fool the watching Danny Maik, but Tony Holland was
distracted, and only the breezy, carefree Des was waiting for
him when he looked up at the sound of his name.

"Tony, I was just wondering if you had any plans this
weekend."

Holland gave her a broad grin. "Always. But I'm known for
my flexibility. What did you have in mind?"

"Well, there's this conference on herbal remedies for
female hormonal imbalances that sounds really fab."

From his desk on the sidelines, Maik watched with
interest as Holland's legendary flexibility twisted in mid-
air like a hanging corpse "Uh, yeah, sure … we could go …"

His conviction tailed off feebly as he reached the end of the sentence.

Gill laughed. "What I really fancy is a trip to the coast, if you're up for it."

"The coast?" said Holland, the relief evident in his voice. "That I can do. Hunstanton and Cromer can get a bit mad on the weekends, but I know one or two secluded spots where we can find a bit of privacy."

If she read anything into the way Holland let the comment hang in the air, Des wasn't letting on. "Actually, the particular bit of coast I want to see is in Essex. So if you're flexible enough to pick me up at my B&B tomorrow morning at about eight, that would be terrif."

"Essex?"

"If it's a problem ..."

"No, not at all," said Holland eagerly. "It's just that we've got lots of great coastline up here. But," he spread his arms and gave her one of his best smiles, "if that's what you want to do, I'll clear my schedule. Probably just as well anyway. Save the girls in Traffic having to fight over who gets to spend time with me."

Gill nodded approvingly. "*Actch*, Tony, I think you dating a lot of woman at the same time is a great idea. Really. Single women spend so much time sorting out the decent blokes from the dross. The more women who get to cross you off their list at the same time, the more can get on with finding somebody suitable. It's like speed-dating, only more useful." She packed her laptop into her bag and headed to the door. "See you tomorrow, then. And you on Monday, Sergeant. Bye."

Holland watched her disappear from sight before turning to Maik. "She was joking, right?" he asked uncertainly.

"I don't think so," said Maik. "I believe she really does want to go to Essex."

* * *

Tony Holland had paid careful attention to Des Gill's driving when they first set off. The weekend traffic was light and didn't really require any great skill to negotiate, but Gill was clearly comfortable handling the MGB, and it wasn't long before Holland found himself able to relax and enjoy the unusual sensation of being chauffeured around.

Taking the MGB was the second surprise she'd sprung on him so far. As he'd arrived, she met him at the door with a change of itinerary. "We'll still go out to Lonely Oak Point, but I need to stop in at the Met first." Gill took a quick look at her watch. The face looked massive on her tiny arm. "It shouldn't take too long."

Traffic had built up at a roundabout ahead and she came down through the gears impressively, managing to slow the car to a crawl without touching the brakes.

Once through the slowdown, she eased the car out into the passing lane and opened it up again. Holland had to raise his voice slightly above the buffeting wind. "I've sussed out why you wanted to come all the way down here today," he said. "It's this nesting instinct in women that I've been hearing about."

Des took her eyes from the road long enough to shoot him a look filled with interest.

"If we went to one of the beaches back in Norfolk, you'd be worried that I'd already been there with some other woman. It'd be like trespassing on her nest. You want to think of this place we're going today as your own nest, not shared with anybody else." Holland tapped his temple with a finger. "Female psychology. Not such a mystery if you use the old noggin."

Des fixed her gaze on the road again and gave a deep sigh. "Honestly, Tony, sometimes it's as if you can see right into a woman's soul. I feel almost naked around you at times. But while it's really unnerving, I have to say, at the same time, it's a hugely sexy feeling."

"Really?"

"Oh, yeah." She nodded and gripped the steering wheel a little tighter. "It's all I can do to keep my hands off you just now. Lucky for me I need to get to the Met in a hurry, or I don't know how I'd be able to control myself."

She opened the MGB up and leaned back, hardly needing to touch the brakes again until they reached the outskirts of London.

In the city, Gill's deft handling of the small car came to the fore, exploiting gaps even Holland's Audi would have had trouble fitting through. She weaved skillfully through a trail of backstreets and eventually pulled into a heavily secured underground car park.

"We're here," she announced as she parked the car. She swivelled the overlarge watch around her arm like a bracelet and reached for the door handle.

"This is it, then? The Met? You know, you never did say why you wanted to come here."

"Didn't I?" She got out and came around to the passenger side. Holland expected her to reach in for her purse, or her computer bag, both of which were tucked behind the seats. Instead she leaned her forearms on the window opening and smiled at him. "I'd invite you to come in, but you'd need to get your security clearance first, and I'm only going to be a couple of minutes. I can get you a transfer application form while I'm here, though, if you'd like. You could try for the profiling department; tell them you specialize in female psychology. I'd back you up."

She eased herself up and began walking towards the building, leaving Holland with a look so ambiguous, he couldn't tell if she had been serious or not. With Desdemona Gill it was always hard to say.

25

They drove beneath a powder-blue sky through country-side awakening to the promise of a new spring. As soon as they had cleared the industrial-commercial chaos of London's East End, signs of the coming season began flickering into view. Early daffodils nodded along roadside verges. Hedgerows, filled to bursting with pointillist dots of green, lined the narrowing roads. Even the fields beyond them seemed to be gathering colour, as if they were sucking the life-giving hues up from the earth itself.

As promised, Des had returned to the car after a few minutes. She hadn't been hurrying, but she was definitely moving like someone with a purpose. She'd flashed a look at the large watch on her wrist as she reached over to fasten her seat belt, announcing, "Okay, Lonely Oak Point."

Des checked her mirror and eased the MGB out past a dawdling Renault. Though there was no oncoming traffic, she gave the sports car a bit extra, as if to celebrate the fact they were open-roading it with the top down on a nice spring afternoon.

"I still don't see why we couldn't have had a look at a beach closer to home," said Holland, in a variation of a comment he had made at least twice before. "There's some belters up there in Norfolk, quiet little coves, plenty of privacy if you wanted a walk along the sand ... or whatever."

"Norfolk is not the only part of England that has its hidden gems, Tony. We've got some fairly spectacular undiscovered country down here in Essex, too."

"We? You're an Essex girl?"

Des nodded. "Born and bred. All of the good qualities. None of the bad."

"Just my luck," said Holland. He fixed his stare on a pub as they passed. "Any chance we could stop for a bite to eat? I'm starving."

She checked her watch. "We can eat when we get there. It shouldn't be too much further now."

Shouldn't be, he registered, as in she didn't know for sure. But he didn't have time to dwell on the thought. Des was introducing a new topic; and it was an interesting one.

"The sergeant certainly seems to love his Motown," she said, heel-and-toeing out of a corner with a skill that Holland would have been proud of himself. "Are you really not a fan of it?"

"Some of the upbeat stuff is not too bad, but lately it's been nothing but this dreck about heartache and loss and all that. I mean, how many ways can you say *I can't find anybody to love me* before it gets old?"

Des returned his smile. "I suppose the good thing is songs were shorter in those days. Even if you don't like something, you only have to endure about three minutes of it."

"Three minutes can be a very long time with some of that drivel he's playing these days," said Holland. "Why all this interest in the sarge's music, anyway?"

"You and he are fairly close, aren't you?" asked Des, keeping her eyes on the road perhaps a touch more firmly than the empty lanes might have required.

"Not particularly. He can be a miserable bugger at times. In fact, he's been even worse than usual lately, with Lauren Salter being gone."

"He likes her?"

Holland nodded. "Though I'm not sure he knows it."

"The people at the station mean a lot to him, don't they? The truth is, you're a pretty tight group up there in Saltmarsh. You remind me of a family, always squabbling and having a go at one another, but really, you care a lot about each other."

"A family? Oh yeah," said Holland derisively. "Put the *fun* in dysfunctional, us lot. Why're you asking? Thinking of putting in a transfer, so you can join the party and sit at the feet of Detective Chief Inspector Domenic Jejeune?"

Gill didn't rise to the bait. When she set her mind on a specific destination, real or conversational, not much was going to deflect her off course. But that didn't mean she couldn't take a break along the way. "If you're really hungry," she said, "that basket behind the seat has some sandwiches. I made us a picnic. Just don't eat them all before we get there."

Tony Holland finished the last of the sandwiches and leaned back on one elbow, taking in the surrounding landscape. On either side, a scrubby patchwork of windswept grassland rolled to the horizon. The remnants of weathered stone walls tracing the old field boundaries was the only sign that humans had ever set foot on this land. In front of him, the grass sloped gently down towards a cliff edge a few hundred metres away. A glinting ribbon of light beyond told him where the water began. Seated beside Holland on the picnic blanket, Des Gill followed his gaze.

"Beautiful here, isn't it?"

"Not bad," he conceded. Holland could see no one walking along the long sweep of the clifftops. *Like our coastline*, he thought. But not quite like north Norfolk. Here, the impact of the relentless coastal winds was more in evidence. Tussocks of grass hugged the ground tightly, and the few shrubs that dotted the landscape were bowed and stunted. Even now, lying down, Holland's hair danced and his shirt rippled constantly.

He looked up as Des drew in a sudden breath. "Did you see that?" she asked, pointing out over the meadow. "It looked like a small owl, but it wasn't flying like a bird. More like some sort of giant moth."

"An owl?" laughed Holland. "In the middle of the day? I think you'd better leave the birding to your hero." He pulled a paper map from his back pocket and unfolded it, holding on tightly as it flapped vigorously in the wind. "I've been having a look at this. I found it in the glove box. I wanted to confirm we are actually still in England." He looked out over the water where it spread from the estuary, under the vast sky, across which swaths of white cloud trailed like tattered banners. "It feels like we're on the edge of the known world out here."

He jabbed the map with a finger at a point where the fringes of the coastal lands fanned out towards the water like fraying cloth. "This is us, right? What I can't figure out is why you chose to make that massive sweep down towards Wakering only to come all the way back up north along the coast again. This road here would have brought us straight out. Your way must've added about fifteen miles to the trip."

Des brushed Holland's hand away and pointed her own dainty finger at the map. "Because that red boundary indicates MoD property. The area is an extension of MoD Shoeburyness. It runs all the way to Foulness Island, over here. They test missiles and ballistics all the time. There's no access to Lonely Oak Point through the property. The stretch of coastline from here to Wakering is outside the boundary, but the only way to get up here is from the south."

Holland gazed out across the wide expanse of water. A thin grey smudge of coastline was barely visible through the haze. "So that's Foulness Island." He peered more closely. Foulness Island. Twenty-five square kilometres of wind-razed fields and overgrown, boggy grassland dotted with low stone buildings, the legacy of a farming tradition dating back centuries that had finally succumbed to the economic pressures of the last few decades.

"Is that why you wanted to come here? To see where those kids were held."

"It can't be more than a few miles' drive from here," said Gill. "I had no idea it was so close."

"Close to what?"

"To where Inspector Jejeune saw his rare bird — the Iberian Azure-winged Magpie." She pointed. "It was in that tree down there."

He followed the direction of her finger to where a single oak tree stood in a mixture of rough brambles and low, scrubby bushes near the cliff edge. Other oaks he had seen this year were already showing some interest in leafing, but this one, bent into the teeth of the winds that funelled in towards the Thames estuary, seemed completely bare. He wondered if it was dead.

Gill watched Holland's face; a map of a thousand thoughts.

She saw his gaze leave the tree and go out again to Foulness Island. "Did you ever read up on that fingerprint trick?" she asked.

He smiled sheepishly. "To tell you the truth, I've been a bit busy. Any chance of the *Reader's Digest* version? I remember he said he'd accept a fingerprint as proof of life when the kidnapper refused the phone call."

Gill nodded. "A separate fingerprint, *actch*, from each hostage. On an item the kidnapper would have to buy, so they could be sure the prints were recent."

Holland waited, his interest piqued now. "So what was it?"

"Ephedrine, the stuff they use to treat shock." Des paused. "A separate hundred-milligram container for each hostage's print."

Holland looked out over the raw, windswept landscape of Lonely Oak Point for a long moment. When he spoke, there was genuine admiration in his voice. "Now that," he said, "was clever." He nodded thoughtfully. "What is it now, one hundred and sixty?"

"Because the kids use it to get high, a hundred and eighty milligrams is the maximum amount of ephedrine anyone is allowed to buy in a single transaction. Any attempt to purchase more than that has to be reported to the local Controlled Drugs police hotline as soon as the person leaves the shop."

And just to drive the point home, thought Holland, *Jejeune had asked the kidnapper to purchase two separate hundred-milligram amounts. He couldn't have looked any more like he was trying to skirt the rules if he'd had it printed on a T-shirt.*

"I take it the hotlines didn't get too many reports of attempted overbuys that day."

Des shook her head. "In fact, when you limited them to those that also included the purchase of rubbing alcohol and a lint-free cloth, in the whole country there was just the one. In a place called Halworth. It's about six miles from Foulness Island. And that was significant for one very important reason."

But this time Holland was with her. Already there, in fact. "Because Foulness Island doesn't have cellphone coverage."

His smug smile told her he wasn't going to need her to confirm it, but she nodded anyway. "There's none here on this side of the estuary either, but Foulness Island is the only dead zone in the area with inhabitable buildings. There are a few places on the island where you can get a signal, but coverage is extremely spotty." She looked out across the field of wind-teased grass sloping away in front of her, the wheat-coloured stems moving like a restless sea. It was a long time before she spoke. "Can I ask you something, Tony? If it came to a choice between a fellow officer and the job, where do you think Danny Maik's loyalties would lie?"

Holland recognized this wasn't the kind of thing you'd ask somebody unless you were expecting a serious answer. He gave the question the consideration it deserved.

"I suppose he'd end up going in the direction of the truth." He looked a touch surprised at his own answer, as if he wasn't quite sure where it had come from. "Whatever that means," he added flippantly. "Sounds like a line from one of his songs. I've got to stop listening to that bloody Motown."

But Des wasn't buying his act. She knew exactly what Tony Holland meant. And even if he was trying to pretend otherwise, she knew that he did, too. "We should probably get going," she said, "otherwise we'll hit the rush hour traffic." They stood and she began to repack the picnic basket as Holland folded up the blanket.

"You know, I've been thinking about that map again," said Holland, as they tucked the picnic items into the MGB's tiny boot. "It's a bit of a jaunt back to Saltmarsh from here. I wonder if we shouldn't turn it into an overnighter. That way we could take our time, have a look around a bit, make it a proper weekend by the seaside."

"That'd be nice," agreed Des. "My exes will stretch to a room for the night. I don't suppose you're on an expense account, though, are you?"

Holland shook his head ruefully and cast his eyes out over the wild, windswept field, and the estuary beyond it, one last time. "Sadly, not. Looks like it will have to be a single room."

"Okay." Des shook her head doubtfully. "It's going to be a tight squeeze, though."

Holland gave her a knowing smile. "Oh, I'm sure we can make it work."

"We?" asked Gill. "I'm talking about you, sleeping in this tiny MGB all night. Still, you did say you were flexible."

26

There are times when it is possible to sense an atmosphere, in a house, in a room, behind a closed door, even. As Jejeune stood on the doorstep of their cottage, he was aware something had changed. But he hardly had time to register the thought before he opened the door.

Lindy was waiting in the foyer as he entered. She had been crying. Her eyes were red-rimmed and her cheeks blotchy. "It's over, Dom."

His heart froze. He stood still, unblinking, uncomprehending. Behind Lindy in the house, the shadow of a figure moved. But there had been no strange car in the driveway. Only Lindy's Leaf.

Lindy reached up and touched his face with an open hand, stroking it gently. She pulled him into an embrace and he could feel her sobbing gently into his chest. The figure behind her morphed into someone recognizable and he took Lindy's shoulders, easing her away from him to arm's length. There was no sadness, he saw now, only tears.

"Damian, Dom. It's over. You did it."

Afterward, he had no memory of shrugging off his coat, or setting down his bag, or being led to the living room. His senses only seemed to return with Colleen Shepherd telling him she could scarcely imagine how much of a relief it must be to him, to them both.

She laid a hand on his forearm, in what had become their version of a hug. "Eric's just popped out to get a bottle of champagne, so we can celebrate properly. Really, Domenic, I'm quite surprised at you, not having any bubbly on hand. I'd have thought you have had more than your share of victories to celebrate."

The details came to him in pieces; Lindy, then Shepherd, then both, talking over each other at times in their efforts to fill him in. As with all of life's defining moments, the final verdict was not clean cut. Damian would remain a wanted criminal in Colombia. He could never return there. But the international warrant had been lifted, the extradition orders rescinded. Damian was a free man everywhere but Colombia.

Damian would rankle at the caveat. Domenic said as much and drew laughs from the women. But he knew his brother well. Banned from the country with the most bird species in the world? There would be endemics, he knew, possibly dozens of them, that Damian would suddenly realize he wanted to see and now never could. But eventually he would come to understand that he was free to travel anywhere else in the world, to enter and exit countries unrestricted. And in a rare moment of self-indulgence, Domenic recognized that it had only happened because of him.

Eric's arrival infused the gathering with new energy. He strode into the kitchen, a bottle in each hand, and emerged with four fluted glasses, Lindy's prized legacy from her grandmother, filled with frothing, golden liquid. Lindy, normally so protective of her kitchen and her treasures, smiled her gratitude towards her boss. She hadn't left Domenic's side since he sat down.

"To Damian, first, I think," announced Eric, holding his glass aloft. "A free man, at last."

They drank, and then it was Lindy's turn. But her salute was not to Domenic. "To Colleen, who brought us the good news."

"I really did nothing," protested the DCS. "I'd asked the Colombian Consulate to inform me of any developments, that's all. Why they chose to let me know before Domenic, I don't know."

At the mention of his name, the three of them simultaneously seemed to recognize the enormity of Jejeune's own contribution. The frivolity faded and there was a solemnity about the way Shepherd formally raised her glass in Domenic's direction. The others followed suit, their faces respectful and sober, gathered like crèche figures looking in his direction. "To Domenic. No man could wish for a better champion in his corner. What you achieved was truly remarkable. I'm sure your brother will never forget it."

They sipped in silence, and it was only at the lowering of the glasses that it was felt the mood should lift.

"I should give Danny a call," said Lindy. "He ought to be here." She was uncertain of the role Maik had played when Damian had visited Norfolk, but Domenic's brother had expressed his gratitude to the sergeant in one of his emails. Perhaps now she could finally get around to asking Danny about it.

"I'm not sure he's at his best, socially, at the moment," said Shepherd uncertainly. "He seems a bit out of sorts. Of course, having to deal with Dr. Jones all the time can't be helping. That man could try the patience of the Dalai Lama."

"Jones, that cadaverous chap one sees loitering in the corridors sometimes?" asked Eric. "The one with the odd name, Mayfield, something?"

"Mansfield."

"Whatever he's called, I would have thought he would have had more sense than to try to antagonize Danny Maik.

He must have a good deal more backbone than it appears," said Eric.

"It's not deliberate," said Jejeune. "He just refuses to allow himself to make any inferences, however logical they might seem to others."

Lindy thought Danny might have welcomed a bit of caution in that regard, given who he spent his days working with. Jejeune's own ability to infer connections he considered logical was not exactly shared by everyone. The "others" Domenic had just referred to included neither Lindy, Danny, nor anyone else she had ever met.

Jejeune took her dubious look at face value. "Imagine you were standing on a street in a strange city and you saw a green double decker bus go by," he said. "You might be comfortable saying that you now knew that the city's buses were green."

Lindy nodded slowly. "Whereas, all you could really know for certain was that one of the city's buses was green."

But Jejeune shook his head. "Mansfield Jones would claim all you could say with certainty is that one side of one of the city's buses was green."

"Blimey, I can see why working with him would drive poor Danny up the wall," said Lindy with feeling. "Great name, though, *Mansfield*. Wonder what the story is there."

"Place of conception, perhaps?" said Eric, taking a sip of his champagne.

"If so, let's hope the idea doesn't catch on here," said Shepherd. "With Tony Holland's antics, I could foresee entire classrooms of kids named *Saltmarsh*."

"That was the old Tony Holland, surely," said Lindy with a laugh. "According to Dom, the new constable seems to have him well reined in. Speaking of which, you could do a lot worse for an investigator than one named Desdemona. Very honest was Shakespeare's Des. Determined, too."

"This investigation," said Eric, with a nonchalance that told them it was merely casual interest, "it's just a matter of verifying the records, is it?"

"She's looking at the whole case, actually," said Lindy confidently. "We met for coffee at the market a couple of days ago. She wanted to reassure me that all this wasn't just a hatchet job on my man. I imagine she'll be pretty thorough, though. I'll bet she's a proper little Jack Russell once she's on the trail of something." Lindy turned to Dom and smiled, placing her palm on his chest in mock comfort. "I don't think you've got much to worry about, though, darling. To say she's a fan of yours would be an understatement. She thinks you could be the goat by the time you're done."

Jejeune's puzzled expression was met by Lindy's wide-eyed nod of affirmation.

"G.O.A.T. Greatest of All Time — it's a *thing*," Lindy said defensively. "I said that was quite appropriate for somebody who told me he was brought up in a stable. Or was that a stable environment? I can never quite remember."

It isn't the champagne causing this giddiness, thought Jejeune. It was the headiness of the occasion, the sense of release, after so many months of uncertainty. So much time and effort and planning poured into a bottomless void of hope; and now, this one single announcement had repaid it all. It was why, too, Lindy's normally razor-sharp powers of observation had failed to notice their guests' reactions to her comments. In her defence, she'd been turned away from them almost the whole time, staring up into Dom's face with a twinkly-eyed sense of mischief. But Domenic had seen them, reactions he hadn't expected — guarded, troubled looks. He'd noticed one other thing, too, in that brief moment before the expressions disappeared behind masks of polite good humour: the reactions were not the same.

Whatever feelings Shepherd and Eric had about Desdemona Gill, they were not shared.

"So I imagine you'll be wanting to jet off to a family reunion in the not-too-distant future, Domenic?" said Shepherd, bringing him back to the present. "I can't see any problem with that, as long as this case has been wrapped up."

"I suppose that means you'll be going too, Lindy," said Eric. He smiled. "Though I'm not at all sure you're as expendable as Dom."

"We haven't really talked about it," said Lindy breezily. She looked across in case Domenic wanted to make a contribution, but he was staring at Shepherd as if trying to commit her features to memory. The ease with which the DCS had moved the conversation on was a testament to her skill, and if Jejeune hadn't been watching for it, he might have found himself discussing an impending trip to Canada without ever realizing how they had arrived at the subject. But his senses were heightened now, and through the lens of what he had just seen, the change of topic took on the appearance of a carefully crafted escape route. Whether Eric's own contribution was part of the plan, he couldn't have said. But based on the man's earlier expression, Jejeune had little doubt he would be as relieved as Shepherd to see all mention of Desdemona Gill disappearing in the rear-view mirror.

Shepherd set her champagne glass down firmly. "Unfortunately, Eric and I have somewhere to be, but before we leave, I wonder if I can just talk shop with Domenic for a moment. We'll let you two discuss the nefarious world of journalism while we pop into the kitchen."

She led Jejeune, gentle hand on elbow, into the other room. "It's wonderful news about your brother, Domenic. Truly, I couldn't be more pleased for you."

Jejeune inclined his head in acknowledgement, but he

said nothing. This wasn't the shop talk Shepherd had come in here to discuss.

"You've been summoned to the high altar. Tomorrow afternoon. An audience with the holiest of holies." She was trying to make light of the news, but affectation wasn't really Shepherd's forte. When she spoke it was generally to deliver a point unequivocally. She seemed to realize her limitations and reverted to form. "It will be about DC Gill's review of the case. If he should ask, please tell the Home Secretary that, much as we love having the Empowered Investigator with us, I am hopeful she'll be concluding her work very shortly. For one thing, I fear she's becoming a bit of a distraction for you, Domenic. I feel quite sure she's the reason you've not yet had a result in the Kowalski murder."

Jejeune was equally sure she was not, but he was more interested in the reason for Shepherd's statement than the accuracy of it. As in their other conversations about the investigator, Shepherd seemed reluctant to continue. "Domenic," she said uneasily, glancing back over her shoulder towards the living room. "The news coverage of that story, it was all above board, as far as you know?"

Was she talking about his relationship with Lindy?

"All the protocols were followed," he said defensively. "We'd only just met, but we had boundaries as to what I'd tell her, and what she would ask. Any information I ever gave Lindy was cleared by the press office." He shrugged. "I had no control over any of the other reporting, the sensationalist parts. There were lots of journalists covering the story."

"But not at the end."

"No. Lindy was the one who broke the news that the girl was safe. That was her exclusive."

"But she didn't report the confession, did she, Domenic? That wasn't Lindy."

Shepherd's look went to the living room again, and in a blinding moment of realization, Jejeune understood. That one taunting detail that had been eluding him, like a butterfly, dancing on the wind: the confession. He'd been concentrating so much on his own role in the case, reliving it, running it over in his mind, that he'd simply breezed over the aftermath, the tidy resolution, the convenient answers to all the troubling questions. *The confession.* Shepherd was right. It wasn't Lindy who had covered the deathbed confession.

It was Eric.

27

Lindy leaned into Domenic as they stood in the doorway watching Eric's car disappear down the driveway. Much as she appreciated the DCS and her boss being here to share the good news with them, she was looking forward to time alone with Dom, to process the idea, to come to terms with it. She was holding the champagne bottle by the neck, two glasses clustered in her other hand. "Let's go and sit round the back," she said. She hot-footed her way across the gravel of the driveway and padded barefoot over the grass towards the rear patio.

It was a beautiful evening, with a soft breeze coming in off the sea and a sky gliding effortlessly through shades of blue towards nightfall. The clear skies promised a perfect backdrop for the waning moon; it would rise through the sky like joy as the night wore on. All in all, their seaward-facing haven seemed about as perfect a place as any Lindy could think of to drink in the new air of a world in which Damian Jejeune was a free man.

She set down the bottle and glasses on a small round table and leaned on the railing, staring out over the sea. Jejeune joined her. "Does Damian know yet?" he asked.

"I've emailed him," she said without turning from the water, "but his pattern seems to be to check his emails around noon, Greenwich Time, so we may have missed him for today."

It seemed strange to hear Lindy speak out loud about her secret backchannel to his brother, the lifeline that had tethered them together since his frantic departure from Saltmarsh. A faint uneasiness welled within Domenic still. Perhaps the caution of holding on to his brother's secrets for all this time wasn't going to be so easy to overcome. For either of them.

"I told him we'd let him know as soon as we had confirmation that the Canadian authorities had been informed of Colombia's decision," said Lindy. "He should probably wait until then before making any grand appearance anywhere, but I'm sure he'd still be safe enough to contact your parents."

Jejeune nodded. Even with glacial pace of international bureaucracy, the Canadian government should have been informed by close of business tomorrow. Damian would then be free to emerge into the light and resume a normal life. The thought was hard to process. He looked at Lindy and she understood. For so long, Domenic had lived under the shadow of his brother's troubles; they both had. And now Damian was free. And so were they.

Lindy went to the table and poured two glasses of champagne. She returned to the rail and handed one to Domenic. They sipped in silence for a moment. "We should probably start thinking about when we're going to go over there," said Lindy casually. "I'll go online tomorrow to see if there are any cheap flights coming up. Will a couple of weeks be enough, do you think? Or will we need longer? Shepherd didn't seem to think it would be a problem for you to have some time off after this case is wrapped up."

"As long as DC Gill's review is over."

"I don't think you've got much to worry about there, Dom. I wasn't kidding inside. She really is a big fan. I mean huge. She probably had pictures of you on her bedroom wall when she was growing up. I do hope she doesn't end up being disappointed in you, Domenic." She smiled at him. "Let's remember, the man Shakespeare's Desdemona admired hardly lived up to her expectations in the end, did he?"

He thought about the two women exchanging details of their athletic pursuits at Wawel that night. In the strictest sense of the word, what Lindy had told Des was true. Every year since they'd been in Saltmarsh, she'd participated in two annual charity runs, one in May and one in September. These were the five-Ks she ran "regularly." But Jejeune knew Lindy chose her words carefully, and even if she would argue that was hardly her fault if a young, fit Des Gill confused the word *regular* with *frequent*, his partner had known exactly what she was saying. A friendship of sorts might be developing between the two women, thought Jejeune, but that wouldn't necessarily prevent each from pursuing her own agenda.

"Did DC Gill ask you anything specific when you chatted?"

On another day, Lindy's antennae might have been up at such a forthright question. But it was not another day; it was the day Damian's freedom had finally been secured, the day the rest of Lindy's life, and Dom's, could begin. Her thoughts were racing with the possibilities, and she was not of a mind to analyze her partner's questions too closely.

"She asked me if I was with you when you saw your Iberian Azure-winged Magpie."

"Most people refer to them as Iberian Magpies these days," said Jejeune.

"Well, of course," said Lindy sarcastically. "The thing has azure wings; it stands to reason birders would want to drop that little detail from its name."

"It's because there's already a species called the Azure-winged Magpie in Asia. Until quite recently they were thought to be conspecific, but …"

Lindy's look suggested that her interest in this subject had ended around the phrase *Most people* …

"Well, she certainly seemed interested enough in your sighting. Not a birder, is she?"

"She's not a birder," confirmed Jejeune thoughtfully. "She's just looking into everything that happened around that time, that's all." Domenic's expression suggested that it might not be all, but Lindy was too consumed with the darkening sky and the play of the dying light on the water, and the all-encompassing beauty of the world and everything in it to notice.

"It was strange," she said, "listening to another woman talk about her open admiration for you. If I wasn't so certain you're deliriously happy with me, I'm sure I'd feel quite threatened." She looked across to see his reaction, but Jejeune was staring at the slow undulations of the water. "A little more delirium wouldn't go amiss, you know."

He roused from his thought and pointed a finger at his face, making a circling motion. "This is me being delirious," he said. He wanted to join Lindy in her happiness, but his restless policeman's mind wouldn't let him. Even now, at this hour of triumph, when all he had worked for had come to pass, when his victory was complete and his brother was free, there was evidence to be weighed, suspicions to be mulled over.

"You've known Eric a long time, haven't you?" The fact that he hadn't even tried to disguise the abrupt change of topic should have set off some alarms, but Lindy had gone back to staring out over the water and didn't even turn at the inquiry.

"Eric's the kind of bloke you feel as if you've known for-ever, but I suppose it's been a good few years, yes."

"He admires you, doesn't he? You have qualities that impress him."

"I don't think he's got any pictures of me on his bed-room wall, if that's what you mean. His dartboard, now that's another matter. What's this about, Dom?" But even with one eye still on the breathtaking spectacle of the fading light over the sea, and a glass of chilled champagne pressed against her chest, Lindy was able to notice that Domenic didn't answer her question.

"The deathbed confession of Vincent Canby, that was quite a coup for Eric." He paused, not wanting to continue on this soft, beautiful evening, but knowing he had to. "Does he ever talk about it?"

Lindy shook her head. "That's no great shock, though. Eric tends not to dwell on past glories. He's the kind of man who always believes there's a new prize just around the corner. That said, it doesn't surprise me he got the confession. He's an old-fashioned newspaperman at heart. A notepad and a tape recorder, and a relentless determination to get the stories the others can't. It was part of the attraction when I agreed to work for him. I've just realized," she said, "I was about as old then as Des is now. I suppose it's a sign of advancing years, isn't it, when you start seeing people who remind you of a younger version of yourself?" Lindy sipped her champagne thoughtfully, as if considering the wisdom of her observation.

The pale moon hung like a giant apostrophe, just above the horizon. A faint haze had started to form around it. *Burr*, the locals called it. Jejeune looked at the moon for a long time, and was still staring at it when he spoke. "It seems an extraordinary arrangement for a dying man to make, to have Eric as the only person in attendance ..."

"Marvin Laraby was there, too."

"Yes, but Eric was the one Canby had made all the arrangements with beforehand. Eric's was the phone number the hospice had, and Canby's wife, for when the time came. If he hadn't called in Laraby to verify the confession, Eric would have been there alone, just him and Canby."

Had it been a different time, Lindy might just have let him know exactly what she thought about this line of inquiry. But the momentous joy of the evening's news came to his rescue and she chose to indulge him. "He'd built trust with Canby. It's what journos do. I know it's hard for you to believe, but there are some people out there who still trust us. A good journalist reassures a source they can be relied on to tell the story, their story. To a man who was dying, probably nothing could have been more important than to know that. You know," she said thoughtfully, "I'd never really considered before just how much it speaks to Eric's integrity that a dying man would trust him with such a tremendous responsibility." The thought seemed to stir something within her and she straightened from the railing suddenly. "Okay, enough talk about your old cases. We've got a beautiful moon, wonderful news, and glasses of bubbly. I'd say we've got some serious celebrating to do. You know, you never did offer a toast back inside. Time to put that right, I think." She took his glass and padded across the patio to the small round table where the champagne bottle stood.

Jejeune leaned on the railing, watching the gentle rise and fall of the sea's swells in the last of the evening's light. She was right. Tonight *was* Damian's night, even *in absentia*, and if Lindy wasn't going to let anybody take his brother's shining moment away, he wouldn't either. He realized she was beside him again, holding out a replenished glass of champagne. He wondered how long she had been there, waiting, watching him like this. He took the glass and raised it to meet the one Lindy was holding aloft. The curious ways of the world, he thought. He'd gone many months without offering a toast, and now here he was being called upon to do so twice in a couple of days. Patterns, coincidences, anomalies. It fell to some people to watch for them, to decide which were innocuous and which meant something more.

"To Damian," he said. "And the future."

The toast seemed to please Lindy immensely, and a smile lit her entire face. She held her glass up high and looked at him.

"To the future," she replied.

28

Highborne was a house that drew its character from its pedigree, rather than its presence, thought Jejeune, staring up at the grand, ivy-clad building. The imposing granite wings were higher than the main facade and seemed to squeeze in on it, making the main part of the building look as if it was sinking inward, receding into the past of which it was so much a part.

If the room Jejeune was ushered into wasn't exactly a replica of the quilted leather and polished hardwood of the cabinet offices, it certainly paid homage to the staunchly masculine decor. Sir David Gresham was sitting in a worn leather chair talking to a man perched uncomfortably on the front edge of a sofa. A table with a bottle and three glasses stood off to one side.

The Home Secretary had lost weight since the last time Jejeune had seen him, and his hair was thinning. There was a slight pallor to his skin, too. Lindy's once-damning verdict that he looked just a bit too much like a politician to ever make it to the top seemed a sad irony now that he no longer possessed the trademark panache of the chosen ones.

"Ah, Domenic. Wonderful to see you. You're looking fit. Keeping well, I take it? Given up that birding business yet?"

Gresham's uncertain expression suggested he might have heard otherwise, and he switched subjects quickly. "You remember Gilo, of course."

The man rose into an awkward half crouch to take Jejeune's proffered hand. The palm itself was disconcertingly soft, but the grip suggested great strength. Simon Giles, Jejeune recalled, even before the man announced it in his polished public school accent. He had a stocky build with shoulders that tapered up strongly into a thick neck. A rugby player, Jejeune had suspected previously, likely a good one if his competitive streak matched the determined set of his jaw.

"Gilo will be sitting in on this one." Gresham's matter-of-fact delivery was that of a man used to making pronouncements that would go unchallenged. "No need for any of that signing nonsense, though. The inspector's discretion has already been demonstrated," he said turning to Giles. "Besides, if the government whistleblowers have taught us anything, bless their cotton socks, it's that a confidentiality agreement is not worth a damn if somebody decides they're going to spill the beans."

Whether Giles's sour expression was a response to the Home Secretary's statement or to his decision to forego the formalities in Jejeune's case, the detective couldn't have said. But the government man seemed reluctant to share anything without a nudge from his Home Secretary.

"Gilo tells me there have been a number of unsavoury types fetching up on our shores recently. Down your patch, Domenic." He made it sound as if Jejeune was personally responsible.

"Organized crime figures," said Giles. "Eastern European. Major players." The man's clipped delivery suggested he was expecting Jejeune to be taking notes. Or at least committing the facts to memory. He needn't have worried.

"I suppose we should be grateful that not everybody in Europe views us as a pariah state." Gresham laughed at his own joke alone. It was a comment that might have played well in the inner sanctum of Whitehall offices, but it seemed strangely jarring out in the open like this, and Giles shifted uneasily. If Gresham sensed the man's discomfort, he did nothing to acknowledge it.

"As Gilo says, it's mainly the higher-level operatives," continued Gresham blithely. "Some seriously undesirable characters, I'm told. There seems to be an established route, of sorts. By boat from the Netherlands to the north Norfolk coast."

"There are certainly closer landing spots," said Jejeune, "but few less populated."

Gresham leaned forward and grabbed the bottle of single malt by the neck. "A wee dram, Domenic?" he asked, waving it at Jejeune. "Gilo here's a teetotaller, but I seem to remember you liked the odd tipple."

Jejeune declined, and watched Gresham as he refilled his own glass. There had always been an element of private school foppishness about the Home Secretary, but Jejeune didn't remember the routine being developed to this degree. The kidnapping of his daughter had changed him, hollowed him out somehow. It was as if the man had lost himself and had now settled on a character to play. Jejeune waited until Gresham had set the bottle down on the tray before asking his question.

"Any particular part of Eastern Europe?"

The men's expressions told Jejeune he had asked the right question.

"Poland. There's a major crackdown on organized crime going on there at the moment. The Polish authorities are trying to cast as wide a net as possible, but those with resources — money, contacts — are finding ways to slip through."

"Do you think there's some connection between this and the case I'm investigating? Perhaps that Jakub Kowalski might have had something to do with this operation?"

"He seems to have been particularly well placed for it," said Giles. "He had access to restricted areas, which would mean away from the eyes of the public. He had reason to be out there, even armed. No one would question him even if he set up a spotting scope and tripod to watch for their arrival. And there's a network of local Polish émigrés to be called upon to provide assistance. For a hefty fee, I imagine."

Jejeune digested the idea. It left a lot of unanswered questions, but there was an undeniable soundness to the reasoning. He wasn't sure if the men were aware of Paulina Kowalski's role in processing documentation for newly arrived immigrants, but it would have been a valuable contribution to her son's enterprise.

"I understand you've been speaking to Curtis Angeren," said Gresham with a deceptive softness Jejeune remembered from previous encounters. It was not to be underestimated. "He told you he had nothing to do with Kowalski's death. Can I ask, Domenic, have you come across anything that makes you believe otherwise?" Gresham's question seemed to have come from nowhere, and left Jejeune slightly wary as he searched for a connection.

Gresham turned to Giles and raised his eyebrows.

"We've been watching Curtis Angeren very closely for a number of months," said Giles. "We know he put the word out that he viewed Jakub Kowalski as a problem. But we have sound information that Angeren was not involved in the man's murder."

The Home Secretary looked at Jejeune significantly. "Ask him where he gets this sound information, and he comes across all tongue-tied, which suggests he and his mob are up to no good, as usual," he said, affecting irritation, but with no real malice.

"The source is reliable," said Giles, in a tone that suggested there would be no further discussion on the matter.

"Nevertheless, if Angeren found out about Kowalski's human smuggling operation, his threat to Kowalski takes on a new light."

"D'you think so, Domenic?" There was lightness in Gresham's tone that had no place in such a sober conversation. "It's a far cry from delivering a few fiery anti-foreigner speeches in public to actually bumping a chap off."

Kowalski had been brutally murdered, and the Home Secretary's schoolboy idiom could do nothing to change the starkness of that fact. But the message was clear now. Another time, Jejeune might have voiced it himself, sparing the Home Secretary the ignominy of having to say it out loud. But being used as a pawn in a larger game never sat well with Jejeune, and for once he chose to use his silence uncharitably.

Gresham could see there would be no help coming and allowed himself a small sigh. "The thing is, Domenic," he said, as if testing the words to see how they would fare out in the open, "Gilo and his mob would prefer you to give Angeren a wide berth just now."

Giles saw Jejeune's doubt. "Angeren has been cultivating connections to ultra-nationalist extremists up and down the country. We're squeezing him tight, cutting off his cash flows, getting banks to lean on him. We want him to bolt to his new friends so we can roll the whole lot of them up at the same time."

"They feel if you start stirring things up at this time, it could put him on his guard," added Gresham unnecessarily. "After all, there's every chance Angeren really is innocent. So if you can see the way clear to letting him slip under the radar for now, I'm sure when the time comes to grab him for this other nonsense, we could manage an honourable mensch for the good DCI here, eh Gilo?"

Giles, who had already seemingly found much to disapprove of during the conversation so far, clearly now had a new candidate for top spot. "Of course," he said mechanically.

"In the meantime, I'm sure you've got plenty of other avenues to explore," said Gresham brightly. "But if you do need somebody fitted up, Gilo's your man."

Gresham's hollow laugh could not disguise the fact that the comment left a maw of awkward silence hanging in the cavernous room.

"Sir David is joking," said Giles eventually.

"Thing is, Domenic, we need to tread lightly until we're absolutely sure we've got him. Curtis Angeren is a bad enemy to make. He's utterly ruthless, and he's very well connected. And while those qualities may be desirable in a politician, they're a bloody nightmare in a criminal."

Jejeune shifted uneasily. Angeren was his only link to Hayes, and at this point his only way of ensuring Lindy's safety. But Angeren still harboured hopes of news on the case. If he thought Jejeune was avoiding him, he would take his revenge by refusing to provide any further information about Hayes. Jejeune couldn't sever the connection now.

"Angeren will be expecting the police to be looking at him for this," he said evenly. "It's why he came to us in the first place. As we continue to turn up new evidence, it's inevitable we'd pay him another visit. If we don't, it will look suspicious."

Gresham smiled indulgently. "Still got that wonderful mind of yours, I see. However, it's decision taken, Domenic, for the time being, at least." Gresham's thin smile didn't disguise the fact that it was an order. He leaned back and considered the room.

"That's it, Gilo. No need for you to stay for the next bit. I'm sure the taxpayer's money can be better spent than by having you sit in on a chinwag between two old friends about the state of play."

Gilo's face remained impassive. He'd spent a lifetime dealing with terse dismissals from higher-ranking officials and this one wasn't going to faze him. He stood and extended a fleshy hand to Jejeune.

"Should there be any developments at your end, you know where to reach me."

Neither man spoke until the broad back of Simon Giles had disappeared from view.

"I've had intel that Caro is to be spoken to," said Gresham without preamble.

Intel. Jejeune had imagined that it was a phrase used only by people on the periphery of such matters, who seemed to revel in such jargon. To hear it coming from a man at the very highest levels of intelligence operations was both surprising and enlightening.

"Needless to say, she's not best pleased at having to revisit that time, but she understands the need. Rather better than her mother, who'd like me to be lopping off a few heads over all this. Understandable, of course, parents would go to any lengths to protect their child, I suppose."

He looked at the detective for understanding. In the past, it had never been necessary to spell things out to Domenic Jejeune. Gresham suspected it wouldn't be now.

"She's doing well, has a wonderful little daughter. No son yet. As a grandfather, one always hopes …" Gresham gave a wan smile. "The thing is, Domenic, if Carolyn does have to go back over it all again, she'd rather it was with you, someone who was there, who can understand what she went through at the time."

"Sir David, my own conduct during the events forms a part of the Empowered Investigator's review. I'm not sure even having me present at an interview with your daughter would be —"

Gresham held up a hand to still Jejeune's protests. "Don't trouble yourself over the details, Domenic." He flashed a mirthless smile of a kind that Jejeune was sure had signalled the end of many objections. "I'll tell Caro it's all set then, shall I? And now, if you'll excuse me, I've some constituency business I should be attending to. It really has been wonderful to see you again."

Jejeune stood to leave. As he reached the door, Gresham called out to him. "Domenic, I am right in thinking there were no breaches of protocol in this one. Nothing coming out of the woodwork at us."

"Nothing I'm aware of," said Jejeune from the doorway.

Gresham nodded his contentment. "Caro is fine, as I say, but there are still days … there have been for all of us. Frankly, I'm not sure how well we'd cope with a major rethink. Any of us."

Jejeune paused in the hallway, the great leather-panelled door shut behind him. It had been an uncertain performance from the Home Secretary, full of false starts and misjudgments. Jejeune could see why so many of his meetings were now scheduled off-campus like this, where his conduct would be less scrutinized. Staying on top in the political world required razor-sharp acumen, and the events surrounding his daughter's kidnapping had taken the edge off Gresham's finely honed skills. He was a political survivor, but he was hanging on now, no longer a rising star, destined for greatness. His time as Home Secretary was surely drawing to a close, but Jejeune wasn't concerned about losing the support of the man who had backed his own meteoric rise through the police ranks. He was only saddened by the way crimes never stopped accumulating victims, and never stopped destroying lives.

29

There are many reasons for keeping secrets in a police station: covert operations, love affairs, deals — above board and below. There are some secrets that come from the stresses of the job: drinking, gambling, abuse of one form or another. But Danny couldn't remember a time when so many people seemed to be carrying so many secrets at the same time.

He'd entered the Incident Room last and it seemed to give him a different perspective, as if, settled in and waiting for him, the group's hidden concerns had been given time to percolate to the surface. DCS Shepherd, for a start, had the distracted look of someone whose troubled thoughts were a long way from this room. The eyes of Des Gill told Danny of hidden secrets there, too. Her gaze seemed to track DCI Jejeune's every move, but the expression Maik caught in the fleeting, unguarded moments suggested it wasn't the admiration he'd seen previously. Holland's own stare, meanwhile, appeared increasingly to be dwelling on Gill. But again, it was not at all in the same way Danny had seen the constable look at a steady procession of other young female officers over the years.

But Shepherd seemed keen to get the meeting underway, so Maik turned his own thoughts to the matters at hand. He waited for a moment to see if DCI Jejeune was going to reprise his leadership role in the summary, but he waved Maik on from the back of the room.

"Right. We've received confirmation on a couple of key issues from forensics." Maik seemed to hurry by the observation, as if perhaps he didn't quite trust himself to venture any nearer the world of Mansfield Jones.

"Did Dr. Jones shed any light on these ducks?" asked Holland brightly.

Maik looked confused. "Is there any reason he would've been able to?"

"Well, he is a quack."

"So we can now turn our attention to motive," said Maik, as if the past few seconds had never existed. "Why don't we start with some ideas as to exactly what Jakub Kowalski might have done that set Curtis Angeren all aquiver? Despite his claims to the contrary, a vindictive Angeren still seems about as good a suspect as we've got. We're as sure as we can be he was behind the attempt to grab Kowalski's belongings at the mother's house."

"I wonder," said Shepherd. "That list: laptop, phone, digiscope, hard drive, iPad. All electronics that would fetch a fair price on the black market. Could it just be as simple as somebody trying to rob a grieving mother of a few bits and baubles?"

"The men didn't ask for Kowalski's binoculars. Or his 'scope and tripod," pointed out Jejeune. "They'd be as valuable as the electronics."

"If we're so sure Angeren is behind it, we should bring him in," said Holland, who apparently felt he might need to redeem himself by showing his serious side.

"We don't have probable cause," said Maik, "and he's hardly likely to come in of his own accord. He's already voluntarily offered his version of events."

"Then we should go round there. Let him know we're not

going to stand for him pulling our chain about not remembering why he was upset with Kowalski."

Maik inclined his head in agreement, but Shepherd stepped in. "There is a new line of inquiry, something that the inspector believes takes us away from Curtis Angeren." She looked at Jejeune to see if he was going to tell them. But he seemed strangely reluctant, so Shepherd continued. "Jakub Kowalski may have been involved in a human smuggling operation, bringing in Polish criminals by boat from the Netherlands."

As an observer only, it was not really Gill's place to make contributions. But she was a serving police officer, and a detective at that, so a point of clarification surely couldn't hurt. "I can't quite see why that takes you away from Angeren, sir. Surely, he's the obvious choice now. Stopping an activity that brings in illegal immigrants, criminals at that. It's a clear motive for a man of Angeren's political views."

"I agree," said Holland. "He's much more likely to take matters into his own hands than report Kowalski to us, where he'd see him getting a slap on the wrist and being out in a few years to start things up all over again. No doubt he'd see killing Kowalski as some twisted act of patriotism."

"I'm told there's no evidence Angeren knew anything about this operation."

Holland looked at Jejeune quizzically. "Evidence is one thing, but it's hard to believe Curtis Angeren wouldn't be aware of an operation to bring in illegals right on his own doorstep. We can at least bring him in and ask him about it. We can have a go at him about the other stuff while he's here."

"What possible justification can we have for asking him to come in?" asked Jejeune.

"I don't know," said Holland in exasperation. "We'll make up a reason if we have to."

Shepherd looked up sharply at Holland. "When we bring anyone in, ever, it will be solely on the basis of evidence that exists, not on what we want to exist, or worse still, that suddenly materializes to suit our needs. There is no place at this station for anyone who thinks otherwise. Do I make myself clear?"

Maik doubted anyone in the room would have missed the point. *Not in my station*, she was saying. *No investigations into questionable evidence are going to play out here.* It was all for DC Gill's benefit, but coming up with creative reasons to question suspects was part of many police investigations, and Shepherd's heavy-handed response seemed over the top. Whatever burdens she was carrying around, they were taking their toll on the crisp professionalism they had come to expect from her. It was a point not lost on Holland.

"Understood, ma'am," he said meekly. "All I'm saying is that Angeren has already put himself in the frame for this, with no help from us. I think it'd be wise to at least bring him in for a chat about this new development."

Shepherd adopted a softer tone, but there was no hint of remorse in it. "While I'd personally welcome the opportunity to remove Curtis Angeren from our orbit for a very long time, I'm not about to sacrifice my career by rushing into anything without a very good reason. Come to me when you've got one, and we'll talk."

"The thing is," said Jejeune, "I believe people may be looking at Kowalski's involvement in this operation from the wrong perspective. Perhaps it was someone else who was running it and Kowalski simply got in the way."

Looking at him now, Shepherd was as sure as she could be that Jejeune hadn't voiced this idea to the Home Secretary. "You have someone in mind, I take it."

"Teodor Sikorski has a poet's soul. He's a lover of natural justice. He would enjoy the idea of taking money from these criminals and using it to assist the kind of people they had victimized in their home country."

There was an uneasy silence in the room. "I'm not at all sure I follow your line of reasoning on this, Domenic," said Shepherd. It reminded Des Gill of a similar comment she'd heard recently. *I'm not following your logic here, Domenic. And that's not good for either of us.* He'd received the benefit of the doubt that time. She wasn't sure he would again now.

"I think Sikorski has a condition called pronoia," said Jejeune. "It's the opposite of paranoia. These people truly believe the world is set up in their favour. And why not; he's intelligent, handsome, charismatic. It would be easy for a man like that to convince a group of admirers to go along with his plans, not ask any questions, and turn a blind eye when needed. Only Jakub Kowalski never bought into the collective mindset. Perhaps he refused to become part of the operation, even threatened to report Sikorski. It must come as quite a shock for someone with Sikorski's condition to finally discover not everyone has your best interests at heart. It might even seem like a betrayal. It was almost certainly Sikorski who told Kowalski about the Ruddy Ducks at Tidewater Marsh. A deserted marsh with restricted access would be a convenient place to kill someone once you'd lured them there. And Sikorski was, by his own admission, the last person to see Kowalski alive."

Jejeune paused and looked at the room significantly. But the silence told him they were still not buying it. Even Danny Maik was having trouble holding eye contact with his DCI. There were just too many gaps, too many conditionals; *might* and *perhaps*, and *almost certainly,* from a DCI who normally seemed so sure about everything.

"There's the money, too," said Jejeune emphatically. "This not-so-anonymous benefactor who is pouring so much of it

into Wawel. If Sikorski is not getting his funds from this operation, where are they coming from? The man's an academic.
They don't get paid well enough to amass personal fortunes,
let alone seemingly inexhaustible ones."

"I suppose we just assumed it was old family money," said
Holland, shifting uneasily in his seat, "that he really was from
Polish nobility. You know, this Count business and all that."

"And we assumed this why?" asked Shepherd, grateful to
finally be able to fasten her queasy, ill-defined sense of unease
onto something tangible. "Because it was easier than doing
proper police work, perhaps? Can we please now go back and
run a proper financial background check on Teodor Sikorski,
one that has less to do with lazy assumptions and more to do
with verified facts?"

She gave Jejeune a troubled look. "We can see where this
goes, Domenic, but I'll be expecting progress sooner rather
than later, or at the very least some indication we're on the
right track. Because on its own, I'm not sure Sikorski's love of
natural justice is going to be enough. The CPS are not known
for their poetic souls."

The implication was clear. Through his past ability to weave
a solid conviction from the most tenuous of threads, Jejeune
had earned some leeway. But Shepherd's look suggested even
her indulgence of Jejeune's extravagant theories had its limits.

Suspicion is insidious. It could have been the tang of all the
other secrets floating around the room, but whatever it was,
as the meeting ended and everyone rose to go their separate
ways, Maik stared after his departing DCI with particular
interest. Danny Maik had never before had reason to question
Domenic Jejeune's motives, and he wasn't sure he did now. But
that was the point; he wasn't sure. There were times he really

enjoyed his DCI's ability to conjure new suspects seemingly out of thin air. This wasn't one of them. Jejeune seemed to be trying to magic away a prime suspect in this case and replace him with a phantom one. And he was ignoring a valid motive along the way. When the three men met at the golf course, the DCI had emphatically rejected the idea of making any deals with Curtis Angeren. But Jejeune had pointedly kept any mention of Ray Hayes out of his report to DCS Shepherd, and Maik knew the scare with Lindy in the marketplace had only heightened his fears about a genuine attack by Hayes. All of a sudden, Jejeune was going to great lengths to find somebody other than Curtis Angeren to blame for the murder of Jakub Kowalski. Perhaps Angeren was as innocent as he claimed, but bringing him in to find out seemed a perfectly reasonable approach, and any time Danny Maik was siding with Tony Holland over DCI Jejeune, it was a sign that something was wrong. Whichever way Maik chose to look at things, the fact was, by introducing this new line of inquiry about Sikorski, Jejeune couldn't have done more to deflect suspicion away from Curtis Angeren if he'd worked out a deal with him to do exactly that.

30

Danny Maik and Lindy stood together on the driveway of the cottage, leaning against the opposite sides of Lindy's Nissan Leaf. She was working from home for the next couple of days, and since Danny was considering buying one, it seemed an ideal opportunity for him to borrow her car and try it out. Especially since his Mini was out of commission once again. The only condition had been that Danny pick her up first from a boozy baby shower at a friend's house and drop her off at home.

"So you're seriously considering going enviro-friendly, are you? Poor Danny," she said with a lopsided grin. "I mean, I was bound to succumb to his constant barrage of eco-twaddle sooner or later. But to browbeat a nice, decent bloke like you into guilt over our environmental sins," she shook her head in mock despair, "I tell you, Danny, those greenies have a lot to answer for."

Maik smiled and thanked her again for the loan. Even in the sober condition that was a long way from where Lindy was now, he knew it was often her way to claim she'd been coerced into something kicking and screaming. In truth, he suspected there was very little Lindy Hey did that she wasn't completely committed to. And that would include driving an eco-friendly vehicle.

"You know there's no audio system in these, right?" She allowed herself a giggle at his shocked look. "Relax, Danny. I'm joking. Play all the Motown you like in there. This car could do with a bit of romance." *Perhaps even take Lauren Salter out for a drive.* If she had said it, she would have blamed the wine. But she knew the damage would have already been done. Talk about the love that dare not speak its name. Lord Alfred Douglas had nothing on poor soon-to-be Sergeant Salter. But then, Lindy supposed there were lots of loves like that. Perhaps, for some people, it was just safer that way.

With one last expression of appreciation, Maik got in the car and drove off. Lindy stood alone in the pale moonlight, watching the car disappear down the driveway. Though she knew Danny was not a man for sentimental attachments, she suspected he'd long had a soft spot for his Mini. But since the catastrophic damage it had suffered in the accident a few months earlier, one problem after another seemed to have befallen it, and she'd seen Danny's gradual acceptance that he was going to have to let it go. Now he was in the final stages of getting ready to part with it, *gearing up for it,* as it were. A sober Lindy would have given the pun short shrift, but this version, who'd perhaps already had one glass of wine too many, found it strangely amusing.

She looked up at the creamy moon, curled on the dark velvet blanket of the night sky like a sleeping child. "Are you shining on Canada, too, I wonder?" she asked, tottering slightly as she craned back for a better look. Not yet, perhaps. *GMT minus 5*, she reminded herself. "So what can you tell me about it then, Mr. Moon? What do we know about the vast Dominion of Canada?"

Surprisingly little, as it turned out. She could manage the prime minister's name, and the nation's capital. The provinces and territories she might have been able to cobble together, given enough time and a glass or two less of white wine. But beyond that, it would be off to the internet for anything more than the most superficial facts about Domenic's former home. Not long after she'd starting seeing him, she had unfurled a large map of the world on her desk at work. Canada took up most of the top left-hand quadrant. And a great deal of it seemed to consist of empty space. Of the regions themselves, Lindy had only the broadest idea. Quebec, the French bit always punching above its own weight, was inevitably going to find a place in her heart. Newfoundland was where God had come up with the blueprints for heaven, according to Damian. The Maritimes were supposed to be enchanting, the Prairies mesmerizing, the Rockies … okay, we get the picture. "But what do we know about Ontario, Mr. Moon?" she asked, gazing up dreamily. "What can we say about that?"

The moon smiled down benignly at her, but didn't want to get involved. Fair enough, she'd answer the question herself. Though Ontario undoubtedly had a couple of urban centres dotted about, as far as she could tell from Domenic's accounts, mostly it seemed to consist of birding areas, possibly even all interconnected, for all she knew. The names came to her effortlessly on the still night air; Point Pelee, Long Point, Carden Alvar. Lindy wasn't even sure what an alvar was. All she knew was, whenever Dom spoke about it, he got the same look on his face as when he held those Leica UltraHD bins at that birding fair last year. She almost would have preferred him to be looking at another woman. Jealous of the optics? *Careful, girl, you're starting to lose it. Time for a drink, I believe. Just one more, to finish off the night.*

She went inside and poured herself a generous measure of wine. She was half-tempted to slump in the chair beside the fire and sip her drink there, waiting for Domenic to return from who knew where. But she'd got Canada in her blood now, and she wanted to delve a bit more deeply. It was a gorgeous night, quiet and still, and her pale, silent friend was waiting out there to continue their conversation. She wouldn't disappoint him.

She went outside again, glass in hand. She was slightly unsteady now; the devil's trident of fatigue, night air, and alcohol were making their presence felt. She'd no idea why she had drunk quite so much at the baby shower. She loved her friend, and her baby, and was happy for both of them. She enjoyed the company of everyone else there, too, even the inevitable banter about ticking biological clocks and the rest. But tonight there had been an uneasiness within her, a feeling she hadn't been able to shake. As a last resort she'd decided she would try to drown it in Chablis. Not the worst way to go, if she was being honest. It had worked, too, for a time, but she could feel the beginnings of her disquiet starting to creep back up inside her again now.

She leaned against the wall of the cottage and looked up. Fugitive grey clouds had begun shifting across the sky, closing in on her friend like doubts. *I behold, upon the night's starr'd face, Huge cloudy symbols of a high romance ...* Another Keat for you, Dom. Lindy closed her eyes, and cradled her glass to her chest. She began swaying gently, allowing her thoughts to drift to that once-forbidden hope, a visit to Canada.

She wanted to see them for herself, these birding sites that had entangled themselves around Domenic's heart. She wanted to understand why they meant so much to him, what enchantments they held. Admittedly, there were other places he'd mentioned that she was less in a hurry to visit. The Nonquon Sewage Lagoons, for example, or Skunk's Misery. Let's face it; any place where even skunks found the mosquitoes intolerable was never likely to make it onto Lindy's bucket list. And although she was sure the Cerulean Warblers you could see there were every bit as stunning as Dom claimed, he'd made the mistake of telling her these pretty blue birds happened to winter in the Caribbean. So she'd wait and see them there one day, if it was all the same to him. But perhaps she needed to see these unappealing-sounding places too, fit them into Dom's past like jigsaw puzzle pieces, to help construct her picture of who he used to be. Would it help her better understand the man he had become? Possibly, but that wasn't her purpose. If she was going to take Dom on full time, it would mean taking all of him, and that included his past.

So why, all of a sudden, these doubts? Why this extra glass of wine in her hand, when she already knew she'd had too much? She took a sip and gave up fighting the truth, letting it come to her in a rush, relief and guilt all tangled together in the sweet, dry taste in her mouth. Because you're scared, Lindy. Because you've been waiting for this for so long now, to go to Canada with Dom, to see the sights, to meet his family, and now it's actually coming to pass, you're not sure if it's what you want to do at all. She looked up at the moon once again, and she could tell he knew. He was looking down at her now; a half-closed unblinking eye, staring right into her soul. "No secrets from you, are there, Mr. Moon," she said, raising her glass. She closed one of her own eyes and tilted her head slightly, as if peering back in this way might help. *Lacus somniorum.* Though she wasn't sure of its exact location, she knew it was up there somewhere. The Lake of Dreams. She had dared to plunge in, and now she was wondering if she should head back to the shore.

C'mon, Linds, she told herself, *it'll be fine. Start with something simple. Hi, I'm Lindy. I'm hoping to be Dom's better half. During the non-birding times, of course.* God, what if they were all birders? Dom's brother Damian was, after all. Perhaps it was genetic. She didn't bother to try to feign interest with

Domenic anymore, but with an entire household full of them, a rigorous indifference might be more difficult to maintain. It might even seem impolite. But to pretend interest? After all, what did she really know about birding? For all the place names she could recite, what could she say about these areas, or why they were important to the birding world? Suppose the talk turned to the Presqu'ile autumn shorebird migration, for example. The words might as well have been interchangeable for all the sense they made to her. No, she couldn't pretend interest where there was none. Her integrity was part of what made her who she was. It was what Eric liked about her, remember? He even told her so, once.

Could she even be another Lindy if she wanted to, one who sat politely, lips buttoned, knees together, no smirking? No, she couldn't, even if the risk of being herself had never been so high, the potential cost of being Lindy so great. She drew a deep, shuddery breath and looked up at the moon again. No, she would just be herself, and everything would turn out fine. Eric would be proud of her decision to keep her integrity intact, after all. She thought about her boss now, how happy he seemed these days, how contented. He'd hardly been able to take his eyes off Colleen Shepherd all afternoon when they'd been here celebrating Damian's news. Neither one of them seemed in any great hurry to take their relationship any further, but that was okay. They were clearly happy enough with where it was. Perhaps it was all that could be hoped for between two strong-willed individuals who had made their way independently in the world for so long. Any kind of a deeper relationship might be a bridge too far for them now. But it wasn't too far for Lindy and Dom. The future was theirs for the making. They had their careers, their home, their love. All that was missing was the next step, whatever they chose it to be. But whatever it was, it couldn't be this, an idling state of suspended animation that seemed to be not only without a clear destination, but with no discernible road to even get to one. "It's all your fault, you know," she told her pale friend, looking up, "filling people's heads with notions of romance and undying love and eternal devotion." Lindy didn't need a love worth dying for. One worth staying alive for would do her fine.

She swallowed the rest of her wine in a single flourish and turned to go back inside. She wouldn't wait up. Wherever Domenic was tonight, he was probably in a better place than she was. But tomorrow was another day. And when they sat down for breakfast in the morning, he would never know the doubts she'd felt tonight.

"That is," she said, looking up at the moon one last time, "as long as you can keep a secret."

31

Darkness is no threat to those who control it. Domenic Jejeune had made a conscious decision to do without the overhead bulbs, relying on the thin beam from his penlight to manoeuvre between the bulky shapes littering the room. He paused for a moment and listened to the still, hanging silence of the deserted offices. Pale light from the street outside filtered in through the glass door behind him and a second silvery trail came in from the side window. Jejeune played his light quickly over the desk beside the window, near the wall. When the magazine had returned to these premises after the reconstruction, Lindy had been offered the chance to take a different spot, anywhere other than the desk she had been sitting at when the wall beside her was blown out in a violent explosion. Predictably, she had refused, quietly defying the forces of fear, challenging herself to confront the demons that had haunted her for weeks after the blast. This was her place, she was telling the world, and nothing was going to force her to give it up. Jejeune allowed himself a small smile at the thought, even as he drew the beam away from the desk and shone it on a path further into the darkness.

He made his way into the office at the back; the one with the door facing out on to the larger room, so all that happened could be seen, heard, noted. Along the far wall of the office was a bank of three filing cabinets; old, battered behemoths from another age, redolent of ink-stained hacks with shirtsleeves rolled up and cigarettes dangling from the corners of their mouths. The Newspaper Room, like so many things now, a mere shadow of its former self, hovering like a work of fiction in the minds of those who had once experienced it. The keyholes at the tops of the cabinets were so rusted Jejeune doubted he could have inserted a key even if he had one. But he eased the top drawer of the first cabinet open and it slid out obediently. He held the penlight between his teeth and began riffling through the files. He withdrew two folders, skimming through the contents quickly, noting what he needed to before laying them on the top of the cabinet, so he could shuffle through the drawer once more, searching for other files.

The jangling of keys is going to be a cause for alarm to any intruder, but perhaps some will already have planned a way of escape. Jejeune had none. At the sound, he quickly stuffed the files back into the drawer, eased it shut, and pressed his back against the wall of the darkened office, next to the filing cabinets. He heard a deep sigh that sounded like irritation as the person entered through the front door, but he couldn't risk peering around the cabinets to see who it was. All he could do was wait. In his panic, he hoped it was Lindy. If it was, things would be bad, terrible. But if it wasn't, they would be worse.

As he stood beside the cabinet, hardly daring to breathe, one thing was becoming obvious. Whoever else had entered these offices, theirs was not an innocent visit either. It had now been about ten seconds since the key had turned in the lock. And they had also decided not to turn the lights on.

Jejeune weighed his options. Keys meant no break-in, so no crime. Yet, at least. He could not spring forward and apprehend the person, in the hope the questions about what he was doing there himself might get lost in the general melee surrounding the arrest. Whoever was now in here, padding through the offices, had entered under the same circumstances as he had. He heard the sound of approaching footsteps and slid down into a crouch, back jammed hard against the wall. If the person hadn't stopped yet, there were only two possible destinations left. One was the kitchen. Jejeune was in the other one.

Still no light, only a thin beam like his own. It puzzled Jejeune, but it alarmed him more. He could think of no legitimate reason a person would decide they were not going to turn on the lights in an office they were visiting in the dead of night. It was exactly what he had done. As he said, no legitimate reason.

He heard the footfall as the person entered the office. Heavy enough for a man. There was the breathing, too. Not laboured, but hardly the delicate respiration of women Lindy's age, which comprised just about everyone else who worked in these offices. But if it was Eric, why would he choose darkness? He, of all people, had the unquestionable right to be in these offices at any hour of the day or night.

Jejeune felt the filing cabinet tilt slightly against his shoulder as Eric opened the drawer. A bead of sweat had begun a slow descent from his temple, and his neck was damp around the collar. He could feel the tension in his calf muscles, cramped into this crouch for so long now, and beginning to ache for relief. But he dared not move. He was less than two metres away from Eric, deep in shadow, but close enough that the faintest movement might rock the filing cabinet, even as Eric was leaning into it, scrabbling through the files in search of the ones he needed.

Jejeune heard a sigh of exasperation and a sharp sound as a file was slapped down onto the top of the far cabinet. The file drawer closed heavily, tilting the other cabinets more force-fully against Jejeune's shoulder this time. The pain in his legs was intense now, his thighs joining the cry for relief from their cramped position. The muscles were starting to jigger with the strain and the sweat was beginning to run freely down his sides and back. Still, Eric seemed unsatisfied, drumming his heavy fingers on the metal cabinet top in a constant tattoo as he ran something through his mind. Jejeune closed his eyes against the pain in his legs, pressing his head back against the wall. He couldn't hold on any longer, he was going to have to move, to stand, to straighten out his legs, no matter what the cost.

Eric moved first, decisively snatching up the file from the top of the cabinet and walking briskly out of the office. Jejeune slumped and straightened out his legs, as quietly as he could but no longer concerned whether it would be enough. Relief flooded back into his joints as the blood began to flow again. He pressed his back against the wall and released a low, quiet sigh.

Eric had reached the door now, and the sound came to Jejeune across the silence of the empty rooms. Six short beeps followed a longer tone and then a series of measured pulses. The alarm. Jejeune had disarmed it when he entered, the code being a shared secret between he and Lindy since she had moved back into these offices. But Eric had now armed it again as he left. And among its other protections, the alarm was equipped with a motion detector.

It was probably no more than a minute, but it seemed lon-ger; much longer. Jejeune had been sitting beside the cabinet, unmoving, legs stretched out in front of him. They no longer ached, but he was not sure how quickly he could move until he tried. And moving quickly was going to be what it was all about, now. Six seconds. Six seconds from the moment his movement was first detected until the alarm sounded, both here in the office and at the monitoring centre in Norwich. A call to the Saltmarsh police station would be followed by a visit from a patrol car, and a casual poke around the doors and windows to check everything was secure, before Eric got a call summoning him back to the offices he had so recently left. In his heightened state of awareness, he wouldn't be buying any false alarm stories. Even if he wasn't sure exactly what had happened, he'd know something was wrong, someone besides him had been in here tonight. And everything Jejeune had been working towards would be compromised.

So, six seconds. To reach the alarm panel, open the cover, and enter the code. Correctly. First time. In the dark. Could he do it? From a sitting position, beside a filing cabinet at the far end of the offices? A lightning quick flash from his penlight had told Jejeune one of the motion sensors was pointing directly at Eric's doorway. It would detect his movement the second he stood up. And the countdown would be on.

He wanted to wait, but for what? No help would be coming. None could. Anyone who came here, anyone at all, was going to mean he'd failed in the task he'd set for himself, the undetected investigation into the conduct of Eric Chappell, a long time ago. What he'd learned so far tonight had taken him a good distance along his route. But it was a long way to the finishing line. And he needed to get there without anyone else being aware of what he was doing. Yet.

He risked one more flash of the light, to map the route from his position to the alarm panel beside the door. He'd been careful coming in, sure-footed in his approach, stepping lightly around obstacles, taking his time. Now he'd need to run, hell-bent for leather, slam into the panel and begin keying in the six-digit code the second he arrived. If he got it right, he could catch his breath for a second, reset the alarm, and slip out undetected into the night. If he didn't…. The thought went unfinished.

He drew his legs in towards him, eyes locked on the monitor, waiting for the steady red eye to begin blinking. He all but convinced himself the beam couldn't see down behind the cabinet when the red light disappeared, as if sucked into the darkness, only to reappear and begin its slow, toxic pulsing. He jammed his back against the wall and forced himself upright, propelling himself forward. He sprinted towards the door, feeling his legs lag as they came to terms with being in motion again. *A cable.* There was taped-down cable somewhere between two desks. He remembered seeing it on his way in, innocuous enough during the day, but surely enough to trip a sprinting man now. He felt it beneath his sole as he ran, and pushed on. As he reached the far wall, his thigh caught the arm of a chair. *Not there before.* Moved by Eric, perhaps, as he left. The collision spun him off balance, and he fought to regain his momentum, recovering enough to fall against the wall, his palms thumping down near the alarm panel. The high pitched beeping had increased in speed now, a frantic staccato of warning. He pried the cover open on the second try and began punching in the code. What if he didn't finish in time? Did he get a grace period while he was trying? Did the alarm decide six seconds meant six seconds, and that was that? He finished the code as the beeps merged into one long agonized wail of sound and he held his breath. Silence. And the slow metronomic pulsing of a green light on the panel.

The night air had never felt so sweet.

32

Danny Maik had seen high walls like this before, but they had been designed to keep people in. Here, he suspected, the aim was the opposite. He and Inspector Jejeune were standing shoulder to shoulder on the rear steps of the redbrick Victorian house they had just been led through. The open lawns and low shrubbery at the front of the house had given no hint of this secluded, walled garden that lurked at the rear. The sun sat just above the wall at the far end, painting a wide stripe of light along the pink gravel path that bisected the garden. A regimented pattern of well-maintained side paths came off the main artery, lying between flower beds that were showing the first green signs of life.

At the far end of the path, a woman was bending down beside a young girl of about three. Behind them, a younger woman waited with the patient indifference that was the tradecraft of household staff everywhere. The mother's hand rested delicately on the child's shoulder as she directed her gaze to something in the flower bed. She seemed to flinch at the sound of the men's approach along the path and snapped her head up to look at them. She straightened quickly and drew her daughter to her, even as it became clear she recognized one of the men.

"Inspector Jejeune," she said. "We've been expecting you, haven't we, Alicia?" She looked down at the girl, as if seeking her agreement. She looked up again and stared at Jejeune like someone looking at a spectre from her past. *Whatever once passed between these two*, thought Maik, *time has done nothing to diminish it.*

"Those are daffodils." Alicia told the men, pointing.

The woman put her hand on her daughter's shoulder once more and guided her to her nanny. "You're a very clever girl, Alicia Montague Weller. You can go into the house now and Jessica will give you a treat. We'll learn some more flowers later."

All three watched the slow progress of the girl and her nanny along the sunlit path. No one spoke until they had disappeared into the house. Jejeune turned and introduced his sergeant.

"Carolyn." She extended her hand and Maik was struck by how delicate and frail it seemed. Behind the woman, sunlight and shadows played across the rough brick texture of the walls, dappling them into latticework patterns.

"You have a nice spot here," said Maik.

"Yes." Carolyn smiled uncertainly and looked around the garden. She nodded as if to convince herself. There was a flicker of movement on the gravel path and Carolyn recoiled from it. A bird gave a short trill, and hopped onto the edge of a flower bed.

"Robin," said Jejeune, and Maik saw him give a slight smile.

Maik looked at the woman carefully. From a distance she resembled Lindy. Though she was younger than the DCI's partner, she had the same lithe build. But the similarities ended at the physical level. In place of Lindy's brash, piratical grin, Carolyn Weller could offer only a tentative, approval-seeking smile. And where Lindy exuded confidence and poise, Carolyn Weller's self-assurance seemed as fragile as a bird's egg. She paused for a moment like someone gathering herself. "There are questions, I understand?" she said. "Part of an inquiry?"

"An internal police matter." Jejeune waved his hand vaguely. The gesture was so out-of-character, Maik suspected it had been a deliberate choice, to alleviate the woman's concerns. It was apparent to Danny, even from his brief time in Carolyn Weller's presence, that anything which would reduce her anxiety would be welcome. In appearance, Carolyn Weller was as well-groomed and polished as one might expect of the daughter of a high-ranking political figure. But hers was an uneasy gloss. Beneath it lay the same brittleness Maik had seen in chronic drug abusers, though she lacked the rest of the identifiers — the personal neglect, the lassitude, the apathy. In their place was tentativeness, a skittishness that refused to let her settle.

"We just need to go over some details with you ..." The DCI hesitated, "About that time."

She led them to a small wrought iron table beneath an awning. "I don't think about it as much these days, you know." Carolyn looked towards the house. "Children give you someone else to focus on, don't they? Another life to consider, besides your own." The comment seemed to make her sad and she fell silent for a moment.

"You told the investigating officers there was a Magpie that used to come around. You saw it from your window."

She nodded. "In the courtyard, between my room and the wing Monte was being held in." Her eyes flickered along the path, over the gardens, but there were no threats coming. She was safe to continue.

"Was something attracting the Magpie?" asked Jejeune. "Was someone feeding it?"

"The windows were locked. We couldn't open them to put out any food. But the bird came every day, anyway. They do that, don't they?"

Jejeune nodded. "Sometimes they do, yes. Did it ever come near the windows?"

"It stole something, didn't it? A pin. The officers told me."

She turned to look back up at the house as if she had heard a noise up there, or suspected she might. At first glance, Maik had thought her blouse was white, but in these shadows he saw now that it was a delicate shade of lavender, too pallid to compete with the rigorous sunlight. He saw marks, too, on her pale skin. They were vestiges of a lost person, tattoo ink and piercings, but all of them discreet. These were not badges of rebellion; they were attempts at masking, at trying to be someone else, anybody who wasn't Carolyn Weller née Gresham, daughter of the current Home Secretary and former kidnap victim.

"It was like being buried alive," she said suddenly, looking down at the interlocking patio stones, as if she could peer back into her memories. "Out there on that causeway, with the fog closing in all around. Except in a way, I suppose I was already dead. I mean, what state is it when you no longer expect to live, when you no longer want to?" She shook her head. "My body was fighting to survive of course, but my heart, my mind, they wanted it to end. It was like I was being pulled apart, and in the middle there was this emptiness, a hollow space as if something had left me: the will to go on, I suppose, the hope and belief that I'd live."

She put her hands together in an attitude of prayer and pressed the fingertips to her lips. Her hands were trembling. The men gave her a moment to return to them, to this table, this garden.

"Forgive me," said Maik gently, "but I've never understood why you didn't run towards the road after you escaped from the house. Why head down to the water in the first place?"

"As soon as we were out of the house, Monte recognized where we were. He was an Essex boy. He'd been to Foulness

Island before, on holidays, day trips. He said there was only one road on and off the island. If the kidnapper was coming back for us, he'd be coming that way. He said we had to run the other way, away from the road. So we did."

Maik nodded thoughtfully. "But you were sure the kidnapper wasn't in the house."

"Monte said not. There were no lights on, no sounds. Monte said he could always hear the TV on when the man was there." She took a deep breath. "I was out there for so long," she said softly. "So long. And then I heard that strange voice coming to me through the fog," said Carolyn. "I didn't know at first it was a Canadian accent, but I knew you had come to save me, to save us both, like Monte said you would. Only …"

Only he hadn't saved them both. Maik saw the light disappear from Jejeune's eyes. He had been too late to save Monte. Despite the boy's faith in him, Jejeune had only managed to save one of them. Maik looked at his boss. Whatever he'd come to ask, surely it was time to end this now, to put these memories back in their box, where they could do no further harm. But Jejeune had one more place to visit, one more memory, one more secret to uncover.

"There was something else, wasn't there, Carolyn? Something you didn't tell me at the time, or the investigating officers. Or even, I suspect, your parents."

"No." But the denial held a refrain of evasion. Maik knew what would follow. Silence, as Jejeune listened to the birds singing in the tall trees beyond the high walls of this garden. And waited.

Carolyn bowed her head and left her stare lingering on the patio stones at her feet. Seconds of the quiet spring morning passed before she spoke. "It was already over," she said, sagging slightly as the long-held secret finally escaped from her. "Between us. That night was meant to be our last date. As friends."

Maik stirred. "You never said anything about this to anyone?"

She gave a slight tilt of her head. "It seemed important not to. It made no difference, really. Besides, let's be honest, half the present government got re-elected on the sympathy vote afterwards, Daddy included. I'm not sure the truth would have played as well in the constituencies." Cynicism didn't suit this inoffensive, wounded creature, and its impact seemed heightened because of it.

"Can I ask whose decision it was to end things between you and Monte?" asked Jejeune.

"Joint. Probably more mine, but Monte was okay with it. We'd gone as far as we could. We both knew it. Sometimes it's like that with a relationship."

Jejeune nodded. Yes, sometimes it was.

Carolyn cast a nervous glance at the house. "If there's nothing else, I should probably go inside. Alicia has a way of getting Jessica to agree to the unhealthiest of snacks. You don't have to go back through the house. There's a side gate. I'll show you."

She led them to a wooden gate discreetly tucked into a niche in the wall. Despite her breeding, Maik wasn't expecting her to tell Domenic Jejeune it had been good to see him again. She didn't thank them for coming, either. Jejeune turned as she opened the gate for them.

"I can't be involved any more, if there do happen to be any follow-up questions from the review of the case. I wanted Sergeant Maik to hear our discussion. If anything comes up, you should feel free to speak to him."

Fair enough, thought Maik, but he doubted any follow-ups would be arising from Des Gill's investigation. He had suspected from the start that Jejeune was here today to pursue a different agenda, one of his own. Danny had been brought along to ensure someone else knew where he was headed, in case something came along that prevented the DCI from finishing it himself.

33

Des drew up at the airfield and parked the pageant-blue MGB near the offices. It had been an invigorating drive. The long shadows of morning still lay across the landscape and the breeze was cool. In the city, she might have put the car's top up on a day like today, but out here there was so much for the senses to feast upon: the smell of the dew on freshly tilled earth, the sound of a Skylark scribbling its song out into the world. She wasn't prepared to shut all that out just to have a warmer drive.

She approached the offices and peered in through the darkened windows to the interior. Empty. Beside her, the large doors to a hangar were open on both sides and light was streaming through. There were two low-winged planes in the hangar and a small two-seater parked out on the tarmac behind it, but she could see neither mechanics nor ground crew anywhere. The airfield appeared to be deserted, and she had all but convinced herself she'd come to the wrong location when she spotted the distinctive grille of Holland's Audi peeking out from the side of the hangar.

Holland pushed his hand down to his side as he saw her round the corner, but the man across from him smiled and pointed at the hand, so Holland lifted his cigarette up again and offered her a guilty grin. "I know, bad habit," he said. "I'll be packing it up any day now."

He was seated on a stack of wooden pallets, leaning back against the metal wall of the hangar, one knee drawn up to support his smoking arm. The man standing opposite him wiped a hand on his once-white overalls and approached Des. "Stan," he said. "I'm glad you could make it. Up there is no place to be trapped with just him for conversation. There's nowhere to escape."

Des smiled at Stan as she processed that Tony's invitation here meant they would actually be going up in a plane today.

"I thought you'd like to see north Norfolk from the air," said Holland, noticing her uncertainty. "You're in for a treat, I can tell you. It's perfect flying weather today." He consulted the skies. "Ceiling at about three thousand feet, excellent visibility, winds south-southwest at about fifteen knots." Holland sounded so convincing, for a moment Des could almost have believed he knew what he was talking about.

Until Stan laughed, anyway. "I'll grab my flight manifest and my gear and we can get underway," he said. "If that's okay with you, Squadron Leader. You can wait over by the plane."

"The Cessna 172 Skyhawk fixed-wing?" Holland asked.

"Or, the white one, as we like to call it."

They watched Stan leave, shaking his head as he went.

"I didn't think you were coming," said Holland when they were alone.

"I had to see someone first."

"About a permanent transfer up here?"

"About a corvid."

Holland looked puzzled, but Des pointed to the corner of the hangar where Stan was now waving them towards the plane. "Looks like it's time for the off," she said.

Holland scooted up from the pallet stack and stubbed out his cigarette.

"Do you think we might have time for a chat when we get back," Des asked casually as they walked to the plane.

Holland nodded. "Sure. We can even talk while we fly, if you like. It's called multi-tasking. Women are supposed to be good at it."

The shadow of the plane tracked steadily across the checkerboard of fields below them. It was the only evidence of movement Des could see down there.

"Not bad, eh?" asked Holland for at least the fourth time. "I suppose this must be what it looks like to your hero when he's got his cape on. Though it wasn't exactly a vintage performance last time out in the Incident Room, was it?"

She met his grin with a serious expression. "We all need our heroes, Tony, even if they have their off days. You could do worse than make Danny Maik yours, you know."

"What, old Captain Sadness? Do me a favour. What am I going to learn listening to somebody who hangs on to lost causes and sad songs?"

"A lot more than if you don't."

Stan smiled as he banked the plane into a gentle, slow turn and pointed down. Below them a river estuary spread out across the land like a wide, glittering fan. "Tidewater Marsh," he told her. "You can't really appreciate the layout of these parts until you see it from up here. It's amazing how much wetland there is down there, isn't it?"

Des nodded and watched as the small plane faithfully traced the thin white fringe of surf breaking along the coastline directly beneath them. Tendrils of shimmering water snaked inland, carving the landscape into shapes and patterns that were undetectable from the ground. Pools of silver reflected back up at them, turning the area into a vast broken mirror of light shards.

"Are you sure this isn't a job-related trip?" Des asked Holland, though her expression suggested she'd already pretty much made up her mind.

"What? Why would you ask that?"

"Because we've made a low pass over the same stretch of coastline three times now. Almost as if, oh, I dunno, say, somebody was looking for something."

For a moment, the two of them sat looking at each other, their silence disappearing into the drone of the engines that seemed to fill the space around them. Holland gave her a guilty grin. "A beautiful woman with brains," he said.

"I know — what are the odds?"

"Oh, I didn't mean it that way. I was just thinking what a great combination it was."

Des looked out the window at the patterns painted on the landscape by the interplay of sunlight and shadow. Whether she was buying the explanation or not, she was keen to get back to the matter at hand. "Were you also thinking of telling me what we're doing up here?"

"Okay. Stan does some contract work for the police, reconnaissance mainly, no active pursuits or anything like that. I just thought you might enjoy coming along with us for the day. I mean, you have to admit it is beautiful up here. The fields with the sun on them, and the water. And on a clear day like this you can see for miles. I think that's King's Lynn over there."

Des didn't follow the direction of the pointing finger and Holland lowered it again in defeat. He sighed. "Fair enough," he said. "The sarge thinks there may be a landing spot somewhere along here where the undocumented immigrants are being brought in. Stan spotted a few potential sites on an earlier run and now we're checking them out more closely." He leaned forward to tap Stan on the shoulder, making a slashing gesture at his throat and pointing further along the coast.

The plane continued tracking the coastline. They passed over Saltmarsh Harbour, where boats with unrigged masts sat in patches of sunlit water like a forest of bare trees. To the west, the cloud-filtered light dappled the fields, appearing almost to set them moving like waves. A mesmerizing palette of earth tones rolled to the horizon, browns and yellows and sepias. The colour promised new life, food — coming sustenance for the people of north Norfolk and beyond. Holland pointed to the peninsula jutting out into the sea just ahead of them. "Whitehaven Golf Club. It can only be a mile or so across the water from Tidewater Marsh. But look how far inland and then back out again you have to go to get there by land." He traced the route with his finger, coming inland from the point where the river spilled its contents into the sea to a narrow bridge across the coast road, and then back out again along the other bank of the river.

"Last time we were up here, I told him a triangle with two long, equal sides like that is called an isosceles," said Stan, turning his head towards Des. "He asked me if it was named after some Latin bloke. You see what I mean about conversation?"

"Yeah, well, Latin isn't my strong suit. But I know about triangles. And I told him, triangulation is how the police track the location of a phone call," said Holland authoritatively. "Three points. Two towers and the phone."

As the plane banked, the land disappeared and a sea view filled their window. From up here, the boats were white dots adrift in a vast blue universe. Des wondered how keen those boat owners would have been to lay out all that money if they could have seen beforehand how insignificant they really were in the grand scheme of things.

"You can do it with two sounds, too," she said thoughtfully. "Triangulation. If you know the exact location each sound came from, and the exact decibel level at its source, you can pinpoint the spot where the sounds would coincide." She paused and looked at Tony. "It's been done." She continued to watch his face, as if expecting he might already have heard about this. But his blank expression told her otherwise.

"All I know is, you try to make that trip from Whitehaven to Tidewater Marsh by road, going inland and back out and all, and it's going to take you the better part of fifteen minutes."

"Even you, Tony?" asked Stan.

"Well, let's say ten for me in the Audi, but at least fifteen if you're trying to do it in some honking great Range Rover."

Des stared at Holland wide-eyed for a long moment, but he just returned her look with one of his irreverent grins.

Holland claimed later that he was the first to spot it, but in Des's recollection they were still looking at each other when a sudden lurch and change in engine pitch jolted them out of their staring contest. Either way, it was Stan who made the first move, pointing down to his left and banking the plane slightly so his passengers could see better. Directly below them, from an isolated building sitting at the edge of a glittering water course, a writhing tower of grey was rising into the sky. Smoke.

"It's that Polish Centre, Wawel," said Holland. "Call it in, Stan, and get us down there, fast as you can."

Stan gave Tony the thumbs up and reached for the radio. Behind him, Des was leaning into the window as far as possible to look directly down. "I think there might be somebody in there," she yelled at Holland over the noise of the deep-throttling engines. "I can see a car parked outside."

"Two," said Holland. He pointed to another, smaller car, parked slightly away from the building. It was sitting at a haphazard angle, as if it had been slewed to a stop by someone in a hurry. Neither of them recognized the car closest to the building, but the other one was familiar to both of them. You didn't soon forget Lindy Hey's lime-green Nissan Leaf.

34

Holland thought Stan might try a landing on the berm itself. From up here, it looked much too short and narrow, but he had seen the pilot pull off some amazing things over the years. If he came in low over Wawel and dropped down immediately, it might just be possible. But Stan decided otherwise. The gravel track that bent through the flat landscape straightened out on its final approach to the berm. Whether this stretch was straight enough or long enough, the pilot was now intending to find out.

He came in low and hard and the small plane bounced once as it touched down. They felt a slight skid as the tyres fought for grip on the loose gravel, and Stan hauled the plane left as it began to drift towards the marsh on the far side of the track. He reined the rolling plane in and brought it to a shuddering stop. Holland pushed open the door and leaped down. Des followed, and they sprinted shoulder to shoulder along the track as it rose towards the berm. Even though they could not see the top of the rise as they ran, they knew where the building was. They headed for the steady stream of grey smoke drifting skyward just ahead. As they mounted the slope, Danny Maik was there to meet them.

"Paulina Kowalski called to say she was in danger. By the time I got here the building was already on fire. She must be inside, but I can't get to her. That metal grille is padlocked. There's a lot of smoke. If she's still alive, she won't have long."

Des had continued running past Maik towards the Centre as the sergeant spoke to Holland. She was standing at the side of the building looking up. Smoke was billowing out of a small opening. "This window's open. I can get in."

The two men turned and ran over to her, looking up as they arrived. "The opening's too small," said Holland. "You'll never squeeze through there."

"Worth a try," she said. "Give me a bunk up."

Maik cupped his hands and boosted Des up as if she was made of feathers. He felt the tiny pressure points of her feet as she scrambled onto his broad shoulders, and then their absence as she reached into the narrow opening and hauled herself up. The two men watched as she corkscrewed her upper body in through the window and twisted her hips around until she was in. They heard a thud as she crashed through onto the floor inside. "Okay," she called. She gave a choking cough. "I can't see anything, the smoke is too thick. But there are no flames. The fire must be at the back."

"Is Mrs. Kowalski there?" asked Maik.

"It's hard to see anything." Des gave another series of rasping coughs. "No, I can't see her." She coughed again. "My eyes are watering. The room is filling with smoke."

"You need to get out, Des," shouted Holland from outside, "while you still can. Climb back up."

"I can't see anything to climb onto. I'll try to head for the front door."

The men sprinted to the front of the building and waited while the smoke continued to billow out from beneath the roof eaves. *The stack of mattresses in the corridor*, thought Maik. If those had been set smouldering, the entire building would be filled with toxic fumes long before any flames caught hold.

Paulina Kowalski, if she was still in there, was almost certainly dead already. Des had seconds, at best, to make it to this front door and unlock the grille before she, too, was overtaken by the lethal smoke.

"She's here!" Des's voice accompanied a slight movement of the wooden front door. Thick smoke billowed out of the narrow opening. Holland moved round slightly and peered in through the grille, but even with the door ajar, the smoke inside was so dense he could barely make out the small grey outline bending over another shape lying on the ground. "She's blocking the doorway. I can't open it any further." Des was wheezing constantly now, fighting for air. "I can't tell if she's alive or not."

"The key to the padlock, Des," Holland was pressing his face against the grille and shouting urgently. "Get the key."

"Not here. Can't see." The words came between paroxysms of coughing.

"We've got to get that grille open," shouted Maik. "Look around, find something to pry it open with, an iron bar, anything."

"There's nothing here!" shouted Holland in panic. "Is there a tow rope in the car? We can tie it the grille and drag it open."

Maik checked the trunk but there was nothing in there.

Holland pointed to the pile of weeds beside the building. "We'll use this. If I can squeeze the root clumps between the bars and bring the vines either side, I can tie them to the back of the car."

"They'll never hold," said Maik.

"They will. You've seen the way those roots bind together. You'll never pull them apart."

"Even if the roots hold, the vines will break as soon as I pull away and put some tension on them."

Holland shook his head impatiently. "I heard Jejeune say this stuff is supposed to be as strong as rope. If we can twist enough of them together, maybe it'll work."

From inside the house came a burst of choking hacks. Black smoke was escaping through the door opening in a steady stream now. The men looked at each other. "We have to try, Sarge. If we can't get that grille open, she's not going to make it."

From the doorway came the sound of a deep, sickening cough, and a single, desperate, breath-starved call. "Tony!"

It was all Maik needed to hear. He jumped in the Leaf and backed the car up to within a couple of metres of the grille while Holland grabbed armfuls of the Frankenweed, looking for the most densely matted root clumps he could find. He grabbed some and ran to the building, trailing the long tendrils of the vines behind him. Maik joined him at the grille and the two men jammed the root clumps through the bars at the far bottom corner, where there would be most play, twisting them sideways, desperately pounding them past their resistance until they were nestled snugly against the bars. As Tony dragged the vines back through the bars and frantically twisted them together, Maik opened the car's tailgate. Together, they coiled the vines around the lift supports, cinching them as tightly as they could.

Maik jumped in and eased the car forward. The weed rope held but the grille didn't move. As he urged more from the engine, one of the lift supports began to bend under the strain. The metal grille twisted away from the door with the faintest of squeals.

"She's going. Give it some more!"

Maik poured on the power. The support bent even more and began to pull away from the car's body as the tailgate buckled downward. But the green cable held firm. The grille twisted further out and Holland tried to squeeze through the opening.

"Not enough," he shouted "Keep going. Keep going!"

Maik gave the car more power, and with a tortured screech, the lift support tore away from the body of the car completely.

Maik jammed on the brakes, but Holland was already undo-ing the weed rope before the car had stopped rocking. He rewrapped it on the other support rod with the rest of the vines and banged the car's rear panel with his hand. There were no more sounds coming from inside the building now. No cough-ing, no choking, no cries.

"Again, Sarge, now!" shouted Holland urgently. "Just a touch more and she'll be able to squeeze through."

"Paulina Kowalski won't. Let me know when that open-ing's wide enough to get them both out."

Maik revved the car again, easing forward into a slow, sus-tained pull. The support held firm, but the tailgate itself began to bend sideways as the car battled against the back drag.

"More," shouted Holland. "Give it one more go."

The car bucked violently as the bodywork continued to bend. But the support held, and the weed rope remained taut. And slowly, the metal grille began to twist away from the door.

"Through." Holland skidded down through the opening and shoulder-rolled into the half-open door, feeling it give under his weight. He got to his feet and peered into the wall of thick, dark smoke that filled the foyer, but it was so dense he could see nothing. Beside him, something moved and he could hear the measured heaves of someone dragging a heavy burden. He couldn't see to help but as he stretched out his hand, feeling for the door, the tiny form of Des Gill lurched past him, hunched over, moving slowly backwards. As soon as she backed through the doorway, she dropped low and rolled through the opening at the base of the grille. Maik reached through to drag the inert form of Paulina Kowalski out after her. Gill came back to help, but as she bent down, she reeled and stumbled back, collapsing heavily on the ground.

Holland had dropped low to escape the worst of the smoke, and he squirmed out through the narrow opening on his belly.

Behind him, dark clouds of smoke were billowing out of the open doorway. His eyes were streaming with tears and the acrid taste of smoke filled his mouth. He got to his feet and leaned against the side of the building, retching violently, until his throat felt like it was on fire. In the distance he could hear sirens, and when he looked up he could just make out blurry flashing lights as fire engines and ambulances made the long, sweeping curve around the track towards the berm, slowing to ease past the parked plane. Holland coughed again heavily and peered around, waiting for his eyes to clear. Then, finally, he looked down in front of him. Through his milky vision, he could make out Danny Maik, resting on his haunches. Beside him, two women lay stretched out on the ground. Neither moved.

35

"Of course I'm not okay with the decision."

Perhaps there had been a second after Holland's entrance, before the diverted eyes and the awkward hesitation in the doorway, when they might both have been able to pretend he had not heard anything. But that moment had passed now and Holland stood still, looking at Des as her gaze slowly returned to his. She waved him into the hospital room with a brief smile, but it was the speaker on the other end of the phone who had her attention. And she had no smiles for whoever it was. She listened carefully for a few moments, nodding her head occasionally, even though the speaker couldn't see her. "I understand. If you'll excuse me, I have to go. I have a visitor. I'll speak to you later."

Holland stood at the foot of the bed and waited patiently while Des set her phone down on the side table beside a small plant with a profusion of pink blooms. Other than this, there was nothing on any of the surfaces, not even a cup of water. Des tugged at the sheets to draw them up a little. She fixed a smile back on for Holland. It was clear the caller hadn't been a well-wisher, but he wasn't going to ask, and she'd made no effort to fill the pulse of silence he'd allowed, so they would move on.

"That's a nice plant, I must say," Holland told her.

She turned her head to look at it. "The nurses tell me some bloke dropped it off last night while I was sleeping."

"Did they comment on what a looker he was?"

"They said he seemed like a bit of a saddo, *actch*," said Des, playing her part, "wandering around the corridors carrying this plant with the name he couldn't pronounce."

"Yeah, well, I believe I told you Latin isn't my strong suit."

Des dropped her smile. "How is Mrs. Kowalski? I'd appreciate some honesty. I asked earlier but nobody wanted to say."

Holland tilted his head slightly. "Not great. She swallowed a lot of smoke. There might be some lung damage. They're going to keep her in for a while and watch her...." He looked around for somewhere to sit, and his eyes found the bottom of the bed.

"Don't get any ideas, Tony. My eyes are like this because of the drugs. Dilated pupils, as you undoubtedly know, signal arousal in women. I just wouldn't want you to get the wrong impression."

"Beautiful woman, lying in bed, giving me the eyes? Never crossed my mind," he said. He chose the uncomfortable chrome-framed chair beside Gill and became serious. "Paulina Kowalski is lucky to be alive, and Danny Maik has been making sure everybody knows why." He looked at her significantly.

"I wouldn't have been able to get her out on my own," said Des. There was a short intake of breath. "Oh my God, Lindy's car?"

"A right mess," confirmed Holland. "From what I could see, they might even have to scrap it." He gave her a crooked smile. "Best thing that could happen to one of those things, if you ask me." He looked as though there might be weightier things on his mind, but the light route was the one he chose to take for now. "So you're doing all right yourself?"

"Just waiting until the results of the pulmonary function test are back and I've had another consultation with the respirologist. Once he signs off on me, I'm on my way."

Holland nodded absently at the news and Des waited to see if there would be another question to which he didn't particularly want an answer. Instead, he made a production of looking around the room before circling in for a landing. He looked at her.

"Erm, in the plane, just before we saw the smoke ..." Holland paused and looked at Des to see if she was going to give him any help, but it was clear that he was going to need to go the distance. "I wondered if there was something you were going to say. About your review."

"Did you?"

It wasn't an answer, but the way she was looking at him now, dilated pupils and all, told him it was the only one he'd be getting. He looked around again, as if there might be another approach lurking in one of the corners of this bright, white room. If there was, he couldn't find it. "Almost forgot." He fished in his pocket and brought out a paperback in a small plastic bag. "Brought you a book. It's a murder mystery," he said, handing it to her.

"Thank you. The doctors have been telling me I need to get plenty of sleep. This should help." She smiled. "Seriously, that's very sweet."

"It's by some Canadian bloke," he said. "I thought perhaps you might get some insight into how they think over there. Help you out with the DCI. You'd better watch your step, though. If you plan on making a habit of this heroics lark, you're going to shove him right out of the spotlight. I can't see that going down very well at all."

"It shouldn't be a problem," said Des seriously. She paused, as if weighing up whether to continue. "That call I just took was confirmation from London. Next stagecoach out of Dodge."

"They're calling you back? Why?" Holland stood to add urgency to his question.

She shrugged. "They sent me up here to do a job, not lounge around in a hospital bed. They've found something else for me to do back at the Met."

Holland gave her a long look. The nonchalance wasn't really coming off. Des didn't strike him as the kind of person who'd be comfortable leaving something half done. He might have expected disappointment, resentment, even, at having been ordered off the case. Of the kind he'd heard on the phone as he entered, come to think of it. "You know, I've never had a lot of time for the bloke," he said grudgingly, "but that business with the ephedrine, I'm beginning to understand how the Home Secretary could get to like Jejeune."

Des nodded. She suspected that the more time you spent around DCI Jejeune, the more you started to understand what all the fuss was about. But she didn't offer to prolong the conversation.

Holland could see that, whatever was going on, there would be no more sharing, no more confidences about her review of the case. Perhaps it would take them both places she no longer wanted to go. It was hard to see your heroes fall. He drew a deep breath and exhaled slowly. "So, that's it, then." For them, he meant. But it wasn't necessary to say it.

"That's it," said Des. The businesslike tone softened. "It was probably never really on, anyway, if we're being honest. You're nice, Tony, really you are. But you're a bit all over the place — lad on the pull one minute, decent, caring bloke the next. I think losing your girlfriend like you did has left you not quite knowing who you are. You need someone who can wait for you until you find out, somebody who doesn't have her own plans to keep getting in the way."

"Like yours would, you mean?" He nodded and gave her

a wan grin. "Cue the soft-focus camera and the twinkly piano music in the background, then, I suppose."

"Just as long as it's not Motown," she said with a sad smile. "But you should think about what I said about Sergeant Maik, Tony. He's a good man."

"Not exactly a great role model when it comes to sorting out your love life, though, is he? I mean, look at the mess he's making of this business between him and Salter."

"Things don't always work out. Sometimes they're not meant to. Like you and me."

"Ah, never say never," said Holland with a smile. "Maybe we'll hook up again sometime. You never know, I might even land that job with the Met — Psychological Profiler: Speciality, Women."

"Yeah, about that…"

Their laughter was cut short by the sight of DCS Shepherd in the doorway.

"I'm glad to see you're in such good spirits," she said. "You're well on the road to recovery, I take it?"

"So they tell me," said Des. Holland stood silently beside her.

Shepherd nodded thoughtfully. "No lasting damage then?"

Gill wasn't sure she would go that far, but she simply gave a shrug.

"You did well, Constable. I want you to know that."

"If the DC hadn't gone in, Mrs. Kowalski wouldn't have made it," said Holland. "We'd never have been able to get to her."

"Yes, Constable, I'm aware of the circumstances." Shepherd paused and looked at him.

"Okay, then. I suppose I'd better be off," said Holland hurriedly. "Make sure you take care of that plant. The book, not so much. I suppose you can leave it in the library when you go. There must be somebody who enjoys that kind of thing." He turned to leave, but stopped at the doorway and looked back.

"It's been a real privilege to work with you, Detective Constable Gill. I mean that." He nodded respectfully to Shepherd as he passed, and she watched him disappear down the brightly lit corridor. The normal spring in his step was noticeably absent.

Shepherd's eyes went to the plastic bag lying beside Des on the bed and then to the plant on the side table. "That's very nice. Did he bring that in for you?"

Des nodded and gave a slight smile. "He told the nurses he thinks it might be called a *Chlamydia*."

Shepherd's eyebrows went up a notch. "Well, let's hope it's a slow-growing one, then. I presume you'll be taking it with you when you return to the Met to take up your new duties. Once you're fully recovered, of course."

Gill's eyes opened a touch wider. There had been no hint of a question in the DCS's comment. Shepherd gave her a frank look. "Tony Holland's goodbye rather suggested you'd already heard."

"They phoned me just before he arrived. Sorry if that's what you came all the way down here to tell me."

"It wasn't, *actch*." Shepherd gave her a small smile and Gill had the courtesy to return it. "I came in to let you know you've been put forward for a special commendation, Constable. I've no doubt the committee will approve the nomination. You showed a great deal of courage going into that building, DC Gill, truly."

"Thank you," said Gill sincerely. "I appreciate that very much."

Shepherd rounded the end of the bed and approached her. "I want you to know I had nothing to do with the decision to terminate your review. I understand you told them you'd come across nothing that warranted further investigation." This time, there was a questioning note to Shepherd's statement.

"They asked me if I had found anything. I told them I had nothing firm. They said wrap it up." Again, the shrug of the narrow shoulders seemed overly casual, but Shepherd ignored the gesture.

Nothing firm. Des could have looked at Shepherd and told her directly, delivered the message unequivocally: *I found nothing.* She hadn't done that. And from a straight talker like Detective Constable Desdemona Gill, the inference was clear.

"I'd like to think you would have come to me if you'd found anything questionable," said Shepherd cautiously. "Any troubling inconsistencies, for example."

"I imagine that would very much have depended on what I'd found."

And just for a moment, Shepherd got a sense of the steel that had taken this young, fresh-faced woman to the heady heights of Empowered Investigator for the Met. But while there was a part of the DCS that admired the honesty it had taken for Gill to deliver her response, Shepherd was not heartened by it. Des Gill was not the type of person to let something lie. Orders from on high or not, she'd find a way to revisit things, eventually, even on her own time. The question was whether somebody else would be clever enough to get there first.

36

A strong wind was blowing in over Foulness Island, and there was enough coolness in the air to remind Domenic Jejeune that out here, spring was still only taking its tentative first steps onto this year's stage. He stood at the edge of the land, where it sloped gently down to the sea. Behind him, the stark, windswept landscape huddled beneath a low sky the colour of pewter. Wild, uncultivated fields spread out in all directions, spongy underfoot and dotted with tussocks of coarse grass and low shrubs. It was harsh terrain, flat and rugged. Less than three metres at its highest elevation, the landscape offered little protection to the few hardy souls that clung on here, scattered across the length and breadth of the island in their farmhouses and cottages. They had been bowed all their lives by the elements that punished Foulness Island, but they had been defeated, finally, by the economic realities of farming in the global era.

Jejeune stared out over the rocky shoreline, beyond which an uneasy sea churned restlessly. A solitary figure stood at the shore, at a point where an ancient ramp of crumbling concrete sloped out into the sea until it finally disappeared beneath the roiling waves. But the figure, he knew, was not looking at the ramp, or the sea. *On the shore of the wide world I stand alone, and think. Till Love and Fame to nothingness do sink.* Fame? Yes, perhaps Domenic might agree with that. His own experience had taught him of the transient, inconsequential nature of public acclaim. But love? Surely, a mother's love endures even when all else has disappeared. As this mother's love had.

He had known she would be here. She had travelled, like him, across the single bridge on the north side of the island that tethered the hundred or so remaining inhabitants of Foulness to the mainland. She would have followed the gravel road built, like so many out here, on top of the ancient sea walls, to park beside the brooding, abandoned building a few hundred metres behind them. It was a modest structure built of rough-hewn Kentish ragstone. At the base of the walls, tufts of pale grass trembled in the constant wind. Jejeune knew the woman had not been into the decaying building. She did not want to see where her son had been held captive. She wanted to look upon the place where he had known his last moments of freedom. Out there, at sea.

The woman did not turn from her vigil when Domenic approached. He stood beside her for some seconds, watching the sea perform its never-ending ballet; rising, rolling, falling.

"I wasn't sure you would come, Inspector. I knew you wouldn't forget, not with that mind of yours, but I didn't think you'd have time. I mean, with that terrible business out there where you are now, the burned body and all…."

Jejeune left his own eyes on the sea as he spoke. "Is your husband any better?"

"He has his days. Still, it's hard, you know." She turned to him and shook her head a little. "Hard," she said again, as if settling on the word.

Jejeune looked at her. She was a small woman, but the weight of her grief seemed to have shrunk her even more. Her hair was wispy and unkempt, the grey-white dominating the black now. *She's stopped trying*, thought Jejeune. Her hair, her clothes, the way she carried herself: it was as if she recognized the irrelevance of personal vanity when you are standing at the site where the world had claimed your only child. He looked at her again, and saw the loss in her face. It struck a note somewhere in his mind. Perhaps he'd seen it before, at the funeral.

The wind dragged its talons across the land, and the scrubby grasses quaked and bent at its passing. Offshore, the grey sea tumbled and rolled into ragged, half-formed waves. Somewhere back inland, a Greenshank called, scarring the air with its high-pitched cries. Individual moments, thought Jejeune. That's where their sense of dislocation came from, these windswept coastal islands. The crashing of a wave, a shorebird's call, a gust of wind. Everything was separated into its own little pocket of time. There was no sense that events were all part of some eternal linear progression, connecting and connecting, drawing you on, pulling you in, dragging you down.

"I did wonder if they'd let me through today," said the woman, as if conversation might keep some of her feelings at bay. "The website said the area was closed for munitions testing, but I came down anyway. The MoD man at the checkpoint was very nice. He told me they'd cancelled the exercises on account of the coming fog. He said I could stay as long as I liked. That was very nice of him, wasn't it, Inspector?"

"Yes," he said, "it was." Another gust came in from the sea, strong and blustery. It rocked Jejeune slightly, and made his eyes water, but the woman stood steadfastly on the rocky shore. She seemed not to mind the cold. Perhaps she didn't even notice it. She just kept looking out, lost in thought, her sadness etched into her features. Again, the image resonated with Jejeune, but he could not say why. He gathered his jacket around him and the woman was quick to seize upon the gesture. "You need a warmer coat on a day like today, Inspector. You don't want to catch a cold."

The mothering instinct, he thought, trying to find a place to alight. Despite her familiar tone, Jejeune had seen her only a few times before: twice here in previous years, and the first time, when he had gone to the funeral to offer his sympathies. He knew she didn't hold him responsible for her son's death. Even by then it had ceased to matter to her who was to blame. He had watched her that day on an Essex hilltop, where the countryside bent away to the horizon in all directions and a priest struggled to find a place for a young man's death in the universal scheme of things. The woman's husband had not been there that day either, unable to face the final goodbye to his son. What was it about a mother that gave her such strength? he wondered. That this small woman beside him could have faced that day with such grace and dignity, even as she was crushed with the inconsolable grief of her loss. It was her love, her mother's love, offering her final act of care for her son, her final duty. It was what brought her here today, to mark the anniversary of her son's death, at this site, on this windswept, desolate stretch of shoreline.

"He had turned his life around, Inspector. That's what helps us now. To know that."

Jejeune had heard the comment before, at other encounters, but he said nothing.

"We thought he might have gone off the rails for good when he was younger. Broke his father's heart, he did, plenty of times. But he got that job, met that girl." She nodded into the wind. "He was happy. He'd turned his life around," she repeated. She was speaking so softly now, Jejeune was no longer sure if she was talking to him at all. The sound of the rushing wind threatened to drown out the words, but she continued speaking anyway. The elements were an irrelevance — the weather, the sea, this metallic grey sky — nothing was going to keep her from her memories of her son. "All the good we saw in him as a young boy, that was all coming back. The last time we spoke, he told us how happy he was. That's what we hold on to now, his father and me."

A lone Herring Gull drifted in, banking on outstretched wings before landing on the beach a few metres away. It picked at the ragged seaweed trapped between the rocks, tearing hard to free some morsel of food and gulping it down greedily. Jejeune watched as it continued foraging along the beach. Without warning, it threw back its head and issued its loud, raucous call into the world. It seemed such an irreverent act, here where two human beings were quietly marking the passing of another. *And yet, perhaps birds have lessons for us, too,* thought Jejeune. They simply go on, fighting for their existence against the hardships of life, day after day. Like this woman before him now, staring silently at a patch of ground, as the waves crashed on the rocky beach and sent incursions of lacy white froth to die like invaders on the stones at her feet.

She leaned forward and placed a hand on the ground in front of her. Leaving something? Or just touching the spot? Jejeune had thought about bringing flowers and laying them here on the shore. But he knew Mrs. Harrison would stay here until the incoming tide forced her back, and she would have been forced to watch as the waters claimed the flowers, as they had claimed her son. He looked at the woman again, her head bowed in thought. He had believed once that if only he could offer her the facts, it may help her to reach some reconciliation with the future she now faced. But Domenic Jejeune was no longer sure what the facts were. At one time, he thought he knew. But everything he was learning was drawing him closer to the realization that he had been wrong. Would it have changed things, to know then what he now suspected? Would it have stopped him from having to stand here today, beside a bereaved mother, grieving for her lost son? Perhaps. But there were times when tragedy was unavoidable, even if you made no mistakes.

The wind had picked up again and the sea was beginning to stir. Under the failing light, its colour shifted through a palette of silver and brown and bottle-green. Even today, the uneasiness of being out of cellphone range troubled Jejeune. He knew the exact configuration of the coverage out here, and how far he would need to go to receive the nearest signal. Four minutes by foot to the northwest. Once, he had used that knowledge to locate two kidnap victims. But why did it matter today that he could not be reached by phone? What could be happening in the world that would be worse than the events that had occurred here? When he looked again, the gull had gone. Perhaps even it could sense the overwhelming sadness of this place. It was time Jejeune left, too, to give Mrs. Harrison the time she wanted, to be alone with her memories of her son.

As he bade her goodbye, she turned to look at him. Her eyes were rheumy, perhaps with the wind. "I never did ask you, Inspector. Did you see him, that day? I thought perhaps from the shore. Or as you were making your way out there."

Jejeune shook his head.

"No," said the woman. "I suppose the fog was too thick by then. I just wondered, that's all."

He left her to her sorrow and began to head back up to the Range Rover. He paused at the top of the rise and took one last glance back. On the horizon, a sinister wall of fog was gathering, sitting low over the water. Soon it would begin its slow roll towards the coast, blanketing everything beneath its damp, lightless emptiness. Somewhere out at sea, a fog-horn sounded. It startled him, but the woman didn't seem to hear it. She was staring out at the gathering bank of fog, too. He knew she would wait until it had engulfed the coast completely, sucking all the light from the day. She would let it enfold her in its grey embrace. Because it was then she would feel closest to her son's last moments on this earth, to what he had experienced that day, when he had waited in vain for Domenic Jejeune to save him.

37

At first, the detectives took the man bending over Paulina Kowalski's bed to be a doctor. He was speaking to her in a low voice, but while she was listening attentively, her face was expressionless. The man finished speaking and straightened and they recognized the noble bearing of Teodor Sikorski. He buttoned his immaculate white dinner jacket and approached the men.

"Inspector, Sergeant Maik. You are here to ask questions? Mrs. Kowalski is still weak. I imagine she will not be able to speak for very long."

"I'm sorry to hear about all the damage at Wawel," said Maik sincerely.

Sikorski acknowledged the comment with a grateful smile. "Thank you, Sergeant. Still, it is in adversity that we may find our better selves. Let us hope we can do so now."

"Were you praying with her?" asked Jejeune.

Sikorski bent his head slightly. "Alas, Mrs. Kowalski is not a believer. I was telling her she will continue to receive her pay from Wawel until she is ready to return."

Jejeune looked at Paulina Kowalski. Her thin face was pale, her eyes were dull and unfocused, and her lips were drawn down sadly. She did not look like a woman who'd been given good news.

Maik nodded. "That is very generous of you."

Sikorski made a dismissive gesture with his hand. "She has no other source of income." He nodded to the men formally. "I will leave you to your questions, gentlemen. I will be outside if you need anything. Perhaps with the drugs, she may forget her English. I would be happy to translate, if you wish."

Jejeune rewarded the Count with a smile of gratitude as he left.

A hospital room wasn't likely to offer Jejeune any great walkabout opportunities anyway, but he seemed particularly keen to get on with things. He took a seat beside the bed. Maik remained standing behind him. Paulina Kowalski lay with her thin arms stretched before her, the mottled bruising contrasting with the stark white of the bedsheets. Maik could see similar bruising around the woman's neck. They covered the preliminary inquiries about the patient's health. The one anomaly the doctor had already revealed to them did not need to be discussed here.

"Can you tell us why you called Sergeant Maik?" asked Jejeune, signalling the end of the pleasantries.

"I heard a noise, in the back room." She paused for a raspy breath. "I was afraid. Then I was hit."

"From behind? You didn't see the person who attacked you?" Jejeune's tone was gentle, looking for clarification, nothing more.

"From behind. I was hit. Knocked unconscious."

"But you were near the front door by then."

Another raspy breath filled the silence. But this one had come before the answer. "I tried to escape. I ran." She flapped a flaccid forearm and the yellow-blue patches on her skin rippled slightly. "So many questions."

Perhaps Jejeune did not hear the comment. "This is the third time you have been targeted, Mrs. Kowalski. Do you know who is doing this to you, or why?"

"I do not. I do not. Whatever these people want from me, I do not have it." Her arms moved erratically on the bedcovers. She twisted her neck and Maik saw the necklace of bruising encircling it like purple pearls. She shifted her position in the bed, and then again, searching for comfort. Paulina Kowalski had been through a great deal recently. There was any number of reasons she should become restless and agitated. But the possibility that she was lying had to be among them.

"We found one locker open at Wawel after the fire. Number 17. It was empty. Was this your son's locker?"

Paulina Kowalski didn't answer.

"The lock wasn't forced. There's a key missing from the cabinet. Did you give it to someone?"

"I do not know where this key is." She flapped her mottled forearm again impatiently. "I am tired now. I can remember nothing more about this day."

Maik moved forward. She didn't want to talk about herself anymore, but perhaps there was another subject she'd be willing to discuss. "You said Jakub liked to get money easy ways, but we didn't find any evidence of a police record."

She shook her head feebly. "My son was not a bad person, Sergeant. To be a criminal you must feel the world has been unkind to you. You must feel it owes you something." She swallowed hard and drew in a feathery breath. "Jakub did not feel this way. He was not angry with the world. He just wanted it to give him money."

"There is a possibility that he was involved in something illegal," said Maik. "It may have led to his death."

Her severe expression softened into a weak smile. Maik seemed to have a connection with the woman that Jejeune had never been able to establish. Whatever she had found in this uncompromising, unexpressive man, Paulina Kowalski was ready to respond to it. "You do not have children, either of you?"

Neither man answered.

"When they are young, it is difficult to believe your children have faults. But as they grow older, you must accept that they do. It does not change your love for them." She turned her head slightly to look at Jejeune. "I ask you to leave this inquiry now, Inspector, all of it. You try to find the person who killed Jakub, to uncover bad things he did, it brings his mother only more pain. You cannot bring my son back to me. I only have his memory now. I wish to protect this. Again, I ask you, as a mother, please do not take my son's honour away from me." She looked at both men again, but saved the smile only for Maik. "Now I must sleep. This you must let me do."

Sikorski was sitting on a bench, deep in conversation with the janitor who was mopping the corridor, when the men came out of the room. A noble bearing and easy charm were passports to many worlds, but there was sincerity to Sikorski's geniality that seemed genuine. Jejeune suspected the Count saw it as part of his bargain with life; he would spread his kindliness in return for the rewards and blessings he received from it.

"Mrs. Kowalski was helpful?" asked Sikorski as the janitor departed. It was just the three of them now in the stark, brightly lit hallway. Jejeune sat beside Sikorski on the bench. Maik stood, facing them.

"She's sleeping," said Jejeune. "The doctor tells me Mrs. Kowalski has very high levels of lead in her system. They aren't life-threatening, but they will retard her recovery. Do you have any idea where she might have been exposed to such levels? Did she come from a lead mining area in Poland?"

Sikorski nodded his head knowingly. "Many rural people of her generation have this problem," he said. "They eat only game that has been shot with lead pellets. They clean what they can see, but small flakes remain in the meat. Over time, all this lead they have ingested accumulates in their system." A shadow of sadness passed behind his eyes. "She was not exposed to lead, Inspector. She was exposed to poverty. We cannot escape the trials of our past. They are like our prejudices. No matter where we move, they stay with us."

The noise of a cart rattling across the far end of the corridor made all three men look, but quiet soon returned to the empty hallway.

"The spare key for Jakub Kowalski's locker at Wawel is missing," said Maik. "Mrs. Kowalski didn't have it on her when we found her."

"The centre is in complete disarray at the moment. Perhaps it has been misplaced."

"The keys to all the other padlocks are still in the cabinet."

"I am sorry. I cannot help you."

Jejeune sat for a long moment, his head bowed in thought.

"Did you see anyone unfamiliar around the centre earlier that day, Mr. Sikorski?"

"That day, no." He paused and the detectives waited. "Curtis Angeren was there the day before. He came to tell me our work to remove the Frankenweed was a sham. He said we should all just pack up and go home." Sikorski looked at Jejeune intently. "He did not mean our homes here, Inspector."

"Did he threaten you?" asked Maik.

Sikorski shook his head. "I asked him why he felt so endangered by us. Why could he not accept our presence here? He said he remembered the lessons of the Battle of Maldon."

Sikorski gave Jejeune a small smile. "The sergeant is a military man. But perhaps in Canada they do not teach much Anglo-Saxon history. A ruler called Byrhtnoth had a band of Vikings trapped on a causeway. The tide was coming in. They had no option but to cross onto Byrhtnoth's island one by one. He could easily have put each to the sword as they arrived, but instead he allowed them all safe passage, so they could organize and wage a proper battle." Sikorski looked at Maik, as if a military man might understand the folly of such a move. "The Vikings slaughtered Byrhtnoth and his men, Inspector, every last one of them. Angeren told me it was an important lesson for those who would accommodate foreign hordes."

Maik looked at Jejeune. It might not be a threat, but it was enough to cast the shadow of suspicion on the developer once again.

"You are surprised, perhaps, that I know this story. But the Polish people must be students of history. To remember the past is necessary. It is essential for our survival. Angeren's tale is simply a new way to dress up an old idea. A historical argument, an economic one, even a patriotic one — they all wish the same thing: *samozachowawczy*, self-preservation. As if they were so many White-headed Ducks, with a gene pool under threat from alien invaders."

"I don't think I'd classify Curtis Angeren as a conservationist," said Maik.

Sikorski looked at the sergeant directly. "Perhaps he is not even a xenophobe. He seeks some gain from his intolerance, but there is no commitment there. There is too much calculation in his ways, too much nuance."

"Nevertheless, I can assure you we will be paying him a visit." Maik cast a sideways glance at his DCI for confirmation, but Jejeune simply stood up. "It's late," he said. "I imagine Mrs. Kowalski will sleep through the night now."

"I will stay," said Sikorski simply.

"You plan to be here all night?" asked Maik.

"She has no one else to watch over her," he said. "In the morning someone from the community will come. They will bring food and bathe her," he inclined his head, "if she will permit it."

As he turned to go, Jejeune stopped and looked at the man sitting on the bench. "Why didn't you tell me it was you who alerted Jakub Kowalski that there were Ruddy Ducks at Tidewater Marsh?"

Sikorski gave a soft smile. "I had hoped he might offer to share the bounty with the community. But he made it clear he saw no reason to do this. He had no connection to us, he said. He owed us nothing."

"I imagine you weren't best pleased," said Maik, "especially after you had told him about the birds in the first place."

"Angry enough to kill, Sergeant?" The Count shook his head. "To take a person's life, you must have a compelling reason, I think. Not a triviality like this."

Jejeune looked at Sikorski for a long moment. *But if you did have a compelling reason, you might see it as your duty to make some great, dramatic gesture,* he thought. *Not to do so would almost seem like a betrayal of the pact you had made with the world. And that would be no triviality. That might even be motive.*

38

Tony Holland had been quiet on the drive out, but it was not the contented silence of a man enjoying the spring morning. He'd driven the Audi fast, pushing it hard into corners, shifting aggressively through the gears, his jaw set firm and his eyes locked on the road. Maik knew the events with Des Gill had opened old wounds, memories of a girlfriend who had died in his arms. When he'd learned Gill, too, would now be departing from his life, he had sunk into a brooding surliness, from which he was yet to emerge.

Curtis Angeren was sitting on a stool in the rooftop bar of the clubhouse. He was looking down at the golf course below, rolling a half-filled glass absently between his hands. When the detectives joined him they could see he was watching a bird. A Magpie had emerged from the rough and was hopping along the far edge of the fairway. Its plumage shone blue-black in the bright sunshine, the white patches dazzling in contrast. For all the baggage Magpies had carried down through the ages, Maik doubted there were many more handsome species in the land.

"They shoot them, you know," said Angeren. "Too many of them, they say. English-born and bred yet they call them vermin."

All three men watched the bird for a moment, strutting around, flicking its tail now and then in jaunty defiance of the world and its prejudices.

"Vermin is vermin," said Tony Holland tersely. "No matter where it comes from."

Angeren half-turned, one elbow on the shiny cherrywood bar top, to look at the speaker. "So, who's this bright boy then, Sergeant?" An idea seemed to strike him. "Don't tell me he's the DCI's replacement."

Maik introduced Holland.

"Welcome to Whitehaven, Constable. Would you like a drink?"

"What I'd like is to find out who set the fire at the Polish Centre."

"That place up at Tidewater Marsh?" Angeren looked down into the colourless liquid in his glass and nodded slowly. "Yes, I heard about that. Much damage, was there? Only I know some people who work in demolition. They could tear down the rest of it and haul it away, if you like. They're very good at what they do. Give 'em a couple of days and they could wipe out all traces of that place. Make it seem if it had never been there at all. Guaranteed."

"Two women almost died in that fire," said Holland angrily.

"Neither of them was English, though, right?"

"Des Gill is third generation British, for Christ's sake," shouted Holland. "Her family have been here since the fifties."

"Then I'd say they've been over here long enough, wouldn't you? It's high time they went back where they came from."

"They come from Essex, you moron." He looked at Angeren coldly. "We're going to find out who set that fire, and when we do, I'm going to remind the arrest team that a serving police officer, an innocent woman, was almost killed in it."

His eyes never left Angeren's face, but the other man wasn't rising to the bait. He took a sip from his glass and smiled at the constable. "Oh, I'd hardly imagine she was innocent, Constable Holland. There's not one of us that isn't guilty of something. It's what happens as you grow up. Only the young die good. Isn't that right, Sergeant Maik?" He took another drink. "But perhaps I detect a bit of personal interest here. You might want to think about who you're consorting with, Constable. Doesn't reflect well on your department at all, you hanging about with that type."

Holland made a move towards the bar but Maik eased his body over to block his path. "Paulina Kowalski was left for dead in that fire, Mr. Angeren. We're treating it as attempted murder."

Angeren inclined his head. "Ah, so that's why you're here." He looked between Maik and Holland. "Well, I don't know about you two, but I can't come up with a single motive I might have for wanting to harm Mrs. Kowalski."

"Unfinished business with her son would be one," said Maik. "That day you were so angry with Kowalski. It hasn't come back to you why that was?"

Angeren bunched his fingers at his temple and exploded them outward. "Gone clean out of my mind."

"So you hadn't heard he was up to anything illegal?"

Angeren looked intently at the sergeant, as if studying his features for clues. But Maik had spent a lifetime making sure his expressions revealed only what he wanted them to, and after a moment, the developer gave up. "I hear a lot of things in my line of work, Sergeant. Some of them are even true. But I can't say I ever heard a small-time chancer like Kowalski was involved in anything major around these parts. Can I ask what particular enterprise we might be talking about?"

Maik seemed content to let the awkward silence between the men go on indefinitely. Angeren held up a hand. "Official police business. I understand. No offence taken." He looked down onto the golf course again. "Pity you never took up the game, Sergeant. You'd probably get some decent distance on your drives with that upper body strength of yours. If you ever fancied a try, I could arrange a few lessons for you. On the house. Not your chirpy friend here, though. I'm afraid the constable would have to pay full whack." He turned to look directly at Holland. "That's the way it is, see — when you own the place, you can always find a way to discriminate if you want to."

"I hear you were up at Tidewater Marsh recently," said Maik, his tone offering Holland a textbook example of how to ignore a comment completely, "giving Teodor Sikorski a history lesson."

"Invasive species control, that's what they're supposed to be working on up there, according to him. As far as I can see, it's just some make-work project to help out a bunch of foreigners."

"It's hardly make-work," said Maik. "More like back-breaking labour."

Angeren was shaking his head to reject the words before Maik had finished speaking them. "The government have already admitted they're never going to be able to get rid of all the Japanese knotweed in this country. So why pay this geezer and his mates to remove it, when they know it won't do any good in the long run?"

"It's a particularly dangerous hybrid species, as I understand it. It has the potential to do a lot of damage."

"It's charity is what it is," said Angeren. "A handout for a bunch of people who shouldn't even be here. Two billion pounds a year. That's what the government pisses away on schemes to control invasives. You know how you get rid of unwanted intruders once and for all? Burn 'em out. A scorched earth policy, that's what's called for." He looked at Holland and gave him a cold smile. "You can tell that foreign lady friend of yours I said so, too, if you like."

This time, Holland made it to the bar. His reflection in the polished wood surface was less than a hand's span from Angeren's. "I don't like you," he said, looking into the developer's face. "I don't like your views, or what you stand for, or your slimy, pretend respectability. And that's bad news for you. I don't know what kind of deal you've got going with Jejeune, but for whatever reason, he seems inclined to give you a free pass on everything that's been going on around here. But you won't get one from me. And that's a promise."

"I imagine we should be checking in with the station," said Maik, leaning into a space between the men that hadn't been there before. "Just to see if any new information has come in." He fixed Holland with a stare. "I wonder, Constable, can I ask you to take care of that, while I just wrap things up here with Mr. Angeren?"

The two men watched Holland's angry departure in silence.

"You're going to have to rein that one in, Sergeant. A bit too much enthusiasm for his own good."

"I like him the way he is. For one thing, he's got very good instincts."

"You know, another man could take some of the comments today as threats. I happen to know DCS Shepherd frowns upon that sort of thing. Still, one man's word against another. I daresay an official complaint wouldn't go very far." Angeren looked down to the golf course. The Magpie was still there, gleaning insects and seeds from the ground.

"A nation of Magpies, that's what we've been reduced to these days," said Angeren bitterly, "through the attitudes of people like your young friend. Grab a bit of tat from this culture, a bit of dross from that one, and what have you got? A pile of crap all cobbled together in the name of *inclusiveness*. Well, to my mind, there's still a lot to be said for exclusiveness."

Maik's look told Angeren he'd heard just about all the philosophical discourses he wanted to for today. "You're interested in this arrangement the inspector and I are supposed to have. I can assure you, Sergeant, I have no idea what Constable Holland is talking about. I do know DCI Jejeune is not interested in any gentleman's agreement to exchange information. I have to say I'm surprised. I'd have thought any plans Ray Hayes might have, imminent or otherwise, would have been of interest to him. But there you are. If he's choosing to do me any special favours around the station now, I can only assume it's because he's seen the error of his ways in having suspected me in the first place."

Angeren reached behind the bar and grabbed a bottle of gin to top up his drink. He didn't offer to pour one for Maik. "Must be hard for somebody like you to see what's going on in this country, a man who's served with such bravery and distinction." Angeren raised his glass. "Your service is appreciated by some, Sergeant, even though I'm sure it doesn't feel like many people care these days."

Maik eyed him warily. The appreciation of a man like Curtis Angeren wasn't really at the forefront of his thoughts when he was doing his military service.

"The thing is, Sergeant, there's still battles to be fought. If it ever crossed your mind that you'd like to continue what you started in the army — protecting our values and keeping our way of life safe from those who'd try to take it from us — I just want you to know, there'd always be a place for you in my organization."

Maik doubted he could have looked more surprised if Angeren had proposed marriage. Surely he must know how fiercely Danny opposed his beliefs. But perhaps it didn't matter. Perhaps there was space on Angeren's exclusiveness ark for non-believers, too, for dependable police sergeants and

Canadians whose jobs couldn't be done by dull-witted natives. As long as you had a purpose, a value to Curtis Angeren, you were considered worthwhile. Nevertheless, Maik felt shamed by the invitation, stained by it, as if perhaps he hadn't done enough to openly declare his opposition to the man and his repugnant views, as Tony Holland had. The feeling stayed with him as he made his way down the stairs from the rooftop bar towards the waiting Audi.

39

L indy dropped the keys to the Range Rover in the basket by the front door as she came in. "Thanks for letting me borrow The Beast," she called out. "But I'll be glad when I can get my own car back. You tell Danny Maik he's got a lot to answer for, destroying my lovely little Leaf just to save the lives of a couple of women. Damned cheek."

She went through to the kitchen and made herself a mug of tea. She'd unilaterally declared herself off alcohol a couple of nights ago, and waited in silence until Domenic had agreed to join her. Tea was their drink of choice now, but he couldn't drink it in the quantities she could. A couple of cups a day was his limit, and she was sure he'd already had those.

She stood for a moment in the kitchen, stirring her tea, staring down into it thoughtfully. She'd been intending to discuss their trip to Canada with Dom tonight, to see if she could get some sort of commitment from him. She had told herself he was busy, that she just needed to be patient, even if she knew patience was really just procrastination without the guilt. But if he didn't say something soon, she was going to have to confront him about it. *So are we going to Canada, or not?* But after the events of today, Canada would have to go on the back burner for a bit.

* * *

Lindy came into the living room carrying her tea and stood opposite Jejeune, who was reading a file on his laptop. "Shepherd hasn't said anything to you about Eric getting a bang on the head recently, has she?"

"No." Normally, Jejeune would have looked up at such a surprising question from Lindy, but he kept his eyes on the file he was reading.

"I think he might be going *gaga*, quite literally."

Jejeune realized no matter how much he wanted to avoid eye contact with Lindy just now, not to raise his head at such an alarming statement would seem suspicious, to say the least.

She took a sip of her tea. "He was ranting on at us about security this morning. He said the last one out on Friday failed to set the alarm. According to him, when he went by later that night, the alarm was off."

Jejeune held his gaze as steady as possible, a task made more difficult by Lindy's unblinking stare.

"That was me, Dom. *I* was last one out on Friday night. And I know full well I armed it. It's like a ritual with us now. Since that spate of break-ins on the High Street last year, we've been expecting to get turned over any day."

"For what? That secret collection of chocolate biscuits you keep in your desk?" He had hoped it might be enough to nudge her off track, but in reality he knew a Lindy affronted was a Lindy unlikely to be deflected by such fluff.

"For your information, there's a lot of sensitive material in our offices: contacts, sources, research documents we're working on. And if any of it ever went missing, we'd have no chance of getting it back. The police round here are bloody useless."

She set her tea down and started searching for something in her purse. Jejeune was still sitting, looking at her. Somehow he still felt to do anything else might alert her to his tension. Besides, it seemed likely that this was simply venting. He settled slightly to the idea of letting Lindy's frustration burn itself out. He'd even help.

"Did you tell Eric you were the last one out?"

Lindy nodded. "I assured him he was mistaken. Quite emphatically, as a matter of fact," she said, allowing herself a small smile at the memory. "But he still kept on giving me the evil eye all morning. Worse still, he turned his anger on that new intern we've taken on. *Why can't she file properly? Doesn't she know what order the letters are supposed to come in?* The poor kid was devastated, and with good reason. I've never seen anybody so meticulous. She could work for Mansfield Jones, for God's sake. If it came to a contest between her filing and Eric's grasp of the alphabet, I know where I'd put my money. Like I said, he seems to be losing it. I'm actually a bit worried about him."

"He's probably just got a lot on his mind at the moment," said Jejeune. "Work things." He needed to straddle a dangerous line here. It was important Lindy didn't harbour any genuine fears for Eric's mental health. Their relationship was important to her, and she would be truly worried if she felt he was showing signs of instability. On the other hand, he could hardly reassure her that Eric's faculties were fine, without revealing exactly how he knew. The alarm *had* been off when Eric entered the offices on Friday night. It was Jejeune who had disarmed it. And while he couldn't speak to Eric's knowledge of the alphabet, there was a good chance the files were out of order because Jejeune may well have misfiled them in his haste to replace them as Eric entered the office.

"What was he doing in the office after hours anyway?" It seemed a reasonable question, one that somebody innocent might ask.

"How should I know?" asked Lindy, resuming her rummage through her purse. "Probably installing spyware so he can track the porn sites we visit. Poor Emma. *Hot Boyz in Thongz* is one of her favourites. She'll be devastated if Eric blocks it." She was smiling as she raised her head. "Relax, Dom, I'm joking. You know you'll always be my number one hot boy, thong or no thong." She became serious again. "Do you really think it's just work? He's been acting strangely for a couple of days now, guarded, not at all like his normal self. I do hope there's no problems between him and Shepherd. He seems so happy. They both do."

Once again, Jejeune was trapped. If there were no problems between their bosses, there almost certainly would be very soon. But they were not of the kind Lindy meant. He was as sure as he could be that they still cared for each other, perhaps even more so now such a major threat hovered over their relationship. He couldn't find it in himself to shut her out any longer.

"You remember that talk we had? The one about you having qualities that have always impressed Eric?"

"Like my Polish folk dancing, you mean?" Flippancy was often Lindy's safety net when she was becoming unnerved by the direction of the conversation. She abandoned her purse search for good and took another sip of her tea.

"Like your professionalism, your journalistic integrity. Eric actually said that, didn't he, when he hired you?"

"Darn that memory of yours," said Lindy, colouring slightly. "Had you not plied me with alcohol that night, I'd never have told you something like that."

"I seem to remember you were fairly well plied by the time you came home," said Domenic simply. "But he was right, Lindy. You would never falsify a story, or manipulate someone to get one."

"Where's this coming from, Dom? Is there a point to all this? If you're working up to asking me for money, I'm afraid you're out of luck until payday."

But he couldn't let it go now. He'd come too far. "The thing is, it's always seemed to me that the qualities people admire most in others are the ones they lack themselves."

Lindy paused with her mug to her lips. She brought up her other hand to hold it also. "Dom, you can't be suggesting what it sounds like. I'm having trouble finding a way to tell you this, dear, but, *erm*, you're wrong. I know it must come as a bit of a shock. Do you want to lie down? Perhaps I should bring you some smelling salts." Her tone was playful, but she looked at him over the top of her steaming mug as she sipped her tea, just to make sure he got the message. She waited a moment to see if he was going to say anything, but he stayed silent. "Come on, Dom," she said reasonably, "you can't seriously believe Eric would ever be involved in anything illegal, even to get such a great story as the Vincent Canby confession."

At this point, Domenic Jejeune wasn't sure if he seriously believed it or not. But he knew DCS Colleen Shepherd did.

"Of all the journalists covering that case, Eric was the one Vincent Canby called in to hear his dying confession, Lindy. The only one."

"I told you. Eric must have built up a rapport with him. He'd earned his trust."

"I'm not sure how he would have done that. They'd never met."

There was a long silence. Lindy set her mug down gently on the table and waited until her face found the expression she wanted. "I know Eric fairly well, Dom, and I know a lot of people who know him even better. There has never been a whisper from any of them about any improper conduct. None. Ever. Do you hear what I'm saying?"

He knew from experience that Lindy's repertoire when she was angry could include a fair amount of pyrotechnics. It was only when she was afraid that she got so calm and reasonable. But he'd done what he could now. She had not been receptive to what he was saying, but it would be important later that he had once brought up the subject. Not much would bring Lindy any comfort when things unravelled, but it would help a little for her to know he had at least tried.

40

"It's not bad, this one," said Holland, as he crossed the room and approached Maik's desk. "So who's this, then?"

While he wasn't exactly taken in by Holland's sudden interest in Martha Reeves and the Vandellas, Maik indulged him and provided the information anyway. When the constable sidled up to a topic this way, it invariably meant the real one wasn't going to be much to Maik's liking. Holland lifted a pencil from the desk and absently twirled it around with his fingertips. Maik had no more information to offer about the music drifting between them, but Holland seemed reluctant to move on. The two of them had engaged in similar standoffs a number of times, and both knew what came next. This time, though, Maik got the sense it would be something beyond the usual request to overlook one of Holland's transgressions. For one thing, the constable's interest in "Nowhere to Run" had started the moment Domenic Jejeune left the room. For another, Holland had left a long, trailing look on the DCI as he departed.

"Des was on to something, Sarge, before they stopped her investigation. And I think the DCI knew it. Did you ever notice how jumpy he seemed around her? His eyes never left her when she was in the room; no looking out the window for birds, like when we're talking to him. He was always just lasered on to her. He closed the physical distance, too, any chance he got, as if he wanted to be close enough to intercept her, if she started taking a conversation somewhere he didn't like."

Maik wondered if Holland realized just how much he'd learned from his DCI over the years. He raised a cautioning hand. "Before we go any further," he said carefully, "you might want to have a think about this. Because whatever it is, there can be no rolling it back once it's started. You know that."

Holland didn't spend much time without some sort of smile on his face. His serious expression now suggested he'd already spent all the time thinking about it he needed to. "A corvid — that's a bird family, you know, Crows, Jays, like that. And Magpies."

Maik had been prepared for the conversation to go in a number of directions, though perhaps not this one. He let his surprise show, but he didn't say anything. Holland was holding all the conversational cards at the moment and Maik was content to let him play them as he chose.

"Des said she'd been talking to somebody about a corvid. I thought she was joking, but she wasn't. Only she didn't go to Mansfield Jones, or some other wonk in the police department, where there might be some official record of her inquiry. She went to Quentin Senior."

"You spoke to him?"

"A casual chat. No alarm bells."

Maik couldn't imagine how Holland could engineer a casual conversation with such an unlikely partner as the leading bird expert in Saltmarsh. But for reasons he couldn't have explained, he found himself prepared to take Holland at his word.

"She wanted to know about Magpie behaviour," said Holland, "like whether one would be likely to move around much in a strong wind. You know, say the kind you might get coming in off the sea. Senior's opinion is that it'd likely hunker down and stay put. Apparently, they're not very strong flyers."

Maik waited. Des hadn't struck him as the birding type, but her questions could just have been a way to find another connection with a DCI she so obviously admired. Only Holland was a good police officer, and he would have already considered that possibility. So there would be more. Martha Reeves had reached the end of her quest for somewhere to hide now, and Maik waited as the silence built between the two men.

"She timed the run we made that day, when we went down to the Essex coast. She tried to disguise it, but I mean, with Big Ben on her wrist, you'd have to have been half blind not to notice. That's the reason we went on this otherwise meaning-less detour to the Met."

"Meaningless?"

"We pulled into the car park and she was in and out of the building within five minutes. No bag, no laptop, no papers. She couldn't possibly have had time to say more than a quick hello to anybody, let alone a serious chat about anything."

"I take it she didn't tell you why she wanted to stop there?"

He shook his head. "No, but I think I know. It was because the Met was a starting point for a journey she needed to retrace. From the third-floor office of Sergeant Domenic Jejeune out to Lonely Oak Point."

The name hadn't meant anything to Holland at the time, but he could see it did to Maik. He saw the recognition flicker in his sergeant's eyes, but he drove the point home anyway. "It's where he saw his bird, Sarge, this Magpie thing."

Maik spent a long time looking at the constable, though Holland had the impression Danny would have continued staring at the same space even if he had got up and walked away. The safe haven of his Motown songs seemed a long way off now. When Maik finally spoke, his voice was as empty as Holland had ever heard it.

"Tell me what you know."

"You know why it all fell apart between Jejeune and his ex-boss, Laraby, right?"

Maik didn't think Holland was fishing. He was fairly sure the constable had the whole picture by now. But he would let him tell him anyway. Holland had drawn up a chair and was sitting beside Maik. He had a blank notepad in front him to diagram his points.

"Jejeune had come up with a way to pinpoint the hostages' location, only it would take a lot of calculations. I don't know, but I'm guessing it had to do with the triangulation of sounds." He paused, but Maik wasn't offering anything. "Anyway, the answers came back from the lab at eight o'clock in the morning and Laraby said he went directly into Jejeune's office to tell him they had their location, but Jejeune wasn't there. He claimed Jejeune had already buggered off to try to find this bird, and that's why everything went pear-shaped on Foulness Island later, because nobody knew where he'd got to, and they couldn't reach him by phone. Only, Jejeune insisted he was still in the office at the time Laraby said he'd come by, and for a good fifteen minutes after. The inference was that Laraby must have sat on the information, probably just as a way to try and screw Jejeune over a bit, and when he finally did take it over and found Jejeune had gone, he decided to lie about it to cover his own arse."

Maik nodded. "The thinking being, Laraby was trying to make Jejeune's life difficult because he was still angry about the way he had been bumped off the negotiations with the kidnapper in favour of a junior officer?"

"His protégé at that," said Holland. "Nobody ever said as much, but yeah, that's the way the brass must have seen it. In fact, the only way Laraby was able to save his career was because he was the one who brought in Canby's deathbed confession. Anyway, the thing is, the first info on this bird is supposed to have been posted at seven thiry-nine." Holland made a face. "Not a quarter to, you'll note, or half past: seven thiry-nine. That's the thing with these birder types, see, they're obsessed with details. I mean, you and me, we see some bird in a tree and that's what we'd say, if we bothered to mention it at all. But with this lot it's *found at seven thiry-nine GMT, in a mature oak tree, grid reference so and so, winds south to southwest, barometer descending.* I'm surprised they don't throw in the shipping forecast."

Maik's look encouraged Holland to get on with it.

"The upside for us is that we have an exact timeline to work with. At 7:39 some geezer posts a photo on his Facebook account of some strange bird he's seen while he was strolling on the clifftop earlier that morning. He's not a birder, and he has no real interest in them, but he decides he'll ask around anyway. *Anybody know what this is? I just saw it at Lonely Oak Point.* Somebody shares it and it finds its way onto Jejeune's page. And, of course, he knows right off what it is: Iberian Azure-winged Magpie. So off he goes to find it, which he duly does. And he's already there and on hand to point it out to a few other people when they show up. But here's where things get a bit sticky. We can't know for sure when he saw the Facebook photo for the first time. He claims it was at 8:15, which is when he left to drive out and take a look for the bird. But really, he could have seen the photo and left the office well before that."

Maik bowed his head thoughtfully. Holland knew his sergeant recognized this wasn't just him having a go at Jejeune personally. It was where the facts led them.

When Maik spoke, it showed him that the sergeant was following along just fine. "I suppose these wonderful records the birders have tell us when it was last sighted?"

"At 9:09. Three people in the group saw it flying away, an hour and a half after it was first reported."

"Lasted about as long as a Norwich City cup run, then."

But for once, it was Holland pointedly ignoring the humour and wanting to get on with things. "That's fifty-four minutes after Jejeune says he saw the photo on his Facebook page." He leaned forward and pulled up a map on Maik's laptop. "These are the directions posted on the rare bird sightings page that day, for people coming from London. There's absolutely no doubt it's the fastest route. These guys were in a serious hurry to get out there. Somebody even phoned the MoD to see if they could get permission to cross their lands, but it was denied. The range was closed for military exercises."

Maik traced the route on the screen. East on the A13, turn off at the sign for Wakering, down along the coast road, and then a long swing back north again and out to Lonely Oak Point.

"Des and I followed that route that day, Sarge. The run took us exactly one hour and fifteen minutes. She didn't set any land-speed records, but she didn't exactly dawdle either. She knows how to handle that MGB. Now as a copper, Jejeune is aware of the dangers of high-speed driving through populated areas, but let's give him the benefit of the doubt. These birders are one finch short of a flock at the best of times. For the chance to see a life-timer, or whatever they call them, we can assume he's going to get a bit of a wriggle on. So say we shave ten minutes off Des's time, down to an hour five."

"It's a tricky business, judging road travel times," said Maik. "There can be lots of variables — road conditions, repairs, weather."

Holland looked at his sergeant, understanding his resistance, expecting it even. He waited, not wanting to tell Maik,
not wanting to have to. But Maik wouldn't cross the distance
to him. "I did the run myself, Sarge. In the Audi, full on, top
end, a clear run all the way." He paused to give the sergeant one
more chance not to make him tell him. But Maik didn't take it.
"Fifty-nine minutes. I'd be prepared to say that drive couldn't
be done faster than that. Certainly not by somebody driving a
Range Rover."

The silence was as profound as any Holland could ever
remember in this room. It seemed so deep, so infinite; he
could have believed it would go on forever. He'd sensed the
reluctance from the beginning, the pulling back from the
information instead of leaning into it, searching for the details,
the way Danny Maik usually did. But as the sergeant looked
at him now, with his eyes holding all the sadness of one of his
Motown songs, Holland could see that he accepted the truth.
Whatever the young sergeant may have claimed in his official
statement, by the time Marvin Laraby came in at eight o'clock
that morning to bring him the information about the kidnap
location, Domenic Jejeune's office was already empty.

41

D omenic Jejeune entered the cafeteria and spotted Mansfield
Jones immediately. He was sitting alone at a corner table,
with his back to the room, staring out the window. Outside, a
small pond had been set up in an effort to beautify a vacant
patch of ground behind the station, but its maintenance had
long been neglected, and now only a sord of Mallards drifted
through the dense mats of New Zealand pigmyweed that coated
the surface of the water.

Jejeune approached the table and hovered over the plastic
chair opposite the M.E. Protocol required him to ask if it was
being reserved for anyone, but in reality there was little chance
that it was. Jones offered it with an outstretched hand.

"I was just watching these ducks," he said as Jejeune took a
seat. "Trying to see what makes birds so endlessly fascinating for
some people." He didn't say if he was being successful, but from
his tone, Jejeune suspected not. He leaned back in the plastic
chair and craned around for another look at the Mallards. On the
grass surrounding the pond, a quarrel of House Sparrows was
bouncing around, picking at seeds. Jejeune checked to be sure
that there were no Tree Sparrows amongst them. There weren't.

"There is no requirement to report a sighting of these particular ducks, I take it?"

Jejeune snapped his head around to find Jones with a faint smile on his lips. "A police station is no place to try to keep secrets, Inspector. These Ruddy Ducks bring all the usual ails of invasive species, I suppose? Outcompeting the native ducks for resources — food, breeding territories, habitat?"

Jejeune shook his head. "That isn't why the government is trying to exterminate them. It's being done to protect the genetic purity of the White-headed Duck population. Ruddy Ducks are cross-breeding with them to the extent that it's feared pure White-headed Ducks might disappear altogether, leaving only hybrids."

"This hybridization, is it easy to spot in birds?"

"In this case, only through plumage characteristics and beak shape. But it can vary in other species. Hybridization between the Blue-winged Warbler and the Golden-winged Warbler back home in Canada couldn't be more diagnostic. On the other hand, between some species it is only detectable at the genetic level."

"Deception sets its own rules," said Jones simply. "It's what makes the pursuit of truth so treacherous."

Jejeune watched as the M.E. shuffled a puce-coloured mix of unidentifiable ingredients around his plate with his fork. He wondered if it was the sickly yellow light from above that made it look so unappealing. Jones noticed his stare. "Vegetarian ragout," he said. "It's the healthiest choice on offer in here."

It may well have been, but for Jejeune it helped if food at least appeared edible. He would freely admit he wasn't the best cook in the world. Lindy said she could never be sure whether the feeling she got after eating one of his meals was indigestion or survivor guilt. But at least his creations looked faintly appetizing. If this was what Jones ate on a daily basis, it went a long way to explaining his undernourished appearance.

And yet, as Jejeune had recently learned, even foods that looked okay could pose hazards.

"I'm told that people who eat game birds killed with lead shot have much higher lead levels in their body," he said conversationally.

Jones looked up, letting some of the greenish puree drip from his fork. "Surely the shot is removed when the bird is dressed?"

"Anything visible is, yes. But microscopic flakes remain, and it's these that are ingested. How significant would the health problems be from something like that?"

Jones laid his fork down again and pushed away his plate, apparently unable to find sufficient comfort in the health benefits of the ragout to overcome his gag reflex. "Lead is a systemic toxin. Exactly how a small continuous intake might impact the body, I couldn't say without further research, but any excessive intake of lead is unequivocally going to be detrimental to a person's health."

"Permanently detrimental?"

"I don't know." Though he hadn't worked with Jejeune for very long, Jones had already come to appreciate that the detective was unlikely to seek someone out in the police cafeteria to introduce a topic of conversation unless it was significant in some way. "I'll look into it." He looked at the detective frankly. "I'm told that you are struggling with this case, Inspector. And I'm told that this is my fault, because I am failing to confirm the necessary facts. But I suspect facts would not help you quite as much as other people may think."

Jejeune regarded Mansfield Jones carefully. In the fluorescent light, the M.E.'s skin had taken on an even more unhealthy pallor than usual. He was right in the wrong way, as Lindy sometimes said. It was not the missing facts that were troubling Jejeune. It was those he already had.

"You no longer have any doubt, do you, Dr. Jones, that the person in your morgue, the body, is Jakub Kowalski?"

Jones pushed his plate off to one side so he could set his arms on the table. He leaned forward slightly. "Dental records are as reliable as DNA, Inspector. The dental profession is aware that records may be called upon to identify a body, as in this case. As a consequence, they are among the most meticulously kept of all medical records. There are a number of regulations and protocols in place which cover the storage, transfer, and release of records, making it extremely difficult to tamper with them. Cosmetic work could re-create someone else's current chart, but the remaining teeth would still reveal the person's previous dental history. I checked the teeth of the corpse in my mortuary against the chart of Jakub Kowalski. It matches. I also checked with the dentists who were listed on the charts, and they verified they had performed what little work Mr. Kowalski had done, on the dates noted. It was Mr. Kowalski's body that was burned in that pit, Inspector. Of that, I no longer have any doubt."

Jejeune was silent for a moment, considering the M.E.'s words.

"I presume this helps," said Jones eventually.

Jejeune looked up at the man and smiled. How to tell him that, for once, certainty was no help at all? Because all the facts he had, all he was now certain of, made no sense. They didn't fit into any pattern of human behaviour he had ever come across. Truths he was once utterly convinced of seemed to be disintegrating around him. His solution must be wrong, though he didn't see how it could be. It was the only explanation for what had happened, the only thing that fit. Mansfield Jones's infallible facts and Jejeune's evidence now all pointed in the same single direction. If the M.E.'s axiom was that facts would lead you to the truth, then Jejeune was already there.

Because he knew now that he had seen certainty before, somewhere it should not have been, in the eyes of someone who should have welcomed doubt. And certainty like that could come from only one place.

"I suppose the compulsion is always to search for new species."

Jejeune realized he'd been staring out the window, and Jones thought he was watching the birds. He smiled at the man's question. There was no cynicism in it, no hint of sarcasm, only the genuine curiosity of someone trying to understand the rules.

"But I wonder if chasing after birds is such a wise strategy. I suspect there may be an argument for staying in one spot."

Perhaps, thought Jejeune. Perhaps if you waited long enough, the birds, like the truth, would eventually find you.

Jones stared out at the duck pond. "I am always intrigued by the idea that something can be so utterly absorbing for some people and hold so little interest for others. Not just birding, of course, I'm sure it's true of all pastimes."

It was the observation of an outsider, thought Jejeune, a stranger to the world of hobbies and recreational activities. There was an eternity of sadness for him in the knowledge that somebody could have no refuge in their lives beyond their work, nowhere to retreat to during those times when there didn't seem to be very much left in your daily life to hold on to.

Jejeune left Mansfield Jones staring out the window. He wondered if it was the man's quest for unequivocal truths, in people as well as pastimes, which left him eating unappealing food alone in the corner of a sterile police cafeteria.

42

Maik saw Tony Holland gaze at the desk vacated by Gill, now cleared of her files and her laptop. As promised, she hadn't disturbed much of Lauren Salter's stuff, but had merely shoved it off to the perimeter. But the strange emptiness in the centre of the desk seemed to mesmerize the constable. Gill had drifted into his life and out of it again and left nothing but empty space behind. Space and longing. Maik's own thoughts turned to the usual occupant of the desk. He missed Salter's stories — about her life, her time with her son, Max. But more, he missed *her*, so often the only hand stretching out to him across the wasteland of human loneliness.

He pulled himself together and looked over the room. He'd decoded most of the secrets he'd seen in here before, but one person still held hers. Off to the side, he watched as DCS Shepherd ran her fingers through her hair and passed her palms over her thighs to smooth out her skirt. She was doing her best to project her normal, efficient, measured self. But a room full of detectives was no place to be trying to hide things, and the signs were there to observant viewers. Maik saw the slightly drawn cheeks and the crow's feet at the corners of her eyes, where the unevenly applied makeup had missed. It was the look of someone who hadn't been getting a lot of sleep lately, and who spent most of their waking hours gnawing on something troubling. But Maik saw something else in it, too. It was that special look of concern that lacked any sense of self. It was the look a parent gets when a child is ill, or a spouse when their partner is distressed.

"I take it there's no question Jakub Kowalski's murder and this fire are related?" she said to the room at large.

"Related, or connected?"

"It's a simple enough question, Domenic," said Shepherd angrily. "You're getting as bad as Mansfield Jones, for God's sake. Is there any chance I might, one day, receive a simple, direct answer to a question?" She was shouting now, frustrated at Jejeune's evasion. And perhaps at other things, too.

Which is why the target of her wrath looked less affected by it than anyone else. Though the others were shocked at Shepherd's sudden rise to anger, Jejeune understood the reason. Shepherd had missed no opportunity to make eye contact with him over the past few days — in meetings, at briefings, passing in a corridor. On every occasion, Jejeune had met her gaze head on, but he had never provided her with that glimmer of reassurance, that faint nod or look she so desperately sought. She knew Jejeune must have completed his inquiries by now. Whatever he had uncovered, it was preventing him from silently telling her that he had looked into Eric's practices and everything was okay. And that meant it wasn't.

"The two incidents are connected," said Jejeune evenly, "but they were not committed by the same person."

"I see. Thank you." Shepherd had recovered from her outburst, but she was not apologetic.

"Whether he committed them, or not, surely the same person is behind them both?" said Maik. "Curtis Angeren's shadow is all over this attack on Paulina Kowalski. He was up at Wawel the day before."

"Was he? I wasn't aware we'd checked on that?"

"Is there any particular reason you thought Sikorski might have lied about that, Domenic?" asked Shepherd, puzzled.

"He was talking to Paulina Kowalski when we arrived at the hospital," said Jejeune. "He claimed he was offering her assistance, but she didn't seem particularly happy to have him at her bedside."

"His concern for her looked sincere enough to me," said Maik, tilting his head slightly as if to bring his DCI, or perhaps his motives, into better focus.

"Sikorski was speaking Polish. We have no idea what he was saying. For all we know, he could have been threatening her to keep quiet about something else." Shepherd wasn't sure whether Jejeune had bristled at Maik's tone, or the fact that he had gone to see Angeren behind his back. But she doubted Maik's current expression was going to do much to ease the situation. It was the one the sergeant used on suspects sometimes; the ones he didn't quite trust. "Surely, you're not trying to suggest Sikorski deliberately set the fire himself?"

Shepherd watched the exchange with astonishment. The two men had blithely dismissed each other's ideas with a brusqueness that bordered on contempt. Their rift couldn't be over something as petty as the damage to Lindy's car, could it?

"In case you're wondering, Domenic, I can confirm the department is prepared to cover all expenses for the repairs to Lindy's vehicle. Just have her submit the bills when the work is completed." She paused for a moment to see if the news had thawed the relationship between the two men. If it had, there were no outward signs. But there were developments with the case that needed discussing, regardless.

"Sorted?" Shepherd nodded. "Good. We move on," she said decisively. "I think perhaps what Inspector Jejeune is trying to point out is that even if Angeren was at Wawel the day before, that doesn't necessarily tie him in to this incident, Sergeant."

Maik looked at Holland. "When DC Gill dragged Paulina Kowalski from the community centre, did she use the standard lift?"

"Under the shoulders from behind." Holland looked at Maik as if to question why the sergeant would ask for confirmation he didn't really need.

"So you're sure she didn't grab her by the arms to pull her."

"There's no way a small woman ..." Holland looked at Shepherd, "person like that would be able to drag a full-grown adult through that gap."

Maik nodded, his point confirmed. "Paulina Kowalski claims she was hit from behind, but she has some fairly severe bruising around her neck and on her forearms. I think somebody grabbed her and forced her to go somewhere with them."

"Somewhere?" asked Shepherd.

"The lockers. I think she was forced to show someone where her son's locker was. That's why the key is missing."

"What would they want from Jakub Kowalski's locker?"

"The same thing they were looking for at Paulina Kowalski's house. Electronics — things that hold data on those illegal immigrants her son was bringing in, the ones whose records she was likely processing for him."

"Then why won't she identify Angeren as her attacker?" asked Jejeune sharply. "It seems unlikely, to say the least, that the woman would protect the man who killed her son. That locker was opened with a key, a key any number of other people at Wawel had access to." He shook his head. "Angeren might be tied to this in some way, but he didn't kill Jakub Kowalski. The last time anyone saw Kowalski was on the Tuesday evening at Tidewater Marsh. Teodor Sikorski said he saw him there looking for the ducks when he left for the day. It seems a reasonable assumption Kowalski was killed later that night."

"Reasonable to who?" asked Holland. "Jones can't give us

time of death, only the approximate time the body was set on fire. The window is any time between that and the last time Kowalski was seen alive."

Jejeune nodded in Holland's direction, as if acknowledging that the point was valid. "Kowalski didn't find the ducks he was looking for. I'm sure I saw the same birds recently. But he was killed with the same kind of ammunition he used to shoot Ruddy Ducks. It suggests he hadn't had time to unload the gun by the time it was used to kill him."

"And you think whoever killed Kowalski must have been able to take a loaded weapon off him and get behind him," said Shepherd, drawing her expression into something approaching approval.

Jejeune nodded. "Most people wouldn't let that happen unless they trusted the person. I doubt that either Curtis Angeren or any of his men would have fallen into that category."

"Unless Jones is right, after all," said Holland. "Kowalski could have been dead, or disabled, before he was shot."

Shepherd looked ashen at the prospect that she may have to tell Jones his ultra-cautious approach had been justified. She might have expected Danny Maik to step in as her champion against Jones's madness, anyway, but the fact that it once again gave him the opportunity to directly contradict his DCI's point seemed to encourage him all the more.

"I doubt Kowalski's gun would have been loaded," said Maik. "Carrying a loaded Brno CZ over the kind of uneven ground they have up at Tidewater Marsh would be a good way to lose a lot of blood. That's a big risk, just because you were too lazy to load the gun at your kill zone."

"Surely duck hunters pre-load," said Jejeune quickly. "They don't wait for the birds to take flight before putting in their shells."

"Kowalski was a marksman. His approach would be more

like that of a sniper. You choose your spot, sight your target, then load. At least, that's the way I'd go about it."

Maik's flat tone suggested no hint of regret at having thoroughly undermined his DCI's theory. Shepherd looked from one man to the other and then back again before leaving her gaze somewhere in between. She knew this was not about car repairs, and never had been. Something much more personal was going on, and whatever it was, she knew it wasn't good for the case. Or the station.

The meeting had concluded without either man conceding any ground. Indeed, neither had offered any further contribution at all, forcing Shepherd to declare an awkward end to the briefing. For his own part, Jejeune was puzzled by the morning's turn of events. But he remained unmoved. Whatever the reason was that Maik had suddenly begun finding fault with his theories, the main point of his argument hadn't gone away. Ignoring the M.E.'s nonsense about Kowalski being dead or disabled first, the victim had allowed someone to take a loaded weapon from him and circle behind him. Even if Maik was right, and the weapon hadn't been loaded, it meant someone had removed ammunition from Kowalski's pocket and loaded the rifle before shooting him, presumably while he stood there and watched them. Neither scenario made any sense. Or rather, they both only made sense in the same way, the one Jejeune was now slowly and reluctantly being drawn towards.

43

Jejeune guided the Range Rover carefully up the steep side of the berm and parked on the top. Before him, the still waters of Tidewater Estuary spread out like glass. Lindy hopped out of The Beast and marched towards the door of Wawel, bending to examine the twisted metal grille hanging from its hinges. "So this is where that sergeant of yours held his demolition derby with my little car?" she said. But her voice held no anger. "It really did save their lives, didn't it?"

"That and the Frankenweed."

Lindy examined the twisted grille again, more closely this time. "It must be formidable stuff to bend metal this thick. God help up us if it ever becomes established out here."

"And this, of course, is what we have been working to prevent," said Sikorski from the doorway. "Welcome, both of you. I trust you have forgiven me, Ms. Hey, for my intemperance the last time you were at Wawel. The drunken ramblings of a disillusioned old man, I'm afraid. The sheer scale of the challenge facing us sometimes seems overwhelming. Invasive species are the second greatest threat to global biodiversity after habitat loss, but sometimes it seems we are even more helpless to control the spread of invasives than we are to prevent the loss of a tract of rainforest. But I think the inspector does not wish to discuss such matters today. You have come to view the scene of the crime, have you not?" Sikorski stood aside from the charred doorway and gave an elegant sweep of his hand. "Please, come inside."

Lindy and Domenic stood and surveyed the scene of heartbreaking devastation. The once-white walls were now smoke-blackened and scorched. The exquisite handcrafted doilies and curtains that had done so much to lend an air of domesticity to the great hall lay soiled and sodden on the floor. Those painted icons and artifacts that had survived the smoke and water damage were stacked in a ragged pile in the centre of the room. It looked to Lindy as if the firefighters' efforts to save the building had caused as much carnage as the fire itself. She looked around, unable to reconcile the abject wretchedness of this space with the room that had so recently throbbed with energy and life. The lustrous wooden floor on which she and Des had danced was now coated with a thick layer of grime, through which a single set of footprints had tracked.

"No one else has been here to help you?" Lindy asked.

Along the hallway, Sikorski picked up the statue of St. Stanislaus that was lying on the floor. He wiped it tenderly with his hand and checked it was undamaged before setting it back in the alcove from where it had fallen. "They will come. When their own wounds have healed. This damage will be repaired and the centre will once again become a place of happiness, of comfort. Resilience is in the Polish blood. It is in the history of the country itself. Some might say it *is* the history of Poland. Sometimes, I think it is not an eagle on the Polish flag, but a phoenix."

The man's optimism seemed so out of place, juxtaposed against the wreckage that surrounded him. But Lindy recognized it contained the hope he was going to need to rebuild this centre. Somehow, the thought seemed to make the act of destruction all the more unbearable.

"That someone could do this ..." Lindy's voice faltered slightly and Jejeune detected the glint of moisture at the corner of her eyes. But the words seemed to stir her from her sadness and she straightened. "We're not having it. I'll talk to Calista tonight and we'll come by first thing in the morning. We'll help you to put Wawel back together as quickly as possible. We'll show those bastards we won't stand for their attempts to destroy this place. They have failed. And will always fail."

Jejeune had been looking around the room carefully since they entered. He had seen the same damage Lindy saw, the patches of dampness in the corners, the smoke-blackened walls, the icons and decorations driven to the ground by the force of the water hoses. But it was what he didn't see that caught his attention.

"There's no vandalism," he said quietly, "no attempt to destroy any of the religious artifacts." He continued looking around him. "I believe the damage to the building was incidental. I think someone wanted to kill Paulina Kowalski. The fire was good cover for their crime, but it wasn't their purpose for coming here."

"Look at this place, Dom." said Lindy, opening her arms and spinning around in frustration. "In the end, does the motive even matter?"

But even as she asked, she could see that to Sikorski it did. His eyes showed understanding of Jejeune's comment and with it a kind of appreciation. Domenic's observations would do nothing to reduce the workload ahead, but it would bring a kind of peace to the process. It would remove the shadows of hate. Instead, the community could take on the restoration project as an act of love, of devotion, free from bitterness and resentment.

"I was wondering if you found that missing key," said Jejeune. "The one to Jakub Kowalski's locker."

"I believe I told you before that I did not know where this key is."

"Actually, you said you couldn't help us."

Sikorski nodded. "Ah, the policemen's precision. I have looked," the Count told him. "Even in all this … I do not think this key is here. Perhaps Mrs. Kowalski's attacker took it with him. Perhaps he was attracted to this bright, shiny key, like the Magpie at your famous kidnapping case."

"It was a lynchpin," said Jejeune. He returned Sikorski's smile, but to Lindy it looked a little forced. And perhaps to Sikorski, too.

"A key to unlock one thing, a pin to unlock another." He lifted his hand. "How these small details of English betray us. Language is the guardian of any culture, do you not think, its protector against outsiders?"

The language and the history, thought Jejeune, *those tiny tripwires set out to catch foreigners, to remind them this was not their homeland, that however well assimilated they may become, they will forever be interlopers.*

Sikorski looked around him at the damage and destruction. "Would you mind if we went outside?" he asked. "I find the comfort of the natural world can help with many sorrows."

After the smell of stale smoke and fire retardant, the freshness of the breeze sweeping in off the marshlands was like a song of joy. Lindy looked back at the building. "It will take a lot of work, but you know Calista, she'll get things moving," she said reassuringly. "I wouldn't be surprised if it was as good as new before we even leave for Canada." She stopped abruptly and turned to Sikorski. "I'm sorry; I know it will take more than a couple of coats of paint for the community to forget what happened here."

"So, you are going to Canada soon?" It was an act of courtesy to change the topic to spare Lindy further embarrassment. Jejeune would have expected no less of a gentleman like Teodor Sikorski.

"Yes, we're going to see ... the birds." Lindy faltered, perhaps still reeling from her earlier faux pas. "Dom misses them." She gave a weak smile and looked across at Jejeune for support, but he offered her only a blank stare.

"You will see birds in Canada that will be familiar to you from this country, though they are perhaps no longer so welcome over there. The Rock Pigeon, after all, was first introduced into North America in Nova Scotia."

"To be fair, Canadians have sent us something that a lot of people wish they'd take back." She linked her arm in Domenic's. "Relax, darling," she said with an impish grin. "I was talking about the Canada Goose."

He smiled back dutifully as he gazed at the setting sun, its brilliant yellow rays coming towards him across the field like laser beams from the west. Canada lay in that direction. Could they simply stay there, after this visit she seemed so keen to take? It would mean giving up all the things he loved here, but he would be prepared to do it, if it meant protecting Lindy from Ray Hayes. Yet even if they somehow managed to forge a new life for themselves out there, the spectre of Hayes would always be hovering in the background. He was intelligent, resourceful, relentless. And he was free to travel wherever he wanted. He would find out where they'd gone, and one day, he would come for them. Jejeune couldn't live forever with that shadow hanging over him, and he wouldn't let Lindy, either. Looking into the sun, he accepted now, finally, what he had known all along. They could never run away from this problem. They could never escape Ray Hayes. And that meant there was only one solution.

"We should be going," said Jejeune.

"You have the answers you came for?"

"Except one," said the detective. "Was it easy to earn Jakub Kowalski's trust?"

"Trust is a precious commodity, Inspector. It should never be given away easily." Sikorski gave a soft smile. "Now you have all your answers, so I will bid you a good day."

By the car, Jejeune paused for a moment at the edge of the berm and looked down the steep slope to the water. Along the shoreline, small curds of white foam had collected — the remnants of the fire retardant that had been used to douse the flames. He watched the white husks for a long time, following their rise and fall as they rode the gentle lapping of the water. Like many acts of violence, the fire at Wawel had left its residue not just in the hearts of humans, but in the natural world, too.

44

Maik and Holland stood side by side at the top of the rise, their ears filled with the sound of waves breaking on the rocks below. Blustery onshore winds buffeted the stands of sea grass that grew along the edge of the jagged shoreline. Along the coast in both directions, brackish marsh blurred the margins between the water and the land. On the far side of the wide estuary, the low, featureless landmass of Foulness Island hovered just above the water. By car it was nothing more than a quick jaunt up to the main road, out past the MoD checkpoint, over the bridge, and down onto the island. But there was another route from Wakering to Foulness, Maik knew. It took a lot longer. And sometimes, you didn't make it at all.

Holland stared out over a wide swath of wet, brown sand spread out below them, so newly exposed by the receding tide it was still glistening. It had the empty desolation of a battlefield with all the human carnage removed. Even from here, it looked to be perilous terrain, capable of swallowing up anything or anyone foolish enough to venture onto it.

"So, what's so special about this place, then?" he asked. "You're not thinking about retiring here, are you? You always said you might like a little place beside the sea."

"The Black Grounds," said Maik, deep in thought. "That's what the locals call that mud. Treacherous stuff, so they tell me. Though you'd only sink up to your waist. It'd be the incoming tide that would finish you off. Comes in faster than a man can run, they say."

"And they wonder why English people choose to holiday abroad," said Holland flatly. He turned to offer Maik another of his patented grins, his eyes watering slightly from the constant onshore wind.

Through the centre of the dark morass, an ancient causeway of crumbling concrete drove out into the sea with a suicidal determination, until it was eventually swallowed by the rolling waves and disappeared from view.

"That ramp there is Wakering Stairs," said Maik. "Doesn't look like much now, but it used to be the starting point for a trip to Foulness Island before the bridge was built."

"*Used to be* being the operative phrase, by the look of it."

"It's called the Broomway," said Maik. "People have been using it to walk to Foulness Island since Roman Times. The route used to be marked by brooms stuck in the sand, once upon a time, but they have long since gone."

"So, what, people just used to walk out from here onto the sand at low tide?"

"A quarter of a mile, straight out onto the tidal flats. The Maplin Sands, they're called. Then you follow the trail for about six miles, as it runs parallel to the coast. There are spurs coming off it to take you onto the island at various points. At least, there used to be. There's only one or two left now."

"Sounds proper dodgy to me. I suppose there have been a few poor sods who didn't make it over the years."

"Hundreds, I should imagine. It would be easy to get disorientated if a sea fog comes in, and a strong wind can turn a low tide into a not-so-low one in a hurry." Maik dropped his voice a touch. "That's what happened to those kids."

"That was here?" Holland's surprise was clear.

"See that tiny shoal right out there, where the waves are breaking?" said Maik, indicating the spot with a jut of his chin. "That's where Carolyn Gresham was when Sergeant Jejeune found her. She was standing on the Maplin Sands, up to her ankles in water, stranded by the incoming tide. She was suffering from exposure when he brought her back to shore, on the verge of passing out. Even if the tide hadn't got her, she wouldn't have lasted much longer. "

Maik began to walk down towards the ramp and Holland followed him. From the shore, the two men looked out at the water. From here, the Broomway looked possible. Despite the small waves crashing against the shore, the water further out seemed calm enough, just barely, to allow a walk across the Maplin Sands.

Holland stared out at the shoal, watching the incessant, irresistible force of the tide-driven water breaking over it. An unconscious human form would have been so insignificant out there, detritus to be gathered up and carried away like so much driftwood, perhaps never to be recovered. "You'd run out of ways to say thank you to somebody who'd saved your kid from a fate like that, wouldn't you?" he said finally. "Talk about a career-builder. Pity it's all about to come crashing down on him."

"I'm not sure it is," said Maik.

"This business with the timing, Sarge. He lied, he had to have done. Laraby was telling the truth when he said Jejeune wasn't in the office at eight o'clock."

"I think he was there," said Maik quietly. "The reason the rare bird site sent everybody on that long loop down south was because they had to avoid the MoD land. Without a pre-arranged permit, they wouldn't have been allowed to cross it. But the sergeant pulled a bit of privilege. He flashed his warrant card, said he was on official police business, and sailed through the checkpoint. It shaved a good twenty minutes off his trip."

The MoD officer Maik had spoken to remembered the time well; the rush that came the night before, when the Emergency Task Force drove onto the island to set up and await their deployment; the stream of police cars the following morning, after the hostages' location had been identified. And before the police cars, earlier that same morning, a single Range Rover, with a single detective sergeant telling him he needed access to cross the restricted area. Maik thought he might have recognized the officer, a past deployment somewhere, maybe, police or military. But then again, he was approaching an age where it seemed he had encountered almost everybody at one time or another. Was this what old age would bring, he wondered fleetingly, an unceasing parade of familiar faces, with names and associations to accompany them, should he be so blessed? Or would they simply be a string of dissociated images, his mind struggling to come up with the connections?

The troubling thought was still with him when Holland spoke again. "So, that's how he managed to leave when he said he did and still get out there in time to see the bird." Holland smiled. "Des will be made up to know he was telling the truth all along." He shook his head. "So, all this is just about him using official police ID to help with a bit of birdwatching, then? A bit embarrassing for a newly anointed Golden Boy, I'll agree, but it's hardly major fraud, is it? Especially when the media had so much else to occupy themselves with then."

Maik knew what Holland meant. The Canadian police sergeant skillfully negotiating for the release of the Home Secretary's daughter, yet still finding the time to discover a new bird for the U.K. list. Heroes didn't come any better packaged than that. And with the media falling all over themselves to polish Jejeune's new image, a minor transgression like his would have soon been glossed over. Even Jejeune himself had no doubt long forgiven himself for this piece of petty self-indulgence. But Maik suspected other mistakes the DCI had made that day had not been so easy for him to forgive.

"So, you reckon this is all over then, the review of the case?"

"As far as the Met's concerned. From the DCI's own point of view, though ..." Maik gave his head a small tilt, "I'm not so sure. I know he's never been happy with this business about the Magpie and the missing lynchpin, but I doubt even he'd be willing to make a fuss over something so insignificant," he said. "The deathbed confession, on the other hand, I think he might still have a few questions about what went on there."

"Good as he is," said Holland, "I don't think even Jejeune is up to talking to the dead."

"No," said Maik thoughtfully, "but he's got a knack for getting past secrets out of the living. I wouldn't rule anything out just yet."

Holland looked out at the sea, an uneasy, rolling mass of grey-white moving like a slowly stirring monster.

"It's not the escape route I would have chosen," he said, "even at low tide."

"They weren't going to run towards the road, not if the kidnapper might still be up that way. The Broomway is the only other route off the island."

But Holland's thoughts were elsewhere now, even as his eyes remained fixed on the heaving seas. "You know, what I still don't get is why she thought she had to keep it a secret, timing the run and all. I mean, I understand that her investigation looked set to drop her hero in the you-know-what, but she could have at least told me what she was up to."

"Perhaps she wasn't sure where you stood."

"You mean she thought I might have slipped him a word to the wise? Come on, Sarge, you don't have to be around me long to realize that's not very likely." There was a heartbeat of silence as Holland digested Maik's look. "What, you mean she thought I might go the other way? Try to stitch him up? Really? I'll admit I'm not the bloke's biggest fan, but even she can't have thought I'd go that far."

Perhaps it was something else then; just an uncertainty on her own part about what she would do if she found out Jejeune really had lied. Would she pursue it, or let it drop? Perhaps she was too afraid to find out, and that's why she hadn't said anything to him. He thought about Des, the Essex girl. *All of the good qualities. None of the bad.* On which list would protecting your heroes be, he wondered. The low, mournful call of a ship's horn drifted to them from somewhere out beyond the horizon.

"Des told me you could pinpoint where somebody was calling from by using two sounds coming from different directions," said Holland. "She was talking about Jejeune, wasn't she? About this case?"

"A story for another day, I think, Constable," said Maik, turning to leave. "We should probably get in that car of yours and start rolling. It's a fair old jaunt back to Saltmarsh and I'd like to beat the rush hour traffic if we can."

Holland stared out to sea a moment longer, wondering if there was something about the story Maik didn't want him to hear. Or perhaps he just couldn't be bothered relating any more tales of the DCI's past exploits just now. By the time he turned to go, Maik was already in the Audi. For an old geezer, he had a surprising turn of speed at times.

45

Eric Chappell greeted Jejeune's entrance to the hide with genuine delight. "It's been quite a while since we managed a day out together at Cley," he said. "I suppose work's been preventing you from getting out much. This awful case of the Kowalski murder?"

Eric detected the tension in Jejeune's silence. It was the reticence of someone wrestling with a difficult decision. "Ah, so even now, I sense this is not an entirely recreational visit. But surely, even an on-duty policeman has time to appreciate an early pair of Eurasian Spoonbills. There they are, over on the far bank. I have to say, I think we should all get a bit more excited about rare sightings of British breeding species, don't you? I mean, a Hen Harrier or a Red-backed Shrike is a wonderful find. But there's nothing like the frenzy over a sighting of one of them as there would be should some Mediterranean overshoot drop in for the day."

An Iberian Magpie would fit Eric's description, but Jejeune knew the reference was unintentional. Eric was not given to petty unkindness. Jejeune raised his bins and watched the tall, elegant birds preening on the edge of the mud bank. Eric joined him and the two men sat in silence for some time, simply observing.

"Thanks," said Jejeune when they finally lowered their bins.

"Well, there's hardly enough space in this bird hide for an elephant, Domenic, so if it's all the same to you, I propose we get on with it. I'd hate to ruin a perfectly good birding day by having a cloud of chariness hanging over us."

Jejeune pursed his lips and nodded slightly. "The first time you met Vincent Canby, was he already in the hospice?"

"Ah, the confession." Eric nodded slowly. "You know, once, I'd almost convinced myself it had vanished from my life for good. Though I suppose if I'd ever imagined someone might cause it to resurface one day, it would be you. Yes, Domenic, the one and only time I met Vincent Canby, he was in a bed in the hospice. And *ergo*, it was there that he delivered his deathbed confession. I have to say, he seemed quite well-versed in the form — got the wording exactly right, without any prompting from Marvin Laraby. You know, *My name is Vincent Canby. In the hopeless expectation of death, I record my dying declaration.* I remember Laraby commenting on it afterward. He said it suggested a lucid mind."

Jejeune nodded. It did. As well as prior planning.

"It was just you and Laraby present, you said. Was Canby a religious man, do you know?"

"I think his form would have read *none of the above*. Certainly, he made no request for any religious figure to be present."

Jejeune paused for a moment. So far, Eric couldn't have made things any easier, but the next step was a world away from the cordial banter they had exchanged so far. "A substantial amount of money was withdrawn from your bank account a few days before the confession. In cash."

Eric stiffened. Though there was a vast expanse of wilderness just beyond the window slats of the hide, it seemed as if the whole world now existed within these four wooden walls. "It's not something we do in this country as a rule, is it, Domenic, check on people's bank accounts? Not unless we suspect them of something."

Jejeune couldn't let Eric's bitter tone deter him. He had started along this difficult path and now the only way to reach the end was to push on, regardless of the obstacles, regardless of the objections.

"There's no record of where that money went," said Jejeune, "but the same week, five months of mortgage arrears on the Canby's house were paid off, in cash. Eight other overdue bills were also paid off in cash, and Andrea Canby's personal account went from a perpetual state of being overdrawn to a healthy, positive balance overnight."

Eric smiled benignly. "Every bit the star they claim you to be, Domenic. I've never doubted it, of course. Even if I did, Lindy would soon put me right."

Jejeune wondered if Eric's mention of her name was an attempt to deflect the topic, to remind him of the mutual bonds they shared — Lindy, Shepherd, birding. But Eric was smiling softly now, and Jejeune knew he had no intention of trying to dodge the discussion or sidestep around it. Not anymore.

"There used to be a comedian here in Britain called Eric Morecombe. Long before your time, of course. Razor sharp wit, but gentle. Not a malicious bone in his body; certainly none of the unpleasant vitriol that passes for comedy these days. That wasn't Eric Morecombe's style at all."

Jejeune waited patiently. Still, the natural world outside the hide ceased to exist for him.

"I particularly remember one lovely put-down he used about bad singers. *All the right notes*, he used to say, *but not necessarily in the right order*. That's you, Domenic. You have managed to uncover all the facts. It's just your order that's a bit off." Eric nodded his head agreeably. "You're quite right.

I withdrew a certain amount in cash and gave it, in various ways, to Andrea Canby. I had contacted her about Vincent." Eric looked at Jejeune. "Your doing again, I believe. You were the one who had mooted the involvement of someone close to the family in the kidnapping. I did a bit of poking around and came up with Canby. Latterly dismissed as a gardener for the Gresham's, a bit of form, in need of money. I thought we might have a winner. So I went round to see him."

A sudden flurry of wings outside the hide had Eric peering through the slat. A small group of Lapwings had dropped in and were settling, faces turned into the wind, their dark green backs shimmering in the sunlight. "A deceit, isn't it?" said Eric. "The collective noun for Lapwings." When he turned his gaze back inside the hide again, Jejeune's was waiting to meet it. He wondered if the inspector had spent any time looking at the birds at all.

"Canby wasn't there, of course. By then he was already in the hospice, close to the end of his stage four, poor soul. But Andrea was. Young, beautiful Andrea. So desperate and so sad, and drowning in debt."

"You had an affair?"

"We did. Of course it never really had a chance of success. A few weeks of mutual needs met. That's all."

"Not quite all, though, was it, Eric? You paid a large sum of money to a man to give you his dying confession, and at the same time you were having an affair with his wife. You can see how, at the very least, there would be questions about how you happened to be the only journalist he would allow to be present to hear his confession."

Eric nodded. "Indeed I can." But he didn't seem bowed by the acknowledgement, or shamed by his actions. "To tell you the truth, Domenic, the money seemed inconsequential at the time. I'd just sold the flat I'd inherited from my parents in Hong

Kong. Even back then it was a ridiculously large sum of money. Andrea had a story: a special-needs child who'd settled well into a school and was now facing a traumatic move when they were evicted. Could've been a sob story, for all I knew. I'm sure I would've bought it anyway. Turned out to be true, as it happens, but the fact is, a few thousand pounds seemed like such a small amount to relieve anyone from such anguish. Perhaps that was even something to do with it, a sense of guilt at having so much, when so little would solve her problems. So I gave it to her. It was a quite uncharacteristic act of generosity, never to be repeated before or since. Just ask the girls in the office."

"So it wasn't in payment for the confession?"

"Had no idea such a thing was even in the offing at the time. I always suspected Canby's confession was his way of paying me back, giving me the only thing he could, the only thing he had left. His story. That was his idea, you see, that I'd make a tidy sum from the exclusive and I'd use the money to continue to support his family. I must say, he had it all worked out: the book rights, the film deal. Of course, none of it ever materialized, but at least he died knowing he'd done all he could for them."

"He didn't mind about your affair? Or didn't he know?"

"Nothing *to* know. It didn't start until after Canby died. I suppose it seems predatory now, but it wasn't. The need to affirm life after the death of someone close, the presence of someone who had been supportive, who understood what she was going through. There may have been a sense of inevitability about it, but it wasn't calculated, I promise you that."

All the right notes, thought Jejeune, *just not necessarily in the right order*. Until now.

When he looked up, Eric was peering through slat again. Jejeune looked outside. The sunlight had turned the scene into a postcard; silent, still, serene.

"Beautiful here, isn't it?" asked Eric. "The sound of the wind in the rushes, the sunlight glinting off the water. It sometimes takes all my will to get up and leave so I can re-enter the real world. Did you ever report those Ruddy Ducks, by the way?" he asked, without turning from the view.

"I called, but somebody else had reported them."

"Really? Who?"

"It was an anonymous call." Jejeune had wondered at this time if it had been Eric. Even now, he couldn't tell. But it didn't really matter. "They said by the time they sent someone out there, he couldn't find them. They haven't been reported since."

Eric withdrew from the slat and shook his head slowly. "Isn't that just the history of humankind, Domenic? Agonizing over whether to do the right thing, and in the end, our own decisions don't really matter a jot." He offered a sad smile. "Poor Colleen," he said. "She must have been beside herself, having to set her best bloodhound on the trail. Suspicion, you see. It does so erode a relationship, doesn't it? The curious thing is, I don't feel any resentment at all. Not a bit of it. I fully understand. Stands to reason I'd only have paid in advance for that deathbed confession if I had known what was coming. In which case, at the very least I'd have been guilty of withholding evidence. The Lapwings are up."

Jejeune joined him to watch the lazy circling flight of the birds, off to find another place to rest, or feed. No thought of motives, or duplicity. No concerns about other lives, other agendas, other pasts.

"Of course, you know Colleen does have a ludicrously high opinion of your skills," said Eric, as the birds disappeared from view. "She'd just about believe you would be capable of uncovering all this without ever having to talk to me." He looked at Jejeune frankly. "I'm not for a minute suggesting that you lie to her. But if she can believe I never knew about her suspicions, I'm sure we'd be able to carry on as before." He paused, and smiled. "And to tell you the truth, Domenic, I'd rather like that."

"*In the hopeless expectation of death, I record my dying declaration,*" quoted Jejeune quietly into the silence that followed. "I've always felt there was something missing from that statement."

Eric nodded emphatically. "So have I, Domenic, so have I. And I do have to say, if one of my writers had been responsible for it, I would have insisted on a rewrite that included that missing piece."

Jejeune looked at Eric for a long time. He didn't need to ask the question, Eric had done so himself. Now he was deciding whether he would answer it. He looked out of the hide again, and when he spoke, it was to the world outside.

"I thought about it a lot at the time, and for a long while after. But I stopped thinking about it as time went on. And that suited me." He sighed. "I might not have trusted myself to go back to it even now, if I wasn't involved with Colleen. But she's been so desperately concerned since all this business started up again, I needed to do it for her sake. I went back to the office a few nights ago and took the file with all my original notes from that time; more specifically from Canby's dying confession. I wanted to be sure my impressions at the time were as I now remembered them." He turned to Jejeune. "It's that missing piece of the declaration, isn't it? Some affirmation, however subtle, that the confession is true."

"Was it?"

Eric smiled sadly, and shook his head, as if in wonder at Jejeune's question. "D'you know, Domenic, in all the many interviews, and police debriefings, and hearings afterward, no one ever asked me that. *What was said*, that's all they wanted to know. *The exact words.* The facts were what they were after.

Not one of them ever showed the slightest interest in the truth." He turned away slightly, and the light from the observation slat fell across one half of his face, leaving the other half in shadow. "You asked me for my opinion, Domenic, and I am happy to give it. Indeed, one might even say I'm relieved to. Because the truth is, whatever else Vincent Canby might have done in his sorry life, when it came to the kidnapping of those two young people, I'm as sure as I can be that he had no involvement whatsoever."

46

Stippled light lay on the uneven brickwork of the walled garden like white moss. Along the gravel path, the buds on the shrubs were green and full. A couple of sunny days and the foliage would start to paint this place with its spring colours. *A time for fresh starts*, thought Danny Maik. He wondered if the coming of the new season had anything to do with Carolyn Gresham's decision to agree to an interview. Or perhaps it was just the right time for other things, too.

At Maik's approach, he had seen the little girl run to her mother and hug her skirt. That sixth sense, he thought, that children have when their parents are upset about something. In this case, that something, he knew, was him. His approach, his presence here.

Carolyn bent to kiss the little girl's head tenderly before easing her off towards Jessica. As before, they watched in silence as the nanny led the girl up the gravel path and into the house.

They crossed to the patio table, set with a full tea service on a dazzling white tablecloth with pink trim. The wrought iron chairs had cushions to match, but they weren't particularly comfortable. Given his choice, Danny would have stood, but Carolyn Gresham seemed to prefer being seated. For one thing, it allowed her to absently swirl the cup handle with a delicate fingertip as she recalled the details of the events Danny had come to talk about. The ones she was revealing now.

The room was always cold, she told him. There was no heater, no light, not even a bulb. The small window let in some light, but the sun never seemed to make it into the room. The house was quiet, too. Monte said he heard reports about them on a TV, but she never heard one. In fact, there were long periods, possibly even an entire day or two, when she had the sense, somehow, that the kidnapper was not there at all.

"That was my greatest fear," she continued, "that we'd simply be abandoned. That something would happen to … this person, and Monte and I would be left there, facing each other's window across that ugly, awful courtyard, unable to reach each other, until finally …"

She was wearing a chiffon dress in pale lemon. *Another bridesmaid's colour*, thought Maik, for no good reason he could come up with. But why not a bridesmaid? She'd already met her own Prince Charming. Three of them, in fact: the one she'd married, the one who had rescued her, and the one she'd lost to the sea.

"The doors to the rooms were still bolted shut when the task force entered the house," said Maik. "I take it you escaped through the window."

"Monte opened it and helped me out. And then we just ran." She paused to sip her tea. The cup rattled slightly against the saucer as she replaced it. "Sorry," she said, "I haven't been sleeping well. It's funny. I think it's gone, and then it all comes back and I can't get it out of my head for a few days." She didn't say it was the detectives' previous visit that had triggered the return of the nightmares this time. But Maik knew it would have been. They had turned over stones, opened old wounds with their questioning. "I expect this will be the last time anybody will have to visit you about this," he said gently. He didn't promise, but his tone did.

"Your cars were both found abandoned in the restaurant car park the next day. The kidnapper must have been waiting there for you. You never saw anyone?"

She shook her head. "Monte walked me to my car that night and I watched him leave. That's the last thing I remember until I woke up in that room."

"The kidnapper never spoke to you?"

"Never. He just slid meal trays beneath the door. Sandwiches. Always sandwiches. And once, a medicine bottle, with a note. *Fingerprint.*" She tried a weak smile. "I suppose it reassured me that he didn't want us to see his face. I thought if he was so determined to hide his identity, he intended to let us go. I held on to that."

Maik noticed she'd adopted a briskness in her tone, a straightforward reportage that might help preserve some distance from the memories.

"And you never had a chance to speak to Monte, either, while you were both being held captive?"

Again she shook her head slightly, making her spun silk hair dance. "There were just the messages in the window of the room where he was being held, on the opposite side of the courtyard. *Be strong, Caro. Hold on.* I would have given anything for something to write with in return. Here he was, giving me all this hope, this courage to carry on, and I couldn't send him a single message back. I found a piece of cardboard, but I had nothing to write with. I even thought about blood, at one point." She looked embarrassed at the melodramatic statement, but somehow this strong, silent man made it seem okay to reveal these thoughts, these secrets she'd held inside her for so long.

"Would you like more tea, Sergeant?" she asked suddenly.

He wouldn't, but it gave her something to do, a situation to control, so he accepted. He watched her as she poured. The sleeves of her chiffon dress rippled gently in the passing breeze. She was like a hologram, he thought, hovering between two worlds. You got the sense she could suddenly begin shimmering and then simply fade away into this soft spring morning. Maik had not known the woman before the kidnapping, so it was impossible for him to gauge how much the incident had affected her. He only knew that it must have. The person who returns from a kidnapping is never the same as the one who was taken. The one who had returned from this kidnapping was a skittish, fragile person who hid herself in a high-walled refuge and started like a frightened horse at the appearance of a songbird in her garden.

"You said you had the sense that the kidnapper left you both alone in the house sometimes. Do you have any idea how he might have got on and off the island? The only road route is by bridge, and he would have had to pass through an MoD checkpoint to cross there. They were checking everybody by that time, so we know he didn't leave that way. They kept a pretty close eye on boat traffic to and from the island, too."

She lowered her head in thought. "I suppose he could have used the Broomway."

Yes, Maik supposed he could. If he had knowledge of it. Or memories. "But he couldn't have got you and Monte to the island that way. Forgive me, but I doubt he could have carried even you all the way across the Broomway to the island." Maik looked uncomfortable, but her smile excused him.

"I have no idea how he got us to the house, Sergeant. As I said, I didn't wake from the chloroform until I was inside the room."

From the house came echoes of laughter; a child and an adult. The maid, playing games to distract Alicia Montague

Weller while mummy talked to that gruff man outside about something that made her sad.

She turned her head sharply at the noise to look back up to the house, but she returned her gaze to him. "My father has always refused to take any responsibility for Monte's death, you know."

"I can't see that he has any," said Maik reasonably.

"He prevented the rescue team from entering. They were there, on the island. They knew the address, but he made them wait. They could have saved Monte. They could have prevented us from ever having to go onto the Broomway. But he wouldn't let them go in."

"Monte was taken by the sea, Mrs. Weller, by the Broomway, as so many others have been over the years. Your father was not responsible for that. No one was." Once, he might have tried the same speech on another person. But he knew it would have met with the same blank-eyed rejection it did now. Maik wasn't sure how much she knew of the rescue efforts. He suspected her father would have sheltered her from them as much as possible. But anyone with Carolyn Weller's intelligence and resources would have been able to find out what she wanted to know, what Maik knew now, that they had honed in on Foulness Island as soon as they received the report about the attempted ephedrine purchase, and that despite their best efforts, they couldn't narrow the location down to any fewer than seven or eight potential locations, scattered all across the island. And that, when Jejeune had provided them with a way to pinpoint the location that day, Gresham had still told the Emergency Task Force to wait. He wanted Jejeune there, to oversee the operation, to guide it with the steady hand that the Home Secretary now trusted above all others. Only no one could locate him. But whatever Carolyn knew, Maik wouldn't be confirming any of it. That wasn't why he had come here today. He had come for answers. And now he had most of them, if not quite all.

"Thank you for your time, Mrs. Weller. I don't believe I need to trouble you further," said Maik, standing. He hoped they would heal in time, this fractured family with their unspoken recriminations and blame. But he wasn't sure they would. Whoever Carolyn Weller was now, Maik knew this was not the same person who had been kidnapped that evening on her way home from dinner with a friend who used to be a boyfriend. Her family could never be the same, either.

As he made his way to the gate, he looked down along the gravel path that bisected the garden so sharply, at the neat plots of tilled earth that ran off perpendicularly on each side. It reminded him of an army barracks, everything precisely positioned and in its place. Even the flowers, when they bloomed, would have a regimented orderliness to them. They would be part of this controlled world that Carolyn Gresham chose to inhabit now. In reality, he had served with men who would have scaled this rough stonework as easily as a ladder. These walls offered no real protection from the threats of the outside world, only the illusion of it. But perhaps the illusion of safety was all Carolyn Weller needed.

He turned to her as she opened the gate for him. "One last thing, if you don't mind. You said before you didn't recognize the accent on the Broomway as Canadian at first. Were you expecting to?"

She looked away. "Monte said he would come. He heard it on the TV. A Canadian detective was looking for us. Monte was sure he would find us. It was the last thing he said to me. *Stay here, Caro, he's coming for us. I know he is.*"

47

Mansfield Jones looked around Domenic Jejeune's office with something approaching a professional scrutiny. "It's always interesting to enter another person's domain for the first time, don't you think, Inspector? There's a certain unguardedness that I find quite appealing."

Jejeune nodded in understanding. Future visits would come with preconceptions. The first visit, when all the sensations, the stimuli, the impressions poured in at once, that was when you got your real insights into a new domain, or anything else.

As the inspector closed a buff file on his desk. Jones could see the name scrawled on the label in black, felt-tipped pen: *Foulness Island*. He looked at Jejeune. "They tell me the review of the case has been concluded. I must say, I found it fascinating how everything unfolded. Particularly your idea of triangulating two foghorn signals to pinpoint the exact location of the kidnapper's phone call."

One short burst only, from two separate sources, a common enough sound off Foulness Island that it wouldn't set off any alarm bells with the kidnapper, but scheduled exactly to fall during a prearranged phone call.

"There was no guarantee it would work," said Jejeune simply.

"But it *did*. And knowing the exact location and volume of the foghorns when they sounded allowed them to triangulate to where they had been detected on the call."

It appeared so logical, now, that the kidnapper would have chosen the closest reception point to where he was holding the hostages to make his calls. Jejeune recalled how much more uncertain it seemed at the time.

Mansfield Jones didn't strike Jejeune as the type of person who would go in for effusive praise, so perhaps this approving look was as close as he got. But Jones wouldn't have approved of other things Jejeune had done that day. His drive out to see the Iberian Magpie while he was waiting for the sound lab's analysis to come back. Going out to a location where he couldn't be reached on his cellphone. There was nothing to approve of in that.

"I came here to tell you what I've discovered about lead shot. It seemed important to you," said Jones. His voice was tentative, uncertain, almost as if apologizing for his visit.

Jejeune offered the M.E. a seat to put him at his ease. In his surprise at seeing Jones in his office in the first place, he had neglected to ask why he had come. But he realized the findings must be significant to bring Jones up here. At least, the M.E. must have found them so.

"The research suggests that two one-hundred-gram portions of improperly dressed game bird meat per week could increase an adult's lead exposure up to eightfold. Based on my own calculations, I am confident that consumption of two game bird meals a week could be enough to cause kidney or heart problems," said Jones. "Furthermore, my research suggests rural people in Eastern Europe often cook game meat in vinegar, which is acidic. It would allow the lead to dissolve and be absorbed by the body more easily."

"Would the effects be as bad on children?"

"Worse," said Jones emphatically. "Pregnant women and small children are particularly vulnerable to elevated lead levels. A young child eating one thirty-gram portion of game bird meat a week would mean their lead consumption was at a level known to affect mental acuity."

He handed Jejeune a paper. "I've prepared a report for you. The section on fetal development is the part I suspect you will be most interested in."

Jejeune scanned it quickly and nodded. It contained the information he had been looking for, waiting for all this time. He had his answer now. He had known beyond doubt that Paulina Kowalski loved her son, cherished him. Yet when he had first gone to give her the news about the discovery of the body, she had shown such an unnatural conviction about his fate; no hope, no disbelief, no desire for anything beyond the truth she was being confronted with. And now he knew why. *We would lay down our lives for those we love*, she had told him. *To sacrifice our happiness is nothing.*

"You weren't to know, of course," Jones's comment brought Jejeune back to the office, where the man was sitting before him, staring at him earnestly. "That the sound laboratory would get their breakthrough so quickly. It would have been an extraordinarily complex set of data to work through — locations, distances, the ambient air quality, the refractivity of water and the effect it would have had on the sounds over distance. There was no reason to expect they would be able to complete their calculations any earlier than they had estimated. By rights, you should have had plenty of time to get out to Lonely Oak Point and see that bird. As you believed you did."

Perhaps. But it was always a possibility the Operations Centre at the Met would receive the results earlier than projected. And he had known, too, there was limited cellphone coverage along that route. After all, he'd based his entire plan to pinpoint the hostage's location on the very fact that the kidnapper could only find a cell signal in specific places on Foulness Island, just across the estuary. And this was why he could never forgive himself for his journey to see the bird. Because when he set out that day, he must have known somewhere in the back of his mind that there was a possibility they wouldn't be able to contact him. And yet he had still gone. So although his actions that day might have been justifiable for the good Dr. Jones, for Jejeune himself they would never be excusable. The knowledge that Montague Harrison had died because of the delay in being able to contact him was something that Domenic Jejeune was never going to be able to escape. Nothing could erase that guilt. Not even his rescue of Carolyn Gresham.

As Jones prepared to leave, he hesitated, lingering a moment longer. "I'm curious about the bird you saw that day." he said. "The Iberian Azure-winged Magpie. I wonder, how could you be sure it was a genuine wild sighting? How could you tell it wasn't simply a bird that had escaped from captivity? I'm told these birds are quite popular in private collections."

"Someone took photos of it that day. The feather wear patterns matched a bird that had been seen in northern France a few days before, and in Carcassonne before that. It represented a progression up from its range in southern Spain."

Jones nodded. "Merely circumstantial evidence, then?" He smiled. "I'm not at all sure the uncertainty of birding would suit me. But I suppose, in the end, only you can decide if you have enough facts to justify your beliefs." He looked at Jejeune significantly. "Though in this case, I would be inclined to accept the sighting as legitimate. I have seen the way you treat information, Inspector. You seem to appreciate that facts should be beacons leading into the unknown, not be mere footprints on a path you have already chosen."

Jejeune nodded. *Beacons.* Like the broom staves that once marked a route across a tidal pathway. But what happened when those markers disappeared, when time claimed them, or the elements, or the sea? Then you were left without anything to guide you. You found yourself alone, out on a narrow, treacherous path, with only uncertainty around you.

Jones paused one last time before leaving. "If you will permit me to say so, Inspector, you should allow yourself some credit for saving Carolyn Gresham's life that day. I cannot imagine what it would have been like for that poor young woman standing on that causeway, frozen in place by her terror, waiting for death to claim her. It's remarkable you found her at all in that thick fog. It would have been like searching for someone in pitch darkness."

Or on a night with no moonlight, thought Jejeune. It was the final piece, the one small detail that brought everything together, that answered the main question: *Why?* A night with no moonlight, with no Bay of Rainbows to see, no Sea of Tranquility, nor any other of Lindy's lyrical features. A perfect night for a human smuggling operation. But if it ran just a little longer than planned, perhaps even the milky light of the early dawn that followed would have been enough for someone to witness it.

One phone call would be all that was needed now, one confirmation, and Jejeune would have his answers. All of them. When he looked up, Jones had left his office. He would likely never appreciate the extraordinary contribution he had just made. But he'd delivered the truth, at last. And perhaps, for Mansfield Jones, that would have been enough.

48

"Good morning, Danny. Welcome. Please come in."

Shepherd's greeting was so effusive Maik thought for a moment she might actually round the desk and come over to hug him. He stood uncertainly near the door of her office, just in case. But the DCS got quickly down to business, even if her radiant disposition remained in place.

"The Inspector here, our brilliant DCI —" she couldn't resist a smile in his direction "— thinks you may have gained some insight from your chat with Carolyn Gresham … or Weller, as she is now, I suppose. It's not my case, of course, but I know it's been consuming a lot of your time," she shot a quick look between the men, "both of you. And extraordinarily enough, it even seems to have had you two at loggerheads. So, if you have found anything to help wrap this thing up and package it off back down to the Met where it belongs, I'd be most interested to hear it."

Maik shifted uneasily. "I'm not sure everything is quite as it once seemed, ma'am," he said cautiously, "though I've not got any actual evidence to back that up."

Shepherd looked across at Jejeune and she could tell that he, too, had found things that did not fit the accepted view of what had happened, the view that was recorded in the case file marked *Pending Review*. And Jejeune, she suspected, might have some *actual evidence*. She regarded the men warily. "As I say, this is not my case, so I can't order you, but I'm advising you as a colleague that revisiting this case will not be well-received. A quick closure was needed. Carolyn Gresham had been through enough. The entire family had. No one wanted the investigation to drag on. Everybody got what they wanted from the findings. We now know for certain that Vincent Canby's confession wasn't coerced, or tainted in any way," a quick look at Jejeune here, Maik noticed, "so opening up the case again can only cause damage. Damage that might linger," she added heavily.

But what of the damage if they did not open it up again? thought Jejeune. Would Andrea Canby not want to learn her husband was innocent? Would her son not want to know his father was not the criminal the world considered him to be? But they were already living their new life back with her family in Bonaire. *Fresh air*. A new start. Did they want this part of their past brought up again? Or were they prepared to let it lie, like everyone else? Perhaps Shepherd was right. Perhaps.

"So, onto the case at hand," she announced. "You've had something of a breakthrough, I understand?" Shepherd's bright energy suggested she'd already left their previous discussion in the past. It was time for her detectives to do the same.

Jejeune nodded. "I'm waiting for one piece of information and I'll be in a position to make an arrest."

Shepherd waited. After several moments of silence, she looked over at Maik in wonder. "And are we permitted to know who?" she asked sarcastically.

Jejeune sighed. It was a function of his work, he supposed, this need to hold on to information, to conceal what you knew, or how much, or about whom, until you were ready to use it to your advantage. It was no wonder it fostered suspicions of secrecy and scheming, even when they were unfounded. But he knew he could get away with it today. He had brought Shepherd the news she had so desperately wanted to hear. Eric was innocent. And now, she would grant him anything he wanted, indulge him in any intrigue he chose. "I just need twenty-four hours."

She looked astonished. Maik did, too. But as Jejeune had predicted, she granted him his request. "Most enthralling, I have to say, but if you're certain it will lead to a safe conviction, Domenic, then why not."

"It will," he said simply.

"And you won't require an arrest team to accompany you?"

"No," said Jejeune. "I don't believe I will."

"Well then," she said briskly, "if there's nothing else, I imagine we all have plenty to be getting on with."

"Ray Hayes has been asking about Lindy."

The sentence seemed to come from somewhere deep within Jejeune, spurting out as if he had no control over it.

In the stillness that followed, Shepherd could only look at him. It was a moment before she spoke. "So, it was him?"

"Not at the church in Elvery. But it was almost certainly Hayes who set the explosion that injured Lindy."

For the first time since she had known him, Jejeune looked lost. Ray Hayes was bringing his war to Domenic, and he had chosen Lindy as their battleground. And the detective had no way of stopping him. He looked so young at this moment. It was easy to forget that he was. He'd achieved so much already and had taken on so much responsibility. But now, he was facing the biggest challenge of his life, and he had no idea how to deal with it. She wanted to offer him her sympathy, but what he needed from her was cold-eyed pragmatism.

"Of course, we'll put everyone on this immediately, Domenic. It shall have full priority. We'll get a description out to all officers."

"I don't believe there's an immediate threat," he said quickly, "Hayes is out of the country at the moment."

She nodded. "Then we'll watch for his return." She paused. "It will be difficult to do more than that now. As you know, there's no evidence against Hayes, or anything we can even use as a pretext for bringing him in, even if he's spotted. We would be able to spare a uniform to protect Lindy, however, in case he slips back into the country undetected."

"I'd like to keep this from Lindy. For now, at least."

Shepherd looked at him warily. "Are you sure that's wise?"

"She's not one to shy away from something like this. I think she'd want to show Hayes that she wouldn't be intimidated."

Shepherd inclined her head slightly. "It might draw him out, tempt him into a mistake."

Jejeune shook his head. "Hayes is not given to making mistakes."

She looked at Maik to see how much of this he already knew. Some, she decided, but not all of it.

"So what do you propose?"

"I have an idea, but I'd like to give it some more thought."

"Of course. In the meantime, if you think of anything else, or need anything from me, you know you only have to ask." She looked at him earnestly over the top of her glasses, as she had done so many times before, in different circumstances. "I mean it, Domenic, anything at all."

Maik approached his DCI as they left Shepherd's office. "Any chance we could take a run somewhere tomorrow?"

"I have to drop Lindy off at Wawel at eight o'clock." Jejeune smiled at Maik. "Her car is still not ready. And then I have something else to take care of. But I could swing by and get you after that."

Something else to take care of. Jejeune must be confident there would be no problems with his arrest, thought Maik, if he was willing to schedule a trip afterward. Maik had never been involved in an arrest yet that had gone entirely as planned, but he had long since ceased to be surprised by his DCI. If Jejeune said he would pick him up, then he would.

"Where were you thinking of going?"

"Foulness Island," said Maik. "There's a couple of things there I'd like to check, before anybody closes the file for good."

There was a moment of silence before Jejeune nodded. "Okay. Tomorrow then."

And with that, he was gone.

49

"This is Eric Chappell. He is a journalist." Jejeune looked across at Eric, as if to verify he was okay with the description. Eric smiled his approval and shook Paulina Kowalski's hand. It was cold and unwelcoming. Perhaps like the woman herself.

She was sitting up in bed, propped against some pillows. She looked around the room uneasily, as if unsure why Jejeune would have chosen to bring this man to her hospital room. And then ask the staff for a few moments of privacy.

Jejeune sat down unbidden in the chair beside the bed. Eric retreated to the only other seat in the room, in the far corner.

"I am here to tell you I know who murdered Jakub Kowalski," said Jejeune.

Paulina Kowalski's expression didn't change. It was still wary, uneasy.

"The lines between right and wrong have been blurring for me lately, Mrs. Kowalski. Truth and facts, morality and ethics; I'm not sure I even know what justice looks like anymore."

Jejeune's candour was shocking. He had been a pillar of moral certitude for so long in Eric's life. If Domenic Jejeune was starting to lose his footing, what hope was there for the rest of them?

"This case challenged all I thought I knew," said Jejeune. "About people, about what they were capable of. The truth seemed impossible to believe, so much so that I even began to doubt the facts." He paused and looked at Paulina Kowalski for a long moment. "But the facts weren't wrong."

Paulina Kowalski shifted uneasily in her bed. Eric couldn't recall the last time he'd drawn a breath. But neither one said anything.

"At the time your son went missing, Curtis Angeren was looking for him," said Jejeune. "He knew that while Jakub was out searching for Ruddy Ducks, he had witnessed criminal activity along the coast; Curtis Angeren smuggling people into the country by boat. Angeren thought your son may have photographic evidence of this. He didn't. But Angeren couldn't be sure. He thought he might find it in your house, or in your son's locker."

Jejeune eased himself back into the chair. He had breezed by the charges of human smuggling against Curtis Angeren so swiftly that Eric was only now beginning to take them in. But Paulina Kowalski was interested in the other things he had said, the ones concerning her son.

"This is all? You say you know this, but I think you do not have proof of any of it."

"No, I don't. But that is what happened. It is why Curtis Angeren was looking for your son. And you knew this. You also knew Angeren's reputation. You knew he was relentless, you knew he would never stop looking for Jakub. He would keep on coming, keep on hunting for him. And when he found him, he would kill him. Only one thing could stop Curtis Angeren looking for your son — if he knew Jakub was already dead."

In the silence, Eric fancied he could hear his own heart beating. Paulina Kowalski sat stock still, watching Jejeune, like prey observing the approach of a predator.

"These are your thoughts, Inspector. You cannot say they were mine. No one you will speak to will ever tell you they have heard me say these things."

"Perhaps not, but you did believe them. And that is why you took your son's rifle from his locker, and the ammunition from your house. Then you found an opportunity where you were sure you would not be observed, and you killed Jakub Kowalski with a single rifle shot to the back of his head. I don't think you killed him at the construction site, although that would have been easier for you. Moving the body must have been difficult. But you knew you ran the risk of raising suspicion if you'd asked him to meet you somewhere so deserted and remote, especially late at night."

Eric watched the reaction of the woman. There was none.

"Once you put the body in the pit, you threw the rifle in and set the body alight. I believe you did all that. You planned this murder meticulously, and carried it out exactly. For a long time, I couldn't believe a mother could be capable of such depravity. To plan such a killing so coldly, and to subject the body to such terrible defilement afterward, that seemed inconceivable. Especially since all the while, I believed you truly did love your son; you cherished him just as you said you did, and you would have sacrificed your own life to save him. Still, I thought I had my answers, everything I needed to give me the picture of what happened. Except for one thing."

Eric looked at Paulina Kowalski, but she had eyes only for Jejeune. They were locked onto him now, burning into his face.

"Why set fire to the body?"

Jejeune waited for an answer.

"You left a rifle beside the body with a recoverable serial number on it. For somebody who'd gone to this level of planning, that wasn't a mistake. It was a deliberate act. You wanted Curtis Angeren to know who was in that pit. And yet the body was burned to disguise the identity. The two facts couldn't both be right. But they were. And the truth was right there in between them the whole time, wasn't it?"

"You were correct, Inspector," said the woman coldly. "No mother who loved her son as I loved mine could ever commit such acts. I did not kill my son. I could not do this. I swear to you. This is the truth."

Jejeune looked at the woman for a long moment. "When I first came to see you in this hospital, the doctor commented on the extremely high levels of lead in your body. Were you aware of them?"

She nodded. "And the reason, I told you. We were poor, we ate what my father and Jakub shot. There were always lead flakes in the birds we ate. We cleaned them as well as we could, but we knew we could not get them all."

"Lead is a systemic poison. In humans, it's stored in the bones for decades, and high amounts are released into the blood of pregnant women. These reach the fetus at a time critical to the development of teeth and salivary glands. They would stay in your child's system throughout his life. But the teeth of the body we recovered didn't show any signs of high lead levels at all. The corpse is Jakub Kowalski, the dental records prove that. But it is not your son."

The scraping of Eric's chair as he sat forward scarred the silence. But he made no apology. He continued leaning forward, looking at Jejeune, at the woman, at them looking at each other.

"You have access to the records of the entire Polish community in this area," Jejeune told the woman, in the same matter-of-fact tone he had used throughout. "Jakub Kowalski is a common name, perhaps the most common Polish name. I'm sure you had at least a couple of prospects to choose from. As long as you had a man of the approximate age and build of your son, the rest of the details could just be left swirling around in the sketchy, incomplete records on file."

Paulina Kowalski sat still, staring straight ahead now. She was wary, but she was not afraid. From the sidelines, Eric could only look on with fascination. Whatever was going on between these two, it was mesmerizing.

"Sometimes, even knowing the truth is not enough, is it, Inspector? As you say, Jakub Kowalski is dead. His dental records say this. I will confirm all the details you will ever be able to uncover. I will say they match my son's history exactly. You need evidence of what you claim, and there is none. There is no evidence left to discover, no witnesses, no proof."

"You are correct. I have no evidence of any of this and no way of getting any."

Eric stirred uneasily in his chair. Even though he'd never seen Jejeune in action before, he had heard enough to expect something special. But telling a suspect you did not have enough evidence to charge them, admitting you could never get such evidence, was madness. It was telling them they would never be prosecuted for the crime they had committed. That they had got away with it. They were free.

Anyone with the intelligence to plan a murder as meticulously as Paulina Kowalski had to understand Jejeune had no case as long as she remained silent. The detective had already explained that he had absolutely no other avenues to follow. If it was as obvious to Eric that the investigation was at a dead end, Paulina Kowalski must surely know that, unless she voluntarily admitted to something, she would never be charged.

"Mr. Chappell is here to officially record the closure of this case," Jejeune told the woman, and at the same time, Eric himself. "At the moment, the facts I am prepared to confirm are that the deceased's name is Jakub Kowalski. I do, however, have sufficient grounds to believe this person is not the same Jakub Kowalski who went missing shortly after witnessing an illegal act on the shoreline near the Whitehaven Golf Club. I have found no evidence to suggest this second Jakub Kowalski has come to harm, and can only conclude that he is alive and well somewhere."

Paulina Kowalski's face had gone ashen. It tightened now into anger, fury. "You cannot say this. This dead person is my son."

"No, Mrs. Kowalski, he is a stranger who you killed because he had the same name as your son, an innocent person whose body you desecrated because you wanted Curtis Angeren to believe your son was dead. Those are the facts, Mrs. Kowalski. And, for once, it is the truth, too."

"Angeren will start looking for my Jakub again if you report this. You know him; he will not stop until he finds him."

"This man you killed was someone's son, too, Mrs. Kowalski, even if, as I suspect, you chose him specifically because he no longer had any family to mourn for him. He deserves justice."

She was weeping now, and she spoke as if she had not heard Jejeune's words. "Angeren has powerful friends. He has contacts, resources. He will find my Jakub one day. And then he will kill him. You cannot allow this to happen."

"I cannot prevent it. But you can."

There was only silence.

"If you confess to killing Jakub Kowalski, I will ask Eric to report exactly this. Your confession will be sealed and I will make sure both the coroner's report and the official police statement make reference to the victim by name only. If people choose to infer that he was your son, no one will correct them. Your confession would mean there will be no trial, no evidence given in public; in short, no way for Curtis Angeren to find out the person you killed was not your son."

After a long moment, Eric withdrew a notepad from his bag and clicked his pen. The simple sound seemed to stir

Paulina Kowalski from her thoughts. There would be no clacking of laptop keys, no pings from notification apps. Perhaps it was comfort of the old ways that finally encouraged Paulina Kowalski to begin speaking.

50

The Beast was parked in a gravel siding at the end of the low, narrow bridge that had brought them over to Foulness Island from the mainland. The two detectives were leaning against the leeward side of the vehicle, which was rocking in the buffeting wind. Maik was scouring the landscape while his DCI looked down at his phone. "I wanted to check messages here because we'll lose the signal as we head further onto the island," he said. "There's a text from Lindy. The garage has called to say they'll drop the car off for her at Wawel, since she can't get in before they close." He shut the phone off and returned it to his pocket. "That helps. It means there's no need to rush back."

A sudden gust of wind kicked the landscape to life, tousling the grasses, setting the reeds trembling in the marshes. The wind had moulded this place, shuffling shingle beds along the shorelines and swirling silt deposits to change the course of the tidal inlets. On a map of this area, the coastline seemed to disintegrate into a series of ragged fragments Jejeune knew to be a network of small islands and interconnected waterways. It was a landscape of barren, raw beauty that crept into a person's psyche and filled their spirit.

"Plenty of birds coming in," said Maik, nodding towards a quicksilver finger of water that traced its way inland. Jejeune looked up as a flock of Brent Geese swirled over the marsh before settling beside it as gently as falling snow. They would be heading for the eelgrass that grew along these margins of isolated marshland, fuelling up in preparation for their northward migration.

"I always enjoyed the birding here," said Jejeune, his voice tinged with sadness. "I came quite a few times, before …" He paused for a moment, and brightened. "In fact, I saw my first U.K. Short-eared Owl just over there." He pointed, but Danny didn't look in that direction. He doubted the bird would be there now, and he doubted even more he'd ever be coming back to Foulness Island to try and find it himself.

Maik and Jejeune wandered among the ruins of the old house. The central block and the two wings retreating perpendicularly from it were all constructed of the same rough-hewn stone, worn and textured by decades of exposure to the elements. Maik settled onto a low wall in an area where the bulk of the house deflected the worst of the winds. Jejeune joined him. In front of them, scattered debris littered the boulder-strewn courtyard — broken fence rails, upturned troughs, bales of hay twined with rusted wire.

"This the one the girl was kept in?" Maik asked, pointing to the right-hand wing.

Jejeune nodded. "She used to look out to see Monte's handwritten messages, held up in that window opposite." He indicated the window in the far wing. "The ones encouraging her to be strong, to hold on."

An iron grate was still in place over the nearest window, but the black paint had been peeled off by the elements over the years and the metal was now rusted and pitted. A steel pin that had once been silver lay on the window ledge beneath the grate.

How scared she must have been, thought Maik, held alone in this cold, stone-walled building, staring out through the black bars at the freedom that lay on the other side of them, wondering if she would ever know it again. How scared until Monte, her former boyfriend, her co-captive, her saviour, had come to remove this pin and set her free.

Maik turned to Jejeune. "How long have you known?" he asked.

"Known?" The DCI continued to stare at the window. "I suppose not until I spoke to Carolyn the other day. I wasn't sure I remembered what she'd said to me on the Broomway, until she confirmed it. But I've had doubts for some time." He looked up and smiled at Maik. "Tell me two things you know about Magpies, Sergeant."

Maik had long ago given up trying to decode his DCI's non-sequiturs. Patience was the key. Patience and compliance. Danny shifted his position on the wall and gave his big shoulders an easy roll. "They're clever, and they steal shiny things."

"Magpies are very intelligent, as a matter of fact. It's probably why the University of Exeter decided to test them in the first place. But do you know what their studies found? No evidence whatsoever that they are attracted to shiny objects. In fact, they seem to be nervous of them."

"Are they sure? There's an awful lot of folklore that would suggest otherwise."

"Think about it. The only place a Magpie would take an object once it's stolen it is to its nest, like the Bowerbirds in Australia. Want to guess how many shiny objects have ever been discovered in Magpie nests? None."

Maik pushed out his bottom lip thoughtfully. It had always been an iffy premise that the Magpie had taken the missing lynchpin from the other window. But it was plausible, just barely. After all, the kidnapper wouldn't have left the window unsecured while he went away. He'd have pinned it shut, just as he did with the girl's window. And it was hardly likely the boy would have stopped to pick it up as he was clambering out. So if no lynchpin was found at the boy's window, a Magpie taking it was as convenient an explanation as any, especially to a couple of investigators who were in a hurry to shut the case down anyway. He said as much to Jejeune now, and the inspector nodded.

"Especially as a Magpie had been seen here. Not to mention they already had a confession. In my experience, people don't tend to look too hard at other possibilities when they think they already have all the answers. I doubt it ever occurred to them that there might not have been a lynchpin at all, that the window had never been locked in the first place." Jejeune shook his head. "I'm not criticizing anybody. I'm not claiming I had the answers back then, either."

Maik looked at him carefully. *No,* he thought, *but you had questions. You always had questions.* Pale sunlight played over the tableau of discarded items in front of them, laying down patches of yellow light. "Carolyn Weller thinks he used the Broomway to get on and off the island, those times when he left her."

"I think she's right. Except when he brought her over. He would have used a boat. Stolen here on Foulness and left waiting on the shore of the mainland, so he could return it to its owner here as soon as he'd finished with it. He wouldn't steal one again after the first reports of the kidnapping. He wouldn't want to raise any suspicion."

"How did you know they'd try to escape along the Broomway?"

"When I got back to the car after seeing the Iberian Magpie, the reception began coming in as I drove. I was getting texts that the Tactical Unit had made their hard entry after all, and there was no one in the house. With the task force blocking the route to the road, the Broomway was the only way they could have gone. I was closer to Wakering than Foulness Island, much closer, so I turned around and drove straight to Wakering Stairs to go out onto the Broomway from that end."

"Did it occur to you that the kidnapper might still be with them, and that he might be armed?" There were times when Maik's tone conveyed as much as his words. More even.

Jejeune shrugged. "I just knew those two young people would be out there, somewhere on the Maplin Sands, and the fog was coming in. I knew I had to get to them if I could."

"Still, it could have turned out bad for you."

Jejeune said nothing. He simply continued to stare out to sea.

Maik bowed his head a little and nodded slowly. "Worse, I meant."

Both men sat quietly for a few moments, letting the wind fill the silence. It was a constant presence out here, a feature of the landscape as real as the grassy tussocks it teased into manic dances or bowed into submission with its force. It swept low across the treeless terrain, washing over everything, seeking out those who might try and find shelter. The constant, unrelenting white noise of its passing would be enough to drive a man insane, thought Danny, if he spent long enough out here.

"Just curious, sir. What was it about what she said to you, out there on the flats, that got you thinking?"

"She commented on the way I spoke. I didn't register it at the time, and afterward I suppose I just convinced myself she meant my words. Eventually, I just forgot all about it. Until I saw her again and realized she was talking about my accent. Monte had told her a Canadian was coming for them."

Maik smiled. "But how did he know? Not from any TV. No light, cold food, no heaters. There was no electricity in that house."

Maik paused. "Does she know?"

The inspector shook his head. "I think she could, if she let herself. If she allowed herself to think about that time, I'm pretty sure she'd realize there were coincidences, a lot of them, that can't be explained away by the version of the truth she wants to believe."

Maik gave a short nod. The coincidences had been what alerted him, too, in the beginning. Of all the people that have ever been kidnapped, he couldn't imagine many were held at a place they were intimately familiar with from their childhood holidays.

"So what was his plan, do you think? Was he just going to stash the money somewhere and then try to get back with the girl after it was all over? The happy couple, once again?"

Jejeune shook his head. "I don't think so. It's hard to believe now, but apparently Carolyn Gresham was a strong-willed woman once. Confident, assured. I'm pretty sure he would have known it was over for good between them. No, I think Monte Harrison saw the money as his severance package, and setting himself up as one of the kidnap victims meant he'd be able to go off and spend it somewhere without ever coming under suspicion."

"So after collecting and hiding the ransom money, his plan was to come back here and wait for them both to be rescued."

Jejeune nodded. "It would have been easy enough to convince the investigating officers he knew nothing about the kidnapper. After all, Carolyn Gresham said the same thing, and she was telling the truth. Once he'd done that, he'd have been in the clear."

"Only you worked out where they were being held, which left him with two options. Stay and play the victim when the ETF arrived, or run with the girl, and hope he could collect some sort of reward from Gresham."

"He had saved him one hundred thousand pounds, and

rescued his daughter. I imagine the Home Secretary would have been more than generous, if not quite to the tune of the full ransom. All they had to do was to make it to the end of the Broomway and Monte Harrison could have cashed in."

Maik looked out at the sea. He thought about his next question for a long time. Not because it troubled him, but because of the trouble it might bring to others. "So do things stay as they are, then?" he asked finally. "As Shepherd advises?"

Jejeune watched as a cluster of Turnstones swooped in and began picking their way among a carpet of glistening, sea-washed pebbles. They moved quickly, meticulously going about their task, untroubled by the wind or the pounding surf or the emptiness of the landscape. It shouldn't stay here. If it did, an innocent man would be forever blamed for a crime he didn't commit. His son would grow up believing his father was a kidnapper, his wife that he was a criminal. But if the detectives revealed their findings, what, then, of Mrs. Harrison's truth, a woman whose only consolation was her son's bravery and his happiness? Was truth a weapon to bring more suffering to someone who was already mortally wounded? And what of Carolyn Weller, who held the memory of her once and forever lover so close, giving her daughter his name in his honour? Or of Sir David Gresham, whom the nation and his colleagues had rallied around so valiantly during his anguish, and celebrated with him so joyfully upon the return of his daughter. Would the truth be welcomed by any of them? No, it would harm these people more than the lie they had now. Things shouldn't stay as they were. But they would.

"Let's leave it here, Sergeant," said Jejeune sadly. "All of it. This is where it belongs."

Maik took one last look around, at the house, the rubbish-strewn courtyard, at the ragged grassy bank leading down to the beach. And out to the Broomway, invisible now, as perhaps it had been then. "In that case, sir, I'm ready when you are."

Jejeune nodded sadly. "Yes, Sergeant. We can go now." And something in Jejeune's voice told Maik his DCI wouldn't be coming back.

They were still twenty minutes outside Saltmarsh when Maik's phone pinged. He stiffened as he read the message, then stared at the screen for a long moment, as if hoping the text might change, or simply vanish.

"The station has just received a call from the garage. Miss Hey's car was stolen earlier today. CCTV footage shows a man in a hoodie hanging around just before it went missing."

"Call her now, Sergeant. Tell her to stay away from that car if it shows up, and to make sure everyone else stays away from it, too. Let's get a unit out to Wawel as soon as possible to secure the area."

"I'll call it in," said Maik as he dialled Lindy's number, "but we're probably as close as anyone else. I doubt the others will be there before us." He switched the phone off with irritation. "It's going to voice mail."

"There's no landline or internet out there either. They lost both of those in the water damage after the fire." Jejeune edged the Range Rover's engine up until the needles were nudging the red lines on the dials and the countryside began to flash by them in a blur. "It could still be something else."

The men had just dismissed coincidence in one case, and discounted it in every other one Maik could think of. That Jejeune was willing to cling to it now as a possibility was a measure of his desperation. The cold, emotionless voice of Curtis Angeren came to Maik. *I'd have thought any plans Ray Hayes might have, imminent or otherwise, would have been of interest to him.*

"It's Hayes," said Maik. "We need to get there now."

51

The hedges were a green-brown smear as the Range Rover sped past them, overhanging branches snapping at the car's bodywork like whips as they passed. They were on the coast road, which ran parallel to the berm on which Wawel sat, and Jejeune could see tantalizing flickers of the building through the gaps in the screen of the hedgerows. It was so close, but the turnoff to the approach road was at least a mile further along this lane. Jejeune saw the open gateway at the exact time Maik motioned to it, and he hauled the steering wheel into the right-hand turn at high speed, the Range Rover rocking as its offside wheels fought to hold on to the road surface.

Now the building was directly ahead of them across this dark brown sea of newly ploughed soil. The men could see cars parked along the berm. Two were near the building, the third a short distance away. It was Lindy's Nissan Leaf. Jejeune asked The Beast for all it could give and the big machine responded. Its wheels left the ground as the Range Rover bucked and dipped over the uneven surface, plowing on so fast it gave the soft brown earth no time to wrap its cloying grip around the tyres. A steady spray of brown rain spattered the windscreen as the car hurtled across the field, and Jejeune was forced to use the wipers, even though he knew his destination lay straight ahead of him. As the Range Rover jolted back down to earth from a sickening upward lurch, he saw a figure leaving the building. He leaned forward and peered hard through the brown streaks dragged across the screen by the wiper blades. The figure began walking along the berm towards the two parked cars. The front end of The Beast dipped violently, and as it reared up again he saw the figure had passed the cars and was heading for the third one. It was Lindy! The car would be unlocked, the fob above the visor. How many seconds for her to cover the distance to the car, open the door, find the fob, and start the engine? Too few. He smashed the accelerator to the floor, but The Beast had no more to give. He began blasting his horn, even as Maik lowered his window and leaned halfway out, shouting at Lindy to stop, back away, not start the car.

She was at the car now and turned for a second, shielding her eyes against the dazzling glare of the setting sun to look at the vehicle racing across the fields. Surely she could tell it was him. But the dying sun's blinding rays were directly behind him, and he realized she would only be able to make out a vague shape hurtling towards her. Abandoning her stare, she opened the car door and slid inside quickly.

Jejeune had almost completed the crossing now, only the final few metres of the field remained. He lay the heel of his hand on the horn without letting up, his other hand keeping his death-like grip on the steering wheel as the uneven, rutted surface did all it could to wrench it from his grasp. Lindy's car sat directly above him on top of the berm and he saw her arm reach up hurriedly. The fob. She was going to start the car and accelerate away from this careering, out-of-control maniac barrelling down on her. The car disappeared from view as the Range Rover hit the base of the berm hard. It bounced upward into its climb, slewing sideways as it rose. When it crested the rise, Lindy's car was less than three metres away. She was panicking now, scrabbling for the fob and reaching forward to press the starter. She was still hunched forward when the car left the ground.

52

The Leaf was sent airborne by the explosive impact as the Range Rover caught it flush on the passenger door. Jejeune saw Lindy's head shake violently and the airbags blast open as the car crumpled and flew sideways off the berm, disappearing down the far side in a half tumble. The Beast skidded to a halt and Jejeune was out before it stopped rocking. The Leaf was lying in the water, the passenger side wheels barely above the surface, the entire driver's side submerged.

Jejeune plunged down the slope and sprinted into the marsh, splashing wildly and falling forward as the deep water dragged his momentum away. He fought his way towards the car and scrabbled up the passenger side, hauling himself onto the small section of the front fender not yet underwater. He bent forward and peered through the passenger window, into the swirl of foamy grey water that was filling the car. He could see the white of the air bag and a dark shape slumped against it. He tried to open the passenger door but the frame was twisted and it would not move. The passenger window was open a crack at the top and he squeezed his fingertips in to try to yank the window down, but he could get no purchase. The water inside the car was swirling around, and it was clear the level was rising. He had to get Lindy out.

He looked around, barely able to make out the shadowy figure on the bank. "Sergeant, a rock, a stick, anything to break the window."

"I'll come across, sir," shouted Maik. "We'll shift it together."

"No time. The car's filling with water. Lindy's unconscious. I need to get to her now!"

The first rock hit the fender at Jejeune's feet before he knew what was happening. It stuck for a second, but slithered off into the water just as he reached down to grab for it. "Another one, Sergeant, quickly."

Jejeune caught the second one but had to pitch so far forward he lost his balance and slid into the water. He clutched the rock to his chest desperately, hauling himself back up onto the car, using only his free hand until he could scrabble his feet into the wheel wells for purchase. Kneeling on the rear door, he raised the rock above his head and smashed it down onto the front passenger window. It bounced so violently he almost lost his grip on it. He tried again, but it only glanced off the tempered glass.

"Closer to the side, sir, where there's less give."

Jejeune obeyed his sergeant's advice and, aiming for the inner edge, brought the rock down with all the force he had left. A milky spider's web flashed outward from the point of impact. Jejeune punched the rock through and leaned into the opening, scattering the glass fragments inside the car. Lindy was resting limply against the driver's door, her head cushioned by the air bag. Jejeune reached in and tried to raise her head into the tiny pocket of air above her head, but she was pinned by something. He gulped a mouthful of air and submerged his head, reaching past her to the seat belt. She hadn't fastened it, but he found the wrap of the air bag was tightly tangled around her chest. He withdrew to take more air and then plunged back under the water that was now almost entirely filling the car.

He tugged furiously until the material peeled away and he was able to move Lindy. He reached his arms under her shoulders and tried to lift her out, feeling himself slipping towards her as his centre of gravity slid forward into the broken window. He hitched backwards, still holding Lindy, but she slipped from his grasp and slumped back under the water. He knew if he tried to reposition, it would be too late. He had to save her now. As he squeezed back in through the window opening, the space seemed smaller, almost too small, and he became aware of something beside him, reaching in over his shoulder, grasping Lindy's collar. Even in the grey murk of the swirling water, the muscle in Danny Maik's arm looked like a bundle of steel cable. Every sinew was taut and twisted as he held on and hauled Lindy back up towards the broken window. Jejeune hitched his arms around her chest and eased her out. She began to stir as soon as her face cleared the water, gasping and gagging for air. There was no room for three on the small, shiny island of the passenger side fender that remained above the water's surface, so Danny slid off into the water and splashed back to the bank. Lindy leaned into Jejeune as they sat together, breathing, heaving, hauling air into their lungs. She opened her eyes and saw him looking into her face, smoothing the wet hair from her brow. She began to shiver.

"Take my hand," he said. "It's over now."

She reached to take the outstretched hand.

53

Jejeune stood uneasily before the seated DCS Shepherd. The midday sunlight flooded into the room through the big picture window behind the desk. Danny Maik, who'd also chosen to stand, was off to one side, in the only spot in the room the sunlight had failed to find.

Shepherd looked at the hand Jejeune was nursing, knowing that beneath the gauze and white bandages, the fingernails were torn and broken, the knuckles still bruised and bloody from his efforts to pry the car window open to free his girlfriend. The DCS saw a small discolouration at the edge of the bandages; leakage from the stitches, perhaps, or just the unguent used to treat the wound, after the shards of glass had been removed.

"How is she?"

"Recovering. The hospital says one more night of observation and then she can come home." Jejeune looked at his DCS to confirm that was not all she was asking. He took Shepherd's stare, along with his own, over towards Maik.

"I found an old friend who had some reading he wanted to catch up on."

Shepherd nodded. "From a chair in a hospital corridor. Yes, I heard. You understand I can't have civilians involved in Lindy's protection."

"Just until she's released," said Jejeune, looking at Maik as if to confirm the terms of the arrangement. "I didn't want her wondering why there was a uniformed officer stationed outside her room."

Shepherd's look suggested the conversation had finally come around to the topic she wanted to discuss. But she veered into the safer waters of the case instead. The DCS was still coming to terms with the knowledge that Jejeune had uncovered Curtis Angeren's human smuggling plot. It didn't help to know they wouldn't be doing anything about it. At the personal behest of the Home Secretary, no less.

"I still find it hard to believe Curtis Angeren, of all people, is involved in an operation to actually bring immigrants *in* to this country."

"I think you'll find Angeren's is a particularly convenient form of prejudice, ma'am," said Danny Maik with what sounded very much like the voice of experience.

She looked at Jejeune. "You have no proof, I suppose?"

He shook his head. "No, but it answered a lot of questions for Simon Giles. They've been putting the squeeze on Angeren financially for some time now, but he always seems to have a ready source of funds. These criminals he's been bringing in would have been willing to pay a high price for the chance to get away from the Polish authorities."

Shepherd considered the information carefully. "Kowalski must have seen something when he was up at Tidewater Marsh and demanded money for his silence."

"Giles confirmed the date Angeren told his people he wanted Kowalski taken care of. It was the day after the new moon. I think Kowalski went to see him that day and told him he had photographic evidence, taken using a digiscope attached to his telescope. It was a bluff. Even with a digiscope fitted, no telescope could have handled the low light of the early dawn after a moonless night. But Angeren couldn't take that risk."

"Once he'd issued his orders, Paulina Kowalski knew it was only a matter of time before somebody in Angeren's network found her son," said Maik. "She sent him into hiding and killed the other person to give Angeren his corpse named Jakub Kowalski."

Shepherd nodded slowly in confirmation. "And Angeren was desperate to find out who had really killed him because he thought they might now have Kowalski's incriminating photos. But just in case, he thought he'd try to find them himself, at Paulina Kowalski's house, and later in the locker at Wawel."

"He was looking for anything Kowalski might have had that could have stored electronic data, like digital images," said Maik.

"He'd have been especially keen to get his hands on this digiscope thing, I imagine," said the DCS.

"It doesn't actually hold photos," Jejeune told her. "They are still stored on the phone or camera that was attached to it. But Angeren didn't know that either." He shook his head. "I should have realized this was about photographs as soon as Paulina Kowalski mentioned the digiscope. It was the one non-electronic item on the list the men asked her about. I missed it," he said simply.

Shepherd breathed in deeply and both men knew the time had come to talk about the real reason they were all in this office together.

"I've given you some leeway to get your breath back, Domenic, but keeping Lindy in the dark about Ray Hayes is utterly untenable in the long term. Apart from anything else, as a serving police officer, I have a duty of care towards her as a member of the public. She's entitled to be informed of the threat against her, and to be offered police protection, regardless of her relationship to you." She paused and looked at the sergeant, still standing in the shadows. "Sergeant Maik suggested you might have some sort of plan," she said. "He seems a little light on the details, however." She gave Maik the sort of dubious look he'd come to expect as par for the course whenever he was in this office. Shepherd swivelled in her chair and raised an eyebrow in the DCI's direction. It was an attempt to encourage Jejeune to elaborate. And, for once, it worked.

There was a long silence after Jejeune finished speaking. Finally, Shepherd drew in a deep breath and exhaled slowly, as she sometimes did when she needed to deliver bad news. "They'd never stand for it, Domenic."

Even Maik seemed to agree, if not in his silence, then in the curiously uneasy at-ease stance he'd adopted, with his legs slightly splayed and his hands folded awkwardly in front of him, resting just above his belt.

"Even if I were to support this idea, which I'm not at all sure I do, I can hardly see it getting official approval. For a start, it seems to compromise what looks like an extremely promising case against Curtis Angeren. I doubt Simon Giles and his mob are going to be eager to enter into an arrangement like this, knowing they'll have to make major concessions to the man."

"They'll accept it," said Jejeune determinedly. "They'll have to. It's the only viable solution."

"But it's not, is it, Domenic? Viable, I mean. It puts Lindy at tremendous risk. It's tantamount to using her as bait."

"No," he said quickly. "As a person, Lindy is nothing to Hayes. His only interest in Lindy is as a means to harm me. If I can make it so he can no longer get to me through her, she won't be in danger anymore."

"We only have your word for that. Hayes is an extremely intelligent individual. Of all those released under the unsafe prosecution probe, the general consensus is that he's likely to be the only one with enough brains to stay out of prison, as he has so successfully managed to do to this point. You've been noticeably quiet, Sergeant. What's your view?"

"I'd have to agree Hayes probably doesn't care about Lindy's fate one way or the other, ma'am."

Shepherd left her eyes on Maik for a long moment after he'd finished speaking. If he'd sensed she was asking his opinion about the wider plan, he'd done a good job of hiding it.

"And I suppose you would be making an application for some lieu days while you took this on?" Her tone suggested the situation would provide still more headaches, but Maik surprised her by shaking his head.

"Probably best if I go about things the normal way, ma'am. At least to outside eyes. Regular hours here, a bit of paperwork at my desk, an inquiry or two if needs be. I can do what needs to be done for this on my own time."

Shepherd regarded the sergeant carefully. For someone who claimed he had no details of Jejeune's plan prior to entering this room, he had made an assessment of his own contributions remarkably quickly. That Maik was prepared to sacrifice his free time, and likely his sleeping hours, as well, wasn't lost on Shepherd. Or Jejeune. The DCI was fighting hard to keep his expression impassive, but even he couldn't suppress a flicker of gratitude for the sergeant's gesture.

Shepherd tried again, as forcefully as she could, while still trying to sound reasonable. "We have to tell Lindy, Domenic. Surely you see that."

But Jejeune was shaking his head before Shepherd even finished speaking. "For this to work, Hayes has to believe it is real. He has to see Lindy's reaction in her unguarded moments, eavesdrop on her conversations with her friends. He'll need to be utterly convinced. And the only way that can happen is if it's real for Lindy, too. She can't know about this, any of it."

Shepherd paused. Her position didn't require her to point out the other consequences, but her compassion did.

"It brings up the other consideration, Domenic," she said carefully. "The personal one."

"It'll be fine. Once this is all over, everything can go back to normal between us."

Shepherd exchanged a glance with Maik. Even he seemed to recognize his fellow emotional Neanderthal was on dangerous ground here, but it was Shepherd who spoke. "I'm not at all sure it can, Domenic. The lies, the deceit, those will be difficult things to forgive. Before you start down this road, it's important to accept that things might never be quite the same between the two of you afterwards."

"No, it'll be fine," repeated Jejeune adamantly. "Lindy will understand. She'll see that this was the only way."

Shepherd looked at him, partly in sadness, partly in pity. The irony, she realized, was that they were in Lindy's territory now. Shepherd had never realized to what extent his girlfriend must guide him in these matters, and how utterly lost and rudderless he was without her by his side. But she could see now that nothing would change his mind. Finally she gave a short nod. "Regardless of my own misgivings, I realize I can't prevent you from doing what you intend to do personally, and it's for that reason only that I'm even prepared to entertain this idea. I'll check Sergeant Maik's progress daily, but I'll expect up-to-the-minute updates about any new developments. And in the meantime, if there is any hint of imminent danger to Lindy, or even the slightest suggestion of unease on her part, or the sergeant's, I'll bring her in to formally advise her of the nature of the threat against her. Is that clear?" Her expression suggested she would be willing to wait for as long as it took to get a formal acknowledgement from Jejeune.

She nodded curtly when she received it. "Good. You can set the wheels in motion with Giles. I imagine Sir David would be willing to weigh in on your behalf, if necessary. I'll get things started on your paperwork. About three weeks, you said?"

"Four."

Shepherd looked at him. "Just so I'm not completely in the dark, what have you told Lindy about the car?"

"As much of the truth as I could," said Jejeune. "That we received a credible threat that someone had sabotaged one of the cars parked at the Polish Community Centre. That our investigation showed the ignition wiring had gone straight to the battery stack, and as soon as anybody pushed the starter, they would have been fatally electrocuted."

"She will undoubtedly assume it was one of Angeren's lot, targeting someone from the Polish community," said Shepherd, pursing her lips distastefully. "Even more so if they vehemently deny it." She looked at Maik "I presume the garage is in no hurry to advertise the fact that someone stole a car from their lot."

"I may have mentioned that their discretion would be appreciated while we conducted our investigation, when I was over there checking out the CCTV footage."

Shepherd waited.

"Nothing," said Maik. "Someone in a hoodie. No face, no build, no identifying features."

"So are you saying it may not even have been…?"

"It was Hayes," said Jejeune flatly.

To Shepherd, Jejeune's declaration would have simply sounded like the conviction of a man determined to protect his partner. But Maik knew it was more than that. It was certainty. Domenic Jejeune had proof of Ray Hayes's guilt. And for Danny, that was where the problem lay in all this. He could accept that, as a person, Lindy was nothing more to Ray Hayes than a means to an end, so that part of Jejeune's plan might work. He could accept, too, that Simon Giles would eventually agree, however reluctantly, to the deal Jejeune was proposing. But the existence of the evidence meant that things wouldn't go the way Jejeune was now selling them to Shepherd. They couldn't. And Jejeune, he was sure, knew that, too.

He had no idea why the DCI had not turned the evidence over, or even why he had taken it in the first place. Maik had seen it as the Leaf was being winched from the marsh; a small filigree bookmark clipped to the visor. He had been the last person to drive the Leaf, and the bookmark had not been there then. Ray Hayes had left it as a calling card, something to let Jejeune know he had come for Lindy, and he had killed her. But it wasn't there when the vehicle recovery team towed away what remained of the car. Somewhere in the chaos of getting Lindy safely onto dry land and away in the ambulance, Domenic Jejeune had removed the bookmark from the visor. And kept it.

54

The door to their bedroom was slightly ajar, and Jejeune observed Lindy through the gap for a long time. She was propped up on pillows, her faithful laptop on her drawn-up knees. Beside her on the bedsheets lay a pad of yellow lined paper onto which she occasionally scribbled a note. As she bent forward, her blonde hair fell across her face. She unconsciously drew it back to tuck it behind her ear, revealing the massive blue-black bruising on her forehead. She was muttering to herself and running through her repertoire of gestures when deep in thought — gnawing on her bottom lip or tapping the pen absently against her lips. Jejeune's heart almost stopped beating at the picture of unaffected beauty.

He touched the door and it swung open. Lindy looked up and smiled.

"I really need to get up, Dom. There's still so much to do, and I'm feeling fine. Honestly."

"The doctor expressly ordered bedrest," he said. His voice sounded detached, normal almost. Not at all the voice of a man on a mission to kill something beautiful. "What are you doing, anyway?"

"Trying to decide what clothes to take. Canada's weather seems to go up and down like an EKG graph during the time we'll be there. It's seems to have been particularly unpredict-able over the past few years. Say," she said, smiling at him, "you don't think the planet's going through some sort of climate change thing, do you?"

Jejeune's forced grin was its own alarm.

"What's wrong, Dom? If you're worried that I won't be ready for this trip, don't be. I'll be fine, probably all healed up long before your hand, I imagine. You look done in. Is it both-ering you?'

"It's fine. A little," he said.

"Well, don't go taking any sick days off just now. If you save them, perhaps Colleen Shepherd will let you tack them on to your holiday time."

Every reference to the trip was another shard of ice plunged into Jejeune's heart. There was such anticipation in her eyes, such joy in her voice at the prospect, he couldn't stand it. He felt the will to do what he had to seeping from him and he knew he had to act now. If he waited, he'd find ways to talk himself out of it, convince himself that there was another way to ensure her safety. And there wasn't.

"Lindy … this trip.… There's a few things I need to work out."

"I know. A couple of extra pairs of socks, or your scope? If you'd agree to take a bigger case, you might have room for both, you know." But even now, Lindy sensed that there was something else in the remark. It couldn't be what she imag-ined, what she had feared all this time. *Not now, Dom.* She stared at him from the bed, unable to speak, unwilling to do anything that might turn this moment, her life, into tiny frag-ments of shattered glass.

"Things I have to work out alone. I don't know how long it will take."

For a fleeting moment, Lindy willed herself to miss the import. It was an abstract problem, something that might involve informing Shepherd, asking for a bit of extra leave. *Alone.* The realization passed through her like an electric current, juddering against her insides, twisting them into water. She felt as if she could no longer support her own weight, even though she was lying in bed. The pressure of the blankets was unbearable. She slouched back against the pillows.

"Oh ..."

She looked at him, at the emptiness in his eyes, the nothingness. What had happened to him? Where had he disappeared to?

"It may not be for too long." He faltered. "I suppose what I'm saying is, I don't know when I'll be back."

Domenic had resolved to say nothing more. He knew words could not repair the damage he had caused; they could only do more harm. But Lindy looked so empty, so crushed; he searched for something to console her. "There are things ..." He faltered to a stop. *Things.* Things even he didn't understand. A swirling mist of guilt and remorse engulfed him.

"It's the boy, isn't it? He was the one who kidnapped that girl. Don't look at me like that. It's hardly my fault if you assume I'm sleeping when you and Danny have your quiet phone calls. I understand, Dom. You've always believed if you hadn't gone birding that day, if you'd stayed around, where they could have contacted you, you could have saved his life. Only things are different now, aren't they? They're so much worse. Because if you had saved him, you could have worked all this out. You would have been able to put it all together and tell everybody what really happened, given them the right answers, so they wouldn't have to live with these make-believe versions of events they're stuck with now. But guess what. They suit them, their versions of the truth. They've helped them to find their own peace in all this. So maybe you did make a mistake, Dom. It's something we mere mortals have to deal with every now and again. Welcome to the human race. But it doesn't mean it ended badly for everyone."

"No, it's not that." But perhaps it was a part of it, too, somewhere in the back of his mind. He was no longer sure what lay behind his motives. All he knew was that he had to drive on, to complete this, finish it.

"Well, what then?" Lindy was shouting now, in frustration, in fear. "Do you think you don't deserve the rewards you got for rescuing Carolyn Gresham, because she was never really in the kind of danger everybody believed she was? Because this boy you've been feeling guilty about for so long, this victim who turned out to be a criminal, intended to let her go all along? And so all the praise you received, the promotion, all of it, you got it all under false pretences. Is that it?"

Was it? His mind was reeling so much he hardly knew what his reasons were anymore. He stared at her blankly, knowing he could offer her nothing.

"Perhaps if I came with you, we could …" But she knew now, looking at his face, that they couldn't.

"I'm sorry," he said.

Anger began to rise inside Lindy at the casual way he'd told her, the cowardly equivocation about whether he might return. *I'm going to bugger off and leave you, but if you wouldn't mind hanging around, you know, just in case….* She had never hated Domenic, but she despised him now, loathed him. She wanted to leave, to get away, to be in a different room. But she knew the only thread holding them together was her presence here. If she left, their relationship would slip away, like a helium balloon, drifting ever further out of her grasp, until all that was left was a tiny, indistinguishable speck that finally disappeared into nothingness. So she remained seated in the bed, helpless, tethered to this moment, to him, even as she crumbled away inside.

"So that's it then, is it? You get to go off and nurse your ego, because your sense of infallibility got a bit banged up, and me, and this place, and your job, and all those lovely people at work who care about you, we all get shoved under the same bus. Well, that's just great, just so long as you get to indulge yourself in your private little heartbreak, you sad, selfish bastard."

Sad? Oh yes, Lindy, as sad as he had ever been. He was crushed by his sadness, destroyed by it. And yet still having to pretend it didn't matter. But selfish? Was it selfish to want to protect her, to save her from being used by Hayes as the weapon in his war against Jejeune? Paulina Kowalski's words came to him again. *We would lay down our lives for those we love, to sacrifice our happiness is nothing.*

Lindy could not know about the sacrifice he was making. If he told her his plan now, she'd avow their love from the rooftops in defiance of Ray Hayes. She would insist that they stay together, fight Hayes, dare him to break them apart. But it would be there every time she walked out of the house, along a street, around a corner; that shadow of uncertainty, of knowing Hayes had tried to kill her, not once but twice, and that he would someday try again. Jejeune thought about Carolyn Weller, a woman imprisoned by her fears in her tiny walled garden. He couldn't permit that for Lindy. It might be the last good thing he ever did, but if he could let her remain who she was, it would be enough. Was it selfish of him to want this version of Lindy to survive, this free spirit with her glorious, uncontaminated innocence? If it was, then yes, Lindy, he was selfish. Guilty as charged.

"I'll go away for a few days," said Lindy finally. "I'll leave tonight."

"You shouldn't … I'll leave," he said. "You can stay here."

"I'm going away."

Away where? Somewhere safe? Away from Ray Hayes? But he knew she wouldn't say. She wouldn't give him the chance to come after her and say he'd made a mistake. She would go away and he would be gone by the time she returned. In the meantime, he would find somewhere to go now, to be away from her until she left. Only then would he return to start packing what he needed. *Needed?* There was only one thing he needed. And he knew he could not have that any longer. Because, as of now, his relationship with Lindy Hey was over.

55

The brightly lit interior of the airport terminal held all the welcome of an ice hotel. Jejeune had long felt there was probably nowhere else that a person could be so surrounded by humanity and still feel so isolated. Everywhere he looked, people were joined in acts of intimacy; warm embraces, solicitous fussing, or just strolling along side by side. And he was alone.

It was understandable. Only three people knew of his travel plans, and none would be making a journey down here to see him off. One had no wish to. Another had willed herself to believe it was a short-term leave of absence only; *Four weeks, Domenic. And not a day more. Agreed?* The third person was setting in motion a plan that was doomed to fail.

The tannoy announced Jejeune's Toronto-bound flight and he moved towards the security check-in to begin his own part in this plan: abandoning Lindy. He had allowed himself one tiny glimpse into her new, post-Dom world before he left. She was staying with Emma, she of the penchant for *Hot Boyz*, he thought with a small smile. It hadn't been much of a stretch for the detective in him to find out, even as distracted and distraught as he was. Emma was a good fit for the purpose; boundless outrage to fuel Lindy's own resentments, encouragement that all of this was Domenic's fault, and re-assurance Lindy had nothing whatsoever to reproach herself for. *You did everything you could to make that relationship work, Linds. Always.* And Lindy would agree with Emma, for a short time. It would keep her angry, keep her away from the cottage, from that place where a man had stood at the foot of her bed and told her he was going away, even as he watched her sorrow sweep over her, engulf her in a wave of pain so deep and wide it was almost palpable. And did it all without flinching. At least on the outside.

And he tells you while you are lying in your sick bed, Linds, a sick bed that he put you in! That's beyond cold. There's calcu-lated cruelty in that. I don't know what got into him, but you're well shot of someone who can sink to that level. Yes, Emma, she was. But he loved Lindy, and he had to protect her. And there was no other way.

The airport crowd swirled all around him, buffeting him with its indifference. He felt like he might spiral off into its vortex at any moment. He needed an anchor, something to draw him back from this abyss, the sight of a single hand upstretched, waving; Lindy, hopping jauntily from one foot to another for a better view over the crowds. *It's okay, Dom, I get it. I know why you had to break my heart. It's because you love me, so much you were willing to pay the ultimate lover's sacri-fice: separation. The only way you could protect me was to leave. I understand that now. And I forgive you.*

But there was no hand, no wave, no terminal-illuminating smile. Lindy wouldn't be coming. So he was left only with the reality of his situation. The first part of the plan would fall into place easily enough. Teodor Sikorski had been called on to help, now that his own financial legitimacy had been estab-lished — a vast family fortune of impeccable provenance. Of his noble bloodline, there had been no mention. Jejeune doubted it had been investigated at all. But that was okay. The people at Wawel needed a nobleman to be their benefactor, a hero to protect them and care for them. It harmed no one if Sikorski remained a Count, regardless of his real pedigree. Jejeune gave an involuntary smile as he thought of Lindy's words about the moon's features on that evening a lifetime ago: *If the truth is going to disappoint you, I say why bother with it. Just make up one of your own.* Sikorski had agreed to scour his network of Polish exiles to find information on newly arrived illegal immigrants. Only one would be needed. And once Sikorski had found him, Jejeune had no doubt this man with the poet's soul, this lover of natural justice, would be able to persuade the person to do what was required. For a man who could convince artists and academics that there was dignity and honour in wrenching invasive weeds out of the soil by hand, getting a criminal to name Curtis Angeren as the man who'd made the arrangements to bring him in illegally would pose no challenge at all.

So Giles would have his man, at last, and in return Maik would exact the price they needed; reduced charges for Angeren in return for information on the whereabouts of Ray Hayes, and sworn testimony that would eventually convict him. Giles wouldn't be happy, but he and Maik shared a pragmatic view of justice, and knew the compromises you had to make to achieve it. In the end, Simon Giles would agree. But Maik's victory would be a hollow one. Jejeune's fingers went to the pocket of his jacket, to the delicate filigree bookmark in a signed, sealed envelope; the evidence he could not turn over. At this point, to everyone else, Hayes was only a suspect. The bookmark was a personal message to Jejeune that Hayes was guilty. But as soon as Jejeune revealed it, he would be forced to recuse himself from the case. His former conviction, his girlfriend the target; he would be too close to the case, too involved. Even Colleen Shepherd wouldn't be able to save him. It was why Hayes had left the bookmark: the final taunt. *I did it, and now you can't even come after me yourself.* Jejeune would be denied further access to the evidence once he'd been removed from the case. But what if there were other, unintended messages on the bookmark, other clues that might one day help him find Hayes and end all this? He couldn't risk handing it over until he knew for sure.

The disembodied voice on the tannoy summoned him once again to the flight that would take him away from Lindy and his life here in Britain. With a final look at the space where he knew she would not be, he turned and began walking to the departure gate. He made his way down a long corridor, thinking about the British spring he had seen on his journey to the airport. It had arrived in its full regalia; flowers blooming, trees budding. The migratory birds were returning in numbers, too. He wondered if he would ever see any of them again. It would take time for Sikorski to get the information about one of Angeren's clients, time for Simon Giles to get the deals approved, but it didn't matter. This short-term leave of absence, Angeren's future testimony against Hayes, it was all a fiction he had sold them to get everyone to buy into this plan. Danny Maik would never find Ray Hayes. Hayes had left Jejeune evidence that he had attempted to murder Lindy. He was facing life in prison if he was caught. So he wouldn't be. The first thing anybody told you about Ray Hayes — arresting officers, prison officials, social workers — was that he was clever. He would go into hiding, stay out of trouble, assume a new identity. Ray Hayes would become invisible. Curtis Angeren would not know where to find him. Nor would Danny Maik. No one would. And Hayes would make sure it stayed that way.

As long as Hayes believed Jejeune and Lindy had split up permanently, she was safe. If they remained apart, Hayes would not hurt her. But there was one other thing they could tell you about Ray Hayes, these prison officials, these social workers. He never gave up. He would never stop watching. And if Jejeune returned to Lindy, because he couldn't stand to be away from her any longer, Hayes would know. And then he would strike, swiftly, suddenly, lethally. Because Hayes would know then that harming Lindy was still the way of causing Domenic Jejeune more pain than he could bear.

The tannoy voice summoned him again, this time by name. *The final boarding call for Domenic Jejeune.*

After all the versions of the truth he had faced in the previous days, the facts and non-facts and half-facts, he entered the departure gate knowing the only truth that mattered: despite Danny Maik's best efforts, Ray Hayes would remain free. And that meant he could never return. Domenic Jejeune's exile from all the things he loved was about to begin.

THE EURASIAN MAGPIE

Few birds have a longer or more complex relationship with humans than the Eurasian Magpie *Pica pica*. At least ten subspecies are distributed throughout Europe and Asia, and together with their closely-related North American counterpart, the Black-billed Magpie *Pica hudsonia*, the Magpie's range encompasses virtually the entire northern hemisphere. Their striking black-and-white plumage and ability to thrive in human environments have made Eurasian Magpies one of the most recognizable species in the world. But this familiarity has bred a considerable amount of contempt. For centuries, the birds have been the object of mistrust and suspicion, and have been associated with a long list of undesirable traits. In Scottish folklore, a Magpie near the window of the house was thought to portend death. In Norway, a Magpie is considered a cunning bird of the underworld, while in Sweden, it is associated with witchcraft. In the myths and legends of numerous other cultures, the Magpie has been branded as a bandit and a thief.

The Eurasian Magpie also attracts its share of critics in the real world, and thousands of birds are legally killed every year by landowners who consider the species to be a pest. There is a particular poignancy to this wanton killing, given that Magpies are known to engage in "funerals" when one of their number dies. Both Eurasian and Black-billed Magpies have been recorded as gathering in numbers around the corpse of a dead bird, laying sprigs of vegetation beside it and then observing a short, silent vigil before flying away.

These funerals are part of a pattern of behaviour which reveals extremely high levels of cognitive functioning. Eurasian Magpies are known to tear food into appropriately-sized portions to match the developmental stage of their young. In captivity, the birds regularly use tools to clean their own cages. The region of the Magpie's brain responsible for higher cognitive tasks is approximately the same in relative size as that of chimpanzees, orangutans, and humans. The Eurasian Magpie is also the only non-mammal species in the world capable of recognizing itself in a mirror. Such data have led many researchers to conclude that the Eurasian Magpie is one of the most intelligent of all non-human species.

It is estimated that the U.K. population of Eurasian Magpies has more than doubled in the past few decades, and it is a testament to the bird's resourcefulness and adaptability that their numbers continue to grow when the populations of so many other bird species are in decline. Noisy, bold, and abundant, the bird will likely never win over all its detractors. But few people would deny that its intelligence, personality, and striking plumage make the Eurasian Magpie one of the most charismatic species in the avian world.

Birder Murder Mystery 1

A Siege of
BITTERNS
STEVE
BURROWS

Winner of the Arthur Ellis Award for Best First Novel

Newly appointed DI Domenic Jejeune doesn't mind ruffling feathers. Indeed, his success has made him into a poster boy for the police. The problem is Jejeune much prefers watching birds to being a detective.

Recently arrived in the small Norfolk town of Saltmarsh, right at the heart of Britain's premier birding county, Jejeune's worlds collide with the grisly murder of a prominent ecological activist. Jejeune must call on all his birding knowhow to solve the mystery. After all, in the case of the Saltmarsh birder murders, the victims may not be the only casualties…

'A new genre is born: the birder murder'
Sunday Times

'Well written…and instructive'
Literary Review

A Pitying of
DOVES
STEVE
BURROWS

When murder strikes a north Norfolk bird sanctuary, why would a killer ignore expensive jewellery and take a pair of turtledoves as the only bounty? And why is a senior attaché from the Mexican Embassy lying dead beside the body of the sanctuary's director? Chief Inspector Domenic Jejeune is all too aware the case is sorely testing as the clues weave from embittered aviary owners to suspicious bird sculptors. For the truth of it is that with murder, everyone pays a price…

'One of the most delightful, old-fashioned
mysteries of recent years'
Daily Mail

'A tremendous whodunnit'
London Free Press

Birder Murder Mystery 3

A Cast of
FALCONS

STEVE BURROWS

As a white falcon circles, a man plummets to his death from a cliff face in western Scotland. At a distance, another watches; later he tucks a book into the dead man's pocket. When the police show DCI Jejeune the book, he knows it's a call for help, and that it could destroy the life he and girlfriend Lindy have built for themselves in Saltmarsh, a north Norfolk village.

Meanwhile, back in Saltmarsh, the brutal murder of a researcher involved in a climate change project highlights his controversial studies. Might there be a deadly connection between the deaths?

'Most entertaining'
The Times

'An excellent mystery whose conflicted protagonist faces hard decisions'
Kirkus

Birder Murder Mystery 4

A Shimmer of HUMMING-BIRDS

STEVE BURROWS

In Saltmarsh a grisly murder precipitates an unfortunate chain of events, forcing locals to question who will be next. Meanwhile DCI Domenic Jejeune is sequestered away in the South American rainforest, hoping for answers that will help his brother's manslaughter case. But there are people on the tour who seem keen to keep their secrets, and the rainforest can be a dangerous place for those who ask too many questions.

'Skillfully written, full of moral ambiguities and artful puzzles, with a spine-tingling final sentence'
Kirkus starred review

'Riveting'
Publishers Weekly